Keep Holding On

Praise for the Walker Family Series

"The instant chemistry between the main characters makes this a delightful favorite, and their easy banter shines with Tagg's smart, witty voice . . . One particularly charged kiss is sure to have readers seeking alternate sources of oxygen! Written in Tagg's engaging style, this latest offering has plenty of dimension and heart."

—***Romantic Times Book Reviews*** on *Like Never Before*

"Tagg captures the familiar cadence of life in a rural Midwest community while bringing gentle compassion to such sensitive topics as grief over the death of a spouse. A thread of historical drama adds an entertaining element of tension to the book's quintessentially American plot, and its inspirational themes are prominent yet seamlessly woven into the dialogue and relationships. An engaging sequel and satisfying read, especially for fans of small-town romances."

—***Booklist*** on *Like Never Before*

"*Like Never Before*, second in Tagg's Walker Family series, follows a close-knit, loving family as they struggle with life's uncertainties and losses. Endearing characters, deft writing, and an interesting historical mystery will intrigue readers, but the real gem is Tagg's well-handled theme of the need to trust in a loving, sovereign God."

—***CBA Retailers + Resources*** on *Like Never Before*

"*From the Start* embodies Tagg's best! Delightful. Endearing. And full of engaging characters and tingling moments reminiscent of our favorite films and stories. I'm thrilled this is the beginning of our journey with the Walkers and eagerly anticipate this wonderful family's next chapter."

—***Katherine Reay***, bestselling, award-winning author, on *From the Start*

"Melissa Tagg's newest book, *From the Start*, is guaranteed to win the heart of readers with this delightful story of a retired football player looking for his future, and a writer trying to figure out how to pen his story—while rewriting her own. Colton is downright swoon-worthy, and this first book in this hometown series about the charming town of Maple Valley, Iowa, scores a resounding touchdown! Tagg just gets better and better."

—***Susan May Warren***, bestselling, award-winning author, on *From the Start*

Books by Melissa Tagg

WALKER FAMILY SERIES

Three Little Words (prequel e-novella)

From the Start

Like Never Before

Keep Holding On

WHERE LOVE BEGINS SERIES

Made to Last

Here to Stay

ENCHANTED CHRISTMAS NOVELLA COLLECTION

One Enchanted Christmas

One Enchanted Eve (coming late 2016)

Keep Holding On

A Walker Family Novel

Melissa Tagg

LARKSPUR
PRESS

Print Edition
Larkspur Press

ISBN 978-0-9979642-0-2

Cover design: ©Jenny Zemanek/Seedlings Design Studio
Formatting: BB eBooks

Connect with Melissa at www.melissatagg.com and stay in touch by signing up for her always fun and never spammy e-newsletter!

To the incredibly special friends I hope to someday convince to move to the same town as me:

Laura Musyoka
Magdalene Landegent
Melinda Parson
Ruby Addink

I had a chance to spend time with each of you during the months this story was percolating in my writer brain. Collectively, you inspired its "best friends" angle.
I <3 you!

1

He'd tell his family tonight. After the wedding. Before he turned himself in to the police.

Beckett Walker pried his fingers from the steering wheel of the rental sedan, wary gaze slanting to the church, its steepled roof reaching into a burning sky. He'd made it on time, at least. Caught a last-minute flight this morning—Boston to Chicago to Des Moines—before wilting in a forever-long line at the car rental counter.

An hour's drive later, here he was in Maple Valley, wrinkled clothes and a gallon of gas station coffee roiling in his stomach. He rubbed one hand over his stubbled jaw. Probably should've shaved this morning. Gotten a haircut or at least taken the time to smooth it back.

"Whatever, I'm here." Whispered words, a tussling of reluctance and resolve.

Until, finally, Beckett slid from the car, dragging with him the suit jacket he'd discarded long before the plane's wheels even lifted from the tarmac. The faintest cool hovered in the early-August air, mingling with the beams of coral and orange sweeping overhead.

Six years. Six years since he'd come home.

He slipped his arms into the jacket, rumpled reflection glinting back at him from the car's window.

"Beck?"

No mistaking his sister's voice, nor the surprise in her tone. He barely turned before Raegan barreled into him. "Beckett Flynn Walker, you crazy . . ."

She let her words trail as she squeezed, then stepped back. She'd ditched her brow piercing and the usual dozen bracelets she liked to cram onto her wrists. But a few streaks of purple colored her otherwise blond hair. At least one thing hadn't changed.

"You crazy what?" he prodded.

She crossed her arms over a shimmering bridesmaid dress. "You crazy . . ." Raegan drawled, then dropped her arms and grinned. "You crazy, awesome brother. I knew you'd show up."

"Not possible. I didn't even know myself 'til last night." He'd meant it last week when he'd told his cousin Seth he probably wouldn't be able to make it to his wedding. After all, it wasn't like this was a normal event with invitations sent in advance and plenty of time to clear his overcrowded calendar—court dates, depositions, meetings. "Who plans a wedding in less than two weeks, anyway?"

"Besotted lovebirds, that's who." She grabbed his arm and pulled him toward the church. Its white exterior glowed against the dusk, faint music lilting from inside. "Seth proposed and Ava didn't so much say 'yes' as 'when?' Too in love to wait, I guess."

Almost the exact wording Seth had used when he'd called with the news. And if he'd figured there was anything else behind Beckett's inability to attend than a crazy workload, he hadn't mentioned it. Despite the guilt, Beckett had resigned himself to missing out on yet another family event with yet another lame excuse.

But that'd been before yesterday's phone call. The

one that might very well change everything. And he'd just known: It was time to come home.

Home. The word coiled itself around his heart—a comforting embrace or maybe a too-tight squeezing hold, he didn't know. Maybe both.

His steps slowed. "I don't want to make a scene, Rae. It's Seth's night. I was going to sit in the back and—"

"Don't be a moron. You belong on stage with the rest of the wedding party."

"I'm not *in* the wedding party." Because he wanted to avoid attention, needed to. If the wrong police officer found out he was home before he had a chance to clear things up . . .

They'd reached the church entrance now, Raegan still pulling him along, and as they spilled into the foyer, suddenly, forcefully, the long-since-evicted memories of his last Maple Valley wedding came squirming back in.

His reckless outburst at the back of the sanctuary. Hundreds of pairs of eyes all bearing identical shock turned in his direction. And the relief on Kit's face.

Relief that'd turned to regret not an hour later.

"Am I seeing things?" His older brother's voice punctured the memory. Beckett had to blink to adjust to the present.

"Logan. Hey."

Like Raegan, Logan went straight for a hug. But when he stepped back, his expression was as much question as it was welcome. "I'd interrogate you about what took you so long, but the wedding's in twenty minutes. We don't have time."

The summer sky poured through the foyer's windows in a cloud of light and color, the scent of flowers and perfume trailing over him.

There'd been lilacs at Kit's wedding. And hers had been earlier in the day.

He dislodged the unbidden echoes with a shake of his head. He should've expected this—all the thoughts of Kit trying to worm their way in. But at least they were only that—thoughts. He wouldn't have to see her. Last he'd heard, she was off in London or somewhere.

"I'll just find a seat—"

Logan cut him off with a laugh and yanked him toward a hallway. "Nice try." He half-shoved him into a bathroom and slapped on the lights. "All right. Strip."

"Huh?" Surprise held him in place as Logan peeled off his jacket, tossed it aside, and reached for his tie. "*Why* are you undressing me?"

The door swung open before Logan could answer. "Beckett!" And that would be his last sibling. Kate squealed, her dress swishing as she crowded past Logan, apparently not caring that she was barging into a men's restroom. "You're really here."

His third hug of the day, third swell of strained happiness. "Hey, Kate." Man, he loved these people—*his* people. Missed them. Wished for the thousandth time the consequences of his own stupidity hadn't kept him away so long.

But it had been for the best, hadn't it? After yesterday's phone call, wasn't he on the brink of what most people would consider success? Busy career about to take a new turn, the kind that came with a uniform and a title bearing so much more weight than junior associate practicing corporate law.

United States Army JAG Corps.

The thrill of possibility careened through him all over again. Travel. Respect. The chance to use his law degree to follow in Dad's military footsteps, maybe even make some kind of difference in the world.

Maybe, hopefully, make up for too many wasted years.

Of course, the phone call had been only the first step—lining up an interview with a field screening officer. He still had to complete the application and impress the board and make it through training and—

Get the Maple Valley police department off your back.

Soaring hope wobbled on fatigued wings. If he couldn't clear his record before that interview, well, there wouldn't be any point to doing the interview.

"I can't believe Raegan was right." Oblivious to his tension, Kate tucked a piece of russet hair behind her ear and punched his arm. "Thanks a lot. Now I owe her fifty bucks."

"Nice way to welcome a guy home."

"You could've called or something."

"What would have been the fun in that? Besides—" He stopped, distracted by Logan unzipping a garment bag. "Don't tell me—"

Logan thrust a shirt on a hanger at him. "Spare tux. Hurry up and change."

Kate nodded. "He's right. We can catch up later. Raegan went looking for Dad. I'll go find a razor."

"I don't need a razor."

Logan rolled his eyes as Kate exited. "Because obviously you've forgotten how to use one."

Beckett met his older brother's eyes—same inky shade as his own. Logan had a couple inches on him, and when they were younger, the height difference had always left Beckett feeling like Logan was looking down on him. And rightfully so most of the time. Logan was the kind of guy everyone wanted to be. Solid. Dependable. Smart.

Even when his life had been in tatters, somehow Logan had held on, come out of the tragedy even stronger.

Now all Beckett saw in his brother's scrutiny was genuine consideration. "You guys were this sure I'd show up?" Absently, he started unbuttoning his shirt.

Logan nodded. "It was Dad's idea to save you a spot in the wedding party. Ava's brother-in-law, Blake, was prepared to stand in just in case. But we all hoped . . ."

Right—Ava. He'd thought he might have arrived early enough to catch Seth's bride before the wedding. Introduce himself and tell her how lucky she was to have landed his cousin. *You got one of the good Walkers.*

But that was before Logan had dragged him in here. "I really can't do this."

"Wait 'til Seth realizes you're in the lineup. He'll be pumped." Logan pulled the tuxedo jacket from the garment bag.

"You don't understand—"

"We already did photos, so you missed that fun. And by *fun* obviously I mean torture. But at least you'll get to stand up with us."

"You're not listening, Logan. I'm telling you I can't do this."

Logan paused, meeting his eyes under the jarring fluorescent lights over the bathroom mirror.

"I've got good reason—"

"Don't play cryptic, Beck." Impatience curled in his tone.

"I'm not playing anything. There are things you don't know."

Logan's gaze darkened. "What I know is, you haven't bothered to come home for seven years—"

"Six." The word came out tinny. Futile.

"You've missed tons of stuff. The only holidays we've spent with you are the ones we came out to Boston for." Barely veiled frustration crackled in Logan's voice. "My daughter hardly knows her uncle."

Beckett watched himself flinch in the mirror. The accusation couldn't have bruised more swiftly if it'd been a punch. But what could he say? Logan was right, and he'd offered too many long-distance apologies over the years to think another would do any good now.

But if Logan would just hear him out . . . Not now—there wasn't time—but tonight. He'd explain why he'd stayed away. Why he'd finally come back. All the ways he was working to make things right.

The door swung open then. "I heard someone needs a razor. I ran into Kate and she gave me this and told me—"

The voice halted the same second Beckett's focus landed on the face staring back at him from the mirror.

Kit.

The razor clinked to the ground.

He stared as the last of his confidence crumbled.

She stepped into the room. "They said you weren't coming."

She'd grown out her hair since he'd seen her last and it dangled past her shoulders in honey-gold waves. She wore a simple navy blue dress and—his gaze traveled to her feet—strappy heels? Since when did Kit Danby run around in anything other than flip-flops?

Since when was she *here*? He swallowed hard.

And then she was smiling that crooked Danby smile that always started on one side before filling out. "I'm so happy to see you."

Logan cleared his throat. "I'll just, um, give you two a moment."

"No." The word released in a heated whoosh. Kate, Logan, neither of them knew . . . He shook his head, felt the tightness course through him and pushed past his brother, intent on the door.

She wasn't supposed to be here.

He flung the door open and spilled into the hallway, unbuttoned Oxford flapping against his thin undershirt. Raegan and Kate stood in a clump of bridesmaids in the foyer. More people, enough of them turning to stare for him to realize what he must look like—half undressed, disheveled, angry.

"Beckett."

Kit's voice sounded behind him, and he turned. He saw the hurt mixed with pleading in her eyes. And maybe something else . . . hope? Did she honestly think they were about to have a happy reunion right here?

But then her expression shifted to confusion, her focus angling behind him.

"Beckett Walker?"

He could feel the hush of the onlookers before he even turned. And somehow, he just knew.

A police officer. In uniform, face older but familiar. Looking none too happy to be here. "You're Beckett."

"You know I am. We went to school together, Hastings." Why, even now, when he knew what was about to happen, did he have to be sarcastic?

"Sorry about this, man." The officer sighed. "Beckett Walker, I'm here to place you under arrest."

2

She should've known not to come.

Kit Danby pushed through the church doors, the strident strains of the post-wedding processional trailing after her, a moisture-tinged breeze glazing over her skin and twisting through her hair. Rain. Soon.

This many years away from Iowa and she could still read the air, interpret its climbs and falls and textures. Could still hear Grandpa's murmur—*"My little meteorologist"*—and listen for nature's whisper.

If only she'd listened as keenly to her gut or her conscience or whatever nagging internal voice it was that'd hissed its disapproval the second she'd stepped into the church a couple hours ago.

Beckett.

She'd known he might be here. Had known he wouldn't want to see her.

So why now, even as she practically fled the building and its trove of memories, was she tempted to go after him?

Because at least with Beckett I know what to expect. As for what might be waiting for her at home . . .

"We're leaving so soon?" Nigel—patient, long-suffering Nigel—hastened to match her steps. His polished shoes clipped against the cement as he caught up with her and reached for her hand. "Not that I'm complaining. After touring your entire town today, I'm ready to find a bed and crash."

"You say 'entire town' as if Maple Valley is the size of London and not, like, a speck in comparison." She pushed out a laugh and gave his hand an appreciative squeeze. He had come all this way with her, after all. Flown across the Atlantic and then, after only a few hours of sleep in a noisy hotel in Minneapolis, traveled down to Iowa and didn't once grumble as she played tour guide.

If he'd picked up on the fact that the extended tour was really just her way of stalling, he hadn't let on. It wasn't that she didn't want to go home—to the house and the apple orchard where she'd spent the bulk of her childhood.

It was just that her older brother might not be any happier to see her than Beckett.

"Well, I had no idea there was so much to see in such a small town." Amusement flashed in his hazel eyes, his English accent so very out of place. "The riverfront, the library, all the antique stores. Seriously, I don't understand how a town this small has so many antique stores."

"And we didn't even see half of them." She tried for a breezy grin but must have failed. Because when she attempted a step toward their rental car, Nigel's grip held her in place. How did he manage to look so put-together after two such long days? From his bald head to his clean-shaven jaw to the astonishing lack of wrinkles in his suit, he didn't appear even the tiniest bit jet-lagged.

"What is it, Kit?"

"Noth—"

"Don't say nothing. I've known you too long to buy

that. Might as well tell me what has your brow crinkling." His scrutiny turned pointed. "Or rather *who.*"

He meant Beckett, of course. Brooding clouds bowed into the trees bordering the church lot.

All through Seth and Ava's wedding, sitting in a pew, Nigel's arm around her, the truth of it had knocked around inside her. *He's here. Beckett. Beckett's here.*

And yet . . . not. Not since shuffling through the church foyer, head down, shoulders hunched. Arrested in front of his family, all the wedding guests.

She'd watched along with everyone else as the Walkers huddled—Beckett's siblings, his father, his cousin. Some she didn't recognize, probably significant others who'd come along in the years since she'd moved to London. They'd decided to go on with the wedding.

"Kit." Nigel's leaden tone finally betrayed his exasperation at her silence. "You fidgeted all the way through the wedding and now we're leaving before the reception. Who's the bloke who was arrested?"

"I . . . He's . . ." The words glommed together, awkward and truculent, under his prodding gaze. "He's just someone I used to know."

"Is he the one who . . . the man you almost married?" Nigel glanced behind her, to the church.

She couldn't hold back her wince. "No." And then, before he could ask any one of the questions trekking over his face, she clasped his hand once more. "Come on. Let's go home." *And stop avoiding the inevitable.*

After a pause, he gave her a resigned half-smile and started toward the parking lot. "Sometimes I think you like keeping me in the dark about what goes on in your head, Kit Danby."

"Or I just like being mysterious." She grasped for a playfulness she didn't feel.

"I can be patient. It took me two years to get you to

go on a date with me. Another eight months to convince you this thing with us is going somewhere. Another four to wheedle my way into meeting your family."

A distant rumble of thunder echoed overhead. "Just my brother, really. Lucas." Far as she knew, Dad was still in D.C., stationed at Fort McNair. Not that he likely would've bothered to let her know if he'd relocated. One of these days she should probably accept the fact that her father had about as much interest in her now as he had when she was a kid—very little.

As for Lucas, his terse email last month was the reason she was here. Just a few hasty lines about how he'd decided to close the family apple orchard, the one Grandpa and Grandma had spent a lifetime cultivating.

No explanation. No answers to her calls and emails in reply.

Days had unfolded into weeks as she'd tried to decide what to do—go home and intervene or stay out of it? After all, Grandpa had left the orchard to Dad, who'd entrusted it to Lucas . . . not her. But she loved the place. Oh, she loved it.

And when she'd received the invitation to the Walker wedding, it'd felt like a sign. The longing to return had simply taken over. She'd go to the wedding. She'd confront Lucas and convince him not to give up on their grandparents' legacy. Two birds, one stone.

The sky's gloamy deepening cast shadows around the churchyard, the first raindrops breaking free as they jogged the rest of the way to the car. Nigel held the driver's-side door open for her and she slid in. He'd driven all of two miles from the car rental lot yesterday before declaring Americans "nutters" for driving on the right side of the road. She'd kissed his cheek and traded seats and wondered for the hundredth time what her friends and family would say about the Brit she'd brought home.

Except there hadn't been any real family at the wedding, and as for friends . . .

The storm in Beckett's charcoal eyes flashed in her mind until a hard blink and the sound of Nigel's passenger-side door closing pushed it away.

"There's just one thing, Kit." Concern hovered in Nigel's voice as he reached across the console to touch her arm. The car's pine-scented air freshener owned the space between them. "You bought a one-way ticket."

She'd known he'd eventually bring that up. "Only because I'm not sure what's up with the orchard. I might need to stick around for a week or two to help out."

"But you packed enough for a month, at least. You closed up your flat." He pulled on his seatbelt. "You haven't signed the contract for the upcoming school term."

Because even before Lucas's email, she hadn't known if she wanted to sign on for another year of field botany for the university where she'd received her master's. It was fine work, she supposed, even if many days it did feel like she was little more than a glorified plant waterer.

She started the engine. "Nige—"

"It's not that I'm trying to pressure you where we're concerned, but if you'd just think logically for a minute . . ." His words drifted into a long sigh.

And then, just like that, just like the patient, undemanding man she'd known him to be since the day they'd met, Nigel simply let it drop. Didn't push, didn't prod. Merely leaned against the headrest and closed his eyes.

She pulled away from the church and turned on her windshield wipers as the rain settled into a steady fall. The quaint town center blurred by outside—brick and pastel buildings, bright awnings, and baskets filled with asters and black-eyed Susans dangling from old-fashioned lampposts. They crossed the midnight blue ripples of the river that cut the town in half, and soon a residential neighborhood gave way to miles of gravel and a stretch of fields, their rise and fall reaching into a veiled horizon.

Until there, up ahead, the familiar sign hanging between two wooden poles. *Valley Orchard.* The mass of trees—almost five thousand of them—spread over a fifty-acre stretch of land. The temptation to park and escape the car, roam the orchard before going to the house, nearly engulfed her.

But no, she needed to see Lucas first. Couldn't put this off any longer.

So she passed the turn that would lead into the main orchard grounds and continued another half mile, eventually curving around to the homestead—the farmhouse and garage situated on a cut-out clearing. The land behind her grandparents' house gave way to the ravine that separated Danby land from Walker land.

How many times had she shuffled down the ravine's sloping decline as a kid to get to Beckett?

"This is it?" Nigel sat up.

"This is it." Except, oh, how the farmhouse had changed since she'd seen it last—its once-white now a dull gray, one shutter hanging crookedly next to a second-floor window. No ivy-entwined lattice climbing the side of the porch like she remembered, no flowers lining the walkway that led from the drive to the front door. Lucas had told her the tornado of 2014 destroyed the deck Dad had built the one too-brief autumn he'd actually spent with them here, but seeing it for herself, seeing all of it . . .

Wonderful memories. Heart-breaking memories.

They swirled together at the sight of the age-worn home that seemed so bereft, so . . .

Empty.

Long grass bent against the wind and the rain. She lurched from the car.

Nigel called her name from behind.

But she didn't slow, didn't stop until she reached the shelter of the front door's overhang. She found the spare key in the empty flower box and let herself in. Hot, humid air billowed into her. No air-conditioning?

"Lucas!" She pried off her sandals and padded into the living room. The furniture was arranged just as she remembered—couch, loveseat, rocking chair. Framed family photos crammed the fireplace mantel. Earthy tones in the carpet and curtains, sprinkles of color—bold oranges and yellows—in throw pillows and a blanket folded neatly atop the couch.

Too neatly.

Something wasn't right.

"Lucas?"

No signs of life in the dining room, the kitchen. No abandoned dishes or articles of clothing. She heard Nigel come in the house behind her as she hurried up the open staircase to the second floor. Lucas's childhood bedroom was empty. Maybe he'd claimed the master.

But no. It sat vacant, untouched.

He wasn't here. Maybe hadn't been for several days, considering how sweltering the house was, how closed-up—every set of window blinds, every drape.

"Kit?"

Nigel's footsteps sounded on the stairs.

Gone. Lucas was just gone. Without a word or a warning.

Even Dad had at least given them some warning.

Nigel approached, something in his hand. A photo

from the mantel?

"He's not here. How could he just leave? Abandon the house and the orchard and—"

Nigel interrupted. "It's him. The guy from the church."

"Who . . . what?"

He held out the frame, and the faces staring back at her registered. A close-up of her and Beckett, arms around each other's shoulders—all smiles and windswept hair. "He's really not the man you almost married?"

Dread-infused confusion over Lucas's absence tangled with the exhaustion pulling on her every nerve. The lingering anxiety over Beckett's arrest. The prickly demand in Nigel's words.

"No." She met his eyes. "He's the one who stopped the wedding."

"This is ridiculous, and you know it."

Dad's voice carried from the front desk of the Maple Valley Police Department building to the stark white, cement-walled cell of the small-town jail. Relief and shame wrestled for prominence as Beckett straightened from his slumped position on the metal bench, a ragged sigh heaving through him as he stood. And something else—the question that'd begun badgering him in the backseat of Hastings's squad car: How in the world had word of his return gotten to the police so quickly?

"I promise you, Mr. Walker, I'm not trying to be difficult." Was that a shake in Hastings's voice? "I'm not authorized to release him. Not yet."

Without even seeing him, Beckett could picture Dad—his height and commanding presence, once-dark hair now silver and his well-creased face that didn't hint at his age so much as his easy laughter.

But he wasn't laughing now. "It isn't enough that you disrupted my nephew's wedding? Now you're holding my son needlessly—knowing he's not a danger, he's not going to run."

"I wouldn't say we know that. Not considering he's conveniently avoided Maple Valley for how many years?"

Wait, that wasn't Hastings speaking anymore. Beckett stiffened. And Dad said the name even as it knuckled into Beckett's brain. "Sam Ross."

"Sorry you had to leave the reception early, Mr. Walker. But as you can see, you're not the only one."

Suddenly it all made sense. Sam Ross had been at the wedding. Sam Ross had seen him.

Sam Ross—Kit's ex-fiancé.

The one who'd stood in front of the church six years ago looking shell-shocked after Beckett had rocketed to his feet and called out an objection as if it were court instead of a wedding ceremony.

"You didn't have to do it, Ross." Dad's tone held rebuke. "Not like this."

"I'm the police chief."

"You were off duty."

"And I'm on now."

Sam knew Beckett was hearing all of this, didn't he? Probably expected him to be back here quaking, mentally backing down from whatever fight was surely coming.

Which was exactly what he should be doing. Because he wasn't the old Beckett anymore—the one who threw caution to the wind and chased mere impulse. The one who interrupted weddings and ran off with the bride.

Who stole a car and ran it into a dumb tree, made a mess of the town square, and then left without a backward glance.

No, he'd come home with the sole purpose of manning up, facing his past, and taking care of this whole thing like the staid, mature person he'd worked to become. Like Logan or Dad would've done if they were in his shoes. Not that they'd ever end up in a situation like this in the first place.

If things had gone the way he'd planned, he would've watched Seth's wedding from a back pew and then come down to the station of his own accord. He'd have used his lawyering skills to talk his way out of the arrest warrant that'd been gathering dust for six years. Then he'd have gone back to Boston free and clear. No police record. Nothing to throw up any red flags when he appeared for his Army JAG Corps interview.

Now the only appearance he'd likely be making any time soon was in court. At least it was a weekend—he wouldn't have to spend all night in jail waiting to appear before the local judge in the morning.

Except maybe that would've been better. He wouldn't be able to make his initial court appearance until next week. Which meant he was stuck in town indefinitely. He needed to call Elliott at the firm, find someone to cover Monday's deposition.

"Ross, let's get this over with," he called from his cell, the riled words out before he could stop them. "Charge me, interrogate me, whatever. Just get on with it."

He heard the ire in his own voice, the frustration-fueled hostility. Silence shifted down the jail corridor in reply. And then footsteps.

"Impatient, are we?"

Sam stopped in front of his cell. An imposing six-foot-six, early gray nipping at his temples. Surprising, really, it'd taken him this long to get to the station. He had to have been positively gleeful sitting through Seth and Ava's wedding, thinking about facing off with Beckett across metal cell bars.

Wait, Kit and Sam hadn't been together at the wedding, had they? Surely someone in the family would've told him if Kit had moved home, gotten back together with Sam.

Maybe if you'd let her say a word instead of charging away, she could've explained.

"I was going to turn myself in, you know."

"No, I don't know—"

"But you just had to have me arrested in front of my family. Classy." It was a wonder Sam hadn't made the arrest himself.

"No more classy than wrapping my father's Lincoln around a tree."

Beckett sucked in a sharp breath, guilt slackening his posture as he pushed away from the cell bars. Bad enough he'd whisked Kit away from her wedding, leaving Sam publicly humiliated, but they'd gone and taken the white car just outside the church doors. The one with "Just Married" soaped onto the window.

Then later, after they'd argued, he'd sped down Main on his own, still in Sam's father's car. Anger had fueled his pressure on the accelerator until he lost control, found himself in the middle of the town square, somehow uninjured despite the wreckage around him.

And yet, so very hurt.

He'd only meant to help Kit, stand up for her, but he'd messed it all up. And when she'd pushed him away . . .

Sam's sneer cut into the sting of his memories. "What I can't get over is how you ran away like a scared little—"

"That's enough."

Dad.

He came up beside Sam, his air of authority—that of a man who'd never entirely shed his soldier-turned-diplomat bearing even this many years later—piercing into Sam's smug control. The police chief's attention shifted from Beckett to Dad, indecision idling for a tension-stretched moment.

"Fine." The word was a snarl. He backed away from the cell. "Five minutes."

As Sam's footsteps smacked down the hallway, Beckett forced himself to meet Dad's probing gaze. An impossible mix of kindness and compassion rested in the brown eyes Mom used to call the color of caramel.

The familiar pang sliced through him. *Mom.* As much as he missed her, at least she wasn't seeing him like this.

"I really was going to turn myself in. After the wedding, I was going to talk to you and Logan and Kate and Rae and then drive over here and—"

"Beck." Dad reached his hand through the cell bars, palm open. He waited until Beckett lifted his arm to speak again. "Welcome home."

Dad's hand was warm, his shake firm.

And something in Beckett crumbled. "I'm sorry, Dad. I didn't mean to . . . I shouldn't have even come to the wedding. Seth probably wants to kill me."

Dad's bow tie hung loose around his neck, and he must've left his tuxedo jacket in the car or back at the church. "Seth is so enamored with his bride you could've burned the church down around them and he wouldn't have noticed."

"I haven't even met Ava."

"She's just as crazy about Seth as he is about her. And as even-keeled as they come. Trust me, they won't be holding any grudges." Dad's focus cut down the hallway. "Unlike our police chief, unfortunately."

"I broke up his wedding." His voice flat-lined.

"Yes, I was there, if you'll recall. Kit Danby looked so skittish walking down the aisle, there wasn't a person there who didn't think you were only doing what she wanted you to do."

That's what he'd told himself at the time, too. Didn't change what he'd done. The hurt he'd caused. And now the shock of seeing Kit earlier this evening pulsed through him all over again. London—she was supposed to be in London.

Yeah, well, he was supposed to be talking his way out of a six-year-old arrest warrant right about now. Not standing inside a barely air-conditioned cell that smelled of bleach and stale coffee.

"Listen, I'll stick around as long as I need to, bail you out, whatever. We'll get this taken care of." Dad pulled his bow tie free and stuffed it in his pocket. "Honestly, I'm surprised they even arrested you after all this time. Shouldn't there be some kind of statute of limitations?"

"Doesn't apply if you leave the state." He'd checked on that years ago. Once he'd crossed state lines, any statute paused. Which meant he could still be arrested, charged, and prosecuted this many years later. If he'd just faced up to his actions at the time . . .

But there'd been law school to think about. His future. The promise he'd made after he'd been too late to say goodbye . . .

I'll focus, Mom. I'll make you proud.

Well, now he had a future to think about again. A new reason to focus. So maybe his homecoming hadn't gone as planned. He could still rally, then get back to the life that was finally beginning to take shape.

"Dad, there's a reason I came home now. It wasn't just the wedding." His fingers curled around the cell bars. "I've got some news—"

Dad held up one hand. "Let's wait until we're

home."

The strain in Dad's voice was so subtle Beckett nearly missed it. It was the slight tick in his jaw that gave him away.

"Not bad news," he added softly. But he couldn't blame his father for assuming. The catalog of his past missteps turned its own well-worn pages in rapid succession: high school parties, lack of focus his first couple years of college. And even after he'd gotten his academic act together and settled on a career path, then there was the mess with Kit's wedding, skipping town, the years of avoidance.

Smack in the middle, his biggest regret of all.

Mom . . .

"Well, then, seems both my sons came home with good news."

Beckett blinked. "Logan?"

Dad nodded. "Refused to say what until after the wedding, but considering the Cheshire smile he had going on, I'd say we're all in for a happy surprise. So let's figure out how to get you out of here and—"

"Nothing to figure out." Sam's words echoed down the hallway ahead of his reappearance. He edged past Dad to open the cell. "You're all processed in the system, Walker."

In the system. Which meant he officially had a record.

As the cell door swung open, Sam thrust a slip of paper toward him. "Initial court appearance first thing Tuesday morning. Expect a couple counts—joyriding, damaging public property, the like."

Aggravated misdemeanors.

Sam's sneer accompanied his curt retreat, final words tossed over his shoulder. "See you in court, Walker."

3

Sunrise still lingered in feathered curls of pink outside the window as Kit slid from underneath Grandma's quilt on her childhood bed. Nigel must have found the thermostat last night, cranked the A/C. The hardwood floor chilled her bare feet.

Nigel . . . that must be him clanging around in the kitchen downstairs. Except . . .

She stilled halfway across the bedroom that still looked the same as it always had—cream-colored walls, lavender chair in the corner that matched the hues of her quilt, white antique desk. Her ears perked to the muted rhythm sounding through the wall—Nigel's snores.

So who was . . . ?

Lucas!

Kit threw a t-shirt on over her thin camisole, decided her striped pajama shorts were good enough, and bounded from the room. She padded past the guest room where Nigel still slept and then picked up her pace as she hurried down the stairs.

All that worry last night had been for naught. Her brother was here now, and even if he'd been brisk in his one email, even if their relationship had never entirely recovered from its fractures, surely they could mend things over the coffee she could already smell and maybe a walk out to the orchard and . . .

And it wasn't Lucas standing at the kitchen sink.

"Willa?"

The woman spun, her sun-streaked braid whipping behind her, her grin as warm as it was surprised. "Katherine Louisa Danby. Honest to Pete, if I was wearing socks, you would've scared them right off."

"But of course you're not." Because Willa Chambers would go sockless and wear sandals right through the dead of winter if it weren't for the nuisance of snow and a pesky little thing like frostbite. "What are you doing here?"

The question was no sooner out than Willa skirted around the kitchen table and gathered Kit into a hug. And oh, if she didn't smell exactly as Kit remembered. Like apples and summer and . . .

Home.

Willa stepped back. Her skin was as bronzed as ever, and extra wrinkles had etched a place at the corners of her eyes and around her still-smiling lips. She would've celebrated her fifty-fifth birthday this spring, right? Had Kit even remembered to send a card?

"It's good to see you, my girl."

Her girl. Automatic tears pooled as Kit gave in to a second, longer embrace. "I didn't realize how . . . how much I . . ."

Willa's palms rubbed her back, so much understanding in her soothing. "I know. I missed you, too."

Willa had been Grandpa and Grandma's only year-round orchard employee since well before Dad had carted Kit and Lucas to Iowa. But from day one of living with her grandparents and meeting Willa—who often spent more time at the orchard than her home in town—the woman had felt more like an aunt than a hired hand.

The closest thing to a mother figure Kit had ever known.

Only when she'd blinked away the evidence of her emotion did Kit pull back. "But I still don't know what you're doing here."

Willa's alto laugh chimed as she returned to the counter. "This being Maple Valley and all, I heard you were back straight away. Came over on a whim, found the door unlocked."

Because apparently old habits died hard. "I wouldn't have dared leave my flat unlocked in London, but here it's a different story." And even if she had thought to lock up, she'd been too jet-lagged and weary to trudge back downstairs last night after making up the guest bedroom for Nigel.

Who'd barely said a word to her once she'd explained just who Beckett Walker was.

"He was my best friend."

She'd tried to explain the rest—in hesitant starts and stops that stuck in her throat. Because she couldn't get past that one word: *was*.

Willa pulled two coffee mugs from a cupboard and poured from the pot she must've brewed. She handed Kit one cup, and even as Kit's fingers closed around the warmth, as the rousing scent wafted under her nose, she lifted her eyes to meet Willa's. "If you heard I was home, then you probably also heard . . ."

Willa simply nodded. "Come, let's go sit on the porch."

She followed Willa through the house and then stepped outside into a morning already thick with warmth. Last night's rain might've ushered in a temporary cool, but there was an edge to this morning's air—a hazy heaviness. She settled beside Willa on the porch swing, its creaks and groans proof of its age and a match for the rest of the house's neglected condition.

How could Lucas have let it get so rundown so quickly?

"I heard Beckett was arrested. Don't suppose you know why."

She blinked at Willa's blunt prying and her thoughts swung back to Beckett.

It had been like this all through the restless night. *Beckett. Lucas. Beckett. Lucas.*

"I have an educated guess." Kit sipped her coffee. "And I would've thought the whole town knew."

It was hard to do anything in Maple Valley without an audience of well-meaning but unyielding busybodies. But something as public as tearing up the town square within hours of busting up a wedding? That was the stuff of local legend.

"You mean this is still about the night of your wedding?"

"I assume so." Although that was six years ago. Beckett would've had plenty of time to get in more trouble since. Which, knowing him, wasn't entirely outside the realm of possibilities. Yet, supposedly he was off in Boston building a successful law career. At least, that's what she'd gathered from the few times she'd allowed herself a glance at his online profile, each time wondering, hoping . . .

Hoping for something that clearly wasn't meant to be. Just like, apparently, her hopes for reconnecting with Lucas. She shifted on the swing. "You don't by any chance know where Lucas is, do you?"

Willa took a long drink. "Can't say as I've seen him all that much. Not since he let me go."

Kit set her cup on the swing's armrest so hard, coffee sloshed over the edge. "Let you go? As in, fired you?"

"Six weeks ago. I could tell he felt badly about it, but when I asked why, he didn't have much to say for himself."

Kit jerked to her feet, paced the length of the porch. *How could you, Luke?* And why? Even if he had good reason to close down the business side of the orchard, the trees still needed tending. Who'd been doing the pruning, the spraying, the everyday maintenance that kept their trees healthy and their crop robust?

"He didn't give any indication of his plans? You don't know where he would've gone?"

"Wish I did. All I know is he hasn't been the same since—"

Her pacing halted as her gaze shot to Willa's. *Don't say it.*

"I don't judge him. You know I don't." Willa leaned back against the porch swing. "But that doesn't mean I don't see what the war did to him."

Willa was being generous—attributing Lucas's changes to a two-word phrase: *the war*. It might've sounded noble if not for the other words lurking behind: *desertion, court martial, federal prison.*

She'd been sixteen when Lucas enlisted and went off to fight in Afghanistan after 9/11. Eighteen and fresh out of high school when they'd learned he'd gone missing. Nearly twenty-one when he was hauled back to the U.S. and had refused to deny the desertion charges.

Her heart ached for her older brother now even as it pumped with aggravation. Didn't Lucas realize what disappearing—again—would do to the people who loved him?

"Didn't he live in one of the Carolinas after he was released from prison?"

Kit brushed willful strands of hair behind her ear. "North. For a while." Almost two years. But that was before Grandpa had passed away. His funeral was the only time in six years she'd come back to Maple Valley, and she'd almost thought she might end up staying. She'd always loved the orchard, always assumed one day she'd come home and help run the place.

But no. Dad had bestowed that responsibility on Lucas.

"I'm sure he's okay." Willa's tone was gentle if not convincing. "Or if not exactly okay, at least safe. He's a grown man who knows how to take care of himself. Maybe he just needed to get away for a while, clear his head."

Kit settled onto the swing once more. "Just wish I knew where he was. And when he's coming back. *If* he's coming back. And as for the orchard . . ."

"Yes, about that."

"You know something?"

"I think your father might be considering selling. Or at least closing the store, the touristy part of the business, and focusing solely on vending. I heard Lucas on the phone a few times."

A feverish worry took hold. "But why?"

"Oh, I don't think your dad's ever had much interest in the place. Lucas never really seemed like a long-term fit, either."

Maybe she shouldn't take it so personally, shouldn't feel such a charge of indignation and heartbreak. But how could they just toss aside what her grandparents had worked so hard to build? Maybe Dad didn't feel a connection to the land—after all, Grandma and Grandpa were his in-laws, not his own parents. He hadn't grown up here.

But Kit had. Lucas had. They were tied to this place.

Willa stretched her arm across Kit's shoulders and let her pause linger before she spoke again. "Even if it's not the best circumstances that brought you home, Katherine, I am glad to see you again."

"You do know you're the only person who still calls me Katherine, don't you?"

Because she'd been Kit from the day she'd met Beckett Walker. Dad had only just moved them to Maple Valley, to Grandma and Grandpa's, and she'd met Beckett playing in the ravine that divided the land between their houses. He was eleven, she was ten, and as soon as she'd introduced herself, he'd promptly declared she couldn't go by Katherine because that was his older sister's name.

"Not Kate or Katie, either. That'd be too weird if we're going to be friends."

"We're going to be friends?"

"How about Kit?"

The memory faded as Willa patted her knee. "You should go out to the orchard. See your trees. Then come on back and I'll have breakfast ready for you and whoever it is snoring upstairs."

"Oh, he might sleep all morning. Jetlag and all."

Willa lifted one eyebrow. "He? This anything I should know about?"

"Don't worry, he's British, which means he's endlessly proper. But yes, he is my . . ." Boyfriend? The word still felt awkward. But that's what this was, wasn't it? That was what Nigel had wanted months back when he'd declared he was tired of, in his words, a relationship that lacked definition. "My boyfriend."

There went the other eyebrow. "So it's a new thing?"

"Not really."

"Huh. Well, you might want to practice saying it a few times before introducing him to anyone around here."

She rolled her eyes and leaned in for another hug before heading into the house. Upstairs, she changed into a pale yellow top over light blue shorts. She toed on a pair of flip-flops she found in her closet, and within minutes, she was back outside, walking the gravel lane that led to the orchard. Her grandparents used to drive their old truck out to the main orchard grounds each day, but it was a short enough distance to walk when unhurried.

The sun had climbed higher in the eastern sky and it rambled over the fields across the road—green and golden and then ebbing to an end as the orchard entrance came into view. She passed under the welcome sign and drank in the sight of her childhood playground.

Most prominent was the long rectangular dairy barn that had been renovated into the orchard's store, its yellow paint weatherworn and pale, a stretching wood porch and quaint shuttered façade tracing the length of its front. Set slightly back and to the east of the main building, a metal machine shed glinted in the sun. Then a large grassy lot with a play area for kids. Grandpa used to talk about adding a petting zoo there.

Finally, at the far edge of the clearing, a concrete foundation and a hollow frame for what would've been the property's largest building. Grandpa had begun building it when she was still in college with the plan of turning it into a special events space he could rent out for additional income—weddings, family reunions, community gatherings. He'd finally laid the foundation the year she'd graduated. *"It'll be red, of course. Classic barn shape with gable dormers at the top and an extended overhang on one side overlooking the knoll. Rustic charm on the outside; elegant, multipurpose space on the inside."*

But that'd been the year before the hailstorm that'd claimed nearly an entire season's crop. After that, he'd either been too short on funds or energy—perhaps both—to finish his plan. So now only the bones of the barn stood testament to his intentions.

Ground still soft from last night's rain slicked under her sandals as she passed between the shed and the barn. Gravel turned to grass in the open expanse behind the buildings and then . . .

Then the trees. They stood together as if waiting for her, patient and beckoning, Grandpa's whisper on the breeze. "*We plant them in rows for better air circulation. Our property is perfect for the trees because it's on high ground, which means well-draining soil and direct sun exposure. There's always at least eight feet between each tree.*"

Out here she could almost forget Lucas's disappearance. Beckett's presence in town, his arrest. Nigel's look of disappointment last night when he'd realized there was an entire piece of her past she'd never shared with him.

Leaves rustled, and dappled sunlight danced through branches. Dew-tipped grass swished over her toes as she tipped her head . . .

And then halted. *Wait . . .*

Her focus paused on a drooping shoot, its shape like a shepherd's crook, black and telling. *No.* Her gaze dragged from tree to tree, taking in too many gray-black fruit blossoms, bending leaves and stems.

Humid air clung to her skin as the reality of what she was seeing sent her hopes plummeting. Fire blight—a bacterial tree disease. Destructive. Contagious. It could take out the whole orchard.

Maybe already had.

What Beckett wouldn't give for the hot water of the

shower to wipe away the past twenty-four hours as easily as it'd washed away the grime of yesterday—a day with too many confined spaces. The airplane, the rental car, the jail cell.

A towel around his waist, Beckett shook the excess water from his hair, then leaned over the bathroom sink. Laughter drifted from below through the open vent, along with the smell of breakfast. He'd wanted to skip it, hide out from his family a while longer. They'd been gracious enough not ply him with a thousand questions when he'd finally been released last night. Or maybe not so much gracious as simply too busy.

Because as soon as they'd all been together at Dad's house—minus Seth and Ava, of course—Logan had announced his news, stunned them all first into silence and then into a celebratory uproar.

Married. Logan had gone and eloped with his girlfriend of only a few months. Beckett still couldn't wrap his head around it. Neat and orderly Logan, the guy who planned every move five steps in advance. And the girl in question—Amelia, the wife and second-newest Walker—had only left Logan's side long enough to hug each member of her new family.

Awkward, that. Hugging a woman he'd never met, realizing she'd probably witnessed his arrest along with the rest of them, wondering what she must think of her new brother-in-law.

He'd never gotten around to sharing his own news, which didn't so much feel like real news anymore. Not after Logan's shocker. It wasn't like he'd even been accepted into the JAG Corps yet. All he had was a very syrupy-sounding story of sitting on a beach near Boston, tired and restless, as his old dream came sputtering back to life. He'd wondered if it might actually be God stirring him up. He'd made the decision right then and there, felt a peace he didn't understand.

Now he had an interview scheduled. September 8, just a little over a month away. He was required to meet with a field screening officer, plus complete a lengthy and intense application by November. He figured he'd get the interview out of the way first, then focus on the written portion of the process.

Last night had put a chink in his plan to handle the arrest warrant before his big day, but surely he could still get it taken care of in time. He had to. Because he was done letting his past keep him from the kind of future he hungered for. One in which he felt like he was actually doing something he was meant for, something worthwhile.

Something that would make his family look at him the way they tended to look at Logan. Or even better, Dad.

Anyway, much as he wanted to, he was smart enough to know there'd be no holing away for long this morning. Thus, the dragging himself from bed. The shower. The attempt at making himself presentable.

But the image staring back at him now appeared ragged, frayed. The damp ends of his hair skimmed his ears and neck, and if he didn't find a razor eventually, what had been a five-o'clock shadow yesterday would end up being the beginning of an actual beard. The circles under his eyes and the yellow glare of the lights over the mirror gave him a hollowed look.

But at least he was clean.

Beckett grabbed his toothbrush from the silver cup he'd stuck it in last night. His niece's princess toothbrush and two others were propped in the holder, as well. He recognized Logan's glasses folded on the counter and Raegan's bright pink robe hanging on a hook on the back of the bathroom door.

He made quick work of brushing his teeth, the voices from below growing louder. Get some coffee in him and a hearty Walker breakfast, and he might be halfway up to handling the questions he knew his siblings wouldn't be able to hold back once he made an appearance downstairs.

What was last night all about? Do you have to go to court? How long are you staying? How's work? What's Boston got that Maple Valley doesn't?

And Kit. They'd ask about Kit.

Beckett slapped off the bathroom lights. He glanced into the hallway before crossing to his bedroom. Not that his sisters hadn't seen him in solely a towel before, but they were adults now and there was Logan's new wife to consider and—

The shriek from across the room and his own shock nearly knocked his breath from him.

"Beckett!"

Kit? One hand flew to the knot in the towel at his waist as he stared. Definitely Kit. Definitely standing in his bedroom. Definitely staring right back at him.

"What the heck, Kit?"

The navy blue comforter from his bed lay in a pile near Kit's feet where he'd kicked it off last night. "You're not dressed."

"Yeah, I usually don't wear clothes when I take a shower." He yanked the towel tighter around his waist.

"I didn't know—"

"Clearly."

Embarrassment colored her cheeks and apparently kept her from being able to look him in the eye, because her gaze hadn't moved from his torso. But he didn't have the same trouble, his focus moving from her ponytail to her t-shirt and shorts to her pale legs—guess they didn't get much sun in England—and bare feet. There were the flip-flops he remembered.

A summer-scented breeze from the open window sent his bedroom door sailing shut, and Kit practically jumped. Awfully skittish considering she was the one to show up in a guy's bedroom unannounced.

"I need your help, Beck." She blurted the words.

"Morning to you, too."

She dropped into the chair at his old desk, pushed up to the wall beside the window. "Well, sorry, you don't seem in the small talk mood."

"Maybe because I was sorta planning to, I don't know, get dressed before entertaining callers."

The red in her cheeks deepened.

"Did someone let you in?"

She poked a thumb over her shoulder. "I . . . uh . . . I climbed in the window."

He ignored the niggle of familiarity that image induced. "Not a fan of knocking?"

Finally, she lifted her gaze and met his eyes, a sudden streak of defiance brightening her ridiculously blue irises. "I've climbed in that window a hundred times, Beckett Walker, and you know it. We always climbed in each other's windows. It was our thing."

"That was a long time ago—"

"Yeah, well, I did it for old times' sake." She crossed her arms. "I thought it might be endearing."

"Try intrusive."

Before he could blink, she stood to snatch a pillow from his bed and chucked it at him. It hit him square in the chest.

"Hey—"

"Put. A. Shirt. On." She punctuated each word with flung items—another pillow, the shirt he'd abandoned to the floor last night, a ball of socks. By the time she'd picked up the last pillow on his bed, he'd moved out of her line of fire, his surprise-turned-amusement finally spilling over into laughter.

He reached for the hoodie over his closet doorknob and scrunched it into a ball before throwing it at her. "Don't get mad at me, Kit. I'm not the one who—"

"What in the world is going on here?"

He froze. Kate stood in the doorway, the clatter of footsteps behind her telling him everyone else was on the way too.

"Kit?" Raegan slipped past Kate. "How did you . . . ?" But her voice trailed as her attention flitted to the open window.

And then Logan. "Let me guess. You took the screen off your window last night so you could sit on the roof and have a smoke before bed."

Beckett rolled his eyes. "I did that one time." Smoke a cigarette, that is. Climbing onto the roof had been a nightly ritual growing up.

And now Dad. "Really, Beck? You had to take the screen off? Tell me you didn't leave it open all night while the A/C was running. And all the mosquitos—"

"Why are you all looking at *me*?" He jabbed his finger toward Kit. "She's the one who climbed in. Started throwing things at me."

"I did not." Kit flounced her ponytail over her shoulder.

His jaw dropped at her bold-faced lie. He spread his arms. "So every untethered item in this room just happened to scatter all over the floor?"

"Hold onto your towel, please." This from Kate.

Dad barely stifled a chuckle. "I gotta get back downstairs before the mini-quiches burn. Everyone, let's leave these two alone." He herded the family into the hallway but stuck his head back in the room before retreating. "Feel free to stay for breakfast, Kit. That is, after you two . . ." He looked between them. "Talk. Or whatever."

And then he was gone, along with everyone else, their laughter trailing behind them.

Kit hauled her gaze from the open door to him, puddles of red still coloring her cheeks, but now something other than embarrassment huddled in her eyes. Longing. He could see it plain as day. Always could read her easier than a picture book.

"Mini-quiches. Your dad's specialty." Her voice had gone soft.

How many Walker breakfasts had she been in on? It was a family tradition and she'd pretty much been family there for a while.

He walked to the open suitcase on his bed and picked out a shirt. "What are you doing here, Kit?" He pulled a plain white tee over his head.

She turned toward the window, obviously meaning to give him privacy to finish dressing. "It's the orchard. I was just out there and I didn't notice it at first but . . ."

He pulled on a pair of tan shorts. "What?"

"Fire blight."

She turned. The fear etched into her expression was enough to barrel past his reserve. "Are you sure?"

Kit nodded.

The half-dozen summers and falls he'd worked at the orchard as a teenager were enough for him to understand the danger of the infection. It could sneak up, infecting trees during humid spring or early summer days, but not show itself for weeks.

"I don't know how many trees are affected yet. I just saw it and panicked and did the first thing I could think to do. Which was come here."

She'd come through the ravine, hadn't she? Just like when they were kids, so many trips back and forth across the creek that separated the properties.

She tilted her head to look up at him. "You helped Grandpa that year in high school when it happened, right? I know I have no right to ask, but I have no idea where Lucas is and I know Willa will help but even so—"

"Kit."

She stilled.

And in the quiet, something shifted. Suddenly she wasn't the woman who'd wordlessly pled for him to rescue her from a wedding she didn't want, only to walk away from him, too, an hour later—hurled words from both of them in her wake.

But just . . . Kit. The one person who knew him better than anyone. The only one who'd known exactly where to find him the day after Mom died, who'd witnessed his sobs and then had the grace not to say another word about it.

"Beckett, I . . ."

Whatever she was going to say dissolved into a strained silence filled only by his own conflicting thoughts.

This is Kit. He'd never *not* helped her when she'd needed it.

This is Kit. The woman whose words, so much more than that car accident and subsequent threat of arrest, had driven him from town.

This is Kit. His best friend, once upon a time.

Finally, a sigh. "We'll need chainsaws."

He refused to let his attention linger on her grateful smile.

"Kit, it's almost ten." Nigel called from the ground

below. "Call it a day."

The groaning of every muscle in her body told her to listen to him. After twelve hours of inspecting trees one by one, mixing bucket after bucket of bleach solution, immersing her chainsaw blade in between every cut of every infected branch—she'd be lucky if she could move her arms tomorrow.

But just enough filtered moonlight laced its way through tree branches to keep her from quitting. "You go on. I want to finish this row." And maybe the next.

"You're exhausted, darling. You never even had dinner."

Because it was too hot to eat. And because every time she stopped for a break, the questions needled her again: Had Lucas known about the blight when he'd left? Did Dad know? And even if she managed to stave it off, keep it from spreading, and save any or all of this season's crop, what did it matter if there was no one to run the place?

Unless you stayed.

That last one—not a question, not a needling. Instead—an inkling, a wondering. Maybe for the first time in a long time, some kind of divine nudge showing her the desire of her heart.

Or she was simply overly tired, and like a parched soul in a dry desert, looking for a vision where there was none. After all, she had a life in London. A relationship. And if Dad had thought she was capable of managing the orchard, he would've asked her to do so in the first place.

"Kit." A thin layer of annoyance hedged Nigel's voice. Could she blame him? He'd expected a leisurely weekend, getting to know her better as he observed her in her hometown. Instead, he'd gotten a day of physical labor under a pummeling sun.

It was tedious work—scouring branches one at a

time, lugging sloshing buckets and heavy chainsaws from tree to tree.

"I promise I won't be much longer, Nige."

If he meant to argue further, she didn't hear it under the buzz of her chainsaw. Willa had gone home a couple hours ago when the sun still lazed in the west, Case and Logan Walker not long after. They'd worked in pairs most of the day—she and Nigel, Beckett and Willa, Case and Logan, three saws between them and as many ten-gallon buckets.

Just as her arms were about to give out from the weight of the pulsing saw, the knotty bark of a limp limb finally gave way to her blade. One more fresh wound. One step closer to eradicating the fire blight before it spread any further. She felt the branch detach just as the ladder jostled under her feet.

"Really, Nige, I can finish by myself."

"What? You're going to climb down to bleach your blade in between every cut and then back up again?"

Her gaze swung from the tree to the face looking at her over the ladder top. Not Nigel. Beckett held out her bucket, and even in the dim of twilight, the day's toll was displayed all over him—sweat-dampened shirt clinging to his chest, cheeks and nose reddened by the sun, and fatigue written into the shadows under his eyes.

"That's what you've been doing since Willa went home, isn't it? Working solo?"

"Yeah, and it's been slow-going." Propping the bucket between his waist and the ladder, he reached around for the chainsaw. She didn't argue but did relieve him of the bucket, then glanced behind her in time to see Nigel's weaving retreat through the web of trees. "I told him to head back. Said I'd help you finish off this tree, then drag you home."

"But I want to at least get through the rest of this

row and—"

"Too dark to be using a chainsaw, Kit."

And yet that didn't stop him from dipping the blade into her bucket and lifting it to a gray, diseased branch. The droning motor kept her from any kind of sarcastic retort.

That and the gratefulness coming off her in waves. Twenty-four hours ago, she'd been convinced Beckett would be happy never to talk to her again. But he'd spent an entire day helping her, wrangled his dad and brother into giving up their Saturday, too.

He'd hardly said a word to her all day, just worked as vigorously as if this was his orchard, as if it mattered as much to him as it did to her.

As if there weren't years of distance and hurt and abandoned memories between them.

He continued on for several more minutes, scanning the underpinnings of the tree for gnarled branches, running his fingers along fresh cuts, while she held the bucket of liquid for him. Did his arms feel as brick-heavy as her own?

Finally, he choked off the saw's whir, scrutinizing the half-stripped tree and then nodding. "This one's good."

She met his gaze over the ladder. "You know, if I go get one of the other saws—"

He shook his head, the first hint of a smile she'd seen all day teasing the corner of his mouth. "Too dark," he said again. "Injury follows you around. You'd end up accidentally sawing off a finger."

"Untrue."

"Broken collarbone from a fall on the ice in fifth grade. Stitches from a shop class project gone wrong in seventh grade. Sophomore year, sprained ankle during a basketball game." His forehead creased as if he was scouring his memory.

"You done?"

"Split lip, sledding accident. Now I'm done."

"Interesting how you were around for every single one of those."

He shrugged. "Pure coincidence." He stepped one rung down, but then stopped when she didn't follow, now eye level over the ladder's top.

"Beck . . . thank you. For today. Willa thinks we might've gotten the worst of it. We've lost a chunk of the crop, but not a devastating amount. But without you . . . you dropped everything to help."

"Wasn't much to drop." His dark-eyed gaze roamed the landscape around her. "You'll need to monitor it closely."

"I know."

"Not just the infected trees, but all the ones around them."

"I know."

Beckett simply peered at her then, quiet and waiting. So not the vocal, boisterous Beckett she remembered.

And that wasn't the only thing different about him. Oh, he still had the dark Walker eyes, the hair, the height. Unlike his older brother's twin dimples, Beckett had only one—barely noticeable unless he smiled just right.

But there was a new depth to his gaze now, a lingering . . . something. Yearning, perhaps, or an ache that hadn't been there before. Or if it had, she hadn't noticed it underneath his usual buoyancy.

"Kit."

He said her name and she blinked—caught staring. She should laugh right now, say something about returning to their roots, reminisce about so many summer nights in the orchard as teens. But the same tightness in her muscles extended to her voice, squashing whatever words might have plucked the tension from the wending air. And instead, in the clammy quiet, realization skimmed over her.

The Beckett Walker she'd known as a kid had gone and grown up—completely and entirely. Become a man. One with broader shoulders and firmer angles and . . .

And who no longer released his every thought and emotion with such carefree abandon.

"Beck, about last night . . ."

There was the proof. The stiffening of his shoulders, the shade in his eyes. He started down the ladder. "Don't want to talk about it."

She shifted the bucket so she could follow him down. "It was Sam, wasn't it? Willa told me he's the police chief now. Do you have to go to court? It's all because of my wedding night, isn't it? I feel so responsible—"

He interrupted her before she was even halfway down the ladder. "Don't. You're not responsible. It has nothing to do with you, and I don't want—"

"Of course it has something to do with me." The bucket knocked against her hip as she climbed down. "You saved me from making one of the biggest mistakes of my life that night. But then we argued, you drove off—"

"I remember. I was there."

Her feet landed in the grass. "So let's talk. Finally, we're both here, back in each other's lives—"

He clamped the ladder closed. "We're not back in each other's lives, Kit. I'm here because I've always liked this place and because, yeah, you needed help. But that's it. As soon as I can, I'm on a plane back to Boston and you'll go back to London, unless by some miracle you actually stand up to your dad and do what you want for once—"

"Don't tell me what I want, Beckett."

"—instead of waiting for someone else to do it for you."

The charge sliced through dense air and the heat of her own rising anger, landing with perfect, painful aim. It stole her breath and stung a wound as open as those marring the trees around her.

"I didn't ask you to stop the wedding." Barely a whisper. And as for what had happened after . . .

"You didn't have to."

Because he knew her. He knew her so very well—always had.

Only now, as he turned and walked away, ladder under one arm and chainsaw in the other, the truth swallowed any chance at a reply.

The truth that, anymore, she didn't know him at all.

4

"Are you sure you don't want a lawyer?"

Dad matched Beckett's hurried pace up the courthouse stairs. The red brick structure stretched to a peak, its massive clock over the main entrance glaring the time in oversized roman numerals. Barely ten minutes until he was due in front of the judge—and the court citation had said to arrive fifteen minutes early.

Why couldn't he have been on time just this once?

"I'm sure, Dad."

Beckett lugged the door open, the muscles in his arms and back protesting even the minor movement. From working under a blazing sun all day Saturday, no doubt. Inside, marble floors and matching columns ornamented a chasm of open space stippled with the occasional desk or office door. He'd only been in the historic courthouse twice, maybe three times growing up. A field trip here, a parking fine there.

Dad used the back of his palm to swipe away the beads of sweat on his forehead. Another August scorcher, but the walk from the car had been minimal.

"You all right, Dad?"

His father chased away a wince with a thin smile. "Just a headache."

"You really didn't have to come."

"I'd feel better if you'd have some kind of legal counsel."

"I *am* my legal counsel. I've spent the last three years working seventy-hour weeks for one of Boston's oldest law firms." Never mind he'd done more pencil pushing than actual courtroom arguing. Beckett skimmed the citation—second floor, Courtroom B. "Plus I did that internship my third year of law school, working for a public defender's office."

Which meant he could recite this process in his sleep. The judge would read the charges, ask if he understood, if he was ready to make a plea.

And yes, he was ready. He'd been an idiot not to get this taken care of before now.

"Isn't there some old adage about a doctor being his own worst patient?" Dad strode beside him.

"Wrong profession. Anyway, I talked to the DA yesterday. Pretty sure he thinks this is as ridiculous as I do."

No way he'd come out of this with anything worse than a fine, maybe a few hours of community service. He'd waive his right to a preliminary hearing, ask the judge to hand down an immediate sentence. Request, too, that his record be expunged upon completion of any sentencing requirements.

Meaning he could apply for the JAG Corps without worry over background checks or security clearance.

So why the niggling undercurrent of anxiety?

On the second floor, burgundy carpet stretched toward a row of closed mahogany doors. Beckett dropped onto the vinyl-cushioned bench lining the hallway outside Courtroom B. Muted voices drifted from inside the room, and down the corridor a woman paced, phone to her ear.

Beckett leaned his head against the wall, kneading the arm that'd taken the brunt of the weekend's physical labor. That chainsaw had done a number on him. And if he was this sore, he could only imagine how Kit must be feeling.

Especially if she'd spent Sunday and Monday working as hard as she had Saturday, which wouldn't surprise him in the least. Fire blight wasn't something to mess with. They couldn't possibly have gotten all of it on Saturday, and if she wasn't diligent—

No. He wouldn't think of her now. He was in this mess in the first place because of Kit.

Except that wasn't entirely fair. It'd been *his* decision to stop by and see her the night before her wedding. His decision to interrupt the ceremony the next day. His decision to drive away in a car that wasn't his own.

And after all that, his decision to let reckless emotion take over.

"How's Kit?" Dad lowered next to him.

Were his thoughts that loud? "Fine."

"Any idea what she's going to do about the orchard?"

"She doesn't think it's her choice to make." Never mind that she'd been in her element taking charge on Saturday. She loved the orchard and could do a fine job managing it if given a chance.

But it'd be a balmy day at the North Pole before Kit was ever honest with the father she barely knew. He'd only met the man twice himself. Mason Danby—Army to the core. Distanced, stern. His own father's opposite in almost every way, which was strange considering Dad had once had a sterling military career of his own.

"Hey, Dad?"

His father leaned over, tying one of his shoes.

"I'm applying to the JAG Corps."

Dad straightened up. "Say again?"

"Found out last week I landed an interview with a field screening officer. It's set for September in Boston, and then the written application is due in November. But they'll do some kind of security or background assessment. It's why I came home. Arrest warrants don't always show up, but I'm guessing for something like national security, they go a little deeper than your general check and—"

"Slow down, Beck. I'm still back at the JAG Corps." Dad's eyes were wide "Really? Military law?"

"I'm bored in Boston." He shrugged and stood.

"You just said you work seventy-hour weeks. And you're bored?"

"Hard work doesn't always equate to meaningful work." He combed his fingers through his hair as he paced. "Not that corporate law can't be meaningful, but for me, it's just . . . not."

"And being a military lawyer will be more meaningful?"

"I think so." And there was a certain merit to it, wasn't there? It felt noble. Or at least respectable. Plus, he'd get to travel, see so much more of the world than he ever had. He'd actually get to litigate cases, argue in a courtroom rather than sit in a cramped office, buried under paperwork.

He just wished he could tell if Dad was pleased with the idea. Was it ridiculous to crave his father's approval so strongly even at age twenty-nine?

"Mind if I ask what gave you the idea?"

"You." He sat once more, met his father's eyes. "Once when I was teenager, you said I should consider joining the Army because I could stand to learn some self-discipline."

"Son, I didn't mean—"

"But it was Mom too," he hastened to add. "We were working on her car one afternoon." The silver 1969 convertible now sitting in his garage back in Boston. Man, he missed the days of tinkering under its hood, Mom at his side reading from a manual, both of them pretending like they had a clue what they were doing. "She's the one who said I should consider going to law school. Said I could argue like nobody's business. I told her it'd be too boring. Next day when I got home from school, there were all these printouts on my bed. She'd done a Google search: 'Exciting jobs for lawyers.' Top result was the JAG Corps."

She'd marked up each page of her research—underlined and highlighted in a rainbow of colors. And on the top page in red ink, in the handwriting he knew so well, a note he'd memorized without even trying: *This doesn't look boring to me, Beck. It checks off all your boxes: Travel, excitement, variety. Something meaningful. And you'd be just as handsome in a uniform as your father.*

"Smart woman, your mother." And then, finally, a grin broke out over Dad's face. "I always wondered if one of my kids would ever follow in my military footsteps. Of your own choosing, that is."

Unlike Dad, who'd been drafted two weeks after turning eighteen. He'd served in Vietnam and then gone on to become a diplomat, though his career had been cut short when Mom got sick the first time. Beckett had been a toddler when Dad had made the decision to give up his illustrious position and move the family back to his hometown so he could focus on taking care of Mom.

"Well, you have my support, of course." Dad rose. "Anything I can do to . . ." He broke off with a wince. He pinched the bridge of his nose, eyes closed.

"Your headache's that bad?"

"Might be bordering on a migraine, if I'm honest. This darn heat and humidity." He lowered to his chair once more.

"You shouldn't have bothered to come along. Head home. I can call Raegan for a ride later. Or if you don't think you can drive—"

"Beckett Walker?"

A uniformed woman stood in the now-open courtroom door.

"Go on, son. I'll just wait out here."

"Maybe there's a help desk or something where you can get some Tylenol or—"

"Mr. Walker." The officer in the doorway tapped her foot.

Dad motioned him on.

The space on the other side of the door wasn't so much courtroom as sparse meeting room. The judge sat behind a simple table. Two narrower tables faced the judge's bench, a scattering of chairs dotting the area behind them.

Beckett ignored the glare of Sam Ross as he covered the distance to the table on the left. He nodded at the DA.

Please let this go well.

The next few minutes passed in a routine march. The judge listened to the DA's scant explanation of the events that led to the charges. One count joyriding, one count damage to public property, both aggravated misdemeanors.

The judge looked to the file in front of her, glasses perched halfway down her nose. "This happened six years ago. We're just now addressing it?"

Her skeptical question should buoy Beckett. And yet, he was beginning to empathize with Dad—his own headache forming as images of the accident curdled in his memory. Spinning out on Main Avenue, losing control, the squeal of tires. His head hitting the window as the car hopped the curb. His seatbelt lancing his chest. The tree, the crash, the shock.

"Mr. Walker has been out of state," the DA's explanation cut in. "There was damage to both private and public property. The car, but also a tree in the town square that was planted by one of the town founders. Historically significant. The damage was enough the tree had to be pulled out."

The judge turned her gaze on him. "You don't deny any of this."

"I was stupid, but it was an accident."

She consulted her notes again. "You drove away from a wedding with the bride in tow in a car belonging to her groom's father. But she wasn't with you when the accident occurred."

He could hear the judge's unspoken questions. What had happened in the two hours between the would-be wedding and his running the car into a tree?

That would be the part of the night he most despised reliving. If he'd have just quit while he was ahead—done the heroic thing, rescued Kit from her wedding and left it at that.

But no. Like a fool, he'd chosen that very night to tell Kit how he felt about her—or thought he felt, anyway. It'd seemed so clear the evening before as they'd walked through the orchard together, reconnecting after such busy semesters. He didn't know why he'd never realized it before—how pretty his best friend was. How smart and winsome and kind. Well, and at the time, how unavailable.

But then just twenty-four hours later, the second she became available, he had to go and spill his entirely new, entirely irresponsible feelings. He'd stunned her, she'd wounded him, and next thing he knew, he was racing through town with an empty passenger seat, under the influence of red-hot emotion.

The judge nudged up her glasses with one finger before pinning him with an unreadable stare. "It's not as if you intended to steal the car. No one was hurt. You could've stuck around, faced up to what you'd done, and this would've been long settled. Were you drinking?"

"I wasn't, Your Honor. I simply wasn't thinking straight."

"You had six years to start thinking straight."

"I had law school. I'd been accepted to Suffolk University in Boston. And then there was an internship and a job offer and—"

"But clearly you knew there was an arrest warrant waiting for you back at home and you were purposeful about evading it."

The buzzing in the back of his head circled around to the front. He couldn't argue that. At first he'd just wanted to get away from Kit. Prevent the humiliation of that night from going one step further with an arrest.

But somewhere along the way, impulse had morphed into intention. He'd known for something so slight law enforcement wouldn't come after him. As long as he avoided town, he avoided his life being interrupted. Could've gone on indefinitely if not for his upcoming need to pass military security clearance.

The DA piped up then. "Your Honor, we realize this is an odd situation, but Mr. Walker has made it clear he regrets acting impetuously and means to make amends."

"He was impetuous the night of the incident," the judge cut in. "But six years of dodging an arrest warrant is willful." She turned to Beckett, lips pressed into a thin line. She paused for a beat before speaking again. "Mr. Walker, you're entitled to a preliminary hearing. You could hire counsel for plea bargain negotiating and if you choose to plead guilty, come back at a later date for sentencing—"

"I'd rather not, Your Honor." The interruption slipped out before he could stop it. "I'm ready to face up to this right now. I *need* to. I've got things . . ." He shook his head, took a breath. "I'm ready to plead guilty and receive my sentence right now."

The judge pulled off her glasses. "You're certain?"

He nodded as the DA spoke again. "We'd be amenable to a fine and perhaps twenty-five, thirty hours of community—"

The judge lifted her gavel. "One-thousand-dollar fine and community service to be completed in state. Four hundred hours."

Beckett's stomach clenched. "*What?* Four hundred—?"

Her gavel hit the tabletop.

Beckett sent a panicked glance to the DA. The man only gave him an apologetic shrug.

Four hundred hours. There was no way he could get that done before his JAG interview and application, not while working full time in another state. "Your Honor—"

"That'll be all, Mr. Walker."

"Eric, you're sure Lucas didn't say anything about his plans? Travel or another job, maybe friends somewhere else?"

Kit read the apology in Eric Hampton's sandy eyes. Eric leaned back in the leather chair behind the desk that filled most of the closet-sized office at the back of the Hampton House. It used to be his parents who alternately filled the seat, much like her own grandparents, partnering to operate what wasn't so much a business as a mission.

In the Hamptons' case, said mission was a transitional home for men coming out of prison or addiction rehabilitation programs.

"Sorry, Kit, he didn't. All I know is, when I contacted him in early July like we always do to ask how many men he could take on for picking season, he said he wouldn't be hiring anyone this year." Eric combed his fingers through hair the same shade as his eyes. "I thought he meant he just wasn't hiring *our* guys, so I pressed him on it. But no, he said he wasn't hiring anyone."

Kit slumped in the well-worn wingback chair opposite Eric. This had been her last idea for discovering Lucas's whereabouts. Grandpa had always hired six or seven men from Hampton House to help during the fall season—his own way of making a difference, he'd often said. Somehow he'd always find time in the busyness of autumn to mentor the men, providing not just seasonal employment, something to stick on a résumé, but also validation, even friendship.

She'd assumed Lucas had continued the Hampton House hiring—which it sounded like he had up until this year. Too, he and Eric had been in the same graduating class. She'd hoped they might've picked back up their friendship—at least enough for Lucas to have confided in Eric his plans.

No such luck.

Which felt like the pattern of her last seventy-two hours. Three solid days of working in the orchard, fighting the blight that had sunk its teeth into her trees. Yes, with all the extra help, they'd made progress on Saturday. But Sunday and Monday had been slower going with only Willa and occasionally Nigel for help, though he'd spent most of his time working on his laptop.

He was getting antsier and antsier to return to London. He was scheduled to fly out on Friday, but he kept saying he didn't want to leave without knowing when she planned to follow.

Thus, her decision to finally take this morning off from the fields. Focus on finding her brother and figuring out what to do about the currently manager-less orchard.

At least she'd made headway in one small way: After a depressing number of unacknowledged calls and emails to Dad, last night she'd tried texting. And this morning, wonder of wonders, he'd actually replied.

Don't know where Lucas is, but Willa is correct. Closing orchard store. Have vendor who will purchase this year's crop.

She'd read the text once. Blinked. Read it again. Didn't make sense. It was one thing to close the store, cease the tourist side of their business in favor of selling their whole crop to a vendor. But someone still had to manage the fields. Someone still had to pick the apples.

Dad, you don't understand. There's no one taking care of the orchard.

Lucas is gone. He fired Willa.

She'd waited two hours for a reply.

Then maybe I'm better off selling the whole place.

The sting had smarted even more than the sunburn on her cheeks and shoulders. It didn't even occur to him to ask for her help? Her brain argued that she shouldn't expect him to. That he, like Nigel, would assume she planned to return to England as soon as things were settled.

Still.

Beckett's badgering words from Saturday night came barging back in. Fine, so maybe he had a point about standing up to Dad. She'd abandoned restraint then, tapping out her next text and hitting Reply before she could rethink it.

This is Grandpa and Grandma's land. It's too important to let go. What if I stayed? There's still time to hire fall help. Willa would come back. We could open by Labor Day.

She'd sent the text at 10:07 a.m. The clock in Eric's office read 12:43. Still no reply.

"I really wish I could help, Kit." Eric stood now, covered the minimal space to the dorm-sized fridge wedged into the corner behind his desk. "Can of pop?"

"No, thanks. I left Nigel out in the living room. I suppose . . ." She rose, swallowing a sigh.

Eric popped the tab on his Mountain Dew. "Keep thinking I'll grow out of my sugar-love one day, but so far, hasn't happened." He took a long drink, eyes on her, and swallowed. "You know, the past couple years, your brother . . . well, honestly, he's kind of reminded me of some of my guys when they first get here. A little haunted."

Which made sense, really. Except that, unlike Lucas, the men here had actively sought help. "You know what he's been through."

He nodded. "And I know assimilating back into the outside world after incarceration is challenging even under typical circumstances. But Lucas's situation was anything but typical."

True. Frankly, she didn't even entirely understand his situation. He'd refused to talk about what had happened in Afghanistan to cause him to desert, to hole away for more than two years. When he'd been hauled back to the States and prosecuted, he'd declined to offer any kind of explanation. The court martial had made national headlines for several months.

"We should've made sure he got counseling or something." Not that he would've been amenable to that. He'd barely acknowledged Kit when she'd attended the court martial. And as for Dad—his and Lucas's relationship had gone from nonexistent to explosive.

Which was what made Dad's decision to hand the orchard over to Lucas two years ago so surprising. Had it been some sort of attempt at a peace offering?

"I don't say that to make you feel guilty or scared, Kit. But if you ask me, there's more going on here than Lucas getting tired of running the orchard." Eric was crossing his office to open the door now. "I just have a general social work degree, I'm not any kind of specialist. But PTSD, depression, I don't think any of it's out of the question." He held the door open for her.

She paused under its frame. "You don't think . . . would he hurt himself?"

Eric's lack of answer was answer enough. Trapped worry battered her nerves as Eric led her through the house. Nigel wasn't in the living room where they'd left him. Had he gone out to the porch? She did her best to smile at the couple men they passed—one with a salt-and-pepper beard, studying what looked like a textbook at a wide table. Another, this one much younger, dusting the bookshelves.

She followed Eric to the entryway.

"The older gentleman is Silas," Eric said. "He's sixty-three and determined to get his GED by the end of this year. The other is Paul—only twenty-two and he's already done two stints in prison." He opened the front door for her. "You know, if you decide to stay and take over the orchard, I've got guys eager for work. Just say the word."

She was too swamped with anxiety to offer any more than a nod—Lucas, the orchard, Dad's silence. And of course, as had been the case for the past two days, Beckett's presence in town hobbling along in the back of her mind.

Now, Nigel's absence.

But it didn't take long after leaving Eric and descending Hampton House's porch steps to spot Nigel halfway down the block, surrounded by townspeople. Was that Mayor Milt waving a clipboard in front of him?

Oh boy.

She hurried down the sidewalk, flip-flops slapping under her feet.

". . . so you can see why we need your signature. We're hoping to get some funding from the state tourism board for a new billboard on Highway 30 and maybe some brochures." The mayor spoke in his usual animated voice, bushy white mustache lifting with every other word.

"I'm sorry, I don't think you understand—" Nigel cut off at the sight of her. He looked relieved.

He looked annoyed.

The poor man. She'd made a mess of his whole visit to Iowa. She reached for his hand, squeezed. "Hi, Mayor Milt. Uh, everybody."

"Ah, just the woman we wanted to see!"

Three others stood with the mayor, including a tall woman with faded red hair, wearing a sundress and a look of warning. "Milt, don't you dare accost the girl."

"This is not the time for patience, Belinda." Mayor Milt's eyebrows wiggled in time with his mustache. "Kit Danby, myself and the rest of the chamber representatives are here to ask you to keep the Valley Orchard open this year."

"Here as in, on this sidewalk? You were searching for me?"

The mayor's grin was wide. "Not searching, girl. We knew exactly where you were. Jim Crayton saw you park down the road. He called Ike, who called me, and—"

The woman named Belinda rolled her eyes. "In other words, dear, welcome back to Maple Valley. I'm the Chamber president, by the way." She shot the mayor another scolding look. "And while I still think we could've waited 'til a better time, the truth is we *are* concerned about the orchard."

Nigel fidgeted with his tie beside her, beads of sweat gathering on his forehead, clearly overheating under the August sun. Why he'd worn a shirt and tie for a day out and about in small-town Iowa, she didn't know. And why had he dropped her hand?

"Not just concerned," the mayor said. "Autumn tourism is our niche in Maple Valley. We've got the heritage railroad, the antique stores. The Valley Orchard completes the trifecta."

"Trifecta?" Belinda crossed her arms. "Really, Milt, must we get dramatic about this?"

"As I was just telling your British gentleman, we're hoping to receive some additional state funding this year for a few promotional opportunities. We've even got some state tourism representatives coming to town in a couple months. The orchard is vital." The mayor held up his clipboard. "Now, since we've heard you're home, we've talked to every downtown business owner in the past two days and all signed a petition—"

"You started a petition?"

"Your family used to have a long-standing commitment to this community, and we're all hopeful you plan to continue that tradition."

Murmurs of agreement fanned through the group.

Milt handed her an envelope. "Now, along with our hope and goodwill, here's a five-dollar gift card to Coffee Coffee—new to Maple Valley since you lived here last. You see? We may not be London but we know a thing or two about progress." He gave her an exuberant pat on her back, and within seconds, the group disbanded.

She turned to Nigel. "I just got ambushed by the mayor and the Chamber of Commerce."

None of the amusement she expected lightened his eyes. "I heard."

"They gave me a petition and gift card for five whole dollars."

"I saw." He started walking toward the car but didn't get more than two steps before turning. "You can't seriously be considering this, Kit."

"I—"

"And what kind of business did you have at a halfway house?"

"I told you, I wanted to ask Eric about Lucas. We always hire several men from Hampton House and—"

"You hire drunks and criminals?"

"Nigel." She snapped his name. "That's the most insensitive . . . I don't even . . . They're *people*, Nigel. Just by coming to stay at Hampton House, they've proven they're trying to make better choices. Most of them have left everyone and everything they know to come to Maple Valley and get away from the negative influences in their old environment. They're trying to start over, and before this year, we got to be part of that by giving them work and good wages and eventually references so they could go on to find long-term employment and—"

She stopped her own rant, surprised at her passion.

She'd never seen such a hard glint in Nigel's eyes. "You said 'we.'"

"What?"

But before Nigel could answer, her phone dinged inside her purse. She took a steadying breath as she reached inside. This wasn't fair to Nigel, any of it. He was getting the brunt of her worry and exhaustion and churning, conflicting longings, and it just plain wasn't fair to him.

She glanced at her phone's screen. *Dad.* His text short and to the point:

Call me.

At least this one thing had gone right. Perfectly, deliciously right. Kit assumed so, anyway, from the piquant scent of basil and garlic mingling over the stovetop.

Kit had found Grandma's recipe for the Italian dish taped to the inside of a kitchen cupboard, but she'd hardly needed to look at the little card, so fresh was the memory of pulling homemade pasta through the cutter and swirling together a dash of spices and sauce.

"Nigel, dinner!" she beckoned, knowing her voice would carry through the house, just like Grandma's used to.

She checked on the garlic bread in the oven before crossing the room to spread a lacy tablecloth over the Formica-topped table she was pretty sure was original to the farmhouse. The whole kitchen was a mix of new and old. Sometime in the past ten years, all the appliances had been upgraded to stainless steel. And yet, the faded curtains over the window by the sink, the country blue border of curling wallpaper, the squeaky hinges on the aged cupboard doors spoke of a space well-loved for decades.

Such was the shape of the whole house, really. Contemporary touches here and there, but no one room fully updated. Grandpa had always been more focused on keeping the orchard running.

A responsibility that was now—finally—hers for the taking. The stilted phone conversation with Dad had sealed it.

She still couldn't believe it. She'd never made a decision this quickly.

Unless you count running away from the wedding.

Well, yes. There was that.

But this was different. This wasn't a decision based on fear or even emotion . . . but on some kind of deep-down knowing. Instinct or intuition, perhaps. Grandma would've called it God's whisper in her soul. But Kit had never had that lifeline to heaven her grandparents seemed to.

All the same, she couldn't deny the tug of her desire, nor the strength it gained with each passing day she spent at home. The sense of belonging. And joy, like a blurry pearl under rippling water, just waiting for her to reach for it.

If this is you, God, telling me to stay, I'm listening.

She'd waited to make the call to Dad until she and Nigel had returned to the farmhouse and Nigel had closeted himself away with his laptop. Despite the heat of the day and the comfort of the A/C inside, she'd chosen to sit on the porch steps to make the call. Less chance of Nigel overhearing.

Not that there was much to overhear. Dad had been brief, formal. In other words, his usual self.

"You're telling me you'd like to move home from

England to run the orchard?"

"Yes, Dad."

"I know you appreciate the old place, but Valley Orchard isn't just a home or a playground. It's a business. I know you've studied plants, but do you really feel you're qualified to manage a business?"

Perhaps she should point out that Lucas hadn't had any business experience either, nor had he spent nearly as many hours as she had as a teenager helping Grandma run the retail side of the orchard. As for her education, she'd majored in botany and had a master's in horticultural science. A far cry from "studying plants."

But she'd hardly ever been able to express her thoughts to Dad, let alone argue with him—as Beckett had so antagonistically pointed out the other night. Aside from that one happy month when they'd first come to Maple Valley, when she'd been convinced he meant to stay this time, she'd hardly spent enough time with her father to know him, let alone know how to talk to him.

"Willa would help," she'd finally managed.

Apparently it was enough. Dad had gone on to list his stipulations: Kit would need to manage not just the orchard fields, the store, the employees, but also the financials—the budget, payroll, vendor sales, and purchases. She would need to strive for a healthy profit by the end of the fall.

"Lucas barely turned a profit his first year, and last year was a wash. If such is the case at the end of this season, I'm going to move forward with alternate plans."

By which he certainly meant closing the store, possibly bringing in an outside field manager to oversee the care of the trees, picking season, and sale of the crops. Or he might just sell outright.

Either way, she had her marching orders, complete with a deadline: Make a profit and make it by the end of the season.

But first . . . first she somehow had to tell Nigel.

She could hear his movement overhead now. He'd been sleeping in the guest room for the past few days—the one Dad had temporarily occupied when they'd first moved here and on sporadic two-day visits in the years after.

"You're going to love this meal," she called. "And you'll finally believe me that I really can cook when I'm working with an appliance I actually understand." Versus the narrow one in her flat back in England with the odd temperature settings.

Come to think of it, she'd need to figure out what to do about her place in London. Maybe she could hire a moving company to box up and ship her belongings.

Nigel's footsteps clomped on the stairs, and he entered the room just as she bent to check the bread again. Another minute or two.

When she straightened it was to see Nigel rooted in the doorway.

Suitcase in hand.

She whirled to set the hot pads on the counter, using the seconds to grope for composure before turning back to him. Grandma's frilled apron and the billow of warmth from the oven heated her. "I thought you weren't flying out until Friday."

His luggage thumped to the floor as she turned. "Found one tomorrow morning. Figured I'd spend the night in Des Moines."

She reached both hands behind her, tampering with the apron knot behind her waist. "But I . . . you . . ." Her fingers strained against the knot to no avail and she gave a frustrated huff.

Nigel left his suitcase, rounded the table, and moved behind her. She dropped her hands when he began working the ties. "I'm not trying to be an oaf, Kit." His smooth accent flitted over her shoulder. "But what's the point in staying any longer?"

"I wish you'd let me explain."

"What's to explain? I didn't have to hear your conversation with your father to know you're thinking of staying. Probably already decided, right?"

The knot released, the apron loosened. Nigel stepped around to face her, surely reading the answer on her face.

"That's what I thought. Never mind that the whole property is run down, the trees are diseased, and one of the buildings isn't even completed. Unless you've got a storehouse of money somewhere I don't know about, I don't see how you could possibly afford to make something of this place. And yet, you're giving up a great job at a great university."

The sound of bubbling wafted over her. *The sauce.*

But the logic in Nigel's string of arguments had stolen her appetite. Everything he said was right. Grandpa might have had trouble keeping the orchard in shape near the end, but Lucas had plain let it fall apart. That skeleton of a barn had sat unfinished for almost eight years.

And there was no storehouse of money.

Which was another of Dad's stipulations. She'd have to work within the orchard's meager budget as-is. He wouldn't be lending any additional resources.

She turned to the stove, moved the sauce pan off its burner, and slid a wooden spoon through the liquid that'd hardened around the edges. *Ruined.*

"The job isn't the only thing you're giving up."

Her stirring stilled. "That's not fair."

Wasn't there any way to make him understand? She hadn't set foot on this land for years, but somehow it still feathered its way under her skin and claimed its space in her heart, breathing reminders of what it felt like to stand in the scenic embrace of a place that was just . . .

Home.

And then there were the murmured maybes, the offers of hope—that maybe if she stayed, maybe if she tried, maybe if she were here . . . Dad might come home. Lucas might come home. They could recapture what they'd lost. Be a family again.

If she stayed.

"Nigel," she began, but when she turned it was to see an empty space in the doorframe and to hear every groan of the hardwood floor as he retreated to the front door. Should she follow him?

She stared at the tablecloth, half whisked off the table after Nigel had brushed past, until an acrid scent yanked her into action. The bread! She snatched the sheet from the oven, the blackened surface of the bread registering through a swell of smoke.

Tears stung her eyes as she coughed.

At a rapping on the back door, she nearly dropped the pan. Instead, it rattled to the counter as she stalked across the room and flung open the door usually only used by family.

Beckett. So not who she wanted to see right now. Not after Nigel. Not after Saturday night. "What?"

He blinked. "You okay? What's burning?"

"Nothing anymore. Do you need something?"

His brown eyes bore into hers. "Yes. A job."

5

It'd been thirty-eight hours and a handful of minutes since Beckett had stood in Kit's grandparents' kitchen and made his case. Begged for a job.

One in which he worked for free.

This being Maple Valley, word had already spread through town that the mayor was petitioning Kit to stay, keep the orchard open. Suddenly, he'd had his answer. Way he saw it, four or five weeks of volunteering at the orchard and he could have his community service done before his JAG interview in September.

That is, if Kit said yes.

And if he could convince the firm to give him a personal leave of absence. Hence the yelling in his ear at the moment.

"Are you even listening to me, Walker?"

Beckett held his phone a good inch away from his ear, the first cool breeze in days skimming over his face as he passed under a flapping striped awning and made his way toward Coffee Coffee. Raegan had assured him it was one of the best additions in town since he'd moved away. Second to Seth's restaurant, of course, which his cousin had opened just last year.

Tuesday night he'd brought Kit a five-pound bag of

candy corn to cushion his request. Yesterday morning he'd had donuts delivered to the farmhouse. Maybe caffeine would work better than sugar.

"Of course I'm listening, Elliott, but there's really no cause to lecture me about responsibility and my role at the firm. I promise I wouldn't be asking for this if it weren't important." Across the street and down a grassy slope, the Blaine River jostled against its banks.

"Of course there's reason to lecture. We've rescheduled two depositions and Carol's been working until ten each night to get the paperwork for the Bleckley case filed." The junior partner at Louder, Boyce & Shillinger, son of Elliott Boyce, Sr., spoke with all the grace of a gong. "A one-week vacation midsummer? Fine, okay. But *a month and a half*?"

"Maybe only a month." He'd just have to work crazy-long hours at the orchard.

"There isn't room for 'maybes' on our schedule. Who do you think you work for? A hokey backwoods firm repping mom and pop shops? We have some of the biggest corporate clients in the country and they expect us to be fully staffed."

Mosaic-topped metal tables dotted the sidewalk in front of Coffee Coffee, and the lilt of some old crooner's song drifted from inside.

"Be glad you're talking to me on the phone, not in person, Elliott. Because if you'd just dissed mom 'n' pop stores out loud in Maple Valley, you'd have started a riot."

This town thrived on local business with a side of seasonal tourism—the heritage railroad and museum Dad had taken over when they moved back to Iowa and Kit's orchard being the main autumn draws.

After walking away from Kit Saturday night, never would he have expected to find himself back at the

Danby house so soon. To be asking to spend the coming month working alongside the woman who'd once called him reckless and impulsive.

It'd stung because it was true.

He clenched his jaw against the memory. If he wanted to make it through the next month or more, he'd have to completely close himself off to thoughts of her wedding night, that's all there was to it. Besides, what was the point in remembering? He had to focus on the present, the future. Despite everything that'd gone wrong between him and Kit, they could help each other now.

"This is all beside the point, anyway," Elliott said—flatly, firmly. "You missed a meeting yesterday, Beckett. Stanley Oil."

Beckett stopped a few paces from the coffee shop's entrance. *Ohhh, Beck, you didn't.* He dropped into a chair at one of the tables outside Coffee Coffee, brunt realization buckling him. Months ago, he'd practically begged for the chance to take the lead on the potential client acquisition. He'd done the legwork, met multiple times with the oil company's rep, finally scheduled a meeting between the Stanley Oil board officers and the law partners.

How in the world could he have forgotten?

"I am so—"

"Look, there's nothing more to say. I hate that I'm the one they're making do this, but as the lowest partner on the totem pole . . ."

Searing August heat clawed at him. Too, a suffocating dread.

"I should've just told you first thing. The partners voted last night to let you go, Beckett."

No. *No.*

"Elliott—"

"It wasn't entirely their choice."

"Don't you mean your choice? You're a partner, too."

"I abstained from the vote due to our college friendship." A friendship that was the only reason Beckett had landed an internship and later a job in the first place. "The officers from Stanley were offended by you not being there, I guess. Like, really offended."

"So firing me is a strategic move." *Stupid. Stupid. Stupid.*

Elliott's silence bulleted from the other end of the call.

Somehow, minutes later, he ended up in the coffee shop, standing in line like a zombie. Shocked. Numb. He'd been fired. *Fired.* The clutter of voices around him, the gurgle of coffee machines, it all felt distant, muted.

Until a sharp voice and a baby's cry plunged into his haze.

"Well?"

His gaze snapped to the girl behind Coffee Coffee's counter. She looked ready to lose it as she attempted to calm the infant pressed against her in some kind of sling. But the wailing only grew louder.

"Well?" she demanded again. Her dark eyeliner matched her jet-black hair, which was pushed back on one side to reveal piercings all the way up her ear. "There's a line behind you, if you haven't noticed."

At the cashier's annoyed words, he glanced over his shoulder. A group of teens, a man reading a book, a girl with a neon green backpack.

He turned back to the counter. "Sorry, I'm still deciding—"

"Order now or forever hold your peace."

Did she have to choose those words? Her nametag peeked out from the sling—Megan. She tried hushing her baby again. The noise of the infant's cries, the rising voices of the teenagers behind him, the annoyingly smooth song playing over the speakers . . . all of it like scraping glass shards over top the grating realization of what had just happened.

He'd lost his job. His income. His safety net if the JAG thing didn't work out.

"You know there's such a thing as a babysitter." Great, and now he was taking it out on the barista.

"And there's such a thing as having compassion for single mothers trying to run a business."

"You run this place?" Hold up, Kate had told him about this girl. His older sister had sort of taken Megan under her wing last year, become the girl's friend last year when she'd needed it most. Kate had forgotten to mention the part about her sardonic edge.

"You think you can do better?" Megan reached into her sling and pulled out her baby. "Here, go ahead, give it a try." She lifted the baby over the counter.

"I—"

"Go on, Mr. Know-it-all."

And because he didn't know what else to do, because no one else seemed to be weirded out by the fact that the pushy young woman who was apparently the manager of this place was thrusting her child at him, he took the baby. Obviously a she, obviously not more than a few months old. She wore a green onesie and a wrinkled expression until . . .

Until the second her head landed against his chest.

Just like that, her cries faded. Her kicking legs stilled.

Megan stared, mouth agape as her straight hair fell over one eye. "I don't believe it."

The fuzzy head tucked into his cotton tee made a sound of contentment. "I don't either."

"You some kind of baby whisperer or something?"

"Does this mean my coffee's on the house?" In his

periphery, he noted the details he'd missed when he'd walked in dazed—the exposed brick wall on one side, the eclectic collection of furniture and tables with multicolored chairs, the backsplash behind the counter.

"And a scone too if you want it." She looked in wonderment from Beckett to the baby nestled against him and then back to him. "Her name's Delia, by the way."

He patted the baby's back, ordered a plain back coffee for himself and an Americano for Kit.

"You're a Walker, aren't you?"

"Family resemblance that obvious?" Something—someone—jostled behind him and his grip on Megan's baby tightened. He threw a glance over his shoulder. "Careful, guys—"

But the teens in line behind him clearly didn't even notice he was there. It was the biggest of the three that'd bumped into him, the other two laughing.

"Aw, Webster doesn't like talking about summer school," one of the shorter ones taunted. "He can play football, but he can't pass basic algebra—"

Beckett realized what was about to happen a second too late. With an angry grunt, the tall kid jutted both arms forward, barreling into both of the others at the same time.

"Hey!"

Megan's outburst was lost in the noise of the brawl. One of the kids fell against an empty chair, the other took a swing at the one they'd called Webster.

It only took a moment for Beckett to hand Delia back to Megan, push his way into the middle of the fray. "Guys, break it up." He managed to pull one of the instigators off Webster, but he missed the flying fist coming from the other direction. Webster's jab landed on his cheek just as another authoritative voice barreled in.

"What's going on here?"

The whole thing was over in seconds. Everyone in the shop had gone silent save for the jazz tempo coming from the speakers. One hand to his cheek, Beckett took in the identity of the other fight breaker-upper. Colton? Kate's boyfriend, the ex-NFL quarterback. He hadn't even noticed the guy in the shop.

"Web, what are you thinking?" Apparently Colton knew the tall kid. He turned to the others. "And you two. You don't have anything better to do than pick fights?"

Colton's NFL size and disapproving stare down—or maybe his air of celebrity—was enough to send them skulking. And the taller kid, the one named Webster, hung his head. "Sorry, Colt, they just—"

"They just nothing. You should've ignored them."

A patron picked up the couple chairs the teens had knocked over, and with an annoyed huff, Megan disappeared into the kitchen. Colton exchanged a few more words with Webster before turning to Beckett.

"You should probably get some ice on that."

"Already taken care of." Megan had reappeared behind the counter, Delia once again perched in her sling—asleep and apparently oblivious to all that'd just happened. Megan handed him a bunched-up towel around a handful of ice. "Closest thing I've got to an ice pack."

"Thanks."

While she went back to preparing his drinks, Colton lingered. Why did he get the sense the guy was studying him? Shouldn't Beckett be the one giving his sister's boyfriend a careful once-over?

Not that Colton needed his approval. All of an hour in Colton and Kate's presence his first night home had made their "perfect for each other" status clear.

"Okay, so we're obviously sizing each other up and that's fine, but once we're done, can we talk?" Colton paid for Beckett's drinks before he could protest. " 'Cause I've got a favor to ask you. You're going to be in town for a while, yeah?"

It was a distinct possibility before. Now, with no job left to return to, it was a cold, hard certainty.

Somehow Kit had to find the words to thank the financial advisor who'd spent two hours of his Thursday morning with her reviewing the Valley Orchard's financial standing. But how was she supposed to dredge up words of gratitude after the horrifying numbers he'd just laid out for her?

They sat side by side in the lean-to Grandpa had always used as an office. No larger than a garden shed, really, but there was room enough for a corner desk beside an ample window. The office was connected to the orchard store. An oscillating desk fan exhaled feeble breaths of tepid air.

Jenson Barrow lifted the glass of lemonade she'd handed him earlier, a ring of condensation wetting the desk where it'd sat. His thin, wire-rimmed glasses perched low on his nose. "Everything make sense?"

Unfortunately, yes. The spreadsheet on the wide-screen monitor taunted her. "I think so. Can't promise I won't call you with more questions later, though."

Jenson swallowed the last of his lemonade with a hearty gulp, then replaced the sweating glass on the desk. "The good thing is, the bulk of your regular bills are set up for auto-pay. But that includes the mortgage, which as you saw is no small amount. So you'll need to watch your spending and make sure you keep enough in that main account."

Except if she was understanding everything correctly, their main account was a flimsy little rowboat barely staying afloat on a thirsty river. Might tip, might swamp, might run into a craggy rock.

Nigel's skepticism echoed. *"Unless you've got a storehouse of money somewhere I don't know about, I don't see how you could possibly afford to make something of this place."*

Yes, well, she didn't understand how he could expect her to just walk away from her home, give up on the land she loved, not to mention her missing brother. So maybe they were even. The knowledge did little to ease the sting of their breakup, though.

And now she couldn't help wondering, what if she'd walked away from that relationship all for the sake of a doomed venture?

"Hold unswervingly to the hope . . ."

The words trickled through her mind, and it took a moment to place them. Right, one of Grandma's recipe cards taped to the inside of a cupboard. Only instead of ingredients, this one bore a Bible verse. Something from Hebrews, wasn't it?

Somehow, that was what she needed to do. Hold on to hope.

"You'll want to learn to use Quickbooks," Jenson was saying now. "Or you could hire someone for the bookkeeping, but of course you'd need to cut expenses elsewhere."

The fan's whir shook the desktop, causing the pooled liquid from Jenson's glass on the desk to dribble down the side. Kit swiped at it with her palm. "I have to admit, this is daunting. Seeing the numbers, grasping the constraints of this business."

Jenson stood. "Yes, but it's a little like farming. A lot of upfront spending, but if it's a good crop, you see the return later."

Problem was that tiny little word: *if*.

She walked with Jenson to his car, gaze lifting to the company of clouds moving in a slow march across the sky. The heat and humidity had been relentless since Saturday, but she could feel the impending break humming over her skin. Cooling rain, a wind to push away the gray canopy overhead and set free the muggy air trapped below. By midafternoon, if she guessed right.

"Mr. Barrow—"

"Didn't we establish you're old enough now to call me Jenson?"

She found a grin underneath her numbers-fatigue. Jenson had been one of Grandpa's oldest friends. Not as constant around the orchard as Willa, but a regular on Friday nights when he and his wife joined her grandparents for game night in the farmhouse kitchen.

"Grandma was always such a stickler for manners, though. She drilled the 'Mr. and Mrs.' thing into us right alongside 'please' and 'thank you.'"

Jenson chuckled as they reached his burgundy Buick—aged but polished to a sun-streaked gleam. "I miss your grandparents dearly, Kit, as does Margaret. Though I suppose that'd be Mrs. Barrow to you."

"I miss them, too." More than she could say. From the age of ten on, they'd been the one constant in her life. Alongside Beckett, that is. "I wanted to ask you, though, Mr.—Jenson, the barn Grandpa started to build . . . do you see any kind of leeway in the orchard budget to resume that project?"

Jenson's kindly eyes turned toward the slat of cement and bare bones of a structure set back from the parking lot. "I wish I did, I truly do. Did you know it was my urging that prompted Henry to take on that project? I kept telling him if he really wanted to improve his financial situation, he needed to diversify his revenue stream. A small event center in a pretty setting like this could do so well. But challenge after challenge rose up in front of him, starting with that hailstorm, and I think he just never had the heart to get back to it."

"I wish I could find a way to complete it. It'd be such a nice tribute to them."

Jenson gave her a consoling pat on the shoulder, then made her promise to call if she ran into any accounting snags in the coming weeks.

Just as Jenson's vehicle disappeared down the lane, another passed under the orchard's welcome sign. Kit lifted her hand to shield her eyes from an errant shaft of sun breaking through a paunchy cloud and tried to make out the form behind the windshield.

Seconds later, Raegan Walker emerged from the car. Her jaunt was carefree and in her hands, two covered coffee cups. "I'm playing delivery girl." Her purple Converse All Stars crunched over the gravel lot as she approached.

"You brought coffee?" Kit hooked her thumbs under the straps of the denim overalls she'd found in her bedroom. Baggy enough they still fit and barely faded. If she was going to run a rural operation, she might as well look the part. She'd completed the look with a white tank top underneath and red handkerchief over her ponytail. "Bless you. I was almost late meeting our accountant this morning, which means I missed my coffee. All I've had is a glass of lemonade, and let me tell you, the effect is nowhere near the same."

Raegan handed her the larger of the two cups. "Well, I can't take credit for this. It's from Beckett, and I have a feeling it's lukewarm at best by now. He meant to bring it himself, but he got tied up with Colton."

She took a drink anyway. Americano, black and perfect even if no longer hot. He'd remembered. "Colton?"

"Kate's boyfriend. Moved here last fall. Former NFL quarterback, old college friend of Logan's."

Ah, she'd seen him at the wedding. Suddenly the size and the vague feeling of recognition made sense. "So let me guess, in addition to delivering Beckett's bribe, you're also supposed to ferret out whether or not I've made any decision on his community service."

Raegan laughed as she fell in step beside Kit. "You know my brother way too well."

The uneven boards of the wraparound porch extending from the main building wobbled under Kit's sandals as she approached the front door. Grandpa had added this porch decades ago, along with the storefront façade running along the front of the long building, disguising its origins as a dairy barn. In the busyness of helping Willa in the fields, she hadn't taken time yet to so much as step foot inside.

"So, have you?" Raegan stopped beside her on the porch as Kit fumbled with a heavy key ring. "Made up your mind about Beck, I mean?"

"Don't know." Beckett expected a quick decision because he was a quick decision guy. Not so, Kit. She could belabor a choice until mentally paralyzed. Free labor was a good thing, of course. But could she handle working side-by-side with Beckett every day, knowing he still resented her?

Kit tried the first key with no luck. At least there were only a few on the ring she'd found in Grandpa's office. Wouldn't take more than a minute to pinpoint the right one.

"I still can't get over the fact that he's even home."

She stopped, turned to Rae. Beckett's younger sister wore a black tank top over a jean skirt and a collection of bracelets on both wrists. From what she'd picked up, his family had been as surprised to see him at Seth's wedding as she'd been. "He really hasn't come home even one time since . . . ?"

Raegan lifted one pierced brow. "Since your wedding? Nope." Her fingers tapped on her coffee cup. "Nor has he ever told us exactly what happened that night. I mean, other than the running a car into a tree part. We all knew about that. What we didn't know is that the arrest warrant was still outstanding. Or what happened with you and Beck." She paused when Kit turned back to the door. "And now I get the sense you're not any more eager to talk about it than he is."

No. She'd been such a mess that night. Said such awful things. No wonder Beck had ditched town without looking back. But to stay away for six years? Surely there was more going on there than a grudge against her. Something else he was carrying around with him, enough to—

Her thoughts cut off when the second key she tried slid into place. A click, a twist, and the door nudged opened. The musty, mingling scents of apples and wood, spice and dust engulfed her. An uncanny flood of emotion accompanied her first step into the store . . . and Grandpa's voice, like a contented sigh.

"You wouldn't know this building used to hold four dozen smelly cows back before World War II. To hear my dad tell it—your great-grandpa—he milked so many Jerseys as a kid that by the time he was an adult and inherited this land, he'd had enough. That's when he decided to make his living off the small grove of apple trees out back."

As a kid, Grandpa had helped bring the orchard to

life. Father and son had cleared additional fields, planted more trees, converted the barn into a two-floor store. Grandpa had carried on the business, raising his family in the same farmhouse he'd grown up in—including the mom Kit only remembered in shadowy snatches.

Kit blinked to adjust to the dim of the store now and let her gaze roam the space. The counters that traced the rustic walls, the shelves made of old pallets and recycled barn wood, all of it was covered in layers of dust. None of the inventory had arrived yet, and light bulbs needed to be replaced in at least half of the old-fashioned frosted glass lamps suspended overhead.

This space alone would take days to clean and organize. Then there was the equipment out in the machine shed to look over, repairs to order. Thirty-five employees to hire and schedule. Payroll to set up, a pre-Labor Day opening to plan, and . . .

She dropped the ring of keys. *Oh my goodness. Ohhh my goodness.* She bent over, hands on her knees.

"Kit?" Worry lit Raegan's voice.

"I don't know what I'm doing or where to start. Why did I think this was a good idea? I haven't even had a chance to get groceries. I've been eating the donuts Beckett bribed me with yesterday for the past three meals and . . ." She gulped for air. "What does a panic attack feel like? I think I'm having one."

Raegan's hands on her shoulders guided her to the stool behind the antique cash register sitting on a glass display case. "Sit. Breathe."

"Did I tell you my dad wants weekly reports from me? No, why would I have told you? Years and years of ignoring me and now he wants to hear from me each Friday, and tomorrow's Friday and the only thing I'll have to tell him is that I panicked and—"

"Shush, Kit. Take a deep breath."

There was nothing to do but obey. Her lungs quivered with each breath and her hands shook. How had she ever thought she could pull this off? And if this was the weight Lucas had felt for two years and counting, no wonder he'd fled.

Oh yes, add that to the to-do list, too: a wayward brother to find.

At a scraping sound, Kit looked up to see Raegan pulling an old barrel over. She tipped it on end and then hopped up to sit on it, directly facing Kit.

"I don't think I can do this, Rae."

Raegan reached forward to press one palm to Kit's knee. She squeezed, then straightened. "I think I said almost those exact words for days after my mom died. I know it's not the same situation, but it's different shades of the same panicky feeling. I'd get up in the morning and a flood of mundane tasks would hit my brain and next thing I knew, I was curled up in bed."

Kit lifted her eyes to Raegan's. She'd been around the Walker house for some of those days, but she'd been so consumed with consoling Beckett, she'd hardly talked to the others.

She'd sometimes wondered which was worse: Losing a mother to cancer so young you missed out on memories—as she had. Or, like Beckett and his siblings, losing her as a young adult—having the memories, but also the pain.

"Oh, Rae."

Tears pooled in Raegan's sky blue eyes—so different from Beckett's. "It's okay, this isn't about me right now. I just wanted to tell you what my dad told me on one of those horrible mornings. He said, 'Today, Rae, let's just do one thing. And then if that one thing goes okay, we'll do the next.' So we made breakfast. And then we washed the dishes. And then we watched *The Price is Right*."

"You do have the most remarkable dad, Rae."

Raegan blinked, the emotion in her eyes and voice gone as rapidly as they'd arrived, replaced with an encouraging nod. "So, let's just figure out what your one thing is."

If Kit didn't come to her window soon, Beckett would fall to his death. Or at least, wind up with his second injury of the day. His cheek still stung from the punch he'd taken this morning.

Though not nearly as much as his pride. He might've been growing restless at the law firm, but to get so unceremoniously fired? For something as irresponsible as missing an important meeting?

And now, the branch outside Kit's bedroom barely holding his weight threatened to snap beneath him.

"Kit," he hissed for the third time. But why was he whispering? The closest neighbor other than Dad was at least a few miles away.

He rapped on the old glass window and said her name again, louder this time. The branch wobbled as a cool gust riffled through the leaves around him.

Finally, the window opened. Kit practically flung the thing off its hinges. "What?" Her hair flopped in an off-center messy knot, and the thin strap of her pajama top slipped down her shoulder. She shoved it up.

He couldn't help a grin at the pure irritation in her eyes. "Gonna let me in?"

"Now?"

"It's ten fifteen. Don't tell me you were actually sleeping. Not Kit the night owl."

"I'm not a teenager anymore. I need more sleep. I'm

old and responsible."

"No, you're not. You're upset. You only go to bed early when you're upset. Raegan said you had a hard morning."

Her lips pressed into a thin line before she spoke again. "Your sister talks too much.

"Whatever. I need you to let me in before this branch breaks. It's not nearly as sturdy as it was when I was a skinny thirteen-year-old."

Exasperation riddled her sigh, but she moved back anyway, giving him space to grasp the windowsill and heft himself through. His left foot landed on a throw pillow that slid over the hardwood floor the second he shifted his weight inside. He ended up falling the rest of the way into the room, landing with a thud at Kit's bare feet.

"Such a graceful entrance."

"Such kind assistance." He stood, taking in her striped shorts and matching sleeveless top. Apparently the cursory review was enough to make her self-conscious, because she immediately yanked the sheet off her bed and wrapped it around herself kimono-style.

He rolled his eyes. "I've seen you in your pajamas a hundred times."

"When we were kids, Beck. It's not exactly the same now."

Moonlight slanted through the still-open window, highlighting the curves the sheet did nothing to hide. And suddenly she wasn't just Kit Danby the childhood best friend or even Kit Danby the college girl who'd broken his twenty-three-year-old heart once upon a time.

But Kit Danby the *woman*. And if he'd thought she was pretty back then . . .

"What do you want, Beckett? And why didn't you just ring the doorbell?"

"We used to climb in each other's windows all the time. It was our thing." He repeated her words from Saturday. "I thought it'd be endearing."

The corner of her mouth quirked. "Try intrusive."

Every encounter with her since he'd been home had been fraught with a frayed tension. But there'd been slim moments—like right now—when the tautness eased just enough to make room for a hint of their old effortless connection. The sun had freckled her shoulders and deepened the streaks of gold in her hair. He had to tear his eyes away to keep from staring longer than he should.

Because he absolutely wasn't going there again.

So his scrutiny traveled around the room instead. The rumpled shape of the blanket on her bed said she still slept in a tight little ball. The white antique desk where she used to do her homework sat in its usual place against one wall. Her *Pride & Prejudice* movie poster was beginning to curl at its edges, and he could still name all three stuffed bears that sat on the lavender chair in the corner.

"Hawkeye, Hunnicut, and Winchester." Named after the characters on *M*A*S*H*.

"Huh?" She followed his gaze. "Oh."

"You're still the only person I've ever met who preferred the later seasons of *M*A*S*H* to the early years."

"And you're still the only person I've ever met who feels the need to argue with me about it."

She and her grandpa had gotten into the habit of watching reruns of the classic show on summer evenings just before supper. Beckett had frequently joined in, gangly limbs outstretched on the shag carpet beside Kit, staying for the meal afterward more often than not.

"Anyway, I don't watch *M*A*S*H* anymore. Not super into anything Army-related this days."

He swallowed. Right. Because of her father's absence

and her brother's court martial. What would she say if he told her about his own plans to trade in civilian life for a military gig?

Kit lifted the sheet over her shoulders now as a breathy wind whooshed through the window. "Seriously, Beck, what's up? I really was sleeping."

"Brought you something. It's out in the yard. Grab a sweatshirt. It got cool all of a sudden." Which she'd probably seen coming. She always could read the sky and predict the weather. Regular *Farmer's Almanac.*

She pulled a sweatshirt over her head, and it mussed her already sleep-tousled hair. "Don't know about you, but I'm taking the easy way out." She started for her bedroom door.

He followed her through the house he could've navigated blindfolded. Weird to think of her now living here all alone. So much space for one person.

Not that he'd been disappointed to hear the Brit had gone back to jolly old England. He'd asked about Nigel the other night when he came begging for a job. Kit had offered only a sparse, "It didn't work out."

Good enough for Beckett. Not that he had a right to any kind of say in who Kit dated. But come on, the man had applied sunscreen to his bald scalp how many times on Saturday? Why didn't he just find a hat?

Kit's steps stammered to a stop just outside the back door when she saw what he'd brought along—the tiny animal tied with a rope to the side mirror of Dad's old truck.

The baby goat mewed at the sight of them, stamping one hoof.

Kit stared at the animal, then at him. "W-why?"

He shrugged. "It's cute?" It really was—tufts of white hair and a circle of brown around its nose, stumpy little legs, and wobbled movements. He walked over, knelt down beside the animal, scratched under its chin. "I figured you're out here all alone, you could use some company."

"So you brought me a *goat*?"

He'd expected some girly oohs and ahhs, not this flummoxed reaction. Kit had her hands on her waist, long, bare legs planted in the gravel. Okay, so maybe it hadn't been his best idea. But when he'd overheard a local farmer at the coffee shop talking about the runt of an animal, the idea had hatched itself on the spot.

Next thing he knew impulse had taken over—because didn't it always with him?—and he was following the man out to his farm. He'd gotten instructions on bottle-feeding and had meant to bring it straight to Kit. But then he'd remembered his niece, Charlie. After a full week at home, Logan and his family were heading back to Chicago tomorrow. So he'd stopped at Dad's to let Charlie see the animal and hadn't been able to tear her away until Logan insisted it was bedtime.

Now here he was—suddenly rethinking the whole thing. Because if Kit was anywhere near as charmed by the goat as everyone back at Dad's, she wasn't showing it.

"You used to talk about how unfair it was you didn't have a pet."

"I was thinking more along the lines of a dog."

He sat on the ground, legs crossed. The goat balanced two hooves on his knee. "Anyone can have a dog, Kit. You can have an adorable baby goat."

"That will eventually grow into an adult goat who wanders off and eats all my grass and bites the paint off buildings and—"

"You don't know that. This might end up being a well-behaved goat."

She knelt beside him, eyeing the animal with something more than bewilderment now. "You don't have to bribe me, Beck. Not with coffee. Not with a cute goat."

"So you admit it's cute?"

"You admit it's a bribe?"

He didn't answer, just nudged the animal toward where she crouched and watched as she petted its head, then its back. "My grandparents used to want to add a petting zoo to the orchard." Her trace of a grin finally spread into the full thing. "And a pumpkin patch and hay bale maze and the barn, of course. They just couldn't ever get financially ahead enough to do it all. Between double mortgages and insurance and regular operation costs . . ."

Responsibilities she'd now inherited thanks to an indifferent father and missing brother.

But couldn't she see the answer was right in front of her? He'd spent so many summers and falls working here as a teenager. He knew how important it was to mulch around the tree trunks in order to trap moisture. He knew what it took to stay ahead of weeds and how critical it was to fix the broken-down fencing at the field borders to keep out deer. He knew how to check soil moisture at a tree's drip line.

"Okay," Kit blurted as if on cue, as if she'd heard his thoughts. "You can volunteer here. As many hours as you need to. I'll sign whatever community service paperwork is needed."

"Really?"

"On one condition."

She stood, and he followed suit. "Anything. I could bring you coffee each day, if you want. Or another animal."

She didn't tease back. Instead, pausing, she played her next words over in her mind—he could see it. She was like Logan in that way, her tendency to work and rework her words before letting them free, sometimes pilfering through them at such length they never made it out.

Whereas his tended to scatter like dandelion seeds at the merest breeze of thought.

"You have to let me apologize," she finally said. There was a surprise firmness to her tone. "You have to just stand there and hear me out. Because I can't work with you every day wondering if you still hate me."

"I don't hate you."

"But did you?"

"Do you want the blunt answer or the nice answer?"

"I want the honest answer."

This was not what he'd come here to do. Yes, seeing her at the wedding last week had thrown him. Yes, helping her on Saturday had messed with the lockbox of stored-away, crushing memories of her wedding night. Yes, the thought of working with her every weekday for at least the next month planted worry in his brain.

Worry that he might once again find himself in the same place he had on her wedding night. So convinced she wanted more than his friendship. So convinced she wanted . . . *him*.

And that was all it took to send him back to that night—she in a dress that hugged her waist and he in a white shirt and a tie he'd loosened when they were barely a mile from the church.

He'd known the night before her wedding, as they walked through the orchard and talked as if classes and college life had never distanced them, that something in her was reaching out for help. He'd known when he hugged her goodnight, when he saw her before the wedding, when he caught her eye as she started down the aisle.

She'd wanted out—desperately. She simply hadn't

known how to do it, what to say. She'd never been a talker—not to anyone but him. She tended to freeze when she panicked. So he'd done it for her. Interrupted the ceremony and whisked her away without any thought as to what came next.

They'd driven for an hour, covering country roads, crossing county lines until finally Kit had insisted they stop. He pulled over onto a deserted, unpaved lane, and Kit got out.

By the time he'd rounded the Lincoln belonging to Sam Ross's parents, she was in tears. He pulled her into his arms, cicadas droning from beyond the ditch of overgrown prairie grass. Cornstalks climbed from the soil in the field beyond.

"It's okay, Kit. You'll get through this. And Sam will, too." He could feel the line of buttons up her back beneath his fingers.

"I don't know how it happened—how it got this far. I was just . . ." His shirt muffled her words. *"I was so upset after everything with Lucas. Sam was there for me. Dad wasn't around, and Grandma and Grandpa were dealing with the orchard, and you were . . ."*

A stab of guilt pierced his heart. He'd been so focused on school. It had been the only way he could deal with Mom's death. But he'd ignored Kit in the process.

His arms tightened around her.

No more. He'd rediscovered his best friend the previous night, wandering through the orchard, talking about everything but her wedding. Their old connection had picked up right where it left off.

And something new had entered the equation. Something that crackled like kindling in a fire.

Beckett cut off the memory with a hard swallow. The rest of it was a blur he refused to walk back into.

"I know you don't want to talk about it. But I hurt

you, Beck. I know I did and I hate that I did and please, just let me say sorry. *I'm sorry.*"

"I'm the one who . . . misread." So completely and totally. For once, though, on the brink of reliving the moment he'd ruined everything, it wasn't mortification he felt. But maybe, surprisingly, something like hope.

That maybe he *hadn't* ruined everything. Maybe they *could* find their way to back to friendship. It hit him all over again, just like it had the night before her wedding, how much he missed her, how much he longed to cross the gulf time and distance had created and reclaim their old bond.

"I don't hate you." He repeated the words—soft and, apparently, convincingly.

Because her every feature relaxed into something like relief. She knelt to pet the goat again, and when she looked up at him, moonlight sparkled in her eyes. "What should I name it?"

6

Kit never should've let Beckett talk her into this.

A man in jeans and a red tee studied the frame of the mostly un-built barn. He rubbed his fingers on his chin. "I mean, seriously, it wouldn't take that long to put up some walls, get you a roof, finish off the interior."

It wasn't so much time Kit was worried about, but money.

Which was why meeting with Drew Renwycke, a local with a startup carpentry business, made no sense at all. But Beckett had been insistent. And in two and a half weeks of Beckett's constant presence around the orchard, one thing had become clear: While her old friend might have changed in some ways, he hadn't lost his ability to bend her will to match his whim.

"Just meet with him, Kit," he'd said two nights ago as they'd worked on repairs to the fence in the south field. He'd been breathless as he spoke while simultaneously heaving a post into the hole in front of him. "Dad told me Drew built an addition onto the railroad museum this summer. Did it for half the price of a regular contractor because he's new. Apparently he renovated almost his entire farmhouse, too—which, incidentally, used to be his grandparents'. You guys have something in common."

She toed the clumps of dirt around the newly placed pole. "You're not listening to me, Beck. I have zero room in the budget." Especially now that she'd managed to hire all their seasonal employees and had put a small fortune into getting ready for their fall opening, just a little over a week away on the Saturday before Labor Day.

Fresh paint for the storefront. New layer of pea gravel in the parking lot. Equipment repairs. Newspaper and radio advertisements.

The past weeks had been a frenzied blur, and if they kept up the pace, they just might be ready to welcome their first batch of visitors on September 5. None of it would be possible without Beckett.

They'd had to get court approval for him to complete his hours at a for-profit business rather than a nonprofit organization, and it'd taken over a week to get the okay. But he'd started helping right away anyway.

He swiped the back of his arm over his forehead before reaching for a horizontal beam to fit into the post. She bent to help. They straightened together on either side of the beam.

"Just meet with him, Kit. Show him your grandpa's blueprints."

"But I don't have any—"

"Money, I know. The two main costs in any construction project: labor and materials. We can get you free labor. I can get Seth and Colton to help. I don't want to ask my dad because, I don't know, he's seemed tired lately and the depot is about to get just as busy as the orchard, but—"

"Beck—"

"I bet some of the guys at Hampton House would help out."

Eric Hampton had been so relieved when she'd called him weeks ago to say the orchard would be hiring, after all. So far, four men had already started working for her under Willa's supervision, picking some of the early-ripening apples—Elstars, Centennials, Ginger Golds.

"As for the cost of materials, I could lend you—"

"No way." The muscles in her arms were beginning to burn from the weight of the beam.

"I'm a lawyer, Kit, working for a private firm. Or *was*. My salary wasn't exactly a pittance, and I'm sure it's more than what you earned doing whatever you were doing."

"I was a field botanist for one of the best universities in England." Which, fine, basically meant she watered plants and took soil samples, but he didn't need to know that. "I'm not taking your money. You've already done way too much."

He fit the beam into place and she dropped her arms, relieved. The sun was little more than a sliver of orange against a haze of pastels in the west, but heat radiated from Beckett. Another swipe of his arm, another beam to lift . . .

And then he'd met her eyes and delivered the clincher. "Think of how much it'd impress your dad."

So here she was, two days later, standing with a man she vaguely recognized from high school. Drew Renwycke's younger brother had been in her grade, hadn't he?

"The foundation's in great shape, by the way," Drew said. "Some of the frame's a little weather-worn, but I could fix that."

He seemed nice, intrigued by the project. What if . . . ?

She did have some savings of her own. Not much, but if she could get some kind of store credit for materials, maybe work out a payment plan with Drew, take advantage of that free labor Beckett seemed to think he could round up . . .

It was crazy. A far-reaching risk.

But what if Grandpa and Jenson Barrow were right about the income potential from a special-events space? What if Beckett was right and there really was some way to make it happen?

What if Dad was impressed enough to abandon his talk of selling? After all, none of the weekly reports she'd sent him so far had garnered any more than briefly worded replies. *Sounds good. Keep it up. Watch the budget.*

She caught a glimpse of Beckett now, crossing from the machine shed to the store. The little goat scampered after him, as much a fixture at the orchard anymore as the man she trailed. Beckett wore jeans so faded they were nearly white over his knees and a plaid shirt, sleeves rolled to his elbows. His Boston Red Sox cap sat backwards over hair that had begun to curl at its ends.

This was the Beckett she remembered. Too busy to bother with a haircut. Too energetic to walk any slower than a near-jog.

She lifted her gaze to the sky. Rain. She could smell it hovering, tucked into pillowy clouds. Patient. The afternoon sun nudged through an opening, casting a yellow-green glint over the landscape.

"So, if I found a way to pay for this . . ." Hesitation slowed her words. "Would you be available? And how long would it take?"

"I'm available. The bulk of my work right now is custom furniture, to be honest. But I've been hankering to take on a bigger project." Drew looked back to the frame. "Far as timeline, depends on what I've got for help."

"If I could get you some volunteer help in the evenings, on weekends?"

"You get me some guys who can follow orders and aren't completely inept around a construction site, I say we can have you up and ready in a month, month and a half."

That fast?

As if sensing her uncertainty, Drew turned from the frame, an appeasing expression on his face. "How about this? I'll take those blueprints and the budget your grandfather worked up, talk to my lumber guy, and update the numbers. It'll be easier to make a decision with better information."

"Thanks, I appreciate that."

With a parting nod, he moved toward the orchard's parking lot. But she couldn't help calling after him. He stopped, and she shuffled to catch up. "Just have to ask, you don't by any chance know my brother—Lucas?"

He grinned. "It's Maple Valley. Everybody knows everybody. I think he was a grade ahead of me."

"Did you happen to talk to him at all recently?"

Drew was shaking his head before she'd finished, as if he knew to expect the question. And why wouldn't he? She'd asked almost every person in town these past weeks about Lucas. "I've only been back in town for the past year or so and it's been a busy one, to say the least. I guess I saw him around a time or two, but we never talked."

She thanked him again and waited until he started his engine to turn.

The sound of Drew's truck rumbling down the lane accompanied her walk back to the orchard office, lingering concern over Lucas tangling with the murmur of optimism about the barn. The breeze ushered in the honey-sweet scent of the clematis just now in bloom. It climbed the outside of the building, reaching for the roof Beckett had patched only yesterday.

She found herself skirting the office entrance and heading instead for the store. Flynnie pranced around the first floor, hooves pattering. The little goat might be a female, but Kit had insisted on naming her after Beckett anyway. Beckett had laughed, said his abnormal middle name might as well be put to good use.

"Hey, Flynnie, you're staying out of trouble, aren't you?" She crouched to pet the animal, scanning the refreshed space. They'd made progress—new shelving, fresh paint on the walls—but the final week before the store opened was when it would really come alive.

Kit rose and turned in a slow circle, imagination spiraling into existence fresh bags of polished apples covering the shelves, glass coolers stocked with gallons of cider and juice. She pictured buckets of caramels and wall shelves with homemade jams and butters and a chalkboard behind the counter with the day's specials and an inspirational quote . . .

A creaking overhead jutted in, giving away Beckett's whereabouts. What was he doing up on the second floor? The stairs were ridiculously rickety, and she wasn't convinced the floorboards were any safer. She'd planned to rope off the space before they opened.

"Beck?"

Kit started up the stairs, boards jostling as she gingerly made her way. She could only imagine a customer's foot going through the old lumber or—

The step halfway up pitched beneath her. She yelped, grasping for the railing with both hands.

Too late.

At her hasty movement, the board beneath her feet gave away, and the next thing she knew, she was pulling the railing off the wall and flailing. Not down the steps but through them, her squeal accompanied by the cracking of wood and the whoosh of dirt and debris. And then a thud as she landed in a twisted heap on her back, broken boards and fragmented pallets strewn all around her.

"Kit!"

She blinked but couldn't see Beckett through the cloud of dust. She could hear his frantic movements, though—his bounding down what was left of the steps and then jumping to the floor.

He was at her side in seconds, crouching down and sliding one hand under her shoulders. "Move, Kit. Make a sound. Say something."

Remarkably, she did. She curled over onto one side, chest heaving in a sudden coughing fit.

Beckett's fingers trailed over her neck and down her back, probably looking for anything bent or broken. Only when she made a move to sit up on her own, did he help situate her. With his free hand, he cleared away the wreckage around her.

"Are you okay? What hurts?"

"Other than everything?" She rasped the words as another spasm of coughing took over.

"I should call 911."

"I'm fine."

"You just fell through a stairway."

Another cough. "Tell me this entrance tops climbing in a window."

"How can you joke when I feel like my heart just did an acrobatic routine?" He brushed a piece of insulation from her hair.

"You were worried." It shouldn't please her so much. Not considering she'd probably wake up bruised from head to toe tomorrow. Not considering the damage she'd just caused and the expense it'd take to fix it.

"Of course I was worried. Because, again, you just fell through a staircase." Beckett punctuated each word, gaze lifting to the hole overhead before lowering to her again. "Think you can stand?"

She nodded, and he helped her to her feet, toeing more debris out of the way and making sure she was steady before dropping his hand from her back. Even then, he stood close, as if ready to reach out if she swayed.

"I told you not to go up there, Beck. I said the stairs were unstable, the wood rotting."

"You're scolding me? Do we need to review which one of us the steps couldn't hold?"

She couldn't help it. Despite the throbbing where her hip had hit the floor, the mess all around her, she laughed.

"I mean, I'm just saying, Danby, maybe you need to lay off the cupcakes and pie."

"Shut up."

"You didn't just fall through the steps, you pulled the whole railing down with you." And now he was laughing even as his dark eyes pinned her with faux reproach and he swiped two fingers across her cheek. A streak of dirt probably.

"What can I say? I don't know my own strength."

A jolt suddenly cut off Beckett's laughter as his attention pinned on something behind her. She turned.

Sam Ross was standing in the doorway, pinched expression pointed and irate and . . . pained. Only a flicker, but there was no mistaking it.

"Sam—"

He spun.

"So, listen, if this is weird at all—"

"It's fine."

The kid sitting across the restaurant table from Beckett was lying through his teeth. Webster Hawks. High school junior. Varsity wide receiver.

Sullen as a storm cloud. Hadn't Colton cleared this with the kid? And how was Beckett supposed to focus after such a long day at the orchard, including those moments in the store with Kit, Sam's sudden appearance—and then just as sudden disappearance?

Beckett lifted his water glass only to find it empty. He'd guzzled the whole thing already? "Truth is, I've never tutored anyone before, and when Colt asked me, I tried to tell him I wasn't the right one for the job."

It'd been three weeks ago that Colton asked for the favor that day in the coffee shop, and Beckett was just now making good on it. Although why his sister's boyfriend thought Beckett would have any success at this, Beckett didn't know. Logan was the brainiac of the family.

But Colton had thrown back at him the fact that Beckett had made it through law school. "Whereas I skated through college on a football scholarship," he'd said. "I'm great helping Web with his long pass. But he barely made it through summer school, and if he can't keep up during his first semester, he's going to end up sitting out games."

It was Colton's description of Webster's past that'd finally swayed Beckett: His mother, a drug addict who'd eventually signed over her parental rights. Several years of foster home shuffling. Finally last year, Webster had landed in Maple Valley right around the same time as Colton.

Beckett lifted his glass again. Found it empty. Again. "Anyway, Colton's a hard guy to say no to."

It was his NFL size. And the fact that Kate acted like he was some kind of hero on a white horse or something. Which, Beckett guessed, he kind of was. Now that he no longer played football, he ran a national foundation from here in Maple Valley and had opened a home for older teens who'd aged out of the foster system. Apparently he was currently working on reeling in some big-name sponsors in an effort to open additional homes in other states.

And of course he was advocating for Webster.

The kid might welcome Colton's intervention in his life, but he didn't seem all that excited about the addition of Beckett. The Maple Valley Mavericks logo on Webster's t-shirt was hidden behind his folded arms, and he'd yet to take a drink of the Coke Seth had set in front of him five minutes ago.

Beckett had picked Seth's restaurant for their first tutoring session in the hope that it'd make Webster comfortable. Well, and because he'd been home for more than three weeks and still hadn't had a chance to stop by The Red Door.

Seth had just opened the restaurant last summer—renovated a historic bank building, basically gutting the inside to turn it into a diner that felt at once both laidback and trendy. From the amber lighting and exposed beams to the hardwood floors and a custom counter made from salvaged Main Avenue cobblestone, the place was a feat of architecture and craftsmanship.

Man, between Colton and Seth, he was surrounded by guys who'd turned dreams into realities. Intimidating and inspiring, all at once. What would it feel like to know you were living the life you were meant to? To have confidence in your purpose?

He'd have that once he was commissioned in the U.S. Army Judge Advocate General Corps, right? When he was providing legal assistance to soldiers and advising commanders. When he wore the JAG insignia—a gold pen crossed above a gold sword over a laurel wreath. Life would feel different then, wouldn't it? Significant. Important.

Finally, Webster plunked his palms to the tabletop. "So are we going to do this or what?"

Beckett lifted his brows. "You got somewhere else to be?"

The kid only shrugged.

"All right, what classes are you taking this semester? What's the most challenging?"

"Algebra, Literature, and U.S. History."

He stifled a groan at the first two. *Thanks a lot, Colt.* But history he could do. "Got a textbook?"

The next hour and a half passed in a series of starts and stops as he muddled his way through the informal tutoring session. He had no idea whether he was doing any good at all, but at least Webster had begun to lighten up.

They'd long since pushed their plates to the far edge of the table when a waiter stopped by to refill their drinks for a second time. Outside the lanky windows that fronted the restaurant, steady sheets of rain fell over the town center. Faint lamplight shone over the street and the green of the square even though the sun hadn't yet set.

"So it's just the beginning of World War I we still need to go over," Beckett said as the waiter moved away. "But I think your ride's going to be here soon."

Webster glanced at his watch. "Yeah, probably."

"You should totally do the music thing I was telling you about. Pick out eight or ten of your favorite songs and reread these chapters while you listen to them. Make yourself focus. And if it works for you like it did me, something will connect in your brain—like your creative and analytical side working together."

Webster nodded.

"Same time next week?"

Another nod. A hesitant look toward Beckett. And then he shoved his textbook into his backpack.

"Webster?"

The teen slurped a final drink from his red glass.

"Is there anything besides school giving you trouble?" He didn't know what made him ask the question. Just a feeling. But even if there was something else, wouldn't Webster talk to Colton or his adoptive parents eons before someone he hardly knew? Beckett could barely pass for a tutor, let alone some kind of wise mentor.

Webster only shook his head, glanced toward headlights streaming past the window. "That's my ride." He slung his backpack over his shoulder. "Thanks for the help."

He started to move away, track pants dragging on the floor, before pausing. "It's a girl I used to know."

Beckett set down his glass as Webster twisted around and returned to the table.

"We were with the same foster family together years ago. She was like a sister. She's a couple years older than me. She used to sorta watch out for me, and when I got a little older I started watching out for her, too. But then she got placed somewhere else. I tried to keep in touch with her, but she stopped returning my texts, and then when I called my old social worker to ask, she acted like I was some creep and used all this legal jargon—"

Webster broke off as if suddenly deciding it was futile to bring up. But Beckett heard the rest of his unspoken words. *"You're a lawyer. Is there anything you can do?"*

"Look, I'm not sure . . ." He wiped his palms on his

jeans, unable to bring himself to so quickly deny Webster. "Colton said your spring semester and summer school were a struggle. This have anything to do with it?"

"I just want to know she's okay." There was something so desperate in his voice, in the way his fingers tightened over the strap of his backpack. "Her name's Amanda Britt."

He should tell Webster there was nothing he could do. That he didn't know a thing about child custody laws and foster care. That what he did know was that confidentiality would likely make getting any kind of lead on his friend next to impossible. He should disappoint Webster now before he got his hopes up.

He should. He couldn't. "Text me your social worker's name and contact info. I'll see what I can do."

Webster offered the closest thing to a smile as Beckett had seen so far. Then he nodded and spun so swiftly he knocked his backpack into a woman at another table. He tossed an apology and was out the door before Beckett could tack on any kind of caution to temper his expectations. The thought of disappointing him . . .

"What'd you say to make him so happy?" Seth stood by the table, watching Webster rush down the sidewalk. His cousin looked enough like both Beckett and Logan, they'd often been mistaken as brothers.

"Something I shouldn't have."

Seth plunked into Webster's abandoned seat. "So what do you think of my restaurant?"

"It's fantastic, Seth. Honestly. Sorry it took me so long to get here."

Seth waved off the apology. "Eh, I was on my honeymoon for two weeks anyway. But I'm glad you're here now, and I'm glad you like it. 'Course, it's not exactly the same without the live music. Bear used to play on

Fridays, and I'm telling you, every girl in town showed up on those nights."

"Bear?"

Seth's jaw dropped. "You don't know about Bear?"

"As in grizzly, polar, black?"

"As in Bear McKinley. As in the dude who I think might've kinda broken your sister's heart or something."

Beckett slapped his napkin onto the table. "Which one?"

"Raegan. Man, where've you been? I thought the whole town knew about Raegan and Bear. He moves to town, she latches on, he announces he's moving to South America to build a church or something. He only just left in June."

And Raegan hadn't said a word to him? She'd always talked to him.

"You. Walker."

The voice jutting in instantly cut off his thoughts as pounding footsteps shook the table until Sam Ross loomed over him. Great. He'd had a feeling after this morning, he might be seeing Sam again. Just how much of that scene in the orchard store had Sam witnessed? And why had he been there in the first place?

"Look, Ross, I'm not sure what your deal is or—"

"What my *deal* is?" Sam's tone was a growl.

"But this probably isn't the place."

"It's a good enough place for me. For what I have to say."

"Which is what?" Foolish question. Foolish decision to stand—slowly—as if facing off.

"You should've just stayed away. You don't belong here anymore. Haven't you messed up enough lives already?"

Now Seth stood. "Listen, this is a restaurant, not a corner bar. So maybe you could just move this whole thing outside?"

Sam ignored him. "It's bad enough you have to come back to town at all, but to rub my face in it—"

"Rub your face in *what*?"

He knew exactly what. Laughing with Kit after she'd fallen through the stairs. The teasing. Him rushing to her side and her looking at him with a sort of wonder in her rich cobalt eyes. Had Sam seen that? He'd been trying to shake off the potent effect of those seconds ever since.

When he'd thought she might be hurt . . .

"You know what."

"Sam, you're the one who had the great idea to arrest me and drag me to court. I'm stuck here in town because of you." *Stop. Stop. Stop.* "I'm working at the orchard with Kit because of—"

Sam had him by the collar before he could choke out the last word. He felt his back hit the wood beam behind him, a chair tip beside him.

"Guys—"

Seth was cut off by Sam's bellow and Beckett's grunt as he broke loose, the last of his self-control disintegrating as he shoved Sam into an empty table.

Kit heard Beckett before she saw him. The thwack of his hammer over slate tile pitched into the hilly landscape that surrounded the Maple Valley Scenic Railroad & Museum.

"Well, Kit Danby, I wondered if you'd ever make it out here." Case Walker emerged from the depot onto the wood boardwalk. Sunset doused the side of the museum in color. The rain she'd predicted earlier today had come in sheets and gone in a flash. A choir of cicadas hummed.

"I stopped by your house first. Raegan said I could find Beck here."

It'd been pure instinct, coming to find him after she'd heard what happened at The Red Door. She'd been at Klassen's Hardware, looking for a part for the apple cider press Beckett had found this morning right before she'd fallen through the stairs. Couple aisles over, someone had recounted the whole thing to Sunny Klassen.

Kit had left the store without paying for the part. Which, great, made her a shoplifter.

Metal track ribboned past the depot building and into the trees. Beyond the station, a rolling hill where she used to sled dipped away from the tracks, lightning bugs dancing in the air. She'd taken the fourteen-mile ride on the heritage railway countless times as a kid. Ticketless, usually, thanks to her in with the man who ran the tri-county tourist spot.

The man now stepping off the boardwalk and opening his arms for a hug. She stepped into the embrace without a second thought. "Good to see you, Case." She'd always adored Beckett's dad, even as his patient, studying ways at times unnerved her. Maybe it was his military background that made him seem so intuitive, so knowing—as if he could read her every thought.

Sometimes she was convinced he'd passed the trait on to Beckett.

Case stepped back. "I keep thinking one of these days you'll take me up on the offer to join us for breakfast. You always used to."

He looked exactly like she remembered—perhaps a few extra lines in his face and a bit of added fatigue, too. But the depot's busy season began right around the same time as the orchard's. Which meant he was likely working just as hard as she to prepare for autumn.

"I will sometime, I promise. I remember how good your quiches are. And Kate's French toast. And Logan's omelets." And Beckett's pancakes, though she'd always refused to admit it—he was cocky enough about them. But even as a teenager, he could whip up such fluffy pancakes they put all others to shame. The Walkers loved their breakfasts.

If Beckett heard their chatter from his post on the depot roof, he didn't let on. Just kept pounding away.

Case followed her upward gaze. "You heard?"

"Someone said they broke a couple tables. Is he hurt?"

"Not that much. Not where you can see, anyway."

She didn't miss the flicker of concern in his eyes. "Sort of feel like it's my fault."

Case turned to her, expression settling into something of a smile. "Kit, my son was getting into scrapes long before you moved to town. He'd get a wild idea about building his own tree house, and next thing we knew he was falling off a branch and breaking his arm. He talked Raegan into letting him cut her hair one time—because he can basically talk anyone into anything."

Didn't she know it.

"She ended up with a mullet. And mind you, this was decades past when it was fashionable."

How had Kit never heard that particular story?

"And it'd take more fingers than I've got to count how many times he came home from school with a black eye or a bloody nose. I couldn't ever even get mad at him for fighting because, more often than not, he was either trying to break up someone else's fight or defend another kid from a bully."

Sounded like Beckett. Hadn't he done the same for her? No, he hadn't fended off a bully, but he'd gotten her through her first day at a new school. He'd helped her un-jam her locker, steered her to her first class, waited with her at the bus stop after school.

And he'd never stopped. Once, when she'd been in tenth grade and terrified of giving her first speech, he'd spent hours practicing with her. And then, on the day of, he'd skipped his own class, managed to slip into the back of Mrs. Horton's classroom. He hadn't just watched her give the speech, he'd mouthed the entire thing along with her.

"Flora and I used to call him our wild child," Case was saying now. "But one thing about Beckett—there's almost always something well-intentioned behind his actions, even if they result in a black eye here or broken bone there."

Or sudden kisses out on a gravel road?

The unbidden thought careened through her, landing with a thud in her stomach. And oh, please tell her Case Walker couldn't read *that* thought. She'd never told anyone—*anyone*—about that. How she'd cried in Beckett's shirt the night of her wedding and then . . .

How he'd kissed her.

Or, well, tried to. In her shock, she'd pushed him away and perhaps for the first time in her life, expressed every exasperated word in her head in a stream of arguments that seemed to astound him as much as his kiss had astounded her.

"I just walked away from a wedding, Beckett . . . my *wedding. And you choose now to impulsively kiss me? Could you possibly have worse timing? Isn't it reckless enough that we're out in the middle of nowhere with a car we basically stole? Are you serious?"*

She'd gone on. And on. And on.

Like the pounding of Beckett's hammer and nails now.

Case cleared his throat, his gaze more penetrating

than probing. He might not know the specifics of the memory charging through her now. But he sensed enough. He nudged his head toward the depot. "Go make him feel better."

That was the thing, though. Once, Kit had been the one who could do that. Beckett could coax her into adventures, help her brave up enough to speak in front of her class—with as little as a smile, charm her into indulging his every whim.

But she'd been the one who could calm him after basketball losses, pacify him after arguments with his siblings. Soothe him as much as possible both times his mom's cancer came back.

But anymore . . . ever since that night . . .

Case patted her shoulder. "There's a ladder around back."

Because it was as impossible to deny father as it was son, she angled around the depot and made her way up the metal ladder. With a cautious heft, she pulled herself onto the roof. Beckett had to have heard her clatter, and still he didn't turn. Ropey muscle knotted in his arms and back underneath a plain black tee, his plaid shirt from earlier discarded on the other end of the roof.

"Beck?" Somewhere in the distance, a coyote's woeful howl lifted into the sky and the crackle of tree branches signaled the scuttling of birds or maybe a squirrel.

Beckett finally looked over at her. So many hours outside had splotched the tops of his cheeks and the ridge of his nose with faint red. If he'd acquired any bruises in the scuffle at the restaurant, she couldn't see them. Yet in the dim light of evening, his chestnut eyes were almost black.

He pulled a nail from the tool belt around his waist. "Don't tell me word got out to the orchard already."

"Actually, I was in town when I heard. So you might have a couple hours before the gossip passes city lines." She crossed the roof in a crawl, its slant messing with her balance.

Three whacks of his hammer and another nail disappeared into tile. "I've tried to stay out of the guy's way. I really have. But there comes a point . . ." He moved off his knees to sit, working his jaw while his gaze reverted to the fiery horizon.

She sat beside him, close enough that their arms brushed. "It's nice of you to help your dad." Especially after working all day at the orchard.

"He's been extra tired lately. Keeps getting these migraines." Heat radiated off his skin—from exertion or emotion or most likely both. He ran one hand over the slate. "Tornado last year practically ripped the roof off this building. Colton helped patch it last year, but I don't think he had any idea what he was doing 'cause it's already leaking."

"I heard about the tornado."

"Logan and Kate came home right after."

In other words, he hadn't. "Beck—"

But he rose to his feet before she could finish a sentence whose path she couldn't see anyway. Mindless of the height, he wandered over the rooftop, checking his work, dropping the hammer into the loop in his tool belt and draping his plaid shirt over his shoulder. Beckett turned back to her. "Coming?"

"You're done with the roof?"

"No, but I had a feeling this was about to turn into a counseling session and I'd rather it not."

Well, maybe it would've if she could've found the words to do as Case had asked—make Beckett feel better. To assure him just because one man held a grudge over something that wasn't even Beckett's fault, he wasn't the consummate screw-up he seemed to think he was.

To let him know that, whatever else had happened after, she'd never stopped being grateful for the moment he said the words she couldn't, rescued her from a wedding that would've been so very wrong and so very unfair to Sam.

"Let me help you finish up." A dance of shadow and dusk colored the grassy hill behind the depot. She stood and shuffled to him. "I promise not to play counselor."

He lifted one palm to the back of his head, rubbing his neck, considering. "Only got one hammer. But I guess you could hand me the tiles."

"Don't sound so excited."

He dropped his arm. "You want to know the truth? I'm still getting used to . . ." He motioned to the space between them. "This. Us. Being . . ."

"Friends again?"

"Is that what we are?" The orange sun bronzed his skin and skimmed over every angle of his face and shoulders and the rest of him. The grazing breeze, the tingle of a leftover mist—for a moment all was forgotten and all was well.

What if I had let him kiss me that night?

The question fluttered in without warning, jarring her enough to make her sway. Beckett laughed again and reached to steady her.

"Friends, yes." She gasped the words, coughed, forced out a wobbly laugh. "At least I hope we are. I accidentally stole a part from the hardware store tonight, I was in such a hurry to get out here and make sure you were all right. If that's not friendship, what is?"

She caught his grin as he turned and started back to where he'd left off. "Thief."

"Says the man currently working on four hundred

hours of community service."

"Touché." He tossed the word over his shoulder.

She followed him across the roof, willing her sudden nerves to settle and her mind to ignore the *what-if* that'd gone tripping through it seconds ago. No reason to dwell on it. Nothing revealing or significant about it. Just an erstwhile flutter of a chance musing.

And even if it wasn't, she had no business letting her thoughts wander *there.* Beckett had inched open that door once, and she'd slammed it shut. The chances of him opening it again were as slim now as snow in a warm front.

7

If Beckett could just forget for a couple hours that technically he was unemployed, barely into his community service, and due in Boston next week for his JAG Corps interview, tonight might turn out to be the perfect mix of rest and entertainment.

If he could forget.

And if he could get Kit to relax.

"Take a deep breath, Danby. This is supposed to be fun." This being Maple Valley's Annual *Empty* Pool Party. Every year on the Friday before Labor Day, the city threw a community-wide shindig in the newly drained pool. Live music, tons of food, probably a rambling speech from Mayor Milt at some point. The man had become an even more animated version of himself since beginning his campaign to impress some state people and bag extra funding or something.

The breezy strain of an acoustic guitar filled the air now, a meandering folk tune that echoed against the pool walls. And beyond the voices and laughter and fencing around the pool, a thousand fireflies danced in the cornfield across the street, stalks gangly and golden under moonlight.

But what were the chances Kit enjoyed any of it? All

day she'd hurried around doing last-minute prep for tomorrow's orchard opening. All day she'd worn the same look—furrowed brow, frenzied eyes.

"How am I supposed to have fun when I should be back at the orchard doing . . . doing . . ." She sat with her legs dangling over the edge of the pool wall, kicking her heels against the cement, keeping time with the staccato of her words. "Well, I don't know what, but I should be doing something."

Beckett couldn't hold back a languid grin. Maybe it was the first hint of autumn in the evening air—a tinge of cool hovering over the pool, the lingering smell of chlorine blending with the loamy scent of grass and grain dust. Maybe it was who he'd seen so far tonight, so many family members and friends, and who he hadn't—namely Sam Ross.

Maybe—most likely—it was Miss Ball-of-Nerves next to him. He'd practically had to drag her from the orchard to get her here. Cajoled her with his plan to stick orchard fliers under the windshield wipers of all the cars in the parking lot. But they'd finished that half an hour ago and she had yet to settle in and unwind.

"I know I forgot to do something. Yes, I crossed everything off my list, but I probably left fifteen things off the list in the first place, so what good was the list anyway?"

"That's it." He reeled to his feet. "You need pizza." Maybe on the way he could find Coach Barton. That was the other reason he'd come tonight. The man had served nearly twenty years in the Air Force before ending up in Maple Valley. He'd be the perfect person to write a letter of recommendation for Beckett's JAG Corps application.

If he could ever manage to talk to him. He'd just been so busy at the orchard. Helping Dad out at the railroad depot. Spending time with his sisters, his cousin.

He'd met with Webster for a second tutoring session, too.

How was it his days could be so full and yet he couldn't kick the feeling that his career, his dream, his whole life had stalled? Had it really been a full month since he'd come home, intending to stay only a couple days?

It was as if God had hit a pause button on his outside life, his real life. That is, if God was paying attention at all.

That was another thing that'd stalled—his faith. There'd been a day not so long ago when he'd honestly thought maybe God was nudging him. Opening doors. Reminding him of his long-ago JAG dream and paving the way.

But then he'd landed in Maple Valley. In jail. In court. At the orchard.

And his future felt further away than ever. Thus the gnawing need to do *something*—even something as small as talking to his old coach and securing a letter of recommendation.

"I don't need pizza." Kit looked up as she spoke. The shade of dusk deepened the blue of her eyes, and after so many days in the sun, her hair had lightened to the color of wheat.

Stop worrying about the future. Enjoy tonight. Isn't that what you're trying to get Kit to do? "Do too. I haven't seen you eat all day."

"Well, I did. I ate a Red Baron, a Gala, and a Haralson."

"Something other than an apple. Just sit. Enjoy the music." He patted her head as if she were a five-year-old and glanced past her to Raegan, sitting on her other side. "Keep an eye on her, will you?"

Raegan gave a mock salute as Kit rolled her eyes.

Beckett scanned the crowd as he wound his way toward the food stands set up near the waterslide, looking for Coach Barton's telltale height. At six foot five, the man wasn't generally hard to spot in a crowd. Ah, there, over by the beverage table. "Coach Barton," he called, nearly bumping into a woman with a plate of pizza in his hurry to catch him.

The towering man turned, grinned, and lumbered toward Beckett, arm extended. "Beckett Walker, I'll be darned." Gray had overtaken what was left of the man's hair, but he still had the athletic energy Beckett remembered. They shook hands as others joined their cluster—Coach Barton's wife, his daughter and her husband, another coach.

"Beckett was one of my star players," Coach Barton told the group. "Gracie remembers, don't you, honey? I used to come home talking about him. I was so sure he'd end up playing professionally."

"More sure than I ever was."

"You could've done it, Walker. Your form wasn't always consistent, but you made up for it with speed and quick thinking. And your three-pointers, hoo-boy. When I heard you quit in college, I had a mind to march over to Iowa City and wallop you."

As if Beckett hadn't gotten enough of a lecture from his college coach at the time. Hadn't made a lick of difference. All the joy he'd once had in the game seeped away the night Mom had passed away.

Not that he'd been there. No, while the rest of the family gathered at her bedside, Beckett sat in an airport, desperate to race home after an away game in Phoenix. *Too late.*

He just hadn't had the heart for it after that, had instead thrown himself into his classes, determined to finally honor Mom's belief in his potential.

"Unfortunately, pre-law and basketball just didn't mix." Forced lightness backed his words now. Up on stage, the folk singer had ceded the mic to the mayor. "Actually, that's what I called you about. I'm applying to the Army JAG Corps this fall, which means—"

His coach's laughter cut him off. "I know what it means, son. You in the Army?"

"Well, yeah—"

"I have a hard enough time picturing you as a lawyer, but in the service? Walker, you're the kid who could barely sit still long enough to watch game tape. You messed up drills, played by impulse, not strategy. Discipline wasn't exactly your strong suit." Coach Barton said it all with a jovial flair, no offense in his voice.

But the skepticism pricked all the same. A churlish wind clambered in, causing a crackle in the speakers hanging around the stage. "All due respect, sir, I was a teenager then."

"True. Still." The coach shook his head. "I just don't see it. But listen, you give me a call again and we'll talk more."

The man turned before Beckett could say another word, which was probably for the best anyway considering the disenchantment knotting its way through him now. Was it really that incredulous, the thought of him donning a uniform to serve his country? Using his law degree for something other than lining corporate pockets. Traveling overseas. Being a part of something bigger than himself.

Was it really so unbelievable?

"Beck?"

He angled, slowly, hesitantly. "Hey, Kate." How much of that conversation had she heard?

Enough. Clearly. His sister's eyes were full of something way too close to pity. "He's just one person, Beckett."

"Who clearly thinks I'm chasing a pipedream." Up on the stage, Mayor Milt was rambling about community spirit and summer's twilight and who knew what. "How is he even still the mayor? You'd think someday he'd get tired of waxing eloquent." Suddenly he wanted to cover his ears, drown out the sound of the mayor's reverberating voice and the echoes of Coach Barton's words.

And all the doubts now piling one on top of the other, impossible to dismantle.

"Beck." She plied him in a gentle tone.

Sometimes he hated it—the way his family members could read him so easily. He'd forgotten what that felt like, living so far away from them for so long. "I don't know what I'm doing here, Kate."

"You're getting that community service off your plate. You're spending time with your family. You're tutoring Webster, which is so great."

She wouldn't call it that if she'd seen the disappointment on Webster's face earlier this week, when Beckett had confessed he hadn't contacted the kid's old social worker yet, nor made any progress on finding his friend. He felt a stab of guilt all over again. Never should've promised to try.

"And what you're doing for Kit. You're helping make her dream possible."

While his own languished. But wasn't it his own fault? If he hadn't come home . . . if he hadn't stayed away so long in the first place . . . if he'd never run that car into that tree . . .

If he'd never spilled his reckless heart to Kit . . .

"I haven't told her about the JAG Corps." The confession slipped from him.

"What?"

"She thinks I'm going to Boston next week just to pack up my office. She hates the military, Kate. Way she sees it, the Army took away her dad and then her brother. We're finally, I don't know, friend-ish again, and I just . . ."

He was just a coward, that's what.

Because, no, it wasn't just about her feelings toward the military that kept him from telling her. It was the uncanny truth that even after years of fractured friendship, hers was still the opinion that mattered most. And if he told her, if she reacted like Coach Barton had . . .

His eyes found Kit now. Eric Hampton had claimed the spot beside her, and she was talking with her hands, animated, finally relaxed.

Kate leaned in for a light side hug. "You have to tell her, little brother."

He did. He would. Just not tonight. Not on the eve of her big day.

Coward.

"You know, you and Kit . . . all of us always kind of thought—"

"Nope." The cut-off was swift but effective. Kate's lips clamped.

He knew what they'd always thought. And maybe, for an all too brief, all too memorable twenty-four hours starting the night before Kit's wedding, he'd started to wonder the same.

But he was wrong and they were wrong and there wasn't a chance he was making that mistake again. For a whole host of reasons, really. But most of all, because he'd finally remembered what it felt like to have his best friend in his life again. He wasn't going to lose her a second time.

"I am not racing you up a tree."

Kit flung the words from her perch on the back of the wagon Beckett had been using all morning to transport orchard visitors from the main lot to this field. They'd reserved the cluster of trees for people to pick their own apples—just for this one September day.

She'd been concerned. Pick-your-own orchards were popular with visitors, but they often ended up with too much fruit on the ground and poorly harvested trees. Not to mention the liability of people balancing on ladders.

But Beckett had convinced her to offer the activity just during opening weekend. Which apparently made him think he could talk her into anything.

"You can bat your overgrown eyelashes at me all you want, Beckett Walker. I'm not doing it."

He stood on the ground with a swell of people around him. And to think she'd been worried about today's turnout. She didn't know whether it was the advertising, the posters hanging around town, the new website Beckett had helped her design, or the fliers they'd used to canvass the pool parking lot last night—probably all of it working together—but the first few hours since opening had been hopping.

"Come on, Danby. All these people are waiting."

"They're here to pick apples."

"They're here to pick apples *and* see me win." He turned to the girl in a cropped black jacket with a t-shirt underneath with the word *Whatever* spread across it. "Right?"

The young mom—Megan from the coffee shop, according to Rae—held a baby wrapped in a thin yellow blanket and had barely taken her eyes off Beckett since the wagon piled with hay bales had left the parking lot. "Well, I don't know about anybody else, but I'm here because you can put my child to sleep in two seconds."

Kit crossed her arms. "See? She doesn't care."

"Also in two seconds I could have this whole crowd chanting for you to accept my challenge, and you know it."

She jumped off the wagon and brushed a piece of hay from the hair she'd left loose today. It had to be a windblown mess by now. This was the first she'd been out to the field all morning, and she'd known Beckett had something up his sleeve when he insisted she join the latest group of wagon-riders. She'd known and had willingly walked right into his playful little trap all of her own free will.

Because she wanted to assess the field, see how many apples had made it into bags and baskets instead of the ground. Because she wanted to determine whether this was something they should do again.

Because Beckett smiled and I couldn't say no.

She squared off with him, head tipped to meet his wheedling gaze. "You can try to get a rise out of me by insisting you'll win. You can shepherd the crowd into chanting until they're hoarse. But there is nothing you can say that will convince me to make a fool of myself climbing a tree in front of everyone."

He stepped into her space, so close she could've puffed and blown the tuft of dark hair off of his forehead. His expression was one of smug knowing. "I will run the cider press all afternoon."

She blinked. Okay, so maybe there was something he could say. She'd spent all of an hour at the press this morning and already her arms ached. "You've got yourself a deal."

He let out a whoop. "Too easy." He turned to the crowd of people spread throughout the trees. "Hear that, folks? We're on. This is happening."

And then her hand was in his and he was pulling her to the tree she knew he would—tallest in the field—and pointing to a lone apple hanging from a high branch and telling her not to fall.

"I'm not going to fall, Beck."

"Says the woman who fell through a stairway in the very recent past."

And then they were racing to the trunk and grabbing for the same low-hanging branch. Laughing. Climbing. Shoving through leaves and branches while the people below cheered, their paths to the top separating and then coming together again.

Until . . .

Kit's fingers closed around the apple just as Beckett's arm snaked around her in an attempt to grasp it first. The branch beneath her feet shook from their shared weight, and she clasped onto the trunk with her free hand. Behind her, Beckett wobbled until he reached for the trunk as well, pinning her between both arms.

She shuffled to face him, still steadying herself with one hand behind her. If her hair had been a mess before, it had to be full of knots and twigs now, and she'd likely broken every fingernail during the climb. She gasped for air, the cotton of Beckett's t-shirt fluttering in her face. "I won."

"You won." His breathing was just as heavy as hers.

"Bet you're sorry you insisted we do this."

His chest heaved as he inhaled, exhaled, slanted his gaze to lock with hers as he caught his breath. "Not even a tiny bit."

Suddenly the crowd on the ground, still clapping and cheering, the rustling of branches, the apple in her hand . . . it all faded as she stared at the best friend she hadn't realized until this very moment how deeply, achingly she'd missed in the past six years.

Of course he'd left a hollow space in her heart when they'd parted ways. Of course over the years she'd yearned for a return to their earlier friendship.

But she hadn't known—or maybe simply hadn't been able to face—how profound the impact of their parting, how bottomless the reach of her longing.

Or how so very different things might be now if she hadn't pushed him away . . .

There it was again. The *what-if.*

As if reading her thoughts, Beckett let his hands slide down the trunk behind her, his eyes never leaving her face until he leaned in—carefully, lightly, and whispered in her ear, "Congratulations, Kit." And then even closer, "Race you to the bottom."

And before she could catch her breath, before she could contemplate the nervous energy tingling through her, he pushed away and began his descent.

"Unfair!" She tried to yell the word, but instead it came out a breathless gasp. *What just happened?* Not until her feet touched the ground did she regain even the barest hold on her senses or still the curious racing of her heart enough to jokingly call, "You let me win."

"I did not let you win." He started toward the wagon as the crowd turned back to their apple picking. But not before she caught the amusement glinting in his inky eyes.

"A hundred one-on-one games of basketball, laps across the swimming pool, races from your house to my house, and you never once went easy on me. Why now?"

He stopped at the wagon. "Katherine Louisa Danby, I did not let you win. You are the better tree climber. Accept it."

"We're doing a rematch tonight."

"Fine."

"You promise?"

"I said fine, didn't I?"

"After closing."

"Fine." He nabbed the winning apple from her hand.

"Stop saying fine."

"Fi—okay." He took a bite, studying her as he chewed.

And why that should make her fidgety, she didn't know. He'd seen her looking worse than this plenty of times. She'd even halfway dressed up today—though by now her dark jeans were dusty and one of the rolled, quarter-length sleeves of her hunter green shirt had unsnapped and unrolled. Her shoes were scuffed, and her necklace tangled in her collar.

She was a wreck. She was a tired, happy, exhilarated wreck.

"You did it, Kit. You made it to opening day and it's a complete success."

The admiration in his voice warmed her. "The crowd could dissolve this afternoon."

"It won't. You're going to make a solid go of this."

Oh, how she wanted him to be correct. It just felt so indescribably *right* to be here. More right than grad school ever had. More right than London and her job at the university and Nigel.

Nigel. Was it harsh to admit she'd hardly thought of him in the passing weeks? They'd exchanged a few emails shortly after he'd left, one stilted phone call. It all seemed so distant now.

She felt rooted to this place—this land, these trees.

And if it was a success—if they could continue to attract visitors all autumn long and keep the fire blight from recurring and pay all the bills, if they could keep the store's shelves stocked and stay on top of field chores and bring in a healthy harvest . . .

If they could do all that, it might convince Dad to let her manage the orchard for years to come. Maybe he'd even begin to show some interest, come home at some point. And Lucas, they could find him and . . .

And she'd have a whole new life.

One she'd owe to Beckett. Because there was no possible way she'd have made it to opening day without him.

"Beckett, I . . . you . . ." Words weren't enough to thank him.

As if sensing her grateful intent and strangely wary, he turned and jumped onto the wagon seat. "Now, if you really want to be a success, you could accept my offer of a loan and get started on that barn. I saw Drew's estimate, Kit. It's not undoable."

She looked up at him, lifting one hand to shield her eyes from the sun. "I can't take your money."

"You could. You're just being stubborn." He reached his hand down to help her up.

She grasped his palm and climbed up beside him. "Anyway, Willa offered too. Apparently she has quite the nest egg." It'd taken Kit completely off guard, but she supposed it made sense. Willa had never married. She lived in the house she grew up in—no mortgage hanging over her head—and she'd inherited money from her parents. "I think the only reason she ever worked at the orchard is she loved the land as much as my grandparents."

"And you, Kit. She loved you."

It was true. Kit had spent too much time over the years bemoaning the people who'd abandoned her—Dad, Lucas, and, well, Beckett. But why hadn't she been more grateful for the people who'd stepped up—Willa, her grandparents, and, again, Beckett? "I always felt like Dad used his Army career as an excuse to stay away. Willa did the opposite—used her career as a reason to stay."

Beckett stiffened on the wagon bench beside her. Was it the career talk? She'd been so consumed with her own work, she hadn't stopped to think how unsettled Beckett must feel these days—no law firm to return to, stuck in Iowa until his community service was complete. What would he do once he was done here?

"Kit . . ." His tone was serious, uncertain. He shook his head, apparently closeting whatever it was he'd intended to say. He never used to do that.

After a pause, he spoke again. "You should do it. Accept Willa's loan. Build the barn, expand the business like your grandpa always wanted to."

It wasn't what he'd meant to say, she could tell, but she latched onto his words all the same. "You think so? What about Dad?"

"He put you in charge. So take charge."

The wagon was beginning to fill with visitors, and soon they were rolling over bumpy grass toward the main grounds. Within minutes, grass shifted to gravel and they were unloading in front of the store. Beckett was chatting with Megan, more cars were filling the parking lot, the bells jangled over the store's front door.

Beyond all the activity sat the unadorned frame of Grandpa's barn. *What if I did it?*

The thought trailed her through the next half an hour as she checked in on the store, restocked a few shelves, set Beckett to work at the press. She stopped to chat with Willa and then eventually made her way to the office, remembering she needed to feed Flynnie. Inside, signs that Beckett had been here earlier were all over the place. His abandoned coffee mug. His hoodie over the chair.

He'd jumped into his community service with both feet. All in. Because that was who Beckett was.

Take charge.

She glanced at the papers on her desk. Drew's budget estimates, Grandpa's blueprints. She plopped in her chair and fingered through them. Drew was convinced he could have the building up in a month. *What if . . . ?*

She pulled a folder from underneath the papers. This wasn't from Drew. Was it something of Beckett's? Community service paperwork she needed to sign? She opened the folder, scanned its contents.

Not community service paperwork. No, instead they were papers about . . . a Judge Advocate Office Basic Course. *This isn't any of your business.* But something that felt an awful lot like desperation propelled her to keep reading. Application instructions. The address of an office in Boston.

An *Army* office.

Her heart plummeted.

Beckett wasn't just heading back to Massachusetts for a couple days to pack up his office. Nor was he as up in the air about his future as she'd thought.

He was joining the military.

"Kit?"

At the sound of the voice, the sight of the figure in the doorway, the snarl of emotions she couldn't even name—hurt? anger?—evened out into stark, suffusing shock.

Lucas.

Now Beckett knew why Kit had jumped so quickly on his offer to take over at the cider press. Only twenty minutes cranking the cast-iron flywheel and he was ready for a break.

At least the roof jutting over the store's front porch shaded the spot where they'd set up the old-fashioned cider press.

"How long do you have to do this?" Raegan peered into the grinder, where a series of serrated stainless steel knives chopped the apples as Beckett turned the flywheel.

"Until we run out of apples, I guess." Which, by the looks of the barrels lined at the edge of the porch, could last until eternity. Kit's crew had done a fine job picking, sorting, and polishing apples in the past few weeks. Although the bulk of the crop was just now ripening, some of the apples that ripened earlier in the season—Bonners, Whitney Crabs, Pristines—had been bagged and either sold at the Farmer's Market or kept in cool storage. "Takes thirty or forty apples just to make a gallon of cider."

The process was engrained in his head from his years of working at the orchard as a teenager. Once he'd chopped a good amount, he'd move the pieces into the mesh-lined tub at the other end of the press. Then he'd use the wooden pressing plate to squeeze juice into another tub. The cider would oxidize into a rich, amber brown within minutes.

The bells jangled over the store's front door as a customer exited. Raegan reached for one of the plastic glasses they'd already filled and handed it to the visitor. Then she was back on her perch, sitting on the porch railing as she had been for the past ten minutes.

She wasn't the only Walker helping out today. Kate and Colton had taken a shift out in the field, and Dad was around here somewhere. Even Logan, Amelia, and little Charlie had driven all the way home from Chicago for the event.

When Beckett had gaped in surprise after they'd arrived late last night, Logan had laughed. "*You do remember calling to invite us, right? Pretty much demanding that we show up?*"

Yes, because he'd wanted to make sure Kit had a good crowd. Figured the least he could do was ensure the Walkers showed up in full force. "*Just didn't expect you to actually make the trip.*"

"*Well, you know how much Dad likes to see Charlie, and with everything else . . .*"

He hadn't known what Logan meant by "everything else," nor the reason for the flicker of concern in his older brother's eyes. It was there and then gone in a blink. Had he imagined it?

"So back to Megan." Rae circled one arm around a porch beam as she leaned down.

"Not that again." She'd been teasing him about the barista on and off all morning. "She does not have a crush on me." Even if she had taken to giving him free drinks whenever he stopped at Coffee Coffee.

"Guess how long she's lived in Maple Valley?"

"Why guess when you're going to tell me?" He reached into the grinder to clear a jam of apple pieces around its blades.

"Two years. And guess how many town events she's been to in that time?"

"I repeat: Why guess when you're going to tell me?" He rose and gave the flywheel another series of turns.

"None. Considering we've got at least one major event each month, that's twenty-four missed events. Until now."

He began scraping the chopped apples into the tub underneath the pressing plate. "So Megan dug up some town spirit. Good for her."

Raegan hopped down from the railing. "All I'm saying is you, big brother, have a fan. And, you know, just be careful with it, okay? From what Kate says, she hasn't had an easy time of it."

At the shift in Raegan's tone, he turned, wiping sticky hands on his jeans. Bracelets crowded both Raegan's wrists and she'd switched out her usual eyebrow ring for a smaller metal stud. The streaks of bright color in her hair had faded to barely noticeable.

Even with her quirky style, her cropped hair, she looked so much like Mom. He and the rest of his siblings had all inherited Dad's darker coloring. Too, the rest of them had all come with some kind of built-in career drive. Sure, Beckett might've taken a little longer to lean into his own ambition, but since the day he'd decided to get serious about his college classes, it'd been an undeniable force.

Raegan? She'd never wanted to go off to college. Never targeted a career goal and gone chasing after it. Never even wanted to leave Maple Valley, it seemed. She said she was content still living at home for now, working a slew of part-time jobs.

But looking at her now, hearing the personal echoes in her light warning about Megan, it made him wonder if she was really as content as she insisted.

"You could've said something about Bear, you know."

She shoved her hands in her pockets. "Who told you about him?"

"Seth."

"Figures." She turned away, propping her elbows on the porch railing.

"This is me, Rae. You used to talk to me."

"That was before you went off to Boston without so much as a 'see you later' and didn't come home for six years."

She made it sound like he'd abandoned the family entirely, which wasn't the case at all. He'd made trips to LA when Logan lived there, Chicago back before Kate moved home. They'd all come to Boston a few times for holidays. He'd emailed and called. Not often, but . . .

But he'd hurt his little sister without realizing it. He'd been so stuck in his own hurt, consumed with his own striving to make up for all the ways he'd messed up. He grabbed a cup of cider and moved to her side at the porch railing. "I'm sorry, sis."

She shrugged. "I just didn't get why you had to leave. For a while there, it felt like everyone was leaving. Logan and Kate. And Mom was gone. And . . ."

And now this guy named Bear, who Beckett didn't know a thing about. Other than if he ever encountered the dude, he might revert to his firebrand days and take a swing.

"Anyway, I wasn't purposely not telling you." Raegan angled to face him. "And it's not like we were ever a *thing*. We were just, like, really close. And then last fall he says he's moving to South America but he doesn't actually move 'til this summer, and Maple Valley's basically the size of a bowling alley so I had to see him everywhere. But it's over so there's no point in talking about it."

Except by the slump in her voice, it sounded far from over. And didn't Beckett know better than anyone that some things just didn't up and go away solely because you wanted them to?

Mistakes. Memories. Arrest warrants.

The guilty voice in his head constantly accusing him of wasting his life. It'd only gotten louder since coming home.

He swallowed a gulp of frothy cider. Maybe it was seeing Kit so focused, so purposeful. He'd watched her yesterday with a couple guys from Hampton House, showing them how to check soil moisture before the orchard opened.

"What you want to do is dig a hole about six inches deep right at the tree's drip line. Grab a handful of the soil. It should be moist enough to make a ball when you squeeze it, but not so moist it doesn't crumble."

She'd had dirt under her fingernails and grass stains on her jeans. Her ponytail had long since loosened and hung limp over her shoulder.

And he hadn't been able to stop the trail of his thoughts: He'd never seen her look so at home. So moored and confident. So effortlessly . . . what?

Captivating. That was the only word for it.

He hadn't been the only one to notice. Eric Hampton, leaning against a tree laden with not-yet-ripe Braeburns, hadn't been able to take his eyes off Kit. The guy had been spending more and more time at the orchard lately. Instead of just transporting the Hampton House residents, he'd begun lingering during their shifts.

Now that was a guy with purpose—running a nonprofit, making a tangible impact on hurting lives.

Longing coursed through Beckett, overwhelming and intense, pungent as the cider in his glass.

But this conversation wasn't supposed to be about him. It was supposed to be about Raegan, her hurt. Yet it seemed he'd lost the right to play the protective older brother. "Well, if you ever do want to talk—"

"Beck! Rae!" Logan's panicked call barreled in from across the yard.

Beckett pushed away from the porch, his cup of cider tipping to the ground. "What is it?"

That's when he saw Kate running toward the wagon.

And Dad on the ground beside it, face in the gravel.

Raegan's shaky voice sounded beside him. "I'm calling 911."

8

The ambulance roared down the road, throwing up gravel and leaving a cloud of dust in its wake.

Everything in Kit screamed for her to jump in her car and follow.

But she had an orchard full of people and there was already a crowd of Walkers on their way to the hospital and . . .

"I'm sure he'll be all right, Kit."

Lucas.

She hadn't had more than a couple minutes to process the jolt of seeing her older brother standing in her office doorway before the chaos of Case Walker's collapse outside had taken over. Now a weary numbness draped over her.

"He was so white. He wouldn't wake up." Fear clenched every muscle.

And there was something else, something Logan had said as the paramedics were loading the stretcher into the ambulance. *"I told him not come today. It was too much. He knew he shouldn't . . ."*

He knew he shouldn't what? Confusion had clouded Beckett's eyes in response, and then he'd climbed into the ambulance. His gaze had found hers in the seconds before the ambulance doors closed. And in that moment, the papers she'd found, the Army application, none of it had been important.

Late-afternoon sun spilled from the sky now, drenching the landscape in fiery light. But a chill grabbed hold of her. She wound her arms around her waist.

"He'll be all right," Lucas said again.

Lucas. He's here. He's home.

She turned, willing her brain to focus. Shouldn't she hug him? Come up with some kind of emotion other than shock? But she feared if she pushed past the surprise, anger might be the only feeling she'd find treading under the surface.

For ditching the orchard. For disappearing again. For scaring her all these weeks.

"Where were you?" She didn't mean to sound so accusatory.

Or maybe she did. Or maybe it was just her clinging alarm. *Please, let Case be okay. Beckett needs him.* The prayer murmured through her.

"Huh, I thought maybe I'd get a 'welcome home' or something." Lucas shrugged. "It's been two years, after all."

For the first time since he'd appeared in her doorway, she looked at him—really looked. The gaunt frame he'd brought home from the Middle East had filled out in the years since his prison release. His dusty brown hair was long enough to be pulled into a disorderly ponytail of sorts; his skin, coppery.

If not for the dull gray of his eyes, she might've said he looked healthier than she'd seen him in years. Almost like the Lucas she remembered from childhood—easygoing, quick to laugh, but always with a protective, brotherly bent. Why couldn't she find the welcoming words he was obviously waiting for?

"You disappeared. You fired Willa. The trees were infected." She spun, suddenly un-numb, overcome. She hastened toward the store.

"It was too much, Kit. I never asked for this responsibility."

She lurched into the store, glanced around. Only one customer wandered through the space. What had happened to their crowd?

And who even cared in light of Case, Beckett, Lucas?

Her brother's footsteps thumped on the floor behind her. He must have grabbed an apple from a barrel, because she heard the crunch of his bite. She moved to the row of glass-fronted refrigerators along one wall. Cold air billowed over her cheeks when she opened the first door. She began organizing the shelves of cider and other juices, filling empty spaces and turning jugs so they faced the front.

"You just left, abandoned the place. I had no idea where you were. Do you have any idea what that felt like, Luke?" Her fingers numbed in the cold of the refrigerator. "It's like it was 2005 all over and—"

"Don't."

The darkness in his tone was enough to make her stop, turn. The refrigerator door bumped closed behind her, and there—there was the brother who'd come home from Afghanistan a tortured mess. Haunted and hollow. Distant.

"I know you don't like to talk about—"

"You don't know anything about it, Kit." He tossed—no, threw—his barely eaten apple at the trashcan already overflowing with garbage. It smacked off the top and rolled to the floor. "So just don't."

"Fine. We won't talk about the war, but we have to talk about the orchard." She stalked past him, picked up his apple, and pressed down on the pile of trash, not even caring about the grossness of it. She pulled up the edges of the trash bag and tried to heft it out. Too heavy. "I don't know what I would've done if Beckett hadn't been around."

"You could've kept the place closed like I planned." Lucas stepped around her and pulled the trash bag from her grasp. "You didn't have to come charging in to save the day. I didn't ask you to." He yanked out the bag.

"I care about the orchard, even if you don't."

"Why?"

She stilled at the sincerity of his question, staring as Lucas twisted the garbage bag handles into a knot and tossed it outside the door. He really didn't know, did he? "Because . . . because this is home. This is the place where we were happy. Don't you remember? We were a family at least for a little while. You, me, Dad."

Didn't he remember that Indian summer? So many evenings picking apples with Dad and Grandma and Grandpa. Listening to Grandpa's stories about growing up at the orchard, wooing Grandma right here in these fields. Sitting on the porch and eating Grandma's apple pie and hearing about the mom she'd never had a chance to know.

And Dad. He'd been carefree and attentive and happy.

He'd been *here*.

"I remember Dad stuck around for a whole month, month and a half." Derision edged Lucas's words. "And then I remember him waltzing in one night and announcing he was heading back to Fort McNair and we'd be staying here with the grandparents. I remember hearing him and Grandpa arguing later that night. I remember you crying your eyes out for the next week."

Yes. Because she'd honestly thought it would be different this time. That Dad would stay. How could it still sting now, the memory of him driving away?

In her youthful despair, she'd actually decided to run away, go back to Colorado, where they'd lived before with one of their aunts, Dad's sister. Beckett—of course—had been the one to find her packing a suitcase. She could remember it so clearly, even now, in the wake of all that had happened in the past hour . . .

He'd told her she had to stay. Reminded her of all the fun they'd had in the past month. Told her they were best friends now, and best friends didn't leave.

Even if fathers did. That's what she'd thought to herself.

But then he'd pushed her suitcase out of the way and hopped onto her bed and launched into a story—of the Spaniards in 1519 who'd arrived in Mexico only to face so many hardships they wished to turn around and go back. Instead, in a show of iron will, they'd burned their ships, forcing themselves to stay and make a new life for themselves.

"You need to burn your ships, Kit Danby."

Even at eleven years old, Beckett Walker had known exactly how to sway her. Just like he had this afternoon, charming her into a tree-climbing race.

Luke went on. "I remember Dad ditching us here. I remember thinking, 'Why in the world can't he take us with him when he's got a desk job?' I understood before, back when he was overseas. But he wasn't overseas most of the time. He was working regular hours, living in a regular house. That's what I remember."

"It must have just been too painful, being around us." She said it by rote, the same old shielding excuses shambling to the surface. "We must have reminded him of Mom. The hurt must have simply been too much."

"Or it was just easier to walk away than man up to his responsibilities."

She couldn't stop her gasp—not at his statement itself, but the irony. Coming from a man who'd left his station in a desert and disappeared for nearly twenty-five unbearable months. Who'd refused to even defend himself during his court martial.

He must've heard it, too. Because his defiant stance deflated. Guilt seemed to press into him. "I'm going to go to the house."

"Luke—"

"You're right, I shouldn't have left the way I did. But I'm back now, and I've got a buyer."

"What?" Vaguely, she was aware of the last customer leaving the store.

"I told Dad at the end of last season I didn't think I wanted to keep this up. He said if I can find a buyer, I can have a slice of the sale revenue."

She sputtered. "But . . . but he told me . . . he said I could have a season to make a profit and . . ."

Lucas stopped under the doorframe. "Probably because he gave up on me doing anything about it. Honestly, I don't think he really cares what happens to this place. He's got his life in D.C. He'll give you some of the revenue, too, I'm sure."

"I don't want *revenue*." This day, it was too much. Such heady excitement this morning and now . . .

She shouldn't even be here. She should be with Beckett. "Luke, we can't sell. Think of Grandma and Grandpa."

"I've got a buyer, I've got the paperwork, I've got everything. It's the owner of the orchard I worked at while I was in North Carolina. Dad just needs to sign."

"He won't—"

Lucas shook his head and turned his back to her. "He will."

Brain tumor.

Beckett couldn't wrap his mind around the doctor's words. The intermittent hum and flicker of the overhead fluorescent light in Dad's hospital room was more nettling than it should be. Just outside the door, a janitor clattered by with a rolling mop bucket, the heavy bleachy odor wafting into the room. And so much white—the walls, the bedsheets, the doctor's jacket.

Dad's face.

He was awake now. Alert, sitting up, but pale.

And apparently not at all surprised by Dr. McNabb's string of jarring sentences. "I'm glad you've already been to Ames for the MRI. Got off the phone with the specialist there a few minutes ago. Sounds like you're already set up for some additional tests in Iowa City?"

Additional tests?

Dad nodded. "Tuesday, actually."

"Will he need surgery, Dr. McNabb?" Kate rose from the edge of Dad's bed. It was the first she'd moved from the spot since a nurse had finally ushered them into the room.

"Honestly, I don't know. That's something testing and the neurosurgeon in Iowa City will determine. If it's not cancerous—"

Beckett's stomach turned inside out from where he sat in the room's one chair, edged into the corner, out of the way.

"—then it'll most likely depend on the location and size of the tumor, the severity of the symptoms. Brain surgery comes with risks, of course, and with some tumors, we have the option not to operate and simply keep an eye on it. Other times, surgery is vital."

Why wasn't anyone jumping in? His sisters and brother—they all just stood there by Dad's bed, still and mute. As if Dr. McNabb was talking about flu symptoms and not something that could . . .

He inhaled so sharply it drew Dad's gaze from the hospital bed. Calm. Reassuring.

Completely nonsensical.

"I'm sorry, Dr. McNabb, can we back up for a second?" Beckett stood so abruptly that the chair scraped the floor behind him. "So this isn't new? You've known about this tumor?" Just saying the word clogged his throat.

The doctor looked from Beckett to Dad and back again. "Perhaps I should let you talk as a family for a bit." He closed Dad's chart and moved to the door. "Case, I think we'll keep you overnight just to be on the safe side."

Dad groaned. "That really necessary, Doc?"

"I promise to stop by before my shift ends and we can argue Iowa versus Iowa State. That way you won't be completely bored."

With that, the doctor left the room, the last of Beckett's patience following him out. He raked his fingers through his hair, alarm pinching his voice. "Dad, you have a brain tumor?"

Not ten minutes ago, he'd been sitting out in the waiting room, half listening to Raegan and Kate's whispered conversation about the hospital's stale coffee and watching Logan bounce Charlie on his knee and assuming the doctor would be out any minute to tell them Dad simply needed to watch his cholesterol or blood pressure or something.

But this? The overhead light flickered again, its plastic panel and the ceiling tiles around it rattling as he grappled to understand. "You have a brain tumor and you already knew and you're going in for more tests and might need surgery and you didn't tell us?"

The darted words ricocheted into silence.

Not just silence. Something else. Unspoken but gradually becoming clear as his attention dragged from Dad to each of his siblings. Logan, Kate, Rae. Not a one of them appeared surprised or even half as shell-shocked as he felt.

They already knew.

It lanced through him. "You guys . . . you already . . ." Suddenly it made sense—Logan's cryptic words last night and then again an hour ago as Dad's stretcher had been loaded into the ambulance. He and Amelia hadn't just come home because of the orchard opening.

Dad straightened against the pile of pillows behind him. "Beckett—"

He couldn't help it, the jagged edge in his tone. "Dad has a *tumor* on his *brain* and you all knew." Nausea twisted his stomach. Or maybe that was just hurt. Anger. Probably both.

"Can we have a few minutes, guys?"

At Dad's request, his siblings shuffled toward the door. But he couldn't look at them. Couldn't look at Dad. Only stared at the glinting silver flecks in the laminate tile floor while that stupid light in the ceiling kept buzzing.

"Beck—"

"Seriously, how hard is it to change a bulb?" He dragged his chair to a spot underneath the light and climbed on it, reached over his head to smack the plastic covering with his palm. When the rattle didn't stop, he hit it again. Waited.

Silence.

"Feel better?"

The sliver of amusement in Dad's voice wasn't nearly enough to quell the frustration building in him. And no, he didn't feel better.

But he climbed off the chair anyway. Stood. Stiff and waiting.

"I've been having migraines for a couple months. Some dizziness. Couple weird vision issues." Dad spoke calmly, evenly. "A few days before Seth's wedding, I passed out in the kitchen."

Beckett finally raised his gaze. Dad's hands were folded in his lap, his posture slack against the pillows.

"Raegan found me, and I came to a lot quicker that time than today. But it was serious enough that I made a doctor's appointment. Dr. McNabb referred me to the specialist in Ames, and I had the MRI about a week and a half ago." A machine with numbers Beckett didn't comprehend blinked beside Dad's bed. "I found out it was a tumor last week, and now I'll go to Iowa City for some more in-depth tests. Probably a PET scan, a spinal tap, couple other imaging tests."

Dad's explanation was a merry-go-round that wouldn't stop spinning. All this had happened without Beckett noticing? That trip to Ames week before last—he hadn't asked Dad what it was about, just assumed it was a regular old errand. The headaches—he hadn't even thought to consider there was something serious going on.

He lowered into the chair, didn't realize his hands were shaking until he tried to trace a rip in the vinyl armrest. "And it might be . . . ?" *Cancer.* He couldn't make himself say the word.

Suddenly he was nineteen years old again, sitting on the couch in the living room at home with his siblings while the recliner by the fireplace swallowed Mom's thin frame, Dad's palms on her shoulders, telling them her cancer was back again.

And this time, there might not be any fighting it.

"There's every reason to hope it's not cancer. Brain tumors often turn out to be nonmalignant." Dad shifted in the bed, pushing the cotton sheet away and swinging his legs over the edge. He leaned forward, coaxing Beckett's gaze once more. "Right now, I just need you to know that I wasn't trying to be hurtful in not telling you. I've been praying about the right timing to tell each of you. You had orchard thing today, which I knew was a big deal, and you're flying to Boston on Labor Day—"

"I'm not. Not if your tests are Tuesday."

"You are not going to miss your FSO interview because of this."

"That's the last thing I'm worried about at the moment." He'd call the JAG officer. Reschedule. Whatever.

God, this isn't happening. Not Dad, too.

Did hurled words tinged with resentment count as a prayer? Even if they did, what was the point? Hadn't he prayed night after night for Mom?

Strangely, despite the unanswered prayer, he'd never stopped believing God was there. Just that he listened. Because despite what he'd always heard in Sunday school, there had to be a point where God moved on from the screw-ups. Gave his attention to the people more likely to get it right.

Beckett scraped his palm over his cheeks and chin. "Will they be able to know if it's cancer or not without surgery?"

"Maybe not definitively. It's like Dr. McNabb said, a lot is going to depend on the rest of the tests." Dad rose to his feet, but not without wobbling. He closed his eyes, gripped the railing along the edge of the bed.

And everything in Beckett told him to reach out, grasp Dad's arm, help steady him.

But he couldn't move. He just sat there, feet cemented to the overly shiny floor as his world tilted. In all his uncertainties in all the years since Mom's death, he'd always had one assurance—Dad. When he'd escaped to Boston and let the gulf between his new life and his home and family span wider and wider, there'd always been the surety of Dad's presence, even if from afar. Even if their relationship bore the strain of distance.

And not just geographic distance. There were things he'd never said to Dad about the day Mom died. Guarded emotion he'd refused to free, to even face. Even so, Dad had still been . . . *Dad.* Strong, always there, always waiting.

Now two words had thrown his entire world off-kilter. *Brain tumor.*

Slowly, Dad lowered himself back onto the bed. But there was a firmness in his eyes as he leveled with Beckett. "We're not going to panic about this, son. We're going to trust God. We're going to—"

The scoff was out before he could stop it, and he hated it. Hated the look on Dad's face. Hated that he couldn't handle this with any kind of even-keeled maturity. Hated the knots twisting inside that drove him to his feet and threatened to drive him from the room.

Not just threatened. "Dad, I'm sorry, I can't . . ." His legs moved of their own accord. "I can't do this right now."

And then he was escaping through the door and down the hospital corridor, past the nurse's station, and around the corner that led into the waiting room. His siblings sat in the same chairs as before, drinking from the same Styrofoam cups, the same drone from the same TV in the corner filling their silence. Logan's wife held a sleeping Charlie.

"Beck."

He pretended not to hear Logan, intent on the revolving door, its blaring red exit sign beckoning. In his periphery, he was aware of Raegan standing, Kate already moving toward him.

He ignored them all and simply kept moving.

Forty-four. Forty-five. Forty-six.

Beckett lobbed the basketball at the garage door in a rhythm that matched his throbbing head. Every bounce rattled against the night's quiet as the ball first hit the garage then the cement, then slapped into Beckett's hands.

Forty-seven. Forty-eight. Forty-nine.

"I thought the goal was to get it through the hoop."

Fifty. The ball met his palms, and he trapped it. Logan's wife, Amelia, stood on the porch steps, hands buried in the pockets of her denim jacket and hair pulled away from her face. She and Logan had arrived home from the hospital half an hour ago, Logan carrying a sleeping Charlie.

Kate and Raegan were still with Dad.

A gust of early-September cool clattered through the wind chimes hanging from the corner of the porch and scuffed over Beckett's cheeks, his bare arms. The opaque night dimmed the rustic wood frame of Dad's house.

"Guess I'm tired. Making a basket feels like too much effort." Easier, apparently, to take out his frustration on the garage door.

Amelia descended the porch steps and strolled to the driveway, coming to a stop just in front of him. "I've been meaning to thank you."

He peered down at her, this woman who'd embedded

herself in his brother's and niece's lives. How long had they been married now? Two months? He'd had only a handful of conversations with her. "Thank me? For what?"

"Logan told me you went out to see him in LA. Earlier this year, I mean. Everything sort of fell apart between us at the end of spring, and he went back to LA and I got the job offer in Chicago." Her hands were still in her pockets, but they moved as she spoke. "Apparently you went out to see him and I don't know what you said, but it must have been good. Because next thing I know, he's following me to Chicago."

And then eloping with her only a few weeks later.

Feathery clouds shifted and separated long enough to release a shaft of moonlight. It highlighted the faraway glint in Amelia's eyes. Dreamy, that was the word for her expression. Head over heels and all that.

It was true he'd gone out to LA a few months ago—mostly because his sisters had called him and asked him to. No way he could've said no to that. Other than Kit, it was rare he was the one anyone turned to for help. He so often felt on the fringes of his family. "I don't think I said anything so brilliant."

She pulled her gaze away from whatever romantic memory it'd settled on a moment ago and instead peered at him. He heard a window sliding shut—probably Logan, making sure Charlie would stay warm tonight—and the distant *hoo* of an owl in the ravine that curved around the back of Dad's property and up along the side. Some nights, if he squinted just right, he could see the lights of Kit's grandparents' house blinking through the knot of trees.

"He hated not telling you, you know."

His attention snapped back to Amelia.

"I was there when Case called a few days ago. Logan

hasn't taken the news well. He's had trouble sleeping. I think it's bringing back lots of memories of your mom. And I know it killed him not to be able to talk to you about it."

He loosened his hold on the basketball, let it dribble to the cement. "But Dad asked him not to say anything and he's Logan, so of course he did the right thing and didn't." He loathed how harsh it came out, the undercurrent of something long-standing and far too familiar layering his words.

Bitterness. Or maybe something even uglier.

Jealousy?

He loved Logan, of course he did. Looked up to him almost as much as Dad. It was just hard sometimes not to compare himself. Logan did the calm, even-keeled thing so well, whereas Beckett was the hothead with the tendency to fight or run away or too often both.

Amelia bent over to pick up the basketball, skirted past Beckett, and eyed the hoop. "I'm so un-sporty, it's not even funny."

"Par for the course around here. I'm the only Walker who ever did the athletic thing. Kate tried a throw a Frisbee once when we were kids—knocked out one of my front teeth." Funny, considering she was now dating a former quarterback. Hadn't been so funny when he was a five-year-old with a bleeding mouth.

Amelia tossed the ball toward the hoop. Missed by a mile. Okay, so she wasn't joking. She laughed and turned back to him. "Told ya."

He shrugged. "Everybody's shot an air ball once or twice."

"Yep. Everybody." She studied him again. "If I tell you something, can you promise not to tell Logan I told you?" He lifted his eyebrows, and she apparently took it as a promise. "Last spring when Logan was home, he had some problems with Emma's folks."

His first wife's parents? Hadn't the O'Hares adored him? Acted like Emma was marrying a prince? "What kind of problems?"

Amelia glanced upward, toward the bedroom window that had belonged to Logan as a kid. The one he and Amelia and Charlie were sharing during their stay. "Had to do with Charlie. Logan was a wreck over it. And this is the part he'd kill me for telling you. He and Rick O'Hare got into it right in the middle of the town square."

"As in, an argument?"

"As in, Logan punched the guy. I wasn't there, but believe me, I heard about it."

"You're telling me, my brother—calm, cool, always-do-the-right-thing Logan Walker—lost his temper and decked a dude in front of a bunch of people." How he could even find a grin under the grime of this day was beyond him. "You're telling me this because . . . ?"

"Because it seems like maybe you could use something to cheer you up a little tonight." She gave him a sisterly pat on the arm. "And because I'm not sure the garage door can take much more."

He kind of liked her, this woman his brother had brought into the family. "You know, I really do feel a little better."

She squeezed his arm before starting for the front door. "Just don't stay angry at him and the girls forever, okay?" She waited long enough for him to nod, then retreated into the house.

Beckett didn't move from his spot on the cement. He tipped his head, stretching the muscles in his neck and back and shoulders as a draught of chilled air flapped his gym shorts against his legs. Stars blinked sluggishly overhead, as if trying to stay awake under the cotton cover of wispy clouds.

His gaze alighted on his own bedroom window on the side of the house, the wraparound porch roof . . .

"You're thinking about heading up and climbing out your window, aren't you?"

Something released in him as he turned. "Kit." She must have walked over, crossed the ravine, and come around the house. How had he not heard her? She stood in the yard, rescued basketball in her arm.

"Don't you ever get worried sometime you'll fall completely asleep up there, roll over in the middle of the night, and topple right off the roof?"

"Probably wouldn't break any bones if I did. I'd land in the rosebushes." They met under the basketball hoop.

She dropped the ball to the grass. "Yeah, but then you're talking thorns and your father's wrath at the sight of your mom's ruined flowers."

His muddled brain didn't know which of her words to latch onto; his tumbling emotion, which feeling to fall into. Worry at the mention of Dad. The familiar pang at the mention of Mom.

Or the talk of flowers and the scent of Kit's lotion or perfume or something and the awareness of how close she stood and how much he'd wished her here without even realizing it.

"I tried calling." Her voice was as soft as the gentleness in her eyes. "I went to the hospital but you were already gone, and then I came here but you weren't home yet."

"I went for a run." Literally and figuratively. "Needed to blow off steam."

"Well, you've got a slew of anxious texts and voicemails waiting for you."

"I honestly don't even know where my phone is."

"It's okay. I got ahold of Kate. She told me everything. I—"

He didn't wait for whatever she was going to say next. Only reached for her like a lifeline. He felt the surprise sway through her as he wound his arms around her back.

But then she leaned into him, her arms wrapping around him just as tightly as he held her.

A minute might have passed—or five or ten, he didn't know—before his hold loosened. But he didn't pull away, nor did Kit step back. "Did I see Lucas at the orchard?"

She only nodded against his chest, perhaps as unready to talk about her own life upheaval as he was his.

"They all knew, Kit."

She tipped her head back, meeting his eyes, and he saw the understanding there. He didn't even have to voice it—how standing in that hospital room, realizing everyone else in the family knew about Dad's diagnosis, had sent him back to the day of Mom's death.

Arriving home to find out he was too late. To hear about how they'd all gathered at her bedside, one by one said their goodbyes.

A shared moment he'd never be able to claim as a memory of his own.

Why hadn't they told him to come home? He'd called, he'd talked to Dad. He'd asked if he should skip his basketball game. Oh, some logical piece of his brain tried to remind him there's no way they could've known. The doctor had said Mom still had weeks. Dad had no idea that morning when he told Beckett there was no need to miss his game that later that day everything would change.

But logic could never quite hush the stormy force of his emotion. It'd blustered in all over again at the hospital today, an unstoppable zephyr. Half hurt, half anger. Would he never stop carrying this around?

And how could he possibly be irate toward Dad considering his current condition?

Kit reached up to smooth a windswept piece of hair over his forehead. Her fingers lingered there, sliding down his cheek until she cupped his face with one hand. "Want to play a little one-on-one?"

He nodded against her palm.

She dropped her hand and stepped away. He fought the urge to pull her back, reaching instead for the ball. Kit pulled a hair tie from her pocket and bunched up her hair. After she tightened her ponytail, he lobbed the ball to her and she moved to the crack in the cement they'd always used as a court line.

Instead of moving, though, she paused after a lone dribble. "Beck, today . . . before everything, I found . . ."

"Yeah?"

But she only shook her head. "Nothing." She seemed to force a smile, a tease. "Just don't go letting me win."

He found a grin of his own. "Wouldn't dream of it."

9

"This town is so bizarre."

Eric Hampton's muttered assessment earned a laugh as Kit walked alongside him, along with half of Maple Valley.

The soft whirr of voices and footsteps pattering over the paved cement of Main Avenue was matched by the sound of raindrops tapping on a rainbow of umbrellas. They moved like a herd across the Archway Bridge and toward Maple Valley High School. Wan clouds draped across the sky, early-evening sun glowing around their underbellies. Shade and light tussled over the landscape and turned the Blaine River a luminous, stormy blue.

Eric held a black-and-white-striped umbrella over the both of them. "Seriously, though, who commemorates a natural disaster with a group walk?"

"Two natural disasters." Kit sidestepped a puddle. A tornado and then a flood had wreaked havoc on the community around this time last year. She might not have been here to experience it, but she'd heard the stories. "We're celebrating the fact that the town got through them." First the walk, then a town meeting in the gym, and later, an outdoor movie in the square.

"With something that looks like a funeral procession?" Eric shifted the umbrella against the wind. "In the rain?"

Fine, the commemorative walk was hilarious—up there with some of Mayor Milt's more outlandish ideas. Like the annual rubber duck race in the river. Or the year he'd insisted the town host a Regency reenactment fair. His own wife had ended up passing out due to a too-tight corset.

But this was what made Maple Valley a place like no other. Besides, she'd needed to get away from the orchard for a while. Away from Lucas. He'd been home less than a week. It hadn't been an easy five days, not with his constant talk of selling and his dark moods, not to mention his nightmares. His first night home, she'd about barreled through his door in panic when she'd heard his yells.

"I still say it's bizarre." Eric ambled beside her.

"I think the locals prefer *charmingly eccentric.*"

"Hate to tell you, but I think we're both considered locals."

It'd been lucky, running into Eric, considering she hadn't brought her own umbrella. They'd developed an easy rapport in all his weeks of transporting Hampton House residents to the orchard.

"So how's Luke?"

And apparently he'd taken to reading her mind. "Honestly, Eric, he's . . ." She halted, catching sight of the figure striding toward her from the opposite end of the bridge. "He's here."

Mindless of the rain, Lucas moved against the flow of the crowd until he stopped in front of her, his expression drawn with irritation. People jostled around them, rivulets of water tipping down umbrellas. "Hey, Luke, I didn't think—"

"You're building the barn?"

Oh. Drew Renwycke had said materials would be delivered today or tomorrow. Guess today was the day. She didn't know when she'd officially made the decision—to accept Willa's loan, spend down her own meager savings, move forward with the project. Maybe it was Saturday night when Beckett had walked her back home after their game of basketball. Or the next morning in church when the pastor had preached on stepping out in faith.

Or maybe it was earlier, back in the orchard store on opening day when she'd remembered Beckett's story. *Burn your ships.*

She'd already quit her job. Moved home. Maybe this was her final act of ship-burning.

"Sorry I didn't tell you, Luke. I hired Drew Renwycke and—"

"Where'd you get the money? Did you even talk to Dad?"

Eric coughed uncomfortably. "How about I let you two talk?" He handed Kit his umbrella, then lifted the hood of his jacket and moved on with the rest of the crowd.

She felt badly, but clearly Lucas was intent on having this discussion here and now, rain or no rain. "I get it if you think it's a bad idea. But Dad gave me management of the place for one season. I'm going to make it count. I really do think it's a smart business move. Look at this town and its crazy love for events. We could probably rent the barn out every other weekend, easy."

They stood at the edge of the bridge now, watching the herd of people move to the school, where the rest of the town meeting would take place.

For one fleeting moment, it seemed like Lucas might actually lighten up. "I've spent the last two years trying to readjust to the quirks of Maple Valley, but this? A commemorative walk to celebrate last year's bad weather? So if we get a hailstorm this year, or maybe a fluke September blizzard," Lucas said, "we can throw a carnival or something?"

"Don't even joke about hail. Don't you remember that year almost an entire crop was wiped out?" It hadn't just been the hail. It'd been the wind, the timing. The fact that the storm had come in mid-September when the fruit was soft enough to slice open under the force of thrusting ice.

Grandpa had had to take out a second mortgage on the house to get through that winter due to the loss of income.

"That's just it, Kit." Lucas's overly long hair waved around his face. "The tornado last year took out half the crop." The crowd glided toward the school entrance, Mayor Milt at the helm. "At any time, a hailstorm or early fall frost or late spring frost or drought or disease or you name it—any of it can wipe away an entire season's hard work, not to mention a year's income." He tugged her back under the umbrella's shade and handed it to her. "Is that really how you want to live and, if so, why?"

Because she loved the thrill of waking up early in anticipation of a day's work. The feel of sun-kissed tree bark. The joy of picking a perfectly round and ripe apple.

"Because I love knowing something I'm doing today—whether it's spraying pesticides or building a fence or pruning—it's going to matter tomorrow. This land is going to be here long after we're gone, Luke. Don't you sometimes feel like we belong to it as much as it belongs to us?"

And that feeling of belonging, that sense of home—there was no trading it in for something better. She should know. She'd looked for purpose elsewhere. She'd walked away only to be coaxed back home by a longing she hadn't even recognized for what it was until . . .

Until that second night home, working in the orchard until after twilight with Beckett.

So much had changed since that night, when Beckett had away from her, refused to talk about what had happened after her wedding. They never had talked about it. Just like she'd never told him about finding his JAG Corps paperwork last Saturday. She kept hoping he might bring it up himself, tell her he wasn't really planning to leave. But she'd hardly seen him this week. He'd spent all day Tuesday in Iowa City with his dad and had been volunteering at the depot more than the orchard.

But it made a hundred kinds of sense—Beckett's plans. He'd love the excitement of traveling to some Army base in a foreign country. He'd love the adventure of it, knowing he'd never get bored.

That was where they were different. The thrill for Kit was knowing where she'd be and what she'd be doing each day. The sense that maybe—just maybe—there'd been some kind of divine plan all along. Like God had guided her back home.

But what if she was wrong about the orchard? They hadn't had nearly as many visitors in the days since their opening. She tried to tell herself lower numbers were to be expected on weekdays, but still. Her crop insurance bill was due in two weeks and here she was spending her and Willa's money on a building project Dad hadn't even approved.

And Lucas—there was a desperation behind his desire to sell and a pain he refused to let her in on. There was a whole history of hurt and hardship she couldn't begin to comprehend. How could she when he'd never once told her what had happened in Afghanistan? In prison?

Or what filled the dreams that woke him up at night?

"I can't just let it go, Luke." Her whispered words were nearly drowned out by the wind. Up ahead, the mayor held the school door open as community members disappeared inside. The rain had slackened to a drizzle. "Why don't you stay? We can run the orchard together."

"I don't want this life." The tumult in his eyes stretched into his voice. "I want to start over. Selling could give me the money to do it." He turned away from her, raked his fingers through his hair, his sigh visible in the way his shoulders sagged.

They were at an impasse, neither willing to give in. At the end of the day, it would come down to Dad, wouldn't it? Not a comforting thought. Why had he given her a chance at running the place if he'd already given Lucas the go-ahead to find a buyer? Did he even read the weekly reports she sent?

She watched Lucas walk away for a few miserable moments before finally turning toward the school to trail the convoy of people heading inside.

She hadn't been in the high school gym in years, but she knew what it'd look like—bleachers that slanted up both walls, flags and championship banners, basketball lines on the floor she'd watched Beckett run during countless games. There'd probably be a set of risers in the middle of the floor where the mayor would give one of his usual homilies.

Maybe she should just head back to the orchard. She wasn't in the mood anymore to be entertained by Maple Valley's quirkiness. But she needed to return Eric's umbrella.

She curved around the corner with the last of the crowd only to see the gym dim and hushed and . . . filled with candles? *What?* Hundreds of them, had to be—they covered every surface, the only glow in the room save for the strands of twinkle lights strung over the metal ceiling beams.

Whoa.

"I was worried you were going to miss it."

The voice behind her brushed over her ears, and she nearly jumped as she spun. "Beck? What's going on?"

He placed his finger over her lips. In the candlelight, his dark eyes danced. "Just watch." He lowered his hand and then used both arms to gently turn her around.

And there, walking across the stage—Colton Greene. And he was saying Kate's name. And the whole room awwed.

"He's proposing? During a town meeting?"

"He's had it planned forever," Beckett whispered over her shoulder. "He was just waiting for the perfect time. I think it's the former NFL star in him that had to do it all public and showy."

But then, just as Colton was going down on one knee, a shrill beeping blared from above. And on its heels, a whoosh—water sprayed from the ceiling as the gym filled with squeals of surprise.

The candles. The fire alarm. The sprinkler system.

Kit's shriek was half scream, half laugh as she took in Beckett's lack of surprise. Water streamed over his hair and down his cheeks, caught in his eyelashes. "I tried to warn him. Told him I went to school here, I know how ultra-sensitive the fire alarms are. At least once a week we all had to file out to the lawn when the alarm went off 'cause someone made toast in the teachers' lounge."

"Or messed up a chemistry experiment." She had to shout over the noise of the gym.

"On accident."

"On purpose and you know it."

"Think Kate will still say yes?"

She looked to the stage, to where Kate had jumped into Colton's arms and was laughing as he spun her around. "I think it's safe to say she will."

But when she turned back to Beckett, he wasn't watching his sister—but her. His gaze was a swirl of uncertainty and desire, and it released a fiery arrow straight into her heart.

Until he snatched the arrow back in a blink and a cough. "Kit, I have to tell you—"

Finally. "I know."

"Know what?" He shook wet, matted hair out of his face.

"I know you're applying to the JAG Corps. I know you're going to leave to go off and be an Army lawyer. What I don't know is why you didn't tell me."

His mouth gaped. "Are you mad?"

"No. Yes. Maybe." All of the above.

Eric walked up then, drenched and laughing. "There you are. My umbrella would've come in handy about thirty seconds ago."

Beckett looked from Eric to the umbrella in Kit's hands. "You guys came together?"

She couldn't read the look on his face, but Eric was saying something else, and in the noise of the gym, she had to angle to hear him. By the time she handed Eric his umbrella and turned back around, Beckett had disappeared.

"Aren't you supposed to be helping me?"

Webster's non-emotive shell made it impossible to tell if the kid was serious or joking—nearly as impossible as it was to focus tonight, despite the calm atmosphere of

Coffee Coffee. Too much swirled in his brain—Dad and the test results they were still waiting on. His unfinished JAG Corps application. The fact that he still hadn't heard back from the FSO office about rescheduling his interview.

And Kit. *She knew.* Had known for days, apparently. And he had no clue what to do with that information.

"Maybe the reason you're not helping me is you actually don't know a thing about—" Webster glanced down at the open textbook on the counter in front of him. "The complex ramifications of the assassination of Franz Ferdinand."

"Um, not that complex. Pretty sure I can sum up the ramifications in three words: World War I." Megan set a mug down in front of Beckett with a thud. "Chai tea. Which, if you ask me, is way too girly of a drink for you."

He eyed the cup with his own dose of skepticism. "Yeah, but Kit's been telling me for weeks if I'd give tea a chance, I might actually like it."

And every time she did, he'd tell her she'd spent too many years living in England. Then she'd tell him to stop being so close-minded about his beverage choices.

Why he'd gone and ordered tea tonight—especially one doctored up with a bunch of cream and who knew what else—he didn't know. Just when he'd stood at the counter and Megan said, "You're usual French roast?" all he could think of was Kit standing in that high school gym, drenched and laughing and . . .

Too many synonyms crammed through his mind all at once—*adorable, alluring, perfect.*

And he was an idiot. An idiot who'd sworn he'd never let himself look at Kit like *that* again. An idiot who'd had the irrational urge to ask Eric Hampton why he felt the need to hang around all the time.

An idiot who was supposed to be helping Webster and, oh yeah, somehow breaking it to the teen that he still hadn't made any progress on finding his friend. At least he'd called the social worker. But Webster wasn't going to like what he'd found out.

"Well?" Megan tapped dark purple nails on the counter. "Aren't you going to try it?"

He sipped, winced. Way too sweet.

"Told you." Megan straightened. "I'll get you a coffee. On the house."

"You can't keep giving me free coffee, Meg. That's no way to run a business."

She grinned. Shocker, that. Maybe Raegan hadn't entirely been seeing things. In which case, maybe he would've been smart to pick a different tutoring locale tonight. But he liked the coffee here *and* the girl who served it. She was her own person—snarky and stubborn. He had a feeling underneath the tough-girl act, she had a sensitive heart. But he'd hate to unintentionally encourage anything he shouldn't.

Webster's heels kicked against the barstool base underneath him. "Look, if we're not going to study—"

"Sorry, Web. My focus is off tonight."

The boy twisted his napkin into a ball. "Don't know why I should care about any of this anyway. It happened decades ago. Doesn't have anything to do with me."

Beckett mustered a smirk. "I think history teachers everywhere might go into a collective faint if they heard you say that."

"I've got enough going on in my own life. Why do I care about a war that started because some dude in Europe was assassinated?"

Beckett took another drink of the tea before remembering he didn't like it. He pushed the cup away. "There's a little more to it than that."

"Whatever." Webster clapped his textbook closed. "Look, the only real reason I came tonight was to find out if . . ." Hesitant expectancy idled in his unfinished thought.

Beckett wasn't going to get a better opening than that. "I tried, Web. I really did."

The teenager's face, usually such a mask of disinterest, turned transparent. He dropped his balled-up napkin, shoulders slumping.

"I called your social worker, and the most I could get out of her is that Amber—"

"Amanda!" Webster slid off his stool. "You can't even remember her name?"

"Amanda, sorry. But the social worker said Amanda is no longer part of her caseload. That's the most she'd tell me."

But Webster was already stuffing books into his backpack and then yanking on its zipper.

"Webster, are you sure it's something to be this upset about? Friends drift apart sometimes."

Webster slung his backpack over his shoulders. "It's not like that with us."

"Is there more you're not telling me?"

"I need to get home for supper."

"Web—"

"I get it. You tried."

He turned and was out the door before Beckett could carve out an argument or at least something encouraging, something to revive Webster's hope. But how fair would that be, anyway, considering the likelihood of his making any further progress on the search?

"Did you really try that hard?" Megan had paused halfway down the counter, rag in hand.

"Of course I did. I argued with the social worker for a good fifteen minutes. Then I talked to a law school friend who's handled a bunch of custody cases, but he said confidentiality—especially with minors—isn't something you can usually get around."

Megan's eyebrows dipped into a disbelieving V.

"I tried," he said again, but it came out slight, unconvincing.

"As hard as you tried to drink that chai?" She cast a glance at his neglected tea.

And just because he was ornery, just because something about this evening—from Kit to Webster to Megan's skepticism now—had him disconcerted and off-balance, he lifted the mug and in a sequence of determined gulps, downed the whole thing.

Megan went back to wiping down the counter. "I'm just saying, you could go talk to the social worker in person. Do that Walker charm thing. I never wanted to be Kate's friend, but she won me over by showing up on my doorstep when I was sick as a dog and making me soup. A few minutes on the phone so would not have had the same effect."

Show up on her doorstep. Why hadn't he thought of that? Maybe because he'd been more concerned with Dad and the orchard and his own stalled plans than keeping a hastily made promise to a kid he barely knew.

But watching Megan now, understanding the impact his older sister had made on her life, it awakened something in him—a desire to be that for someone else. Obviously Webster already had Colton in his life. His adoptive parents, too. But for some reason he'd reached out to Beckett for help on this one thing.

What would it hurt to drive over to Ames, see if he could wrangle some information from the social worker in person?

Megan cleaned the length of the counter, then shook her rag over a garbage can before tossing it in a stainless steel sink. He waited until she faced him again to speak. "You know you're actually kind of a genius?"

She rolled her eyes, removed his empty cup. "Just for that, I'll get you that coffee I promised."

There was that smile again. More of a smirk, but still. Raegan's admonition rebounded, reminding him to be careful. "Hey, Meg, just so you know . . ." Man, this was going to be awkward. But he had to say something, didn't he? Wasn't that the right thing to do? "I don't come here expecting free coffee or . . . like, expecting or looking for anything else. I mean, you're great, but—"

She froze, coffee pot in midair. "You are not actually serious."

"I just don't want you to think—"

She plunked the coffee pot back under the machine. "You think I . . . you . . ." She pointed back and forth between them, eyes going wider with each word. "You've got to be kidding me. You're *old.*"

Um, not what he'd expected. "I'm what, seven or eight years older than you?"

"You're starting to get those crow's feet things by the corners of your eyes."

"Some girls might call that charming."

"And even if I was into older guys, which I'm not, you don't have a job." She took off her apron and slapped it on the counter. "You're living with your dad. Technically, you're a convict."

"You really know how to make a guy feel good about himself, you know that?"

"I don't give you free coffee because I think you're my knight on a white horse or something. I give you free coffee because apparently motherhood has made me soft, and I hate making a guy pay when I know he doesn't currently have an income." She reached for the pot once more, poured a cup, and set it in front of him with a clunk. "Then there's the fact that you're holding a grudge against your dad, who, far as I can tell, is just about the greatest guy to walk the earth."

At the pitch of his eyebrows, she nodded. "Yeah, Kate and I talk. She says you're mad at all of them, too."

"I'm not mad." His fingers closed around the coffee mug.

"Well, she says it's been weird in the house ever since you found out about the tumor. It's probably why Colt proposed today, so Kate can hurry up and marry him and get out from under the same roof as her brooding brother."

He took a long drink of the bitter brew. It scorched his throat.

Megan pushed a chunk of black hair behind her ear. "Sorry. I was a little harsh on that last part."

"Just the last part?" He never should have started this conversation. It'd gone from awkward to amusing to biting. No, Megan hadn't meant to claw at him. But he felt scraped and raw and exposed all the same. He'd been less than composed Saturday at the hospital, sure, but he thought he'd done an okay job appearing fine in the days since. He'd gone with Dad to Iowa City earlier in the week. Conversation might have been a little stilted, but he'd tried.

But clearly trying wasn't good enough lately. Not with Webster. Not with his family.

"Beckett, I—"

"It's okay, Meg." His phone buzzed.

"You're really lucky to have the family you do." Dark eyeliner couldn't hide the softness in her eyes. "If I have a crush on anything, it's the entire Walker clan. I like you guys." She reached for her bunched-up apron atop the counter. "In a completely innocent, platonic way. Okay?"

He slid his phone from his pocket, scrounging up the closest thing he had to a good-humored expression. "Okay." He glanced at his phone screen. The text was from Raegan.

Dad got test results. Wants to talk to all of us together.
Come home.

It was time to stop avoiding Sam Ross.

Kit's searching gaze ambled over the activity of the almost entirely tarp-covered town square. The lawn was a kaleidoscope of colored plastic laid by a troop of community members—a solution to the rain-soaked ground in preparation for tonight's "Movie on the Green." Folding chairs were being set up over the tarp, facing the massive screen hanging in the band shell. On the fringe of nightfall, only street lamps and twinkle lights wrapped around the spindly trunks of trees—newly planted since last year's tornado—lit the grounds.

Surely Sam was around here somewhere, wasn't he? She'd asked a couple people, but so far, no one had seen him.

"I suppose it didn't occur to anybody to just move the whole shindig indoors, did it?"

Kit turned to see Drew Renwycke walking toward her with a woman beside him in a maroon knit cap and jean jacket. It was the woman who'd spoken, and Drew was chuckling. "Clearly you aren't a Maple Valley native, Maren. We don't like to let weather or circumstances interfere with our fun." The couple reached Kit. "Hey, Kit, meet my girlfriend, Maren Grant."

Kit pushed her fluttering hair out of her face and

shook Maren's hand. "Ah, I heard about you—the writer from Minnesota, yeah? Have you met Kate Walker?"

Maren laughed. "Everyone asks me that."

"Because having two novelists in one little town is big news around here." Drew circled one arm around her waist. "Kit's the one whose barn I'm building."

Maren's eyes sparkled. "Right, the barn that's going to be an event center. Adorable idea. Maybe I can do a book-signing there someday."

"I'd love that. When's your next book coming out? Drew here says he can have the building up by mid-October."

Maren patted Drew's chest. "If anyone can do it, this guy can."

Was it Kit's imagination or did Drew flush at his girlfriend's praise? This couple might be able to give Kate and Colton a run for their money in the lovestruck category. Or Logan and Amelia. Or Seth and Ava.

Was something in the air around here?

"Back in the day, farmers threw barn-raising parties and put up whole structures in a day. So, a month isn't all that big of an accomplishment." Drew pulled Maren closer. "But anyhow, I've got a good crew of guys coming out to help on Saturday. And to answer your question, Maren's next book is out in November, so you should definitely be able to host that signing."

The cinnamon scent of apple cider drifted in the air, and the crackle of plastic tarp underfoot sounded all around them.

"I hope you know how grateful I am, Drew—not just for taking on the project, but for whatever fancy budget work you did to get the numbers looking so reasonable." She hadn't had to borrow as much from Willa as she'd thought. And if others were as quick to book the barn for small events as Maren seemed to be, maybe she'd be able to pay Willa back sooner than planned.

If only her optimism wasn't so clouded by worry over Dad's reaction. Had Lucas alerted him already? Would he be angry?

But he shouldn't have any right to be. She hadn't used orchard revenue on the project.

Because there isn't any revenue. Any money they'd made so far this fall had all gone toward payroll and their semi-annual insurance installment. Ending the season with a decent-sized profit was a far-off dream at the moment.

"Hey, I'm just happy to have the work." Drew interrupted her tense worries. "Owning your own business comes with a whole set of risks and challenges, which of course, you know."

She did. All except for the actual "owning your own business" part. She was simply managing the orchard on borrowed time.

They chatted a few more minutes before Drew and Maren moved off. People were beginning to claim seats as Kit wandered to a table at the back and bought a cup of hot chocolate. Early autumn tinged the night air, and she burrowed her chin into the collar of the burgundy puff vest she wore over a long-sleeved navy blue shirt. The warmth of her cup seeped through the frayed yarn of her homemade cream-colored mittens—a gift from Grandma a half-dozen Christmases ago.

"I heard you were looking for me."

The voice came from behind. *Sam.*

"You heard right." She turned, slowly, a prayer trailing as she did. *Please, God. Let this go well.* She'd put it off far too long. "Hi, Sam."

He must be on duty—or just recently off—because he wore his uniform. Midnight blue with a black belt around his waist. Straight Roman nose and gray at his temples. Polished as ever—a little like Nigel, really—but with a rigid edge to his clear-eyed regard. "Kit."

Had he read the letter she sent him weeks after their would-be wedding? Had her heartfelt apologies done any good at all? Would saying the words in person now, so many years later, make a difference?

"I was looking for you. I, uh . . . I . . ." A sincere speech she'd practiced a hundred times stalled in the shadow of this man she'd once promised to marry. He seemed a stranger now. She tried to conjure up the familiarity she should be feeling—scoured her memory for flashbacks. They'd started dating the year Beckett went off to college. She'd been missing her best friend and Sam just sorta drifted in. He'd been kind and funny and dependable and, well, there.

Their relationship had intensified her junior year at the University of Iowa. Because after everything with Lucas, she'd needed something—anything—to hold on to. And by then, Beckett had been so focused on classes and getting into law school.

The truth slammed into her all over again—the reality of how unfair she'd been to Sam. She'd fallen into their romance from a place of hurt and longing. She'd truly cared for him, but not the way a future wife should've. It'd become so clear in the weeks leading up to the wedding and then magnified on the eve of the event, when Beckett had found her out in the orchard.

She'd used Sam, hadn't she? And then she'd run out on him before it was too late to change her mind—but not too late to hurt him.

If he saw any of the remorse palpitating inside her now, he didn't show it. Only stood with arms crossed, wary and waiting. Clearly, six years had done little to diffuse his resentment.

"I'm so sorry, Sam. And I know those words don't

come anywhere close to making up for what I did—"

"You've got that right."

She felt the flinch travel through her. "If I could take it all back—"

He didn't drop his arms so much as fling them. "Which part? The part where I proposed and, like a sucker, thought you meant it when you said yes? The part where you waited until you were halfway down the aisle to throw me over for another guy?"

"It wasn't for another guy."

"Or how about the part where you and Beckett Walker"—his voice dipped into a growl when he said Beckett's name—"stole my dad's car?"

The twinkle lights dotting the square blinked off and then on again, a signal that the movie was about to begin. Regret and guilt tumbled together, leaving her defenseless against Sam's condemning words. Had she really thought this conversation would go any other way? She couldn't even lift her gaze to meet his eyes.

"Everything all right here?"

Beckett.

The tension radiating from Sam amplified. As quickly as relief slid in, it dissolved. *Bad timing. Really bad.* "Everything's fine." *Lie.* She dumped the remainder of her hot chocolate in the grass peeking out from the edge of the tarp. "Sam—"

Sam angled past her. "You can't even let us have a conversation without butting in, Walker?"

She spun. "Beck—"

The Warner Bros. logo splashed onto the screen over the band shell, its roar cutting her off.

Sam stopped in front of Beckett, his whole body stiff and accusing. Beckett didn't make a move, his dark eyes swimming with a calm Kit barely recognized.

"Sam, please."

He glanced over his shoulder at her, fists clenched at his sides. "Please, what?"

"Please, listen for one second. You don't have to accept my apology. You don't have to forgive me. But you need to hear me when I say Beckett wasn't the reason I walked out on our wedding."

Sam stilled, and it was enough to prompt her on. "Yes, he interrupted the wedding. Yes, he got me out of there." She stepped to his side. "But I'm the one who made the decision. I'm the one who hurt you."

Sam's posture deflated, his shoulders losing their puffed readiness. "You're not worth it, anyway."

He said it while looking at Beckett, but Kit felt the sting of his words even as Sam turned and walked away.

The jarring triumph of the opening music from *Casablanca* crashed in. She could only watch Sam's retreating form, wordless. The tarp underneath her feet shifted as Beckett moved closer.

"You tried, Kit."

She let herself look at him. Hair in desperate need of a trim, the light of the movie screen highlighting the tiny scar along his jaw that a couple day's worth of scruff didn't hide. Granite eyes so . . . disheartened.

"Your dad?"

He nodded, looking around the square. "Do you think Maple Valley has finally gone overboard? So many twinkle lights."

"There can never be too many twinkle lights." The impulse to reach for his hand nearly took over. But Sam was still in her line of sight and he would think the worst, of course. Still, she hadn't seen Beckett this beaten down since his mom . . . "Talk to me, Beck."

"They don't know if it's cancer yet. The spinal fluid testing was inconclusive, but the tumor markers are a little high. Instead of a needle biopsy, they want to go in and do a full surgery. Because of where the tumor's sitting and the symptoms . . ." His voice was ragged. "They want to do it right away, but Dad wants to wait. He wants to get through Depot Days first, which is ridiculous. A silly town festival isn't anywhere near as important."

The opening lines of *Casablanca* filled the night around them, and she couldn't take it anymore. She reached for Beckett's hand. Sam could think whatever he wanted. "What do you need?"

10

No doubt this wasn't exactly what Kit had in mind when she'd asked he needed. But she'd asked and he'd answered honestly and here they were, four days later, on a road trip that felt an awful lot like an escape.

"The bottom line is, I'm just a better driver than you, Beckett Walker."

A line of reddish-brown brick townhomes rambled by as Kit steered her car down the Chicago suburb's residential neighborhood. Late-afternoon sunlight sifted through aged trees, their tawny leaves waving in the breeze.

"Believe whatever you want." He shrugged in the passenger seat. "We both know you never could've navigated your way here without me."

"Bert and I would've been perfectly okay without you."

"A girl who names her GPS is not perfectly okay. She's perfectly peculiar." He tapped the window. "One more block."

He still couldn't believe she'd actually agreed to come along, but maybe Kit had her own reasons for wanting to get away from Maple Valley for a while. If he'd had his way, they would've ditched town right away last week.

But he'd needed to get over to Ames first to see Webster's old social worker. Too, he'd promised his help to Drew Renwycke over the weekend on Kit's barn.

Besides, better for Kit that they were taking off on a weekday. The orchard wasn't nearly as busy during the week and she'd feel better leaving things in Willa's hands for a few days.

Originally, he'd only thought to travel to Boston—pack up his office, his apartment. But after visiting with that social worker, he'd decided to make a stop in Chicago, as well. They'd crash with Logan and Amelia tonight. Tomorrow he'd meet with Webster's friend's new DHS case manager.

They'd catch a flight to Boston tomorrow night, then drive his own car back to Chicago on the weekend to pick up Kit's vehicle. A convoluted travel itinerary, sure, but it meant hours alone in a car with Kit. Somehow in recent weeks he'd gone from dodging her company to craving it.

"Hey." His tone beckoned a momentary glance from Kit.

"Yeah?"

"Have I told you yet how glad I am you came along for the ride?" He probably would've spent the whole trip today fretting about the future, about Dad, if not for Kit's presence.

"Only ten or eleven times. Might as well make it an even dozen." She tipped her sunglasses onto her forehead, strands of hair slipping from her ponytail as she did.

He fought the urge to reach across the console and brush them behind her ear.

"Better yet, explain to me how in the world you got that social worker to tell you where that friend of Webster's is now. What's her name again?"

"Amanda. And I guess I'm more persuasive in person."

Kit looked away from the road just long enough to scold him with her eyes. "You *flirted* with her, didn't you?"

"I didn't flirt—"

"You did. I know you. And now you're going to do the same thing to the social worker in Chicago."

"You don't know that. What if this one's a man?"

"You are something else, Beckett."

"Hey, I did what I had to do to get the information I needed." He'd found out Amanda's birth mother had temporarily regained custody and then promptly broken parole by moving across state lines and getting high at a Chicago club. But by the time law enforcement and child protective services got involved, Amanda had already settled in a new school and reconnected with extended family in Illinois.

So a new social worker had taken over and a relative had temporary custody until Amanda's eighteenth birthday, which apparently wasn't that far off. Perhaps that information might have been enough for Webster. But Beckett had a feeling the boy wouldn't be satisfied until he'd heard from his friend himself.

"I didn't flirt," he reiterated. "I just made an eloquent little speech, if I do say so myself, while being friendly and nice."

"You flirted and you know it."

"There's a difference between throwing out a compliment or two, being a little bit charming, and actual, legit flirting."

"Whatever."

He was tempted to argue. Show her just what he meant. But instead, perhaps because he liked the idea a little too much, he straightened in his seat. "There, the brownstone on the corner."

Kit slowed the car and turned into the driveway. "So this was Kate's house?"

"Yep, she moved home in February, I think, and hadn't really gotten around to deciding what to do with the place by the time Amelia and Logan took off for Chicago this summer." He released his seatbelt as the engine cut off. "Apparently Amelia had a job offer here and Logan followed her like a lovesick puppy."

Which was funny, considering. Kate had moved home in large part for Colton, leaving an empty house in Chicago. Logan had taken off for Chicago with Amelia and left an empty apartment in LA. And though not for the romantic reasons of his siblings, Beckett now had a deserted place in Boston.

"You say 'lovesick' with a smirk, Beck, but it's the sweetest thing ever and you know it."

"And anyway, they eloped and Kate offered them the place with the promise that they let her crash here once in a while when she needs to get some writing done."

"Funny—the thought of her leaving quiet, small-town Iowa to come to Chicago to write. You'd think it'd be the other way around."

"Yeah, well, you've seen Dad's house. He's basically running a bustling B&B at this point. Plus, there's this not-so-little distraction back home in the form of Colton Greene."

He started to open his door, but she stopped him with her next question. "Why the JAG Corps, Beck?"

His fingers slid from the car handle to the armrest. "What brought that up?"

"Talking about your siblings and their careers and big moves, it just made me wonder. Why military law? Why now?"

"It checks off the boxes. Travel, excitement, variety.

More than that, I want to feel like I'm doing something meaningful. I want to feel like I was made for it—like you and your trees." At her questioning look, he elaborated. "Corporate law was interesting at first. But it got boring fast. Then one evening this spring I was hanging out at Salt Island—this beach I like north of Boston—and, I don't know, it's like the idea of joining the Corps rode in on a wave or something. It'd been in the back of my head forever, but somewhere along the way, I'd completely forgotten about it. Got distracted, drifted. I do that sometimes, I guess."

Kit nodded. "I understand. That's how I felt in London. Like I never fully belonged. Like I was living someone else's life."

At some point, they'd slipped from the car, met at the trunk. A sharp wind scraped over his cheeks and wreaked even further havoc on Kit's ponytail. She wore the same faded jeans he'd seen her in a hundred times and a plaid flannel shirt she'd told him once she would've been laughed out of London for wearing.

"I came home and turned right back into the farm girl I used to be," she'd said.

Yeah, well, farm girl looked good on her. As did messy ponytails and cheeks brushed with cold, Chicago sky no match for her blue eyes. She reached for the overpacked suitcase he'd teased her about eight hours ago.

He nabbed her hand now, before she could pull out the suitcase. "Wait."

"Oh, come on, it is *not* that heavy. No matter how much you exaggerated earlier, acting like you were carrying a bag of cement blocks and—"

He quieted her with a step forward. And then he did what he'd wanted to earlier. Reached with his free hand to tuck her loose hair behind her ears. He didn't miss her sudden inhale, nor the way his own senses instantly stood at attention, awareness thick in the miniscule space between them. "Thank you. Even dozen."

She blinked, glanced down at their entwined hands. And when she looked back at him, for the first time he could ever remember, he couldn't read her eyes, couldn't hear her thoughts.

But when her gaze trailed mere inches, down his face toward his lips, he felt it—the tug of her desire. Or maybe that was his own. Or something shared.

"Uncle Beck!"

Charlie's voice hurdled into the moment so forcefully he practically thrust Kit's hand away. Which must've amused her as much as it startled her, because her laughter joined the sound of Charlie's pattering footsteps running toward them.

His niece was in his arms in seconds, her hands reaching around his neck for a hug.

He tried to catch Kit's eyes once more over Charlie's shoulders, but she'd hidden her flushed cheeks in the trunk, reaching in to pull out her suitcase. So instead he planted a kiss on Charlie's head. "How's my favorite niece?"

The four-year-old leaned back to place both her hands on his cheeks. "You need to shave."

Kit laughed again, and this time when he glanced past Charlie, he met her gaze. And something freeing and flawless glided through him.

And then Logan and Amelia were emerging from the house and a round of hugs followed, all the while Charlie tugging him toward the brownstone. "You have to see my bedroom. It used to be Aunt Kate's only it looks different now 'cause my mom painted it."

There was no mistaking the delight that played over Amelia's face as Logan's daughter referred to her as

Mom. Nor Logan's look of pride. To think, just six months ago Charlie had barely spoken at all. Concern about his daughter's speech delay had been just one of the reasons Logan made the decision to take a break from his busy speechwriting career in LA and spend some time in Maple Valley. Now look how his life had changed.

Logan pulled Kit's suitcase behind him, and Beckett slid his duffel bag over his shoulder. Charlie pulled away and raced into the house, Amelia and Kit on her heels.

"Thanks for letting us crash here," Beckett said as he followed Logan up the cement steps.

"Of course." Logan stopped on the top step, resting one hand on the metal railing and the other on the handle of Kit's suitcase. "Listen, Beckett."

Beckett paused two steps below, sensing what was coming before Logan went on. "It's okay, Log—"

"No, I need to say it. I'm really sorry about not telling you." Sincerity rimmed his eyes.

"Dad asked you not to."

"And he had reasons that all stemmed from a good place. But that doesn't mean it wasn't hurtful to you. If I'd been in your shoes . . ." He matched Beckett's shrug with one of his own. "Anyway, I'm sorry."

"Apology accepted." Perhaps surprisingly, he meant it. There was too much else crowding his mind these days to let useless anger at his brother take up space.

Eventually, you need to have this same conversation with Dad. Needed to let go of so much more. But for now, for these few days, he just wanted to forget.

Logan appeared relieved at Beckett's easy acceptance, but he didn't move to the doorway. Only peered at Beckett.

"You waiting for something? We can hug it out if you want, but we hugged back at the car and that seems like enough. Handshake?"

Logan shook his head. His wedding ring glinted in the sun as he pushed down the handle of Kit's suitcase. "Nah, just deciding how long I'm supposed to wait before I taunt you about Kit."

"Say again?"

"You brought her along."

"So?"

"So, I looked out the window when we heard the car in the driveway."

The implication settled in. "I'm trying to think of the name of that nosy neighbor lady on that old show with the chick who twitches her nose."

"Mrs. Cratchett. *Bewitched*."

"That's the one." He shifted his duffel bag to the other shoulder.

"I'm just saying, you were standing awfully close and I kinda think if Charlie hadn't escaped from the house—"

"Shut up." He budged past his brother.

"Is that any way to talk to your host?"

Logan's laughter followed him into the house.

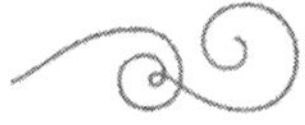

Kit flopped over in the daybed in Charlie's room—formerly Beckett's sister's room. She tried fluffing her pillow, flinging off the comforter. No use.

Restless energy barred her from sleep. She should've known not to have that second cup of coffee after dinner. But it'd smelled so good—crème brûlée flavored, a perfect complement to their dessert of pumpkin cheesecake. That on top of the dinner of lasagna and breadsticks had put her into a blissful food coma earlier this evening.

Or maybe it was the laughter, the conversation that had filled her with what could only be satisfaction. Pure, unadulterated satisfaction. For a few hours there, she hadn't thought even once about the orchard or Dad or Lucas. It should've been enough to quell the effects of caffeine and lull her into a contented sleep.

But she'd been lying here for nearly an hour, eyes that refused to stay closed tracing the pattern of curtain-muffled moonlight on the carpet. Finally, she slipped from the pink sheets of Charlie's bed and padded barefoot to the doorway. Maybe a glass of water would help.

She tiptoed past the bedroom that belonged to Logan and Amelia, where Charlie was bunking tonight, as well. Apparently the little family had decided to make an adventure of it. Charlie had insisted that Kit look in earlier. "*We're going camping in the house. We've got sleeping bags and pillows and blankets and everything.*" She'd spied the bed edged against the wall and filling most of the rest of the room, a tent.

They should win some kind of award for being the cutest family ever. Logan and his daughter and brand new wife. Even from the brief time she'd spent around Amelia, she'd been able to pick up on the bits and pieces of the woman's own hurt-filled past. A broken marriage and unwanted divorce. Forgotten dreams only recently revived. Logan, of course, had lost his first wife in a tragic accident.

Now look at them—so happy this house practically thrummed with it.

One hand glided along the railing leading down to the first floor, where Beckett slept on the couch. She hurried into the kitchen, hoping the running faucet wouldn't wake his sleeping form. She filled her glass and stopped the water, lifted it to her lips, and—

"Can't sleep?"

At the whisper over her shoulder, she jerked and whirled. Before she realized what she'd done, she doused the whisperer in water.

Beckett sputtered, but even in his own shock, he managed to stop her from shrieking with one finger to her lips. He caught her toppling glass with his other hand before it could hit the floor.

Water trickled down his cheeks as he grinned and reached around her to set her glass on the counter behind her. Her alarm-filled surprise swept away in a wave of awareness. He stood so close.

And smelled so good, both soapy and masculine—the tips of his hair still damp from the shower she'd heard him take in the bathroom across from Charlie's room. Or maybe—more likely—from the water she'd just thrown in his face.

"Sorry." She murmured the word against his finger. Behind her, the faucet dripped.

"What? You don't think I got clean enough during my first shower of the night?" Even in a whisper, his voice still held its usual rich timbre.

"If you hadn't snuck up on me—"

"I wasn't sneaking."

"Then you must walk like a mountain lion or something, all quiet and careful-like."

Did he realize he'd pinned her to the counter? One hand still perched behind her. The other, he'd lowered from her mouth and instead angled around her opposite side to fiddle with the faucet until the dripping stopped. "Mountain lions walk quietly?"

"I don't know," she hissed into his chest. "Probably."

And then, with a telling reluctance, she slipped under his arm and away from the counter. Away from *him*.

When he turned around to her, amusement filled every nook and cranny of his expression. And maybe even a smug knowing. As if he could hear every note of the instantly and absurdly nervous hum feathering through her.

Don't be ridiculous. This is Beckett.

Beckett who managed to make sleep-tousled hair and a faded old tee look almost alluring.

Not almost. Entirely.

"Sorry I woke you up. And threw a glass of water at you."

"Stay up for a while. I couldn't sleep, either. Let's get a snack." He turned to the fridge.

"You're actually hungry after that dinner we had?"

The open fridge lit his profile. "That was, like, four hours ago." When he turned back to her, his impish grin widened as he pulled the lid off a Tupperware container. "I knew it. One piece of cheesecake left."

Any argument died at the sight of the dessert. "I'll get the forks."

He lifted one eyebrow. "Did I say I was sharing?"

She grabbed two forks from the dish rack in the sink. "You're too much of a gentleman not to."

"Quite right." He said it with a proper lilt, then nudged his head toward the living room. He pushed aside the blanket Amelia had spread over the couch earlier and dropped onto the sheet-covered cushion. He looked up at her. "Well?"

It's not a bed, it's a couch.

And this was Beckett. *Beckett.* There was absolutely no reason for the flutter of nerves accompanying her movement as she sat.

No reason except the firm outline of his arm against hers and the fact that he smelled like a darn forest.

"Fork?" He snatched one from her hand and cut into

the cake. He held up the bite in front of him before shaking his head and handing the fork to her with a sigh. "Now I'm such a gentleman, I'm giving you the first bite."

She curled her legs beside her as they ate, Beckett's familiar quiet slowly chipping away at her unease until she'd almost entirely relaxed.

"Speaking of gentlemen, tell me about Nigel."

So much for relaxed. "Why?"

His shrug nudged her. "I don't know. The guy came all the way to Iowa with you, helped out in the orchard that first day. I mean, kind of feeble-ish, if you ask me. Took a thousand breaks."

"Don't be mean." She couldn't help a giggle.

"But then he was gone and you haven't mentioned him once. Awfully stoic for a breakup." There was something tentative in his voice.

"Actually, Nigel said he doesn't know how we can technically call it broken up when I was never fully committed to begin with. He says I never let him in."

And he was right, wasn't he? Which was worse—the way she'd held Nigel for so long at arm's length? Or the way she'd let Sam in too far, knowing all along it wasn't what she truly wanted?

"I don't know why I do it, ruin relationships. Lucas says it's a Danby family trait, walking away." She reached over Beckett's arm for another bite of cheesecake. "That's not the person I want to be and yet, if I look at the evidence, I'm usually the one pushing people away."

She chanced a glance at his face, wondering if his mind had suddenly rewound to the same moment hers had. The gravel road. The almost-kiss.

His Adam's apple bobbed as he swallowed. "I think sometimes," he said slowly, "there's a fair amount of pushing away on both sides."

Except, the night of her wedding, he'd done the opposite of pushing her away. She dared to let the memory in—how it'd felt those few potent minutes wearing her wedding dress, buried against Beckett, feeling so very free and so very lost all at the same time.

And then she'd felt his lips on her forehead, her cheek. Her breathing, her heartbeat, the breeze . . . everything had stilled.

Until his head dipped and she yanked away, fear and confusion and an anger he didn't deserve all unleashed at once.

"Your turn." She blurted the words, a near-frantic attempt to silence her memory. "You have to have had plenty of girlfriends over the years." He'd never been short on dates in college.

He stuck his fork into the last bite in the Tupperware container. He lifted his fork and offered it to her. She shook her head.

Only after he'd swallowed it and then slid the container onto the coffee table did he answer. "No one."

"At all?"

"Well, there's this girl—Piper from law school. She's with another firm in Boston. We're kind of each other's standing 'plus one.' You know, for corporate events, weddings, whatever. But that's all it is."

"Does she know that?"

He laughed. "She's the one who came up with the idea. We were both ultra-focused on making partner as soon as possible. No time for dating or relationships or all that."

They shifted into a comfortable silence, the clock on the wall over the window ticking away the seconds as Kit tried to convince herself it wasn't relief tingling through her. It shouldn't matter to her whether Beckett had dated anyone, or if there was someone waiting for him back in Boston.

But it mattered. No matter how much she denied it, it mattered.

"Besides, Piper has green eyes."

The comment seemed to come from nowhere. "What?"

He moved on the couch so he faced her, his gaze capturing hers. "I've always preferred blue ones."

She swallowed. "That so?" She squeaked the question.

"And not just any blue eyes, but impossibly blue ones. Logan would have a word for them—luminescent or cerulean or, I don't know, something fancy." He leaned closer. "Blue eyes that glimmer with playfulness and shift with your mood and take on every stunning shade of every sparkling ocean, depending on the lighting."

When had he reached for her hand? And what was he doing? And how was she supposed to breathe with his face so close to hers, uttering such melting words right into her ear? Her heart was about to pump its way out of her chest—a swirl of delight and fear turning its beat erratic.

"And that, Kit Danby," he said, his breath warm over her cheek, "is legit flirting."

She sprang away, voice and words and heart sputtering. "Y-you . . . you're awful!" She pushed him hard, and he let himself topple from the couch, laughing all the way down. "You're—"

She didn't even know what, so instead she just attacked him from above with a throw pillow, her own laughter bubbling.

"I'm sorry, it was just too easy."

She hit him again, and he lifted his hands in surrender but didn't stop laughing.

"I hope you wake up Charlie and Logan comes down to yell at you."

"So worth it." He climbed back onto the couch.

She tried to keep pummeling him with the pillow, but he plucked it from her hands with ease, cackling a dozen more apologies he clearly only half meant. Only when their laughter finally subsided did he flop back against the couch.

"Just for the record, I have no idea what color of eyes that social worker back in Ames had."

Good. She didn't voice it. Minutes drifted into an hour or maybe two as they talked more of the night away. She told him about her hopes to impress her father, lure him home. He regaled her with stories of famous military lawyers and the interesting cases they litigated. She filled him in on her travels while living in England.

Eventually, the clock over the fireplace told her today had turned into tomorrow. And the steady, heavy breathing beside her let her know Beckett was on his way to falling asleep. Or maybe already had.

For a moment that stretched with undeniable perfection, she just existed, resting in the cocoon of her best friend's arm that had at some point stretched around her, the warmth of him beside her. Impulse glided in, heady and undeniable. She ignored every nudge of restraint, every warning bell in the back of her head, and leaned close to his ear.

"I wish I'd let you kiss me that night, Beckett Walker."

"You didn't have to drive me, you know."

Logan steered his sedan into the right-hand lane. Tuesday-morning traffic zipped around them, sheer clouds coasting in and around the Chicago skyline. "I know I didn't." Logan lifted the travel mug Amelia had sent him out the door with. "But I wanted to."

Beckett twisted open the lid of his own mug. The dark roast aroma wafted over him, and if he didn't think he'd scorch his throat, he'd guzzle the entire thing. Grogginess clung to him like a second layer of clothing.

Too many hours awake with Kit.

And then too many hours awake without her.

"I wish I'd let you kiss me that night, Beckett Walker."

She'd thought he was asleep. He nearly had been before she leaned over to whisper the words in his ear. What he hadn't stopped asking himself since was, why in the world he hadn't just opened his eyes and pulled her onto his lap and kissed her right then.

He took a long drink, sputtering when the coffee burned his tongue.

"I told you, that fancy coffeemaker of Amelia's is insane. Gets the stuff so hot." Logan flipped down his sun visor. "You have to wait, like, half an hour 'til it's drinkable."

Beckett took another drink anyway and then, at Logan's raised eyebrows, pointed to his mouth. "Burned off all my taste buds with the first swig, so now it doesn't matter."

Logan took the exit and laughed. "Okay, moment of honesty?" He glanced over at Beckett, then back to the road. "I didn't just offer to drive you because I'm the nicest older brother you've got."

"I don't know, Seth's older than me and he's like a brother, too, and—"

"Can it. I offered to drive you because I'm under orders from my wife to get the deets on you and Kit."

"You didn't seriously just say 'deets,' did you?"

"And you don't seriously think you're going to sidetrack this conversation, do you?"

The GPS on Logan's phone cut in, giving orders to turn left and continue for three blocks. Then the only sound in the car was Logan tapping his steering wheel and Beckett twisting and untwisting the lid of his travel mug.

Until finally Logan cocked his head. "Well?"

"You told me to 'can it.'"

"Fine, whatever. Just know Amelia's back at the house working on Kit."

Poor Kit. He should've known not to leave her alone.

"My wife and I both have newspapering in our blood, little brother. We follow stories until we have all the facts."

"Yeah, we're not a story, though." Parking on both sides of the street narrowed Logan's lane. Reminded Beckett of downtown Boston traffic. Claustrophobic.

"Don't get me wrong. Amelia will be a hundred times subtler about it than me. But that's only because she's more polite. She doesn't know Kit as well as I know you."

"And what do you think you know?"

"I know we heard you both up last night. And even if we hadn't, we would've seen the empty Tupperware and two forks in the sink."

Beckett shifted against his too-tight seatbelt. "Way to go, Nancy Drew."

"And I know you and Kit acted all kinds of awkward this morning. We're talking, way past comical levels of awkward. I swear, she says 'good morning' to you and you're tongue-tied for the first time in your life. You bump into her when you're both going for the coffee and she suddenly matches Charlie's bedroom walls."

Pink. Bright pink.

The GPS cut in again, directed Logan west, noted the destination was on the right. Thank goodness for that. Freedom from Logan's interrogation.

"Look, if you don't want to talk about it—"

"I don't."

"Okay." The tease had slackened from Logan's tone. He pulled up in front of a glass-fronted building. Metallic lettering over the curved entrance spelled out *Department of Human Services*. "But if you ever do, I'm around, you know?"

Beckett stuck his travel mug in the cup holder in the console between them and reached for the door handle. Same thing he'd said to Raegan a couple weeks ago. "I know."

And honestly, he did. For all his years of geographic distance from his family, even with all he'd missed, he'd never—not once—doubted that his siblings cared. Truth was, he'd always known all it'd take was a phone call, a text, and any one of them would appear on his doorstep in Boston.

He'd simply let the shame that drove him from Maple Valley hold him back. Too, the burrowed, lingering wound of missing his chance to say goodbye to Mom.

"I'll go find a place to park and hang out. Just text me when I need to pick you up."

Beckett nodded and opened the car door, stuck one leg out, paused. He looked back at Logan. "She's my best friend. Even after all this time, she's still my best friend."

That was why he hadn't opened his eyes last night. That was why he hadn't made a move as she'd stood from the couch and carried the Tupperware and forks to the kitchen, then padded upstairs to Charlie's bedroom.

"You don't want to do anything to mess it up."

"I've done it before." And suddenly, Beckett had the urge to forget this errand that probably wouldn't amount to anything anyway. Go find a park somewhere and sit on a bench and tell his big brother everything.

But a car honked behind them and he jerked. "Sorry. Text you when I'm done."

He closed the car door before Logan could respond and angled around it. *Focus. You're here for Webster.*

The kid who somehow reminded him of himself. Part cocky athlete. Part lost and uncertain.

Fluorescent white light spread through the open interior of the office building's lobby. He stopped at a receptionist's desk and asked for Kelly Polanski, the name Webster's old social worker had given him.

Soon he was following an intern down a hallway. The building aged as they moved farther in, shiny marble flooring shifting to worn carpet, office doors crammed together like too many hangers in a closet. Eventually they stopped in front of a door with Kelly Polanski's name in the placard beside it. The intern knocked, then stepped aside so Beckett could enter.

An ebony-skinned woman rose from behind a desk too big for the confined space. She reached one arm over the paper-covered surface to shake his hand. "Have a seat, Mr. Walker."

He lowered into a chair with a ripped cushion and scratches in its wooden armrests. "Thanks so much for agreeing to meet me today. I know you said your schedule's tight." He'd called from the road yesterday, fingers crossed that she'd be willing to meet him on such short notice.

She had, but with obvious hesitation that clearly hadn't waned in the hours since. "You want to talk about one of my current case files."

"Uh, not the file, Ms. Polan—"

"Kelly." She laced her fingers atop her desk.

"All right, Kelly. It's not the file I'm concerned about, or even any specifics on where Amanda Britt is, but—"

"Mr. Walker—"

It was his turn to interrupt. "Beckett."

"Beckett, I'm really not even comfortable talking about this girl by name. You explained the situation yesterday. And I am sympathetic to your . . ." She glanced at her screen. "To this Webster's predicament. Assuming there's nothing untoward in his desire to know where she is—"

Beckett's grip on the armrests tightened. "Believe me, there's not."

"I want to believe you, of course, but I don't even know you. And a person doesn't work in child protective services for long before developing an unfortunate tendency toward skepticism. This is a teenage boy we're talking about."

The air in the room was fraught with restrained friction. The lawyer in him urged Beckett to argue, persuade this social worker to hear him out. But he couldn't blame her for her position. He'd done his homework. The chances of trying to work the system or lawyer his way to any kind of information for Webster—slim to none.

No, his best bet was to draw on his years of experience settling disputes *outside* the courtroom. Except Kelly Polanski clearly wasn't one for smooth talking or emotional swaying.

"Look, I'm not here to ask you to break any kind of confidentiality policy or rule. I'm not even here as a lawyer right now." He absently traced the lone, long scratch in the wooden armrest with one finger, searching for the right words.

"That's why I think you should consider being a lawyer, Beck."

Mom's voice. Somehow it stole into the room and settled over him.

"Because I'm always arguing with you?"

She'd laughed. *"Because you're great with words."*

"Kate's the writer, Mom. And Logan."

"They're both great with the written word. You're great with the spoken word. I'm not kidding, Beck, sometimes when you get all oratorical trying to talk your way out of a punishment, you almost convince me."

The memory hovered in the tiny office, filling him with confidence—or maybe conviction—and he leaned forward. "I'm just here as the friend of a kid who wants to know someone he cares about is safe. That she's all right." He pulled a folder from the leather messenger bag he'd carried in. "This has copies of Webster's class attendance, his grades—which could admittedly be better, but he's working on them. It has a letter from his football coach, his adoptive parents, and a guy named Colton Greene—you might've heard of him, ex-NFL quarterback. He runs a nonprofit in Maple Valley and also mentors Webster. All attesting to his good behavior, work ethic, you name it."

Kelly's lips curved into an almost-grin. "I thought you said you weren't here as a lawyer."

Beckett leaned forward. "Amanda used to text Webster regularly and she hasn't for a while. He's worried. I've seen it firsthand." And frankly, wondered about it. But Webster had assured him there wasn't anything more going on than one friend concerned about another.

Kelly opened the folder, gaze skimming its contents. "Maybe she doesn't want further contact."

"If that's the case, okay." Beckett nodded. "Webster will have to learn to deal with that. I'm just asking you to check with her. And if she wants to let him know she's all right, his email and phone number are in there." He motioned to the folder in her hands.

She closed it. "Okay."

"You'll talk to her?"

"I'll consider talking to her."

It was as good as he was going to get, he could see it in her firm posture. But she hadn't said no. And there'd been that half-smile. Reason enough to hope.

11

For the second day in a row, Kit woke up in an unfamiliar bed. The sound of dishes clinking, the smell of something tantalizing and sweet, lulled her eyes open, but she couldn't make herself lift her head from the pillow.

Not from this perfectly bunched mound with its perfectly soft pillowcase in this perfectly dark room. And these sheets, the heavy duvet, so warm and comfortable.

Where in the world was she? What time was it?

She slid one arm free of the haven of her bed and reached for her phone on the nightstand. She tapped its screen—ten-thirty in the morning? She bolted up, the cogs of her memory finally churning.

The plane trip from Chicago to Boston late last night. The cab ride to Beckett's apartment in the brownstone with the split foyer. His bedroom. His voice insisting she sleep in here and she too tired to argue.

Those must be some heavy curtains on the windows—not a slice of light filtered into the room. She switched on the nightstand lamp and gave the bedroom the once-over she'd been too exhausted to last night. Dark beige, almost-brown walls. Even darker furniture that matched the leather pinned headboard she leaned against now. Laundry hamper, closet door, a tie hanging over the doorknob.

Beckett wears ties. And inside the closet she'd probably find suit jackets and dress pants and nice shoes. *Beckett wears ties and works in an office and argues cases in front of judges.*

The same Beckett who climbed trees and drove hay wagons at home.

Except, it wasn't his home. Not permanently, anyway.

She slid down against the pile of pillows in Beckett's bed, wishing away the unwelcome thought that he had an entire life she knew nothing about.

A knock at the door made her blink, and before she could make her voice work, the door cracked open. Beckett's head ducked in. He grinned. "Oh good, you're awake."

Yes, with her hair in tangles and the makeup she'd been too fatigued to wash off most likely smeared under her eyes now. "Barely."

He trounced into the room and walked to the window. He pushed the curtains aside, and light thrust over her.

"Really, Beck?"

He was at the side of the bed in two long strides. "I figured it out."

"Figured out what?" She forced herself to sit up.

"How you're going to convince your dad to keep the orchard in the family." He dropped onto the bed beside her, apparently oblivious to her bedhead and what she was wearing.

And, uh, not wearing. She pulled her sheet up over her shoulders. "Why are we talking about this now?"

"Because it's a brilliant idea." He leaned against the headboard with his legs stretched out, as if this was a completely normal locale for catching up on business. "Lucas won't stand a chance."

"I'm not at war with my brother, Beck."

"I know that," he drawled. "But you said he's already got a buyer, right? You're going to have to step up your game. For all you know, Lucas and his buyer are working up a deal right now."

"Why are you trying to stress me out? I just woke up."

"You won't be stressed when you hear my plan. I'll explain over breakfast." He clasped her hand and pulled her up. "Don't worry about what you look like. I'm still in my pajamas, too." His pajamas apparently being a pair of track pants and a t-shirt. A far cry from her pink striped flannels and flimsy top. "Let's go. I'm making pancakes."

He still held her hand and tugged her toward the door. "Beck—"

He let out an exaggerated sigh. "Fine. Brush your teeth, wash your face, do whatever you need to. But don't dawdle." He started for the door but stopped halfway there. "And pajamas are mandatory."

"Why?"

He grinned. "Because you're cute." And with that, he disappeared.

She groaned. And then giggled. And then had a heart attack when she saw her face in the mirror in his master bathroom.

Ten minutes later, she emerged from the bedroom—still in pajamas as ordered, but hair parted down the middle and pulled into two braids, teeth brushed, and yesterday's makeup scrubbed away.

Beckett's first-floor apartment was a maze of small spaces. Across from his bedroom, an alcove carved into the corridor wall housed a small desk with a window looking out onto the tree-lined street. A twin alcove just a few feet down held a crammed-full bookcase. The hallway led into a circular den with a mahogany-hued leather couch and matching recliner with a reading lamp standing beside it. More bookshelves and a TV along one wall.

The den led into what was probably supposed to be the dining room—sans table. An arched opening on the opposite end spied on the kitchen.

She moved through each space with a studying eye, seeing signs of Beckett in every room—the pillow and sheets on the couch where he'd slept, the sweatshirt draped over a lone chair in the dining room. In the kitchen, the man himself.

The smell of pancake batter sizzling on a griddle beckoned her into the room, where Beckett held a spatula in one hand. "Finally. You took forever."

"I took a few minutes."

He looked eager. Way too awake. Way too . . .

Handsome. She'd been trying to ignore it for weeks, since that night in the orchard. But what was the point in denying it any longer? They weren't kids anymore.

She was a woman, and he was a man. One whose once skinny arms were now rounded and strong. Whose shoulders stretched wider than she remembered and whose chest, as she'd discovered on Logan's couch, made an awfully firm but comfortable pillow.

His gaze angled to hers, and she felt the flush climb all the way from her toes. "Beckett Walker's famous pancakes." She grappled for a lighthearted tone, but her voice refused to cooperate.

But if he'd noticed her ogling or her embarrassment, he let it go. "I've perfected the recipe some."

She willed her nerves to settle. "And added blueberries, I see."

"Had to run to the market for those. And for milk. And eggs. And basically everything."

"You've been to the store already? When did you get up?"

"Not long ago." He handed her a plate already prepared with two pancakes slathered in syrup. "Sorry I don't have a table. Never got around to buying one. You could eat on the couch if you want." He pulled a fork from a nearby drawer.

"Nah, I can eat standing. I need to hear about this plan of yours."

"Good." He flipped a pancake. "Here's what I'm thinking: Remember how the mayor keeps talking about state tourism board folks who are coming to town in October?"

Remember? The man hadn't stopped talking about it in weeks. She took a bite of a pancake, closed her eyes. "Oh my word."

"I know they're good, but focus."

"I don't know if I can. These are amazing, Beck." She crammed in another bite. "But yes, I remember. Clearly Mayor Milt is angling for state dollars. I think he honestly thinks Maple Valley is on its way to becoming a true tourist trap. Iowa's very own Coney Island or Atlantic City."

"Well, I say we talk him into making the orchard the centerpiece of his pitch. Put on a charming evening event. Lights, music, moonlight tours, that kind of thing." Beckett's spatula scraped against the griddle as he slid off a perfectly golden pancake. "We pack the place with people, go all out for one night. *And* we get your dad there. He'll see firsthand how important it is to the economy of the community."

She paused halfway to another bite. "Forget for a minute that this only gives us a month to plan an event, an event I don't even have money for—"

"That's the beauty of it, Kit. We get the city to pay for it. They invest a few dollars in hopes of attracting additional state funds. Spend money to make money and all that. You're just playing host."

"But what makes you think my dad would come?" He'd missed countless birthdays and holidays. He hadn't even come to her graduation ceremony. "Why would he show up for this?"

Beckett flipped another pancake before turning to look at her. "Maybe I can talk to him. I'm great at talking people into things, remember? I've got a social worker in Iowa and another in Illinois as proof."

He joked, but she didn't miss the flash of compassion in his eyes. He knew more than anyone the stages of hurt and anger she'd gone through over the years because of her father's continual absence.

"Surely I can convince him to leave his office for one night."

Kit lowered her gaze, voice soft, as she set down her plate. "You know, I don't begrudge him his career. It's just that . . . he wasn't serving overseas most of the time he was gone. He was in D.C. He could've had us with him. We were already short one parent. I barely have any memories of my mom. Why couldn't he have at least given me good memories of him?" And was it pitiful to still carry with her the hurt?

"I'm sorry, Kit. Maybe I shouldn't have brought him up."

She traced one finger through the syrup on her plate. "No, I'm sorry. Here your dad is . . ."

Beckett looked away. He'd avoided every mention of his dad the past couple days. She didn't know what to say. Or what to do. Or why she couldn't, for the life of her, get ahold of the emotions whirling around inside her. She felt like a snow globe—tipped upside down and shaken, a flurry of nerves and worry and . . .

And an attraction so strong it scared her.

Because eventually Beckett would leave, too. She'd known it all along, of course, but it felt so much more real here. Yes, he was here to pack up his belongings, essentially bring closure to his life in Boston.

But he wouldn't be unpacking those things in Maple Valley. He'd bring a few boxes home, but he'd already told her he'd rented a storage unit for the bulk of his stuff. Maple Valley was only a pit stop.

He turned off the burner, and when he looked at her again, it was as if he'd heard every one of her thoughts. A glimmer of urgency filled his eyes. "Let's have fun today, Kit. Let's go for a drive. I can take you to Beacon Hill or a beach or something."

"But your office, your apartment."

"We can stop by the office real quick and save the packing for tonight. We'll stay up all night if we have to. Or I'll just hire a packing company. Whatever. Let's forget everything else. Just for today."

"Okay." Just for today.

Because it was beginning to feel like today was all they had.

Beckett should've waited to do this until the weekend.

And he shouldn't have brought Kit along.

The elevator dinged as they reached the seventh floor of the downtown office building. "I should've just let you take the car and get an early start on the tourist-ing." He waited until Kit stepped out of the elevator to follow. "There's not that much in the office to pack up. I could've done it myself."

Behind her, a wall of paneled glass windows peered in on the capacious offices of the Louder, Boyce & Shillinger Law Firm. Gray walls and birch furnishings overtop marbled flooring in swirls of white and copper. He could still remember his first gaping tour of the prestigious firm, picturing himself in one of the corner suites with the Boston skyline views along two windowed walls.

And to think, he'd come so close.

"Ashamed to be seen with me, are you?" Kit studied the aerial photo of the office building on the wall opposite the elevator doors as she teased.

And he studied her. Navy blue sweater with sleeves that reached only to her elbows. Jean skirt over brown leggings and boots. She'd left her hair down for once and it reached past her shoulders in unruly waves. "Not even close."

She turned to see him watching her, and for at least the hundredth time since he'd whisked her away from Maple Valley, she smiled and blushed and gave him that look that honestly made him think maybe she saw him differently now.

And it—she—took his breath away.

"I wish I'd let you kiss me that night, Beckett Walker."

"I just . . ." *Talk. Words. Focus.* "You could be doing something fun while I do this. There are these gardens I know you'd love. I mean, to me, they're just a bunch of plants and flowers, but with your botany background—"

She shifted the jacket dangling over one arm as she interrupted. "I did way too much lone sightseeing in London. This time I've got you with me and you're telling me to strike out on my own? I don't think so,

Beck." She nodded her head toward the offices. "Besides, I want to see where you work."

"Worked." He plodded to the gray wood door and opened it for Kit. "We'll make it snappy, though, so we can get on with the exploring."

And maybe, if he was lucky, no one would notice them.

"Beckett Walker, in the flesh!"

No such luck. Elliott Boyce, Jr.'s, boisterous call turned nearly every head in the oblong open space at the front of the floor. And then he was standing in front of Beckett, his handshake quickly turning into a light hug. "How are you, old man?"

Beckett eyed Kit over Elliott's shoulder. "Our birthdays are two days apart. I've got a whole forty-eight hours on him."

Elliott stepped back. "Making you the old man and me the jaunty, spry youngster." His gaze latched on to Kit. "Please tell me this is the 'personal reason' you ditched the firm for. I might not look it, but I've got a romantic streak like you wouldn't believe."

Ditched the firm? That was the quite the spin. Especially from the guy who'd carried out the firing.

Kit's laugh was pure amusement. "Kit Danby." She held out her palm for a handshake, but Elliott instead took hold of her fingers and lifted them to his lips.

Beckett felt his own jaw drop. "Did we suddenly step into an English parlor?"

Elliott's gleaming grin was as shrewd as it was annoying. "Mock my impeccable manners all you want, Walker. I don't think you'll find the lady complaining."

"Except the lady would kindly appreciate having her hand back." Kit pulled her palm from Elliott's grasp with a tone half scolding, half teasing.

And wholly curious, he could tell. Was she trying to

picture him working here, in a polished suit just like Elliott's, with an office and assistant and overcrowded calendar? Was it as discordant a scene in her mind as it felt in his just now?

Had it really been only six weeks ago he'd spent more hours each week amid this drone of ringing phones and clacking keys and closed-door conference rooms than his own home?

Elliott smoothed his lavender tie. "Honestly, I'm a little surprised to see you here after the way things went down. You should hear all the rumors flying around about what made you miss that Stanley Oil meeting. Mysterious illness. Criminal background. Secret lover." His repeat glance to Kit wasn't nearly swift enough. "Though, judging by your tan, I'd go with sudden inheritance and life of luxury on an island somewhere."

"Actually, criminal background is a lot closer to the truth."

"You're not serious." Elliott turned to Kit. "He's not serious. Is he?"

Beckett strode past Elliott, toward his old office. "We're just here to pack up my stuff," he called over his shoulder. "Won't take long and we'll be out of your hair."

He heard Kit's double-step behind him until she caught up and laced her arm through his. "*He's* a character," she whispered.

"Good guy, but total goofball."

And then Elliott's voice again. "But your stuff isn't in your office."

Beckett paused, turned.

"That is, it's not your office anymore." Elliott slid his hand along the tall half-wall separating the open space of assistants' desks from the row of office doors. "You've been gone for over a month, Walker. Your stuff was packed up weeks ago. It's downstairs in one of the storage rooms. Didn't I text you about that? Security can let you in. You're lucky you showed up when you did. After sixty days, it all goes to the dumpster."

Of course. Had he really thought he'd find his office just as he'd left it? That the firm wouldn't replace him? Some lucky intern or recent law school grad had scored a quick climb up the ladder.

While his own prospects dwindled. He hadn't even managed to get his interview rescheduled yet. Not that he hadn't tried. He'd given up on rescheduling the Boston meeting and instead begun contacting law schools in Iowa. Army reps usually began meeting with prospective JAG officers while they were still in school.

Perhaps that's why he was having so little luck. He was a non-traditional applicant. One who'd already missed an interview.

"Well, this is great. Saves us some time." The cheer in Kit's voice was over-much, which meant she sensed his plummeting mood. She released his arm to instead grasp his hand. "Let's find the storage room and get on with our day. Nice to meet you, Elliott. Maybe you could have someone call down to the security desk to let them know we're coming?"

And then she was leading him back the way they'd come, past the sprawling receptionist's desk and out to the elevators. "Nice place, fancy offices, but way too stuffy for you, Beck. I don't blame you for ditching it." She punched the elevator's down button.

"Didn't ditch it. They fired me."

"Maybe so, but look at it this way, you're down to only forty hours of community service left. You never would've gotten that done so quickly if you'd still been working here and—"

The elevator dinged, the doors opened.

And Elliott Boyce, Sr., stepped out, a glare that could only be meant for Beckett darkening his expression. "Beckett."

"Mr. Boyce."

Kit's fingers tightened around his as they traded places with the man.

"Someone let you know where to find your belongings, I trust."

Beckett nodded from inside the elevator.

Boyce nodded from outside.

The elevator doors closed.

"Don't do it, Beck." Kit's tone was soft, but firm.

"Do what?" The air inside the elevator was strained.

"Start second-guessing your whole life because of a dirty look from a dude who fired you. Besides, you have plans."

"Only twenty percent of the people who apply to the JAG Corps get in, Kit. Most of them are younger than I am. And don't have a criminal record."

She laced her arm through his. "I meant your plans for a fun day today, silly goose. But if you must know, even if that percentage was lower, I'd have no doubt you'd get in. You're Beckett Walker."

He glanced down at her, drinking in the encouragement in her voice, her eyes. She looked at him as if she truly believed him capable of anything. It was a terrifying feeling.

It was a thrilling feeling.

And if she kept looking at him like that, kept smiling, if she kept her arm tucked through his, and if the elevator door didn't open soon . . . well, he'd have to give in, that's all. Find out if she'd really meant what she said the other night on the couch.

"I should've let you kiss me . . ."

The elevator door opened. Kit let go of his arm.

"Come on, let's go get your stuff."

"Forget it."

"But—"

He reached for her hand. "It's nothing but a few pens and a stapler and an employee handbook I'll never look at again. Let's go."

A tingling salt-tinged breeze whipped through Kit's hair as Beckett steered his old convertible along the road that traced the rocky shore north of Boston. Cold huddled in the seaside air underneath a sky laced with frothy clouds.

"I'm numb and my hair's going to be so knotted after this I'll need to shave it all off."

Beckett's wind-ruddied cheeks lifted with his smile. "You're the one who insisted we drive with the top down."

"Clearly not my best idea ever." She had to yell to be heard above the engine, the tires whirring over pavement, the sound of the Atlantic Ocean crashing into the coast.

She'd known part of the reason they'd come to Boston was to pick up Beckett's car. It just hadn't clicked until she saw it that it was *this* car—the classic, sleek Cadillac, the one his mom had driven as a teenager and then had refused to sell years later. It used to sit in the Walkers' garage, covered by a heavy gray cloth. But the year Beckett turned fifteen, Flora Walker had given him the car as a birthday gift. Mother and son had spent a whole year fixing it up before Beckett got his driver's license.

A thousand happy memories had poured in when she first saw it in Beckett's garage this morning—coasting Maple Valley's downtown on hot summer nights, laying on the hood and looking at the stars in Painter's Field, sitting on a stool in the Walkers' driveway while Beckett tinkered with the engine and told her about the trip down the Pacific Coast Highway he and his mom would take eventually.

He'd loved to talk about that trip—a trip they never got to take.

Windy waves of cold rolled over her. This morning felt like forever ago after such a sublime day of wandering Boston. They'd spent most of their time in the Beacon Hill district—roamed the narrow brick sidewalks lined by historic rowhouses and stood at the metal gates in front of the Massachusetts State House.

Now they were heading north to Gloucester and Beckett's favorite slice of Massachusetts beach. Salt Island, worth the forty-minute drive, he'd assured.

Honestly, he could've driven her anywhere and she would've gladly settled in for the ride. Or he could've taken her back to his apartment for nothing more than an evening of packing boxes and she'd have been happy.

Because he was there.

"I need one of those head scarves like Grace Kelly always wore in old movies whenever she was driving." Surely the misty air had long since faded her makeup, and of course, her hair was a mess. She'd traded in her nice jacket hours ago for a thicker fleece zip-up she'd found in Beckett's back seat.

Beckett only laughed and turned the car onto a twisty side road and past a sign pointing to public parking. Within minutes, he paid a ridiculous amount of money and tucked the car into one of several open spaces.

"Usually you're lucky if you can park around here, but with it being so chilly tonight . . ." He stopped. "Are you sure you're not going to freeze? We can go find a restaurant or something instead."

"No, I want to see this place. You said this is where you came to study before exams, where you brought your family the last time they came to visit." Where he'd made the decision to apply to the JAG Corps. He'd told her more about it the other night. How he'd come out to the shore on a Sunday after an eighty-hour workweek. Prayed for the first time in months and felt a peace he didn't understand.

So similar to her own feelings these last weeks at home, in the orchard—all the purpose and belonging and direction she'd been missing for so long. God's whisper in her soul, just like Grandma said. It had echoed into every corner of her being.

But where her awakening had grown roots, deep and embracing, Beckett's had set him free—like the wind blowing a leaf from its branch.

Don't think about that today. Tomorrow she'd return to reality. Today she was a leaf, too, plucked from her perch and carefree. Following the tug of the breeze and the whim of her best friend.

"When the tide's lower you can actually walk on a sandbar out to the island," Beckett was saying now. The sound of their footsteps over the wooden walkway's weathered boards was lost in the wind scraping over rippling coast. On the opposite end of the bridge, white sand splayed over the tiny island.

When she stepped off the walkway, her boots sank into the sand, and Beckett's grip tightened. Cobalt water lapped at the shore as he led her to the far end of the island, past only a couple other clusters of people.

Soon Beckett was spreading the blanket and they were settling onto the soft ground. She burrowed into the high neck of his fleece jacket, hands hidden inside its overly long sleeves. The faint scent of his cologne lingered in the coat along with the saltiness of the sea air.

"You going to be warm enough?"

"Plenty." As long as he didn't mind her huddling so close to him.

Which apparently he didn't. Because he reached behind them to the leftover length of blanket and pulled one corner over her shoulders, the other over his.

God, if you could just let tonight last for the rest of forever, I'd be okay with that.

The prayer tripped through her mind as Beckett watched her watch the ocean—she could feel it, the heat of his stare, even as she drank in the horizon. It'd become so familiar in just these past ten or eleven hours. As if some invisible barrier that used to stand between them had finally gone and collapsed.

"So how does it compare?" His breath feathered over her face.

"Huh?"

"You've never been to the Atlantic coast before, but you were telling me last week about that trip to Spain you took a couple years ago. The beach along the Mediterranean."

"Right. Costa del Sol." She'd stayed in a flat along a sloping seaside, the walk from the white stucco balcony with the orange tiled flooring consisting of more than two hundred steps to get down to the actual shore. "Well, I was there in March, so it wasn't warm at all. But I put on my swimsuit anyway and tried wading into the water. It was this gorgeous shade of turquoise that tumbled under a moody wind. The sea was so forceful that I was barely in knee-deep before it knocked me over."

"Good thing you took all those swimming lessons."

"I'm serious, Beck. I could barely stand up. Every time I tried, waves just kept knocking me back down. I was choking on saltwater while laughing my head off."

"I think I would've liked to see that."

"Pretty sure I swallowed a gallon of water. And it was so cold my fingers and toes were blue. Probably my lips, too."

His glance dropped to her mouth and then just as quickly away. "And?"

She closed her eyes around the memory. "And I can still remember lying in bed that night with the windows open. The room was freezing, but it was worth it to hear the waves."

"You're a good storyteller, Kit, you know that?" A drowsy quiet curled in the air around them. Beckett's midnight eyes were fastened on the water, something distant and contemplative in his gaze. The wind ruffled his hair, and minutes passed before he spoke again. "It's too bad we weren't on speaking terms when you were abroad. I could've demanded you send me postcards. I'd like to go to Europe someday."

Maybe the Army would send him there. Maybe *he'd* send *her* postcards.

The unwelcome thought propelled her to her feet.

"What?" Beckett lifted his eyes.

"Let's go wading."

"It's going to be freezing, Kit."

"I know, but if I can survive the Mediterranean in March, I can endure the Atlantic in September." She bent over to unlace and yank off her boots, movement almost frantic. Off came her socks, and she rolled up her leggings.

Beckett just sat there, staring.

"Don't wimp out on me, Beck."

His inflated sigh gave way to obedience. He rose and kicked off his own shoes while she tested the water. A squeal pitched from her the second it touched her toes.

"Told you!" Beckett chirped, still safely ensconced in

sand.

Just for that, she waded deeper, icy water licking up her ankles and the chill climbing her spine. "It's refreshing." Her teeth chattered through the lie.

Beckett laughed and followed her in, his own gasp colliding with the whoosh of the wind. "If I get frostbite and my toes fall off—"

"Stop whining." She reached her fingers into the foamy blue and sent a splash his way.

Which, of course, was a mistake. Because, of course, he splashed back.

Within seconds she was half-doused and wholly frozen, shrieking and laughing and on her way to losing her footing.

If not for Beckett's darting arms.

He caught her before she could fall, and she landed against his chest.

And yet, something told her she was far from safe. "Don't you dare push me all the way in. Don't you dare." She yelped the command.

"I'm not going to push you in."

But his impish grin and baritone laughter convinced her that was exactly what he was going to do. Which was why she clasped her hands together around his neck. "I'm not letting go. You push me in and you're coming down with me."

Her hair whipped around her head, wet strands matting to her face. She couldn't feel her toes, couldn't catch her breath, couldn't stop laughing . . .

Until he stopped.

Stilled.

Arms holding her in place and eyes locked on hers. "You said you wished you'd let me kiss you that night."

The shiver raced through her. "Y-you heard that?"

He lifted his hand to brush her hair from her face,

one finger trailing over her cheek as he tucked it behind her ear.

"Beck." Her voice was a whisper even as her heart roared. She loosened her arms from around his neck, but they only made it as far down as his chest. "You're going to leave. You're going to spend six weeks at Fort Benning in Georgia learning leadership skills and military tactics."

"You read up on it?"

"Then after that, you'll go to Charlottesville for ten and a half weeks of officer's training." She should push away from him, make her numb feet move. But it was as if the sandy floor beneath her held her in place. "You're going to leave," she said again. She'd promised herself not to think about it, but it was a promise she couldn't keep.

"I haven't left yet." His soft words sifted over her cheeks as his fingers tipped her chin.

And finally, as he closed the last breath of space between then, lowered his lips to hers, she stopped fighting. Her hands slid around his neck once more as he kissed her once and then again.

Both his arms crushed her to him as a third kiss intensified. And there was nothing left to do but lose herself in his hold.

12

"I have to say, Beckett, if every one of my parolees was as diligent as you about completing their service hours, my job would be so much more pleasant."

The parole officer Beckett had been assigned to nearly two months ago moved her computer keyboard to the side and folded her hands atop her desk. Sylvia Jones—early fifties, snow white hair cut in a blunt bob. He'd found her intimidating when they first met but quickly discovered she had a soft spot for cooperative parolees.

What she didn't know was he'd almost turned unintentionally uncooperative today, would've forgotten this meeting altogether if not for the ping of his phone's calendar reminder.

Today, this week, his brain was anywhere but here.

One week since he'd broken all his own unwritten rules and kissed his best friend. Since everything he'd ever imagined about kissing Kit Danby proved pale in comparison to the real thing.

The rest of that night and even most of the drive home the next day had felt idyllic, almost spellbinding. When he'd let himself kiss her again, just before leaving Boston, it hadn't been nearly as feverish as the night before. He'd been slow, deliberate, memorizing the feel of her, almost as if . . .

As if this couldn't possibly last. As if he stood somewhere between everything he'd planned and hoped and worked for . . . and something else so very unplanned, yet staggering and remarkable. And he didn't know which way to lean—toward the everything or the something. Knew only he couldn't hold on to both.

The feeling had only intensified the closer they drove to Maple Valley—in separate cars after picking up Kit's in Chicago.

"You don't look nearly as happy as I thought you would." Sylvia's voice budged into his wayward thoughts, her forehead wrinkled above her thick-rimmed glasses. "You're done, Beckett. Free. You've got all four hundred hours in and then some."

He straightened. "Wait, what?" He'd still had forty hours to complete before his Boston trip. He'd only managed seventeen at the orchard since returning.

Partially because he was spending so much time helping Dad at the depot. Mostly because he was avoiding Kit. Not because he didn't want to see her, but because he did. Because he yearned to throw restraint to the wind and forget the past, ignore the future, focus only on the present. A present in which he'd happily kiss Kit breathless every chance he got.

But wouldn't that be reverting to the old Beckett? The one who acted on impulse and spoke without thinking and hurt the people he cared about most. Starting something he couldn't finish *would* hurt her. Probably already had in some ways. Of all the career moves he could've made, he'd honed in on the one thing that, to Kit, only ever spelled out loss.

She was trying to be supportive, he knew. But he also knew her well enough to recognize the underlying dejection she tried to hide.

He forced himself to focus. "I should still have twenty-some hours left."

Sylvia shook her head. "Your math is off. Trust me, I reviewed the numbers multiple times. I've never had someone work off that many hours so quickly. You're free to go, Beckett. Your obligation to the court is complete."

Free to go.

Her words trailed him as he left the office in the Department of Corrections, as he walked toward his car parked along the curb and then thought twice and continued on down the sidewalk. He'd told Kit he'd come out to the orchard today so they could plan for tonight's town meeting, during which they'd pitch Beckett's plan to host the tourism board members at the orchard.

But he needed space; he needed to think. *Free to go.* This was what he'd worked for all this time. This was why he'd come home, why he'd stayed home, why he'd gone to Kit pleading for a volunteer position despite the warning of his gut.

Back then he'd been so consumed with leftover angst from her wedding night, the night she'd pushed him away when he'd tried to kiss her. Now he actually *had* kissed her and he was just as churned up as before. Maybe more so.

Coffee. He needed coffee. Or maybe a burger at The Red Door. Something. But before he could decide what, his attention snagged on the sight of someone pushing a broken-down car up the middle of Main Avenue—and not having an easy time of it.

Instinct kicked in and he crossed the street to help. Not until he was close did he realize whose straining form pushed the car.

"Go away, Walker." The words lurched from Sam

the second he saw Beckett approaching.

"I would, but you're holding up traffic and you're not going to get anywhere pushing this heap of junk alone." The caustic reply was out before he could stop it.

Sam grunted as he gave the car a shove. Rust had eaten its way up the side of the vehicle. "I don't need or want your help."

Maybe he *should* leave Sam to He-man his way to the car repair place on his own. Well, not entirely on his own. That was Hastings in the front seat steering, wasn't it? The officer who'd arrested Beckett his first night home.

But a honk from the car behind them compelled him to move to Sam's side and thrust his weight into the car.

"I said—"

"I know what you said." Beckett gritted his teeth as he pushed.

A surly wind grappled through the trees in the town square on one side of the road and set to flapping the awnings of the businesses lining the other side. They passed Klassen's Hardware, Baker's Antiques.

Beckett's arms strained against the trunk. "Maybe you should consider getting a new car."

"Maybe you should consider shutting up."

Two more blocks and they'd reach the car shop at the end of Maple Valley's stretch of downtown. "Listen, as long as we're both here, not glaring at each other across a set of cell bars or rough-housing in a restaurant, maybe the time is right to finally say—"

"There's nothing you've got to say that I want to hear."

"Maybe not, but I'm going to say it anyway."

Sam jerked to a stop and threw up his hands, before yelling to Hastings. "To the right, Hastings. To the curb." His palms slapped back onto the trunk.

The officer leaned out his door. "But we're almost to the garage."

"To the curb!" He started pushing again.

But Beckett had stopped. "What are you going to do? Hire a tow truck to get the car the rest of the way?"

The car bumped into the curb. "Sure. It's worth the seventy-five bucks not to have to listen to you any longer." Mindless of Hastings, Sam started down the sidewalk.

Beckett glared at the man's retreating back. "I'm not sorry, you know."

Sam froze for only a second before spinning. He covered the distance to Beckett in three long strides, cheeks red, his entire body rigid and pulsing, as if ready for a fight. Maybe he should just let the man pummel him once and for all.

"What did you say?" Sam's eyes were dark.

"I'm not sorry Kit didn't marry you. She would've been miserable, and you would've been too eventually. I'm not sorry I helped her do the thing she couldn't do on her own." Why hadn't Sam decked him yet? "But I am sorry about how I did it. I could've had better timing. I could've gone over to her house before the wedding. I could've talked to you."

"I wouldn't have listened." Sam's arms were crossed, his voice tight, but his jaw twitched. Possibly the first sign, however brittle, of understanding.

"It was a mistake—waiting until the last minute. For that, I'm truly sorry."

He waited for Sam to say something, anything. But when he finally did, it wasn't what Beckett had expected. "Are you staying, then?"

"What?"

"In Maple Valley. Just want to know if I'm going to have to get used to seeing you day in and day out."

"I . . . I don't . . ." The breeze carried away the words he didn't know how to say.

Stay? It wasn't like the thought hadn't drifted in and out of his brain the past few days. Weeks, really. But every time it did, there was another right on its heels. *And do what?*

Chores at the orchard might help him fulfill his community service, but he couldn't do that forever. He could pass the Iowa bar and hang up his lawyer's shingle here in Maple Valley, but how would that lead to any more long-term fulfillment than his job in Boston?

Sure, Logan had given up his dynamic career for Amelia, at least for the time being. Dad, too, when Mom got sick. But the difference was, they'd both had a chance to chase their own dreams for a season first. Was it completely selfish to thirst for the same opportunity?

"Dad!"

A child's voice came barreling in, along with the rattle of training wheels and then the child herself. She braked her bike in front of Sam and jumped into arms that were no longer crossed.

Beckett's eyes met Sam's over the mass of curly hair sticking out from the girl's helmet. But Sam looked away before Beckett could read any kind of explanation for what he was seeing.

"Where's your mom, kiddo?"

The little girl pointed over her shoulder. "In the square. She says we can take the training wheels off soon, but I said I don't want to unless you're there."

A woman sat on a bench in the square. But whatever book she'd been reading was now in her lap facedown as she watched the sidewalk meeting.

Sam kissed the girl's cheek and set her down. "Why don't you ride on back to your mom? I'll join you in a minute, all right?"

The girl nodded and hopped on her bike. But before turning around, she looked at Beckett. "My dad's a cop. He drives a car with a siren, and he has a gun. And he got me this bike."

Hold up, Sam was her *father*?

"Go on now, Mackenzie." Sam leaned over to give her bike a push. When he rose, it was to meet Beckett square in the eye. "You might as well ask."

"When . . . who . . . are you married?"

"No." His chin jutted out with the word, and yet, something in him visibly softened. "You weren't the only one who . . . made mistakes that night. The night of the wedding. I'm surprised you didn't know, this being Maple Valley and all."

Understanding landed in pieces as overhead clouds rolled, folding into one another in a gathering sheet of gray. Sam had been hurt and angry. He must have found temporary comfort—or at least distraction—with another woman.

Sam's eyes were on his daughter now, biking down the sidewalk. "She's not a mistake, though. Never was, not for a second."

"Are you and her mom—?"

Sam shook his head before Beckett finished the question. And yet, there was a flicker in his eyes, a shadow of longing. "That's why I went to the orchard that day in August. Figured I should tell Kit before she heard it from someone else. But then I saw her. You."

Maybe for the first time, Beckett looked at Sam—really looked at him. And for once, it wasn't Kit's ex-fiancé he saw or even the cop who'd put him behind bars.

But someone who'd weathered a storm of his own and, for all his bitterness, had been able to do something Beckett hadn't: He'd stayed. After the humiliation of being jilted; after, presumably, a one-night stand; after getting a woman pregnant . . .

He'd stayed.

Sam started to walk away but paused, his attention curving back to Beckett. "Look, I've been over Kit for a long time. But the two of you showing up in town again, seeing you together, it messed with all the closure I thought was already a done deal. And I'm not going to lie, arresting you—that felt good." He glanced to the square, to his daughter and her mother, both watching him now. "But I've got two really good reasons to make myself get over this all over again." He looked to Beckett once more. "So if you're going to be sticking around, I'll try to play nice."

Beckett couldn't have been more surprised by the change in Sam's demeanor if he'd suddenly embraced him. "Fair enough."

A single nod and he turned to walk away. But not before one final soft warning. "Just don't hurt her, Walker."

At least Kit could depend on someone to show up at the orchard when they said they would.

Eric Hampton appeared through the labyrinth of trees. He'd been out here all afternoon, working alongside Paul, Bill, Jose, and Bessemer from Hampton House, raking around the trees, creating circles of mulch and leaves about a foot and a half away from the trunk. Come winter, the mulch would break down and feed the earthworms below, who then did their part aerating and loosening the soil.

Later in the fall, they'd wrap the trunks with plastic

protectors, even paint them to prevent winter sunscald. They'd do a round of pruning, as well.

Eric leaned on his rake and glanced at his watch. "About time to head back, fellas."

Was it really almost five p.m.? And Beckett still hadn't shown up? That town meeting was in just a couple hours, and supposedly she was presenting a plan for using the orchard to wow the tourism board. But this had all been Beckett's idea. He'd promised her he'd use his arguing charm to make her case. Maybe he'd decided to wing it tonight.

"It's killing me how much work you've done around here without pay, Eric." Kit propped a bag of mulch against a tree and moved to Eric. "As for your guys, I wish I could pay them three times what I do."

"We wouldn't argue." The joking call came from a row over—Bessemer. The man's first name was Horace, but he'd told Kit straightaway his first day working at the orchard to use his last name.

She'd picked up pieces of each man's backstory in the weeks they'd been under her employ. Paul's astounded her the most—only twenty-two and already two prison sentences under his belt. Drug-selling and a slew of burglaries. He'd gone through an addiction rehab program before transitioning to Hampton House.

All because an uncle had introduced him to cocaine at the age of seventeen. Certainly, Paul had a choice. He'd always had a choice. But working with these men was a continual eye-opening, a practice in empathy. How could she judge Paul's choices knowing where he'd come from, *not* knowing what it must feel like to be part of a family where recreational drug use was a given?

No wonder Grandpa had felt so strongly about employing individuals who might otherwise not be able to find work.

"Some of these men will lead productive, law-abiding lives from here on. Some of them will relapse, give in to their old ways. But all of them will have experienced, at least for this one season, what it feels like to be affirmed, to be needed and valued."

Grandpa's words filled her anew, the echoes of his voice so clear out here among the trees. Chicago, Boston, she'd had a blast, had needed to get away. And Beckett . . . *Beckett.* He'd quite literally swept her off her feet on the shore of Salt Island, and she wasn't sure her feet had come even close to touching the ground again.

But this was home. This was what she was supposed to be doing. Not just nurturing trees, but investing in people—her employees, visitors, these men from Hampton House. Why, she was even helping Drew Renwycke get his own business off the ground. She'd been amazed when she got home after midnight on Thursday to see walls and a roof already enclosing the barn.

"Seeing these guys gainfully employed and, even more, happy—that's payment enough for me." Eric lifted the still half-full bag of mulch she'd set aside and started walking toward the truck.

"You're good at your job, Eric."

"As are you."

"Actually what I'm good at is surrounding myself with people who can help me. Willa, Beckett, lots of former employees who graciously came back after Luke let them all go."

Eric stopped, hoisted the bag into the truck bed. "How's he doing these days?" Concern filled his taupe eyes, and the breeze lifted his hair. For the first time it occurred to her what a nice-looking man he was. No, he didn't send heat bolting through her like Beckett. No pulse-racing and fluttery nerves, either.

How had she ever looked at Beckett the way she looked at Eric now? What had changed?

Everything. Nothing.

"Kit?"

Lucas, he'd asked about Lucas. "He's okay, I guess. He's still upset that I don't want to sell, and I know he's angry about the barn project." And yet, he hadn't told Dad. She had no idea why. "But he gets in these moods. Everything will be fine and then next thing I know, he's stomping up to his room and slamming his door and I'll hear him up there pacing. He gets nightmares, but of course, he won't talk about any of it."

The other men were ambling in their direction now, carrying rakes and empty mulch bags.

"Do you ever feel unsafe? Does he get violent at all?" Eric asked the questions slowly, carefully.

"No, definitely not, he wouldn't . . ." She was interrupted by the memories of Lucas throwing his uneaten apple in the store, barging toward her on the Archway Bridge, so much anger in his eyes. And then there was the medicine cabinet in the second-floor bathroom. She'd noticed its cracked glass yesterday and asked Lucas what had happened. He'd shrugged and walked away, but not before she'd glimpsed the Band-Aid on his knuckles.

Could Eric read her uncertainty? "You're living in that house alone with him, Kit."

The guys were jumping onto the truck bed. "I'm his sister. He wouldn't hurt me."

"Even so, if things start to feel weird, if he seems erratic, just tell someone, okay? Beckett or Willa or me, whoever." Eric rounded to the passenger side. "If he's struggling with PTSD or some other mental illness, it's nothing to be ashamed of, but it's also not something to ignore."

That was the thing, though. From the day Lucas had

come home from Afghanistan, he'd been intent on ignoring whatever had happened that had caused him to go AWOL. Assuming something had happened, that is. There had to be a reason he'd deserted, disappeared. There had to be a reason he'd refused to stand up for himself during his court martial.

But he'd been as tight-lipped then as he was now.

Kit climbed into the driver's seat and started the drive back to the parking lot. She thanked Eric again when she dropped him and the others off at the Hampton House van, tried not to worry when she saw only two other cars in the lot.

It's late in the afternoon, and it's a weekday. It's okay there's not a crowd.

But the low numbers, Eric's words, worry over Lucas, all of it cluttered her thoughts as she drove to the house. And Beckett, where was he?

She sent him a text and then, with only ninety minutes until the meeting, hurried upstairs to shower and change. She took longer than usual, not even trying to deny the extra care she took with her clothes and hair had everything to do with seeing Beckett tonight.

But forty-five minutes later, still no Beckett. She made a sandwich and ate, sent another text. Read the notes Beckett had made for their presentation. Man, he was a bad speller. Finally, with only twenty minutes left until the meeting, she headed outside once more.

And ran smack into Lucas crossing the porch. He grabbed her arms, whether out of shock or to steady her, she wasn't sure, but his grip pinched. He grunted an apology and released her.

"Luke, I haven't seen you all day."

His eyes, the color of soot, held only a hint of the blue in her own. Like Mom's, Grandma had once remarked. Kit had made it a point to find an old scrapbook and compare. Grandma was right.

"Been out" was all he offered now.

"Well, listen, uh, you should know . . ." Would this make him even more upset than the barn had? "I'm heading to the town meeting. Gonna ask the council to host an evening event for the state tourism board here. Well, not just the board. We'll invite the whole town. I'm going to try to get Dad here, too. It's Beckett's brainchild, really—"

"Of course." He pushed past her toward the door.

"Of course what?" A coil of tightly packed clouds overhead threatened to break open any minute.

"Of course it's Beckett's brainchild."

"He's trying to help me, Luke. He knows how important the orchard is to me."

Lucas leaned one arm on the doorframe, his heel kicking the swaying screened door behind him. "He knows he can barrel in and play hero and you'll worship the ground he walks on like you always have."

"I don't—"

"But he'll let you down eventually. He'll get restless and leave. And you'll be stuck with only a bunch of trees and a failing business. Have fun with that."

"It's not a failing business."

"I have eyes, Kit. The past two weekends' numbers weren't nearly as good as opening weekend. You were gone four days this week—none of them saw more than a handful of visitors. Go ahead and build your barn and plan your event, but it's not going to stop the inevitable. Dad and I are going to sell, and there's nothing you or Beckett Walker can do about it."

He disappeared inside, the door slapping closed.

She just stood there, dismay needling through her. Only when her phone buzzed, did a thread of hope curl in. But no, it wasn't Beckett. Just Willa asking her why she hadn't yet arrived at the meeting.

She pushed the speed limit on the way into town. Green tinted the landscape, the bullying wind forcing what crops remained in half-harvested fields into a full bow. Scattered drops of rain dotted her windshield.

Luke's wrong. Beckett will be at the meeting. We'll convince the council. Drew will finish the barn. Dad will come home. Everything will work out.

The city hall meeting room was packed. The townspeople never failed to make a good showing at these meetings—which probably had more to do with the free coffee and social time afterward than the agenda itself.

Yet the one person Kit needed was nowhere to be seen. She slipped into the empty chair Willa had saved her. Beckett had to show up. He knew how much she hated public speaking. He'd promised.

But forty minutes later, when they reached the line on the agenda that read "Valley Orchard Proposal," there was still no sign of Beckett. Mayor Milt looked at her expectantly.

Willa patted her knee. "Go on, Kit. You've got this."

"But Beckett—"

"Isn't here. And it isn't his orchard, anyhow."

Except it wasn't hers, either, as Lucas had been quick to remind her. But she had to fight for it, public speaking fear and all. She thought of Paul and Bessemer and the others. She thought of Grandpa and Grandma.

She rose on wobbly legs and made her way to the front. She'd deal with Beckett later.

Beckett knew who stood behind him without turning around to look. So he didn't look. Only gave a halfhearted effort to cast a flat stone skipping across the creek's shallow ripples.

"You've never been patient enough to master that."

Kit was right. He heaved the next rock and stood.

The weathered boards of the makeshift bridge—more of a walkway, really—tremored under his feet. Untamed brush, tall grass and weeds, climbed the brushy inclines on either side of the ravine that separated Dad's land from the orchard property. Stray raindrops pattered in the twisting creek.

"I'm sorry, Kit." A gust of stalwart wind sent crinkled leaves spiraling down.

"That's it? You don't show up at the orchard all day and then you don't show up at the meeting tonight. And all you have to say is you're sorry?"

She'd dressed up for the meeting. No flannel and jeans tonight. Instead some kind of wraparound dress thing that accentuated her figure and tights and heels. He could count on one hand the number of times he'd seen her in heels. How had she walked down the ravine in them? A flash of lightning glinted through tree branches.

She looked beautiful.

She looked angry.

She looked hurt. And that was the worst.

"Where have you been? Not just tonight. I've hardly seen you all week. And when I do see you, you're skittish and awkward. If this is about Boston, if you're worried I have some kind of overblown expectation . . . well, don't."

It was full-on raining now. The only thing keeping them from getting soaked was the canopy of leaves providing a flimsy cover. But with the lightning, the grumbling of clouds, the piercing wind, it didn't make sense to stay out here stalling, fumbling for an explanation he didn't know how to give.

He truly didn't know why he'd missed the meeting. Didn't know why he'd felt the near-frantic need to spend the afternoon finally completing his JAG Corps application, making phone call after phone call in an attempt to set up a new FSO interview. Didn't know why he hadn't been able to think of anything else after talking to Sylvia, running into Sam.

All he knew was, those words, "free to go" and "don't hurt her," had collided into each other on a loop until he'd lost track of time and missed being there for Kit.

Just like he'd missed that Stanley Oil meeting. Just like he'd missing his first FSO interview.

Just like he'd missed Mom.

"Is it Webster?" Kit wrapped her arms around her torso. "Has he still not heard from his friend?"

"I don't know." He'd told Webster about the encounter with the Illinois social worker last week the day after returning. He'd been grateful, but not as relieved as Beckett had hoped. He was beginning to wonder if what he'd told the social worker was true—that Webster simply wanted to know Amanda was okay. Was there more to that story?

"Is it your dad?"

"Kit—"

"How's he feeling? I know he's got Depot Days next weekend. Were you helping him and time got away from you?"

Her forced optimism was enough to tempt him to lie. But he'd never lied to Kit, not about something that mattered. *Don't hurt her.* "You should have a coat, Kit. Let's go—"

"No. You owe me an explanation, Beckett. You left me to make a presentation on my own and—"

"And did you?"

"Did I—?"

"Did you make the presentation?"

Her arms wound tighter as she shivered. "Yes."

He pulled off his jacket and slipped it around her shoulders. "Did it go over well? Are they going to let you host the tourism board?" Another flash of lightning.

"Yes."

"Then there's nothing to be upset about."

"Except that you said you'd come out to the orchard today and you never did. Except that you weren't there tonight. I had to stand behind a podium with my knees knocking and my voice shaking and stammer out a speech I wasn't prepared to give, one that was your idea in the first place."

The rain was falling harder now, breaking through the cover of the trees and landing in splotches. He couldn't hold back anymore. "What do you want from me, Kit? I've worked four-hundred-plus hours at the orchard. I have fixed fences and fought tree disease, repaired equipment and picked enough apples to feed a small country. I came up with a plan for you, and I'm sorry I missed presenting that plan, but you don't need me fighting all your battles."

She dropped her arms. "All my battles? Really, Beck?"

He closed the space between them. "I have goals, too. I have things I need to be working toward, too. And my dad needs a major brain surgery and might have cancer and I can't figure out why in the world he's insisting on waiting. Some guy broke Raegan's heart and Webster's still worried about Amanda and—"

A crash of thunder cut off the rant he'd never meant to give. Kit didn't deserve this. The storm wreaking havoc inside him wasn't her fault. Her face was only inches from his, hair matted to her forehead and cheeks, tears filling her eyes. Why was he doing this to her?

And how, rain-soaked and shivering, swallowed up in his jacket, could she still look so exquisite?

"Beckett." She whispered, she trembled.

And he couldn't help it. Breath heaving, his hands found her waist and his lips found her forehead, her cheeks, her nose. The rain grew louder. Her skin was cold, her lips waiting . . .

And then she jerked, stumbling backward, gaze dropping to the ground, lifting to the trees. That was when he heard what she heard, felt it hitting against him. *Hail.*

"I have to go." She spun and started up the hill, heels digging into the grass.

"Kit, I'll take you—"

She ignored him and kept running.

13

Kit awoke to the sound of Lucas's terror.

His yells thrashed through the house, a sound even more eerie than last night's storm. She slipped from her bed and crossed the hall to Lucas's room. Cold hardwood chilled her feet as she lifted her hand to knock lightly on his door. "Luke?"

Nothing.

Not even the soft moans that sometimes followed his nighttime bellows, which meant he might be awake in there.

"I'm here, Luke. If you want to talk."

No response. Just like every other time she'd tried. But today the silence pricked even sharper. Last night's hailstorm had brought all her worries about the orchard to a jagged peak. After leaving Beckett, refusing to let him accompany her home, the only thing she'd been able to do was sit at the kitchen table fretting, until finally dragging herself to bed for a night of tossing and turning.

But the storm had done something worse to Lucas. When she'd arrived home, she'd found him sitting in the dark in the living room. She'd asked if he was okay, received only the barest nod in reply before he shambled upstairs. She'd listened to his pacing—louder, more rapid than ever before. And then the nightmares . . .

She didn't know how to reach him. Hadn't a clue where to start.

Kit returned to her own room and dressed quickly—the faded overalls that'd become everyday wear and a long-sleeved gray tee made of long-john material. She grabbed an oversized flannel shirt as a jacket and then padded down the hallway and through the house.

The sun was pale, as if it, too, had been worn down and burnt out by last night's storm. It nearly blended in with flaxen clouds that brushed through the sky. Even here, the hail and wind damage was obvious. Broken tree branches strewn across the yard. Autumn mums limp and lifeless in their paint-stripped flower boxes.

She started for the fields, ground slippery and soft under her tennis shoes. The air was cool and still, like it held its breath, waiting and worried.

"Morning, Kit." Willa emerged from the nearest field, the hems of her own coveralls muddy. "Didn't think I'd see you so early."

They reached each other at the field's border. "Same here." Although, she should've known. Willa's care for this land nearly rivaled her own. She'd worked even longer hours than Beckett these past two months, giving far more than she was getting—at least as far as a paycheck was concerned.

"I don't want to know, do I?"

Willa draped one arm around Kit's shoulder and turned her away from the field. "There's no need to go looking and making yourself feel worse than I reckon you already do."

"It's that bad?"

Willa squeezed her shoulder. "I'd say seventy-five, eighty percent of the remaining crop is on the ground."

No. The air whooshed from her lungs.

"And from what I can tell, a lot of what's left is cut into."

She'd known. Somehow she'd known as the wind hurled itself against the house last night, as hail struck the roof and windows and smattered to the ground, she'd known. She'd seen it happen before.

The crop could often survive a hailstorm if it happened early enough in the season because the fruit was still hard enough to withstand the hit. This far along, though, when the apples were soft and when the wind added its battering force, the loss was unavoidable.

But eighty percent?

"What are we going to do?"

Willa squeezed her shoulder again before dropping her arm. "We'll get a crew out here today to clean up the mess and salvage what we can. We'll likely need to find a vendor to help stock the store for the remainder of the season."

Buy apples from another orchard. With what money? Everything they'd made so far had gone into paying employees and building the barn and making repairs to buildings and machinery. At least they hadn't let their insurance lapse, but it'd take weeks, maybe months, to see a claim fulfilled.

Perhaps she could ask the bank for a loan. But even that would take time.

"This isn't a death knell for the orchard. Your grandparents made it through seasons like this. There are probably farmers all over the county waking up to similar shock this morning." Willa fidgeted with the clasp of her overalls before touching Kit's elbow and steering her the way she'd come. "This is a part of agricultural life."

"I know that. It's just . . ." Her footsteps shuffled in wet grass. "I was so sure God was telling me to stay, to run the orchard, make it a success again. Something like this happens, and I have to wonder, what's the deal? It's not just the storm. It's Lucas and Dad and Beckett . . ."

"What about Beckett?" Willa's tone had gone gruff, protective around the question.

Yes, what about Beckett? He'd gone from distant and sullen to exploding and then to looking at her with enough desperate desire to summon her own. This wasn't a man playing hot and cold with her affections. This was Beckett. This was a man hurting.

And she felt as helpless to reach him as she did Lucas.

"I don't know what to say about Beck." She stopped as they reached the house. "I only know I can't help wondering if I got it all wrong. When I first came home, I honestly thought maybe God led me here. But if this is where he wants me, why is he making it so hard?" Chilled, gluey air gathered around her.

"Kit, when God calls us to something, it doesn't mean we're never going to have setbacks. And if we go doubting his direction every time we face a challenge, we'll end up stagnant and frustrated, tied up in knots."

"Maybe it's not his direction I'm doubting so much as my ability to hear it, to recognize it." She swiped her fingers along the porch railing, sending rivulets of lingering rainwater to the ground.

Willa's pause stretched. "You know, I always loved how your granddad called you his little meteorologist. Not many a kid can earn a term of endearment like that."

"Yes, well, not many a kid gets a kick out of reading books about air pressure and movement."

Willa chuckled, but her gaze held steady and serious. "The thing is, for all we know about weather and its patterns, some of it is still a mystery. Fronts shift out of nowhere. Temperatures defy seasons and predictions.

Patterns change." Her gentle voice beckoned. "Sometimes God whispers. Sometimes he shouts. He doesn't always communicate the same way twice, and frankly, sometimes we're going to get it wrong. But part of faith is embracing the mystery—all the while knowing that even when we're confused, God is faithful. He's trustworthy."

Willa's words sunk into her bones, filling a hungry, empty space she hadn't even fully realized was there. If it could just last, if she could truly grasp the assurance in Willa's words . . .

If only she could believe hope wouldn't let her down with the next catastrophe, that her own heart wouldn't drift . . .

"He doesn't ask for perfect hearing or a life free of missteps, Kit. Just your trust."

"What if I don't have that kind of trust? What if my faith isn't as strong as yours?" *What if I lose the orchard?*

What if Dad never came home and Lucas never healed? What if Beckett left for good? What if Case had cancer?

Could she still call God trustworthy and faithful if life and people and circumstances let her down?

"*Hold unswervingly to the hope . . .*"

Willa tucked Kit's hand through her arm and climbed the porch steps. "That's the beauty of God, my girl. Even when we're tempted to let go, he keeps holding on."

Beckett knew exactly where to find his father.

Soggy leaves and storm-tossed branches littered the spacious grounds in front of the Maple Valley railroad museum, but other than an eave spout hanging askew, the depot didn't seem any worse for wear. But with the annual Depot Days event set to kick off tonight—Friday night fireworks followed by a Saturday of train runs and other activities—Dad had probably risen with the sun.

Beckett crossed the yard, stepping over the train tracks ribboning from the depot station. They disappeared into rolling hills veiled in misty gray, wrapped in quiet.

He ached to know how Kit was doing this morning, how the orchard had fared. But she'd insisted on going home alone last night. He'd tried calling her once, after eleven p.m., while the storm still raged. She hadn't answered.

"Dad?"

He found his father Windexing the glass display cases that lined two walls of the museum. Wan sunlight from a bank of windows did little to brighten the room, not on such a cloudy, pale morning.

"Beck." Dad straightened. "I didn't expect to see you here, not this early."

"Whereas I fully expected to see you." At least Dad had been better about not working such long hours lately. He'd begun to recognize signs of headaches and dizziness before they hit full force. Thankfully there'd been no more collapses in the weeks since the orchard opening.

Still, he had to squelch the urge to scold his father for working so hard, insisting on going forward with Depot Days. Couldn't he have at least put someone else in charge?

"There's coffee back in the office, if you want. Extra cups, too."

It was all the invitation Beckett needed. He wandered back to Dad's cubbyhole of an office, his attention hooking on a framed photo of Mom sitting on his father's desk. Whoever had taken the photo had caught Mom mid-laugh, the blond hair and blue eyes she shared with Raegan glinting under a halo of light that also highlighted the slight bump on her nose. It was one of Beckett's favorite family stories—how Logan had tried peewee baseball one year and during a practice game of catch with Mom had ended up breaking her nose.

Seriously, he was the only one in this family who had any business playing sports.

He found a mug and poured himself a cup of coffee, not needing to taste it to know it'd be strong and dark. Dad liked his coffee muddy.

"Baseboards need polished," Dad said simply once Beckett returned.

Beckett found the lemon polish and went to work. Silent minutes passed. Dad was more comfortable in silence than anyone Beckett had ever met, even quiet, slightly introverted Logan.

But the silence of the past few weeks, the silence of right now—it was different. Strained with too many unsaid words. Ever since walking out of Dad's hospital room, all the things he wanted to say, to ask, the emotions tumbling into each other, they'd jammed and refused to budge.

The only one that seemed to break free was the one he most loathed to feel: an irrational, indisputable anger.

It was part of why he'd fled to Boston. He didn't want Dad to see. The realization had been soaking in for days now. This wasn't new anger. This was quiet and prowling.

And it filled him with shame.

He swiped his rag along the floorboard, the tart scent of the polish assailing him. He crouched his way around all four walls, only rising once the full circumference of the floorboards gleamed. When he straightened and turned, it was to see Dad watching him while leaning over a case filled with mementos from the depot's history—old railroad photos and tools, stamps and coins and handwritten letters. "So should we get on with it already? You've been crawling out of your skin lately, son. Is it me? The Army application? Kit?"

"Dad—"

"If it's Kit, then we definitely need to talk. I promised Flora I'd always make sure to pry into our children's love lives."

"Even when your children are no longer children?" Beckett draped his rag over the polish bottle and stuffed it behind a counter.

"Especially then. Generally I try to be at least somewhat subtle about it—"

"If this is subtle, I'd like to see what your version of blatant looks like."

Dad eyed him with something like amusement. "Suit yourself. We can go back to taut silence and cleaning if you want."

"No, Dad, I want to talk." He did. That was why he'd come out here, wasn't it? Hadn't he been wishing for weeks for the kind of easy relationship the rest of his siblings shared with Dad? To be able to talk to Dad like he'd once talked to Mom. It was a soul-deep craving—for guidance, wisdom, *something*.

"Do you love her?"

"Of course I love her!" Beckett dropped onto a stool behind the counter, flinging his frustrated reply harder than he'd meant to. "I've loved her since I was eleven." Perhaps not in the same way. Okay, definitely not in the same way.

Dad gave a hearty laugh. "Yeah, well, you haven't been kissing her since you were eleven."

"How do you—"

"Got a brain tumor, Beck, but I'm not blind."

"How can you joke about it?" The question slipped from him before he'd realized it. It stole any lightness, any mirth from the space between them.

Dad's fingers clutched the edge of the glass case. "Son, if you don't think I've had some trouble sleeping lately because of this thing, you're wrong. I've pondered what surgery might mean, wrestled with the thought of not being around to spend at least a couple more decades watching my children grow into the amazing people I've always known they are, seeing Charlie grow up and any other grandkids I might end up with . . ."

Beckett shifted on his stool, dread and discomfort dragging through him.

"I've met with my estate lawyer and updated my will and made sure all my affairs are in order—"

He didn't want to hear this. "Dad—"

"I'm not immune to what's happening here."

He ached to say something, refute or reassure or just *something*. But all he could do was sit here looking at the father he'd too often taken for granted and hear the same flood of pleading prayers he used to say for Mom rush through him once more.

Please don't take him away.

"So why are you putting off the surgery? This whole thing could be over by now."

Dad's pause stretched so long Beckett thought perhaps he wasn't going to answer. And maybe he wasn't. Because instead of acknowledging the question, Dad reached into the display case beside him and pulled out a book—the depot's old guest register. Creases wrinkled its water-splotched cover.

"Colton found this about a half mile from the depot after the tornado last year. Can't believe it survived."

Dad fingered through a couple pages before stopping and setting the book in Beckett's lap. "Check it out. Colton found this, too."

He looked to where Dad pointed, gasping as he recognized the handwriting. *Flora Lawrence.* And right underneath, *Case Walker. 1979.*

"That's the year the depot and museum officially opened after the Union Pacific donated a final mile of track."

He knew the story. Dad had been between assignments with the Foreign Service Office, and Mom, though living in New York at the time, working at the foundation she'd helped open, had come home for the weekend. After several years apart, a series of stops and starts, they'd reunited during the first-ever Depot Days festival.

He traced his finger over Mom's name. "I wish I could hear her voice, just once more."

"I never feel closer to Flora than during Depot Days." Dad spoke slowly, his tone willing Beckett to look up and meet his eyes. "If I'm going to have a tumor scraped off my brain, face months of recovery and possibly radiation or chemo, then I needed this one thing. It may sound silly, it may sound illogical, but I needed it. I asked the neurosurgeon if a few more weeks would make a difference, and he said, unless the symptoms got worse, probably not."

Dad sounded so . . . human. Uncertain and miles from invincible.

"I just needed to feel close to her. I miss her, and I needed to feel close to her."

The welcome sign underneath the depot's open front door tipped against the wind, its creaking filling the silence. Unbidden tears—so long denied—pooled now, blurring Mom's name in the book on his lap. And emotion, tangled and inescapable, knotted his whisper.

"Why didn't you tell me to come home?"

It was the wrong time, the wrong place. His father had just confessed his fear and hurt. But maybe that was why Beckett couldn't stop his own now.

It came in a deluge—the hurt, the anguish, soul-wrenching regret.

"I would've skipped that basketball game, Dad. I called you, I asked how she was doing. Why didn't you tell me to come home?" He blinked, but it was useless. Hot tears streamed down his cheeks.

"Oh, Beckett, I didn't realize . . ."

"I would've come home."

He felt his shoulders, his whole body shake as a sob overtook him. He felt the book slipping from his lap and falling to the floor. He felt weeks—no, years—of bottled up grief breaking free.

He felt his father's arms.

"I got a call from Eric Hampton today."

Kit whirled at the voice sounding from the cellar stairs. A lone bulb from a dangling string provided the only light in the dank space. They wouldn't be able to keep the overflowing bags and barrels of fallen apples in here long. The air was too damp. But there simply wasn't enough refrigeration elsewhere.

Lucas descended into the cellar. Hard to discern his mood in the dim lighting. Would this be the brooding Lucas who spent his nights pacing until he collapsed into another round of nightmares? Or the Lucas who then and again threw out a joke, played with Flynnie, even spent hours today helping collect apples in the field?

It'd been vital that they clean up as much fallen fruit

as they could as quickly as possible. Apples that had been on the ground more than twelve hours could end up with bacteria, making them a health hazard to consume raw. With so much of the crop damaged, they had to save what they could.

"Willa says maybe her original estimation was wrong," Lucas said as he sidestepped a barrel. "The entire east field is unscathed. We maybe lost only sixty, sixty-five percent of the crop."

Only? It was still far too much. She didn't know what they were going to do from here. Some of the damaged crop was still salvageable, could be bagged and sold as "seconds" in the store. But ending the season with a profit seemed more unlikely than ever.

It wasn't just the crop loss. They'd need to re-mulch, which meant buying who-knew-how-many bags. She still hadn't purchased hay for the bales they'd place throughout the orchard in winter. The hay bales attracted mice, the scent of mice attracted bumblebees, and the bumblebees helped pollinate come spring. The storm had knocked over several of the younger trees, ripped out the limb spreaders in others.

There was just . . . too much.

But Lucas had said "we." Had he finally begun to feel some ownership of the orchard?

At least the barn was just fine. Drew had been hard at work all day today, alongside several of the volunteers he'd rounded up. Finishing that project, hosting the tourism board, it might be her only chance now. Drew had worked right up until half an hour ago when he'd left to pick up his girlfriend who was in town for the annual Depot Days festival.

Would Beckett be out on the field in front of the depot with everyone else, watching the fireworks that always kicked off the weekend event?

She propped a lid atop the barrel. "Eric Hampton called?"

Lucas folded his arms and leaned against a shelf crowded with empty mason jars and apple cider jugs. "Yeah, and I don't think I need more than one guess to figure out who gave him my number."

At least he didn't sound irate. "What did he want?"

"Something about joining some softball league. But I'm not quite naïve enough to believe my pitching arm is the only reason he called. The guy has a counseling degree, if I'm not mistaken. I'm his next project."

"Or he's simply noticed that, since you've been home, you haven't had much in the way of a social life."

The jars on the shelf rattled as he pushed away. "Look, if you asked him to talk to me, Kit—"

"I didn't." Not exactly.

"I'm not mad. But a little pop psychology isn't going to do anything for me."

"But talking to someone might. And if you won't talk to me—"

"Then I'm certainly not going to talk to a dude who apparently doesn't have enough to do helping a bunch of former inmates." He plucked an apple from a plastic bag.

"Luke—"

"And no, I don't need a reminder that I fall into that category."

"I wasn't going to say that, I was going to say, don't eat that apple. That bag isn't from today. Those are ones waiting for compost. They fell before they were ripe, which means they probably have codling moth larvae."

"I don't know what that is, but it sounds gross." He dropped the apple. "Listen, Kit, I need to tell you something."

She hated the instant dread his words ushered in, was

so tired of feeling like she was fighting a losing battle.

"That buyer I told you about. He wants to come see the place in person. He owns an orchard up in Minnesota, and he's making a visit next week. He's going to stop here on the way." Lucas hurried through the explanation, obviously worried at how she'd handle the news.

But honestly, tonight, she just didn't have it in her to argue. "Fine."

"Even if we sell, Kit, he'll probably want to hire an onsite manager. I'm sure he'd give you the job."

"You wouldn't want it?"

"I told you, I want out. I want to start over somewhere else."

"And do what?"

He looked around the dimly lit space. "I don't know, but not this. I don't want a life where some tree disease or one measly storm can endanger your livelihood and wipe out months of work."

Her phone dinged, and she was instantly desperate for it to be Beckett. He'd missed that town council meeting and bit her head off at the bridge. He'd confused her by kissing her one minute and avoiding her the next. And yes, last night she'd needed to get away from the intensity of him, them.

But tonight . . . tonight she needed her best friend.

And maybe he needed her. Because it was true, all those things he'd said at the bridge. He'd spent weeks and weeks helping her, while his own goals teetered. He had his own set of frustrations. What had she done to help him?

She pulled her phone from her pocket and, despite everything, grinned when she saw the screen.

Fireworks. Watching from the roof. You coming?

"Gotta run, Lucas."

"Beckett?"

He had to ask?

She didn't bother stopping at the house to change, just hopped in the truck and drove the short distance to the Walker house. Clouds muted the last hint of sunset, the blue-gray sky void of glinting stars. No matter. Soon enough, booms of color would light up the night.

She knocked only once on the Walkers' front door. Surely everyone else was out at the depot. She made her way through the house, so familiar even after all this time. The expansive kitchen where she'd so often joined the family for breakfast. The comfortable living room where she'd frequently seen Case and Flora Walker watching old movies late at night as she left after an evening of hanging out with Beckett. The stairway, even now, cluttered with abandoned shoes and folded clothing waiting to be taken up to bedrooms.

Beckett's bedroom door was open, as was his screenless window. She climbed through.

"That was fast." He was lying on his back, arms folded underneath his head. He looked tired but comfortable, almost . . . tranquil.

Without a word, she crawled to his side and, after only a moment's hesitation, stretched out beside him. The warmth of him seeped through her jacket, his presence the balm she'd longed for all day. How had she let herself go six years without seeing him, talking to him?

How would she say goodbye when it came time for him to leave again?

"How are you, Kit? How's the orchard?"

A hazy moon slouched behind lacy clouds. She didn't answer. Only scooted closer.

"Objection. Non-responsive."

"The fireworks are going to start soon. I don't want to ruin the ambiance by talking." But she shifted onto her side, up on one elbow, so she could look at his face. He hadn't shaved today, but he must have showered recently because the tips of his hair were wet and he smelled clean. And good.

"What?" His eyebrows lifted at her studying gaze.

"How are you? Last night you seemed . . ."

He fingered a strand of her hair. "I'm fine."

"Objection. Vague answer."

"You don't know your court objections, Kit."

No, but she knew him. Something had changed since last night. But instead of pressing him, she settled once more beside him, this time with his arm outstretched beneath her shoulders.

The hushed sky waited. Elsewhere, the rest of the town gathered on blankets and lawn chairs in an open field. She could picture the clusters of people, the line of cars along the gravel road leading to the depot. Just like on the Fourth of July, kids would run around with sparklers while they waited, and parents would call out words of caution.

She'd always loved the wait almost as much as the fireworks themselves. Tonight was no exception.

"I went to my mom's grave today." Beckett's voice was soft. "With Dad."

"You did?" She felt his nod against her cheek. A distant squeal cut into the night. A trail of light, then a burst of color and a boom. "And?"

"And the fireworks are starting. I don't want to ruin the ambiance."

Perhaps that was best. Enjoy the lit-up night sky, the sound and the brilliance, while it lasted. It'd be over soon enough.

14

Kit stared at her computer monitor, had to read the lines twice to be sure she wasn't projecting her own wishful thinking onto the screen.

But no, she'd read Dad's email correctly the first time. He was coming home. He was coming home!

"Flynnie, this is so exciting I'm not even going to get after you for eating your own pillow." The little goat pattered over the office floor, nosing a fluff of cotton from the pillow she'd destroyed.

The shrill pulse of a power tool sounded from outside, no doubt Drew hard at work on the barn. He'd promised her a tour of the inside today, and an update on its progress. Now more than ever it was vital the project finish on time. Eight days until the representatives from the state tourism board would be here.

And Dad.

Hopefully a crowd of community members, too. The mayor and city leaders, Belinda and the Chamber of Commerce—everyone was going all out with plans to impress the state reps. This was what Maple Valley did best—pull together as one.

And ever since she'd stood up at that town meeting, Valley Orchard had become the centerpiece of their plans. They'd dubbed it "An Evening at the Orchard." There'd be guided walks and even a scavenger hunt by lantern light through the grove, wagon rides and cider. Apple-bobbing and other games for kids. And inside the barn, a dance with music provided by the antique victrola she'd found in the store's attic after the stairs were repaired.

She petted Flynnie on her way out of the office, leaving the door open so the animal could traipse along behind her if she wished.

The urge to text Beckett or, better yet, show up on his doorstep, nearly caught hold of her. But she'd been trying so hard since last week to give him space from everything orchard-related. Now that he'd completed his community service hours, he wasn't obligated to be here. She'd sensed his relief when he'd told her Friday night after the fireworks about being done. She'd had to squelch the rise of her own panic.

But she'd had a few days to adjust. To wrap her mind around the thought of not seeing him around the place every day anymore. It was best this way, wasn't it? Preparation for when he'd eventually leave for good.

A hodgepodge of leaves and dust scuttled across the gravel and grass. Only a few cars filled the parking lot but, for once, Kit didn't let it bother her. Because not too many bags of apples filled their shelves at the moment, either. Better to save their limited inventory for weekends, anyway.

In front of her, the barn gleamed bright cherry red against a backdrop of trees in varying shades of amber and fading green. The trim running up the barn's corners and around the gable dormers was a pure white—exactly the classic look Grandpa had envisioned. Unlike in a utilitarian barn, though, long windows were tucked into all four walls, skylights in the ceiling.

"Hey, Drew," she called when she spotted him rounding the corner of the barn, hefting what must be one of the countertops for the kitchenette at the back of the building. Someday when she had more funding available, if the barn proved a popular event destination like she hoped, maybe they'd put in a full commercial kitchen. But they'd make do with a little kitchenette for now.

"Here for your tour?" Despite the chill of the October day, perspiration dotted his forehead. The man had worked long hours every day except Sunday for the past month. Somehow, once the craziness of the coming weeks was over, she had to find a way to thank him.

"If you've got time, absolutely."

"Follow me in."

The massive barn doors, rigged on metal sliders above, were already open, but they were mainly for show. A second set of doors, sturdy and containing weather-resistant glass, were propped open with a pair of ten-gallon buckets.

The smell of paint and sawdust mingled as she stepped into the open space. The cedar floors were still covered in tarps and the interior drywall was in desperate need of paint.

"I know it looks sparse now, but this is the part where it moves quickly." Drew leaned the countertop he'd been carrying against the wall. "I've got an electrician coming to look at all the wiring tomorrow. The plumber has already finished with the kitchenette and the bathrooms."

Light spilled through the rafters overhead. They'd talked about building a second floor in what would've been a typical barn's hayloft. But with limited funds, they'd had to forgo that part of the project. And now, she decided, she liked it this way. It was open and airy and perfect. If they ever needed more space, they could expand outward instead of upward. "I love the way the skylights make it feel even bigger than it is."

Drew led her through the rest of the main room, pointing out features, explaining what still needed to be completed. "We'll have a half wall up by the end of today that will partially close off the kitchenette."

"And you still think we can be done by the fifteenth?"

"I think we can be done plenty before that if everything continues to go as planned. Four or five days and this place will be looking great."

"It already looks great." She turned a full circle, and by the time she faced Drew again, tears filled her eyes. "My grandparents would've loved to see this. My grandpa, especially. You took his vision and made it a reality, Drew."

Clearly her emotion made him uncomfortable. He looked to the ground, folding his cap in his hands. "It's been my pleasure. Truly." He lifted his gaze and grinned. "Besides, I kinda need to propose to Maren one of these days. We're both getting sick of driving back and forth between here and the Twin Cities. But seeing how she's a writer and I'm a one-man startup business, well, I appreciate the work."

She blinked away her tears. "Is Maren going to move here or are you moving there?"

Drew returned to the countertop. "She's moving here. She stayed here for a few weeks last Christmas and was totally charmed by the town. Calls it enchanting. I keep trying to tell her the right word is bizarre, but she only laughs me off. She's crazy about Maple Valley."

"And our resident carpenter."

His smile spread as he hefted the countertop. "Can't argue with that."

She couldn't deny the pang of envy that tried to slither in as she left him to his work. But no. There was too much to be happy about today. The barn was coming along. Dad was coming home. Even after the hailstorm, there was still a chance this season might be a modest success.

Certainly, there'd be no massive profit. Grandpa had always made the bulk of his revenue selling crop to fruit vendors—the store was only a small slice. Less crop equaled less income.

But at least there'd be no major debt. All the barn expenses had come from her own account, thanks to that personal loan from Willa. So maybe, just maybe . . .

She stepped into the ochre light of a harvest sun, caught sight of Flynnie bounding across the yard, the new autumn mums she'd planted just yesterday brightening the walkway to the store . . . and Lucas walking with a man she didn't recognize toward the machine shed.

Rickety confusion lingered for only a moment before realization set in. Of course.

His buyer.

"Why don't you email him?" Beckett tossed the question over his shoulder as he trekked through Dad's house, Raegan trailing him while the doorbell dinged incessantly. Someone out there needed a lesson in patience.

"I'm not emailing Bear."

He thudded down the carpeted stairs of the split foyer, about ready to cover his ears if whoever was at the door didn't lay off. "Then call him or Skype him or something. He's in South America, not Timbuktu."

Raegan's footsteps thumped behind him. "I'm not

calling him, I'm not Skyping him, I'm not anything him. He's been gone for three months, Beck. I'm over it."

He toed a shoe out of the way and reached for the door. "You're not over it."

Hadn't he just found his sister minutes ago, slumped in Dad's recliner, staring listlessly out the window? That was a pining girl pose if he ever saw one. "I'm just saying, do something. If you miss the guy—"

"I don't."

He pulled the door open.

"Finally."

"Webster?"

The teen budged in, shaking the hood of his sweatshirt off his head and looking past Beckett and Rae. "Is Colton here?"

"Uh, no. He doesn't actually live here."

"But your sister does, so I thought . . ." Webster rubbed his palm over his close-cropped hair. "Never mind."

He turned to leave, but Beckett grabbed hold of his hood to stop him. "Not so fast. If something's wrong, you might as well spill it."

"But Colt—"

"Is spending the day with Kate. Trust me, you won't find him in Maple Valley." Apparently they'd decided to try and plan their whole wedding in one day. And Kate had said she wanted her fiancé all to herself while they did so. Wasn't a chance that would happen in town. Colton Greene might have been a national celebrity even before moving to Maple Valley, but from what Beckett could see, around here he was a downright superstar. He'd helped sandbag during the flood last year, then opened up a nonprofit right here in town. The community had embraced him so fully, it wouldn't surprise Beckett if one day they all forgot he wasn't even a native.

The man's entire life, his career, all his plans, had changed on a dime. But instead of clinging to his old life, Colton had found a way to start fresh in a new place with a new dream.

Which was exactly what Beckett was trying to do. Which was why he had to finish that JAG Corps application once and for all, do whatever it took to get another FSO interview. So far, his calls and emails had gotten him nowhere. He was running out of time.

Webster finally sighed and kicked off his shoes. "You got pop?"

Beckett swallowed a laugh. "Always. Everyone in this house is a caffeine addict."

He led Webster up the stairs, realizing Raegan had disappeared at some point. Probably figured this was her best chance for escape from his brotherly badgering. He just hated seeing her this way. Oh, she put up a good front most of the time. But he'd caught her distanced expressions when she thought no one was paying attention. She'd picked up a fourth part-time job, too. He had no idea how she managed to juggle her schedule, but he had a feeling the juggling was her way of staying distracted.

All he knew was, his little sister wasn't nearly as content as she professed to be.

Then again, what right did he have to be giving any kind of romantic advice? He'd gone and fallen for his best friend. Hard. She was his last thought at night and his first thought in the morning, lingering around the edges of every thought in between. She was, quite simply, his favorite person in the world.

"I'm just saying, do something." His words to Raegan. But what was *he* supposed to do? He could no more stay in Maple Valley, career-less, without a purpose, than he could ask Kit to leave the orchard.

"You just gonna keep standing there or what?"

Beckett blinked, the blast of cold air from the refrigerator door he'd apparently opened billowing around him. He moved aside. "Help yourself."

The kid downed half a can of Dr. Pepper before walking a slow circle around the island in the sprawling kitchen. It'd always been the family's gathering place. Beckett hated to think how many Walker breakfasts he'd missed these past six years.

How many he'd miss when he left again.

And Dad—what would he do in this massive house when Kate married and Raegan finally moved out? Seth had already moved out of the basement and Beckett, of course, was on his way out eventually.

"This is a nice house," Webster said after another long swig.

The kitchen opened into a dining room with patio doors that overlooked the spacious backyard. Fallen leaves blanketed the lawn, the throng of trees leading into the ravine looking barer by the day—especially after that storm last week.

"What's up, Web? School? Football? Did Amanda ever get in contact with you?"

He set his pop can on the granite countertop. "I need a ride to Des Moines."

"Your parents—"

"They're really busy."

He'd met Webster's adoptive parents a time or two—Laura and Jonas Clancy. Nice folks.

"Besides, I haven't told them . . ." Doubt clouded Webster's face.

Beckett opened the fridge to grab his own soda. "Look, you don't have to talk to me if you don't want. We can stay strictly tutor and student and that's fine. But I did go to Ames and then Chicago just to harass a couple social workers for you. So I *can* be helpful, and at the moment, looks like I'm all you've got available."

Webster dropped onto a stool at the counter, fiddled with the top of his pop can. "Thing is, I wasn't entirely honest with you."

"About?" he prodded.

"My reason for wanting to find Amanda."

Beckett plunked his can down. "Webster, I vouched for you. I said you were just a friend who was concerned—"

"I was. I am. I just . . . here." He pulled his phone from the pocket of his hoodie, tapped a couple keys, and slid it to Beckett.

"You want me to read your text messages?"

"The foster parents Amanda and I lived with for a while had a twenty-year-old son, Jake, who'd stop by all the time, stay overnight sometimes. Total creep, I couldn't stand him. He hated me. We got into it a few times. But he liked Amanda and, who knows why, but I think she liked him and he's bad news. Don't know if he's dealing drugs, but he's doing them. My birth mom was always strung out. I know the look."

Beckett's heart lurched at that. "But Amanda's in Illinois now."

"Read the texts. They're from Jake."

He picked up Webster's phone, scrolled through the messages.

Guess who I've been talking to? Calls me every night. Does she call you?

Amanda says hi.

Took a road trip to Chicago this weekend. Did a little sightseeing if you know what I mean.

"Yeah, this guy's a piece of work."

"I thought he was just being his stupid bully self at first, but then Amanda finally texted me, too. Last week. Said she doesn't like living with her relatives, after all, and she's leaving the minute she turns eighteen. Said she already has a place to go. I haven't heard from her since."

The pieces were beginning to fall into place. "But that doesn't mean—"

"She turned eighteen on Saturday!" He knocked over his empty pop can as he jerked to his feet.

"And let me guess, this Jake lives in Des Moines."

"In a crummy apartment with two other dudes. He invited Amanda once when we were still living with his parents, and I went along 'cause I had this feeling if I didn't something would happen. And I have the same feeling now."

Beckett sighed. "So you want to drive down there and what? Barge in?"

Webster's chest puffed. "If I have to."

Huh, maybe Webster had the right idea. Just go after the girl, consequences be hanged. "Webster, you told me Amanda was just a friend. If this is a male ego competition thing—"

"It's not. She is just a friend."

He'd heard that one before. From his own lips about a thousand times. "Even so, if she's eighteen, she's not a minor anymore. She's old enough to make her own decisions, even if they're bad ones."

Webster shoved away from the counter. "Thanks for the pop."

"Webster."

But he was already skulking through the living room. He bounded down the steps. "I'll find someone else to give me a ride."

"Will you just wait a sec?" He marched after the

teen, but Raegan's voice from the stairway leading to the second floor stopped him.

"Beckett! Beck! Your phone was ringing in your room and I went to grab it so I could bring it to you but it'd been ringing a while by then, so I answered." She about ran into him on his way to catch Webster. "It's a JAG officer. He's calling to schedule an interview."

The front door slammed. He looked from the door to Raegan to the phone in her hand.

"You shouldn't be working so late."

At the sound of Beckett's voice, Kit pushed a tree branch out of the way and leaned over the side of her ladder. A pale harvest moon danced in his eyes as he tipped his head up. Past him and stretching over the rolling field, rows of trees brushed in shadows of black and blue by the dark tarried in various states of survival after last week's storm. Some with craggy branches half bare, many stripped of most of their fruit.

But there'd been this hearty patch of trees in the east field that somehow entirely escaped the storm's path. With one hand, Kit balanced the half-filled basket atop the ladder. "You forget, though, I love the apple-picking part of the job. Especially when it's a Honeycrisp tree."

Beckett ascended the opposite side of the ladder until he met her at the top. "Because Honeycrisp are your favorite. Because while they taste good picked straight from the tree, they can develop even more complex flavor after being stored for a time in a dry, cool place. And they can survive temperatures of negative forty degrees."

She stared across the ladder's top at him.

"What? I listen when you talk, Kit Danby." He propped his arms on the top of the ladder. "What are you thinking right now?"

She was thinking about when exactly it was she'd stopped seeing him as just the kid she used to go fishing with. How it was possible to turn breathless at the sight of someone she'd seen countless times before.

When he was going to leave and just how she'd get along without him.

"Well?"

"I'm thinking I've missed you the past few days."

"You're not alone." His gaze dropped to her lips, and for an evanescent moment, she thought for sure he'd lean over the ladder and kiss her. Instead, he reached for her basket. "Willing to call it quits for the night? It's past nine and I've got something to show you."

She nodded and climbed down the ladder. He grasped her hand as soon as her feet touched the ground, her basket under his other arm.

His steps were unhurried as he led her from the field. She forced herself not to look around, scour the trees that hadn't been as lucky as the few at the edge. What had that man, the potential buyer, seen when Lucas gave him a tour? A devastated crop? Or trees that would only stand that much stronger next year after having their load lightened too early this season?

She leaned into Beckett. "How's your dad? Surgery's next week, right?" He hadn't told her much about his conversation with Case last week, only that it'd been a long time coming.

"It's next Friday, day after the big orchard event. Sorry I haven't been much help with that, by the way. I seem to be really good at big ideas, but not always at making sure they play out."

They emerged from the line of trees bordering the

orchard onto the public grounds. Stars glistened like a scattering of gems across the sky.

He stopped. "Even if it's not cancer, it's his brain, you know? One slip of the surgeon's hands and everything from his speech to his vision to his mobility could be impacted. I mean, maybe he's had the right idea all along, putting off the surgery. He gets headaches now and then, but a person can live with that. And if it's not cancer . . . I'm rambling."

"I don't tend to get tired of your rambling, Beck."

He set the basket of apples on the store's porch, looked at her for a long moment. "Come on."

"Why? Where?"

"The barn. You'll see." He tugged her toward the structure, heaved open sliding doors, and before they'd even entirely parted, the glow from inside beckoned her.

Twinkle lights—strings and strings of them—were wrapped around every beam and thrown over the rafters. They draped like ribbons back and forth overhead and turned the empty space into an enchanting hollow.

"You said there could never be too many twinkle lights." He stepped up behind her, his presence only deepening the magic of this moment.

"When did you . . . ?" She was too breathless to finish the question. He must've climbed the scaffolding Drew hadn't taken down yet in order to get up to the rafters. "Why . . . ?"

"Because you've had a rough few days, and I knew it'd make you happy. And because Kate and Colton were planning their wedding today and they aren't sure where to hold it and I told them the barn would be perfect. They'll be over here in a little while to look around."

"Are you serious?"

"And also because I've got something to celebrate." He came around to face her and pulled a sheet of paper from his back pocket. "But first, I need a signature. Sylvia called me today. My community service isn't officially done until you sign the paperwork. I should've brought a pen, though."

"Good thing I was too lazy to go looking for a hair tie today." She reached around behind her hair to pull out the pen she'd twisted her hair around on the way out to the field. The faintest, unwelcome trace of hesitation accompanied the scratching of her pen as she signed. It felt too official, too much like an ending.

And yet, he had to have spent hours hanging all these lights. For Kate and Colton, yes, but also for *her*.

She mustered a deep breath as she handed the paperwork back, and when she met his gaze, she realized he'd read every one of her trickling thoughts. But all he did was pocket her pen.

"You just stole my writing utensil."

"Because your hair's so pretty down and loose like this."

The rich timbre of his voice made her shiver. Or maybe it was the lights. Or the heady combination of the cool night air mingling with the warmth of Beckett's closeness.

"Is that what we're celebrating? Your community service being done?"

"No, something else."

"So tell me."

"One more thing I want to do first." In a sure step forward, he filled the space between them and lifted his hands to her cheeks. He traced her lips with his thumbs, and his voice rasped. "The thing I've been thinking about every day since Boston."

His kiss was soft at first, tentative and feather-light. But not for long. The moment she leaned in, he shifted, kissing her with enough intensity to send scurrying thoughts of anything outside the barn doors.

She was lost. She was found. She was *home.* All those years of friendship with Beckett. How had she not known?

The rhythm of her heart hadn't a hope of steadying; her breath, not a chance of catching. His fingers moved from her face to her hair and then down her back until he'd nearly lifted her off her feet. She gasped, tightening her own hold.

Until he pulled back, eyes the color of midnight. "Kit."

She couldn't find her voice underneath her trembling emotion.

"I got a new FSO interview."

She blinked, cold air stilling in her lungs as her feet touched the ground.

"It's next week, Thursday. In Des Moines, at Drake." His hands were still clasped behind her back, his sentences darting one after another, as if by blurting them fast enough, he might lessen their effect.

"Thursday? That's when the tourism board is here."

"I know, and I'm really sorry. But it took so long to get this thing lined up."

Movements sluggish and unsure, she disentangled herself from him. That was what he was celebrating? "Okay. Um, well, I'm glad it . . . that you . . ." *No.* No, she wasn't glad. And if she lied, he'd see right through her. He always did.

Before she could entirely pull away, he cupped her face in his hands. "What if you came with?" There was a hushed intensity to his question.

"What?"

"Not to the interview. I mean later. If I get in. I know you have plans for the orchard, I do. But imagine for a second it wasn't a factor, and you could pick up and go somewhere new. Have an adventure." His hands slid down her shoulders, down her arms. "With me."

Before he could grasp her hands, she scrambled backward. "I can't just pick up and leave, Beck. I'm in the middle of the season and I've got a major event next week and Dad's coming home—"

"He is?"

"And Lucas is traipsing around with this prospective buyer."

"Maybe that's a sign, Kit."

"So I'm just supposed to walk away?"

"It wouldn't be immediate. And why does it have to be walking away? Why can't it be walking toward something?"

For all of a dizzying moment, she let herself latch onto the hope in his voice, the romance of what he was asking her. Except . . . "What exactly *are* you asking me, Beck?"

As if sensing a chink in her armor, he caught her hands. "I'm asking you to come with me."

"As what?"

"As . . ."

His pause said too much and not enough. "You don't even know what you're asking me. Have you really thought about this? Planned any further ahead than the next kiss?"

"If that's an offer—"

"I'm not like you, Beckett. You got a phone call from an Army officer in August and within twenty-four hours hopped a plane to Iowa. I spent a month deliberating after Lucas emailed me this summer. I'm not like you. I'm not . . ."

His eyes darkened as he dropped her hands. "Not what?"

Impulsive. Reckless. She'd called him those things

once. She wouldn't again. Tears pooled in her eyes. How was this happening? Two minutes ago her every emotion was soaring on wings of hope and anticipation and . . . love?

Yes. *Yes.* She loved him. *Oh,* she loved him.

But she also loved her home and this land and the way she felt when she poured herself into it. It was a part of her.

So is Beckett.

But they'd only just discovered this new layer of their friendship. It had been all of—what, two, two and a half weeks?—since he'd kissed her on the shore of Salt Island. They'd never even talked about it. And now he was asking her to jump with no sense of whether she might land in grass or sea or a pile of rocks.

"When God calls us to something, it doesn't mean we're never going to have setbacks."

Willa's words. But this wasn't a setback. This was her heart laid bare and bleeding.

Because she knew, somewhere crazy-deep and convincing, that she was supposed to stay. That she couldn't cut and run. Even if it was hard, even if Dad was doubtful and Lucas was persistent. Even if another storm came charging through. Even if Beckett left.

Burn your ships.

But why, *why* did Beckett have to be one of those ships, drifting away from her all over again right in front of her eyes? His back was to her now, one hand combing through the hair so obviously in need of a cut.

Maybe if for once she could do what he'd done so many times before—find the right words, convince him . . .

To what? Give up *his* dream? How was that any more right than her walking away from the orchard? "Beck—"

"I should go."

"Don't. We can talk this out." Hot tears pooled in her eyes.

He turned to face her under the frame of the barn door, moonlight silhouetting him from behind. "I don't think we can. We both knew, didn't we? It's why we skirted around it for weeks." He shook his head, gaze softening underneath his hurt. "It's okay, Kit. Maybe this was just another one of those big ideas I can't make play out. But I'm not walking away angry this time. I promise."

But he *was* walking away.

And the ache was simply too much.

15

This was what Beckett had been waiting for. All this time—the paperwork, the references, the endless phone calls trying to land another interview. All for this.

And he was about to blow the entire thing.

Focus. You just have to focus.

But how was he supposed to do that with Kit in his head? Maybe a week should've been enough to dull the bruises of their argument in the barn. Maybe he should be able to sit here thinking about his future instead of feeling his present crumble. But he'd never been good at "shoulds."

And he was pretty sure Field Screening Officer Adam Hunter wasn't buying his pretense of calm.

The walls of the claustrophobic study room off the Law Library of Drake University seemed to close in on him as the JAG Corps representative scribbled a note on the paper in front of him. The paneled glass in the door window rattled as a student with a backpack lumbered past.

"Right. Okay, then." The officer looked up, hazel-eyed gaze even and unrevealing. If Beckett had to guess, he'd place the man in his mid-forties. "We've covered the basics—degree, work experiences. What I'm curious about, Beckett, is why now?"

"Excuse me, sir?" He fingered his collar, wishing he hadn't cinched the tie around his neck so tightly earlier today. But he'd been distracted as he'd knotted the thing in the bathroom across from his childhood bedroom. Thinking of Kit. Thinking of Dad and his surgery tomorrow afternoon.

Thinking of Webster. At least there was one person he wasn't letting down. He'd convinced Webster not to go racing off to Des Moines on his own last week. Told him if he'd just wait, he could come along on Beckett's trip.

"But anything could happen in a week. If Amanda's with Jake—"

"Then that's where she wants to be. She's not a little kid, Webster. You can't force her to leave." His response had been a little too sharp, a little too personal.

Webster was waiting for him out in the library now, his patience likely wearing as thin as Beckett's concentration.

"All the rest of the individuals I'll be speaking with on this campus visit are still in law school. Even a few first-years." Hunter glanced once more at the folder on the table—the one with the paperwork and letters and transcripts that summed up the last decade of Beckett's life. "Whereas you're three years into the private sector. What sparked your interest in the JAG Corps?"

Lines he'd rehearsed climbed up his throat—a few even made it out. His lifelong respect for the Army thanks to his father's service and long-time interest in military law. His dissatisfaction with corporate firm life and his desire to do something different.

"I know it's probably a different route than many of the men and women you interview, but—" Beckett cut off as his cell phone blared from his pocket. He flinched, fumbling to yank the thing free. "I'm so sorry, sir. I can't believe I forgot to turn it . . ." His voice trailed as he caught sight of the screen. Kate? Why in the world would she call now? When she knew Beckett was in the middle of this interview?

"Do you need to answer it?"

The officer didn't so much as cock an eyebrow, but Beckett heard the hint of reproof behind the question.

"Uh, no." He silenced the phone before abandoning it to the table. "Again . . . sorry."

Hunter nodded before making another note in the open file in front of him. Probably something along the lines of *too dumb to turn off his phone before the most important interview of his life.*

Beckett could kick himself.

Behind the officer, a sliver of a window looked out on the law school's Cartwright Hall. Across 27th Street, residence buildings were clustered into the center of campus. Steely clouds didn't roll so much as tramp through a sky gray as the walls of this room. If Kit were here, she'd whip out the cloud classification and predict whether they carried rain.

Snappish regret tunneled through him. Beckett had tried to leave the emotion behind where it belonged—back in Maple Valley, back in last week. But it'd proven as impossible as trying to rake leaves in the rain. It clung to him now, soggy and stubborn and threatening to undo him in front of the man he most needed to impress.

The officer closed his file. "You're prepared to deploy?"

The question caught Beckett off guard. "Uh, yes, sir. I mean, that's one of the reasons I started looking into the Corps in the first place. I want to serve. I like the thought of traveling."

One corner of Hunter's mouth actually lifted. "This

wouldn't be sightseeing."

"Oh, I realize that. Of course. It's just—"

His phone. Again. This time just vibrating, but against the tabletop in the tiny room's emptiness, it might as well have been a roar. He slipped it the quickest glance. *Raegan?*

The first needle of concern threaded through him.

"Mr. Walker—"

He snagged the phone and lowered it out of sight. "Sir, I can't apologize enough. Clearly, my family—"

"That's part of what we need to talk about. Deployment is tough on a family. I've seen it cause divorce, people missing funerals or the births of their children." The officer leaned forward, palms flat on the table between them. "I watched the dawning play across a kid's face just an hour ago when he realized deployment would mean missing entire NFL seasons."

"Well, I'm more of a basketball guy, so we don't have to worry about that."

He waited for the officer to crack a smile. Clearly a practice in futility. "Officer Hunter, can I speak plainly?"

"That would be what we're here for."

Beckett had to work to keep the frustration from his tone. How many times would he have to defend this decision? Argue his way into convincing somebody—anybody—that he'd thought this through? That he knew what he was doing. "I'm not here on a whim. My path might've been a little unconventional, but I have worked hard to prepare for this potential transition. I understand what deployment means."

Except do you really?

That voice again. The one sagging with doubt. The one that'd gotten louder the longer he was home. The more time he spent with his family.

With Kit.

But Officer Hunter appeared to accept his words at face value, because he offered a nod and laced his fingers in a relaxed pose. "All right, then. Let's talk a little about past leadership experiences."

Just as Beckett opened his mouth, his phone pulsed for the third time, surprising him enough that he dropped it. He nursed a caged groan.

"I think you should probably go ahead and answer." It wasn't a question.

Beckett's limbs dragged as he reached for the phone. Logan this time. He was going to kill him. "I'll just be a second." No use apologizing again.

He jiggled the door handle, dodging the officer's eyes as he slipped from the room. He wrenched the phone to his ear. "*What?*" In long, juddered strides, he darted down the library aisle, titan-sized bookshelves reaching to the ceiling.

"Whoa, you answered? Great, I'm probably interrupting your interview—"

He yanked open the library's glass door, cold air smacking into him. "Not probably. You are." The growl of the clouds matched his voice.

"I'm sorry."

"Do you have any idea how important this is for me?"

"You're angry, I get it. You can take a swing at me later if it'll make you feel better."

He paced the cement walkway. "One swing is so not going to cover it."

"Would you just shut up for a second?"

Beckett tipped his head toward the pallid sky, churlish wind raking over him. Logan's pinched tone, its volume, stole away his tumbling exasperation and replaced it with instant worry.

Logan never raises his voice. And he wouldn't call

now if it wasn't important.

"Is something wrong with Charlie?"

"No, take the next ramp." His brother was talking to someone else. Amelia?

"Logan?"

He heard the phone shift. "Sorry. Charlie's fine. She's with me and Amelia. We're on the way to Iowa City."

Iowa City. But why today? Dad's surgery wasn't until tomorrow afternoon. A band of students walked past him, laughing and oblivious.

"Dr. Ostler's first surgery tomorrow got postponed and they're moving Dad's up. He'll go in first thing in the morning, so we're all heading there tonight."

Beckett pushed away from the wall. "In that case—"

"Don't cut off your interview. You're only a couple hours from Iowa City. You'll get there later tonight and it'll be fine. You've got plenty of time."

Except the last time he'd thought he had plenty of time . . .

"If you guys are all on your way, then I should be too." He started down the sidewalk toward his car, then shook his head and turned. He should at least let Officer Hunter know why he was leaving.

"Beck, I wouldn't even have called yet if I'd thought you'd answer. I figured your phone would be off and it'd go to voicemail."

"Probably the same thing Kate and Rae thought."

"They called, too? I guess we all just really wanted to make sure, well . . . I know Dad didn't want . . ." Logan's voice grew distant again as he gave Amelia more directions.

Didn't want Beckett to feel like the last to know again. "Logan—"

"It's going to be fine, Beck. And I'm really sorry I interrupted the interview."

“Did you talk to him? Is he doing okay? Are you doing okay?”

“Everybody’s all right. I promise.”

He heard the almost-crack in Logan’s voice, the strain. Something trenchant and cold grated over him as he stepped aside so a student could exit the library. The sudden desperation to be with his family consumed him, and if he’d thought he hadn’t been able to focus before . . .

“Go in there and give one of your best lawyer arguments and convince that officer you’re a JAG. Okay? We’ll see you later tonight.”

Beckett hung up a second later and retraced his way through the library, gaze pinned on the door leading into the study room. He could see Officer Hunter through the narrow window, just sitting there, waiting. Was there any point in finishing the interview? He’d already bungled it—his lack of focus, his phone.

“Beckett, what is it?”

Webster. He’d completely forgotten.

“We have to make this fast.”

“I know, you’ve said that twenty times already.” Webster zipped up his sweatshirt and started toward the decrepit-looking building.

After cutting his interview short as graciously as he could, everything in Beckett had wanted to backtrack on his promise to the kid. Skip going to this Jake guy’s apartment and head straight to Iowa City, Webster in tow, whether he liked it or not.

But Logan was right—Iowa City was barely two hours away and it wasn’t even seven yet. There was plenty of time to make a quick stop, just long enough for Webster to make sure his friend was okay.

If she was even here.

What in the world would make a girl *want* to live here? Crumbling brick and cracked windows, overgrown weeds lining the walkway to the front door. Par for the course in this neighborhood, it seemed.

"I'm not feeling great about this, Web." Wasn't feeling great about anything at the moment. He'd walked away from an interview he was well on his way to bombing even before Logan had called. What if he'd finally, once and for all, blown his chances? And now he was about to enter a building that could've made an awfully convincing haunted house without any effort at all.

"Now you see why I'm worried about her?" Webster yanked open the front door.

"But you don't know that she's here. For all you know, she's still back in Chicago doing just fine."

"So why won't she text me back?" His voice echoed as he moved toward the cement stairwell just inside the door. "And if you're right and she's not here, then good. At least I'll know that much."

The smell of burnt toast permeated the air, muffled voices rising from every direction. They climbed two sets of stairs before spilling into a corridor, painted walls chipped and peeling. Webster stopped in front of Apartment 327, the 7 at the end hanging crookedly.

He hesitated only for a moment before lifting his fist. Beckett hung back, waiting. This felt wrong. Was it just worry about Dad?

Webster knocked again, harder this time. "Jake! Open up."

A door across the hall opened and a man stuck his head out. "Oh. Thought you were the police."

"The police?"

The man stepped out, shirt unbuttoned, revealing a potbelly. "Called 'em fifteen minutes ago at least. Bad enough imagining what that kid's dealing out of there, but the shouting tonight—I lost patience."

Webster stiffened. "Shouting? Is there a girl in there?"

The man shrugged and Webster whirled back to the door, pounding now. "Amanda, are you in there?"

"Web, if the cops are on their way—"

Webster kicked the door, and it sprang open.

"Webster!" But he'd already barged inside, calling for Amanda. His panic became Beckett's. He hurried in after Webster, the smell of something pungent and sickly sweet wafting over him. Pot. Probably something else, too. "We can't be in here, especially not . . ." His focus snagged on a kid sprawled out on a couch, arms and legs draped over the sides. What had they walked into?

Webster had already disappeared into a bedroom. The sound of footsteps on the stairwell registered.

"Webster, we need to leave *now*."

"Amanda!"

He followed Webster's voice, passing a kitchen he didn't have to look into twice to know it wasn't meals they were cooking in there. He found Webster in a bedroom, kneeling over a bare mattress, shaking a girl's body.

Webster flung a scared look over his shoulder. "She's breathing, but she's definitely high on something."

"Hey, what's going on here?"

The kid from the couch stood in the doorway behind them. He looked from Beckett to the bed to Webster.

It happened too fast: Webster's guttural yell. "I'll kill you!" His lunge across the room. The clash of bodies and fists.

Beckett sprung toward the brawl. “Webster, stop—”

They crashed into a vanity with a broken mirror, Beckett reaching desperately for Webster, trying to pull him free. Until a pair of arms yanked *him* away. He fell backward against a closet door while the police officer who’d come charging into the room wedged himself between Webster and the guy who must be Jake.

He cradled the arm that had hit the closet door, elbow throbbing, breathless. “You all right, Web—”

“Neighbor was right.” A second officer marched in. “It’s all right there in the kitchen. I’m going to call Buckley to get him down here for bagging and pics.”

Webster shot him a helpless look before glancing at the bed again. The girl—Amanda, he assumed—was sitting up now.

“Sir,” Beckett said, “the one in the hoodie and myself, we don’t have anything to do with this.”

“Save it for the station.”

This couldn’t be happening. If they were arrested, it could be hours before they were let out. Worse, they could be booked overnight until an arraignment and . . .

Dad.

“You don’t understand—” He tried again, but the sinking feeling in his gut was confirmed by the officer’s head shake and the clatter of handcuffs.

Autumn was finally here to stay. Kit could feel it claiming its territory, raking through tree branches that shivered against a moaning wind. It wasn’t quite the stunning fall day they’d all hoped for as they’d planned for the state tourism board’s visit. But at least those ashen cirrus clouds didn’t carry any rain.

The thumping of the machine shed's door, its jangling hinges, carried across the span of dusty yard to where she stood on the store's porch, watching the mayor lead their esteemed visitors around the orchard.

But where was Dad? Lucas should've returned from the airport an hour ago.

He's not the only one you're watching for.

She took a tattered breath, couldn't deny it. There was a piece of her that still hoped Beckett might whisk in like he had so many times before—always there, right when she needed him most. Of course he had that interview in Des Moines, but it was only an hour's drive back. He could still show up.

But after a week of silence, did she really expect it?

She'd wounded him. He'd walked away. They'd been here before.

She'd thought so many times of going over to the Walker house, forcing him to talk to her. But what would be the point? Nothing had changed. She couldn't give up on the life she'd begun to build for herself here, not when she'd worked so hard, invested so much.

Plus, it wasn't just about her—it was about Grandma and Grandpa's legacy and all her employees, the guys from Hampton House. She'd heard that buyer of Lucas's—he didn't plan to keep the orchard open as a tourist spot, but solely as a fruit farm. He'd probably hire fewer workers, work them longer hours, and pay them lower wages.

Show me that I did the right thing, God, please.

"Milt's gotta be happy. I think the state reps are duly impressed." Willa's voice emerged from the store.

Kit jumped. "I didn't realize you were back there."

"Eric and I traded places. He's leading the next lantern walk, I'm manning the store for a while. Not that we've got much business at this point. Most people are having fun outside or dancing in the barn."

Dusk cast shadows all around, but just enough light remained to showcase the colors of what leaves remained on the trees. The field behind the orchard buildings was a tapestry of fiery reds and oranges and yellows. Lanterns placed throughout the grounds glowed from all directions.

Music and laughter, pirouetting light, drifted from the barn. All the final work on the building had been completed in the last week. Floors stained and walls painted. She'd washed every window herself just yesterday and then spent the entire afternoon and evening decorating the interior—tulle wrapped around beams, refreshment tables set up along the walls and ornamented with fall-themed centerpieces.

And of course, the twinkle lights.

The pang hit her again.

"You can't just stand here all night waiting, Kit."

"What is it with the men in my life not being here when I need them to be?" How many birthdays and holidays had she spent just like this—looking out a window or standing on the porch of her grandparents' house, just sure that *this time* Dad would show up? All those months during the war of having no idea where Lucas was, and then his repeat disappearance, though much shorter, this year.

And Beckett . . .

But it wasn't fair to include him. When she'd needed him this fall, he'd thrown himself into helping her. Early mornings, late nights, he'd worked so hard to make *her* dream possible. It was only lately he'd begun to drift.

But then, that was Beckett. He had a way of diving into things, all in, and then eventually pulling back when things didn't turn out the way he'd planned or he got tired of them. Basketball, his corporate law career, even the car he used to work on with his mom . . .

She sucked in a breath. Was that why she'd really said no that night in the barn? Because underneath all her other sensible objections was an underlying fear—that eventually he'd grow restless with her, too? That what had seemed exciting and romantic and had tugged on his Beckett Walker impulse would one day seem as tedious as his former job?

An eerie haze hovered in the air—one that didn't make sense. It wasn't warm enough, nor the clouds thick enough, to warrant trapped moisture. Perhaps she didn't know her Iowa weather as well as she'd thought.

"Maybe your dad's plane was late landing."

"Maybe."

Willa nudged her head toward the barn. "Go have some fun, Kit. Help Mayor Milt charm those state people. You put a lot of work into tonight. You should enjoy it."

But she'd put in the work so Dad could see it. And he wasn't here. Why wasn't he here?

She was halfway to the barn when she heard the spark. More like a boom, actually. What in the—

"Kit, what was that?" Willa's voice carried over the yard.

But Kit was already running. It couldn't be what it sounded like, but she raced to the side of the barn to make sure, dreading she'd find . . .

Exactly what she found. The electrical box sparking and smoking.

She jumped back as it blasted a second time, her shocked yelp covered up by the sound of a crackling. *No . . .*

She had to put it out before the wind fanned the baby flame, carried sparks to the roof or the trees. *If it turns into a full-blown fire . . .*

She had to get the people out first. She ran around to the front of the barn, but the crowd inside had already begun to realize something was wrong. Buzzing concern was rising throughout the room, and by the time she'd pushed in, people were scurrying for the door. "Stay calm!"

But then she saw it, what they must've seen—billowing smoke through the window. Just that fast, the fire had begun to climb. Mind spinning, she pushed through the frenzied crowd, frantic gaze landing on the tablecloth spread over a table.

She forced her way to the table, wrenched the linen free, and started weaving her way back to the exit. Someone screamed as shattering glass sounded over the chaos.

Please, no . . .

By the time she was back outside, hungry flames licked at the east wall, aided by barreling shafts of wind. Smoke clouded her vision as she stumbled to the fire. Desperate, determined, she thwacked the tablecloth at the fire. Tears stung her eyes, and her heart battered the inside of her chest, stilted prayers clogging her throat with no hope of making it past dry lips. Sparks leapt from the blaze as the fire clawed its way higher.

"Kit!"

Lucas came careening around the side of the barn.

"Help me, Luke."

"It's too windy. The blaze is already too much."

Her lungs burned, and a moan wracked her body. Even so, she flung the tablecloth at the fire once more. She lifted it again, only to be stopped by Lucas's arm around her waist. She struggled against him, but his hold was tight and his labored steps firm.

Within seconds he'd towed her away from the building, her half-charred tablecloth dragging along with her.

Somewhere behind the crackle and hiss of the flames, Willa's voice barked information to a 911 dispatcher.

"You okay?" Lucas yelled to be heard over the pandemonium.

"Where's Dad?" It came out a near sob.

The glow of the fire highlighted the regret in his eyes. "He didn't come, Kit."

"The flight didn't get in?"

He tugged the burned linen from her hands and let it drop to the ground. "It did. He just wasn't on it."

She sank into his arms and cried.

16

6:47 a.m.

Beckett burst through the doors of the hospital. This was wrong, it was all wrong. He should've been here last night with his family. He should've had the chance to talk with Dad, laugh with his siblings, pretend what was to come wasn't scaring them all.

But it'd been nearly one in the morning by the time the police had finally let him go. He'd wanted to leave right then, but common sense had forced him to find a hotel, get at least a few hours of sleep. Besides, Dad wouldn't be awake in the middle of the night.

At least he was here now. He could see Dad for a few minutes before the surgery.

6:48.

He'd tracked the turnover of every minute since leaving Des Moines. One hundred and seven minutes on Interstate 80. Six minutes snaking through Iowa City traffic to get to the university hospital. Two minutes parking.

He jabbed an elevator button, groaned at its slowness as it lugged him toward the surgery floor.

6:51.

At least Webster's parents had been able to get to Des

Moines. They were taking charge of Amanda, too.

The elevator dinged and he surged free, following signs with arrows and a maroon stripe on the wall in a half-jog until he arrived at the surgery wing's family waiting room.

6:52.

Winded and harried, he spurted into the room. "I'm here."

They were all there, scattered across the room. Logan and Amelia, Charlie still in her pajamas. Colton and Kate. Raegan. Seth and Ava.

"Where's Dad? Is he already in a room? Do I need a visitor badge or something to see him?"

Logan stood. "Beck—"

"Well, where is he? Why aren't any of you with him? He shouldn't be waiting alone."

His brother moved toward him. "He's already been taken into the operating room."

His breath left him in a whoosh. "But you said . . . you said eight or eight-thirty. It's not even seven."

Logan's eyes brimmed with apology. "I know. I didn't realize they'd take him back so early for the anesthesia."

At some point during Logan's explanation, Rae had wandered to his side. She leaned in for a partial hug. "He knew you were coming, Beck."

Everything in him constricted and bellowed, his nerves balled so tightly he might just come undone—right here in front of his family.

"I know how much it meant to you to be here, to get to see him . . . before." Logan. But a buzz in Beckett's head made it hard to hear him.

He felt Raegan's surprise when he pulled away. Felt the eyes of all his siblings, his cousin. Knew somewhere deep down he should take comfort in their presence and understanding.

But this was too much. Too familiar.

Before the crippling anguish could break free, he turned and fled the room.

17

Just a building. Just a collection of wood and metal. Maybe to see it reduced to blackened rubble shouldn't wound Kit so. But the reality of what she was looking at speared through her with such force it buckled her legs.

She landed with her palms in wet ground on either side of her, gravel digging into her knees. The bitter scent of smoke and ash still clung to the air this Saturday morning, nearly thirty-six hours after the fire.

It wasn't just the loss of the barn itself. It was seeing Grandpa's dream charred and destroyed. He'd poured that concrete foundation himself. He'd framed the building's outline. He'd envisioned its final design.

"Don't you love the idea of it, Kit? Valley Orchard will become a gathering spot year-round for this community. Weddings and family reunions and birthday parties. We're in the business of nurturing life, my girl."

Had there ever been anyone as buoyant and joy-loving as Grandpa?

Beckett.

Yes.

But that was another dream seemingly lost.

"Kit." Willa's gentle voice came up behind her. She'd stayed the night with Kit and Lucas on Thursday. Made them breakfast. Stayed again last night. And now she'd come with Kit to meet with the fire marshal.

"It's ruined."

Willa stood next to her. "But it's the only building that was ruined—none of the other buildings, none of the trees. Which is amazing considering how windy it was Thursday night. And nobody was hurt. That's the main thing."

She'd nearly forgotten about the tourism board members in the panic of the fire, the commotion of the crowd. By the time the fire department had settled the blaze, the weather had calmed and almost everyone had dispersed. Only Willa and Lucas had lingered.

No Dad. Lucas had told her later that, when Dad didn't show up at the airport, he'd called his cell number several times before finally trying his office number, only to find out from an assistant that a last-minute meeting had come up. Apparently Dad had emailed her the night before, but she'd been so busy with event prep she hadn't bothered with her inbox.

But wasn't this important enough that he could've called? Would it have been that hard to pick up the phone and *talk* to his daughter?

The boot-shaped footprints of the fire marshal and his assistant who'd come out this morning cluttered the ground around her. She'd been surprised they wanted to come on a weekend. If they hadn't, she'd likely still be holed up at the house.

"It would've worked, Willa. The building, I mean. Thursday night I had two different couples ask me about hosting weddings here." Not counting Kate and Colton. Although would they still want Kit involved in their wedding after the way things had ended with Beckett?

Why am I even worrying about this? There's no building. There won't be any weddings at the orchard.

"It can still work. The foundation's okay. Walls can be rebuilt."

"With what money? I spent my savings on this place. I spent *your* savings. We've lost the back half of this season's crop."

A biting wind swept over her as she watched the fire marshal round the barn, faced streaked with cinder. She stood, ready to hear his verdict as to what could've possibly caused a blaze to erupt so quickly. He stopped to inspect something near the ground.

"Kit—" Willa began.

"Please don't tell me this is just a setback, Willa, and that I shouldn't give up. I know it could've been a hundred times worse. I know the mature thing to do is buck up and square my shoulders and move forward. But I'm not there. Not yet."

Something of a smile flitted over Willa's face before she spoke. "I wasn't going to lecture you."

"Sorry," Kit muttered.

"In the past two weeks, you've been through a hail-storm and a fire and—judging by a certain young man's absence of late—maybe some heartache, as well. Last thing you need is an old woman's sermon." Willa's silver bangs shaded deep-set eyes brimming with compassion.

"You're not an old woman," Kit said.

"Tell that to my creaking joints. But what I was going to say is, you're not in this alone."

"Dad didn't even show up."

"His loss, Kit. It's always been his loss." Willa shielded her eyes from the sun with one hand. "I don't know if you remember this, but that month or so your father was home when you first moved here, I was around quite a bit."

"You've always been around." *Unlike Dad.*

Would she ever stop thinking thoughts like that?

Weighing everyone else's presence against Dad's absence?

"But I was around perhaps a bit more than needed during that time. I had supper almost every night with you kids and your grandparents and Mason. There were quite a few nights when your grandparents would turn in early and I'd stay and watch a TV show with the three of you."

Where was this going? And why was Willa reminiscing now of all times?

"You and Lucas would fall asleep, and your father and I would talk."

"Willa, are you saying—"

"I'm saying you aren't the only one who has wished from time to time that Mason Danby wasn't so blind to what all was waiting for him back in Maple Valley."

Kit simply stared. She'd had no idea. No earthly idea. "I didn't realize . . ."

"Oh, a silly woman's long-ago fanciful wish of inviting herself into someone else's family, it's not at all the same as a daughter's hurt. But sometimes knowing another person shares at least a hint of your grief, well, it can help."

"I'm not sure it's grief I feel as much as anger."

Flynnie ambled across the yard, coming up beside Kit and nudging her head into Kit's leg.

"Which is understandable. But allowing grief a little space to breathe, that can be awfully healing. Grief about your dad. Grief that you never got to know your mom. Grief about the fire and the barn and Beckett."

She might have cried if not for the tears she'd emptied in the past day. "What would I do without you, Willa?"

The older woman pulled her into a hug. "That's something you won't have to worry about for a long, long time, Lord willing."

The fire marshal's uncomfortable throat-clearing interrupted. Kit swallowed and stepped back. "I'm ready."

"Definitely electrical," he said as he pulled off his baseball cap and swiped his palm over his forehead. "Obviously a lot of it's charred, but it's easy enough to pinpoint where it started. Electrical box in the east wall."

Kit nodded. "That's where we saw the sparks. But it doesn't make sense. This was new construction. It's not like the wiring was old."

The fire marshal nodded. "True, but things like this happen. I was out at a fire a few months ago a couple counties away. Brand new house in a subdivision. Family had only moved in three weeks prior. Electrical fire started in the basement and consumed the entire house."

A fluke. She'd lost Grandpa's dream to a fluke.

"Although, it's also a possibility something chewed on some of the wiring. You're out in the country. Squirrels or chipmunks could've gotten to any exposed wiring. Or . . ." He looked down at the animal still nudging her leg.

Ohhh. She'd had Flynnie in and around the barn with her every day in the past week. She hadn't watched her closely. It was possible . . .

Kit closed her eyes as the probability pricked through her. When she opened them again, it was to see both Willa and the fire marshal eyeing her with twin concern.

"I can't believe my own pet might've caused the damage. Or an electrician's mistake." Or God was simply trying to get through her thick skull once and for all that she didn't belong here. That it hadn't been his voice urging her to plant herself here, grow roots, and watch a dream blossom.

She'd been holding on to a feeling, but look at the facts: the hail, the buyer, the fire, the barn. How much more had to happen before she got the message?

She hugged her arms to herself, her sweater flapping in the wind, several loose strings knotting from its frayed hem.

"I'll work up an official report," the fire marshal said. "I'm really sorry about the damage, Miss Danby. If there's anything else . . ."

"No. But thanks for coming out so quickly."

He shook her hand, then Willa's, and started for his vehicle.

"I have no idea what to do next, Willa." She'd closed the orchard for the weekend, obviously, but it might as well be for the season. She wasn't like Beckett—she didn't know how to charge forward without thinking and planning and lining up all her details.

She was sapped of energy and, worse, of desire.

Willa squeezed her shoulder. "You're not in this alone. You'll get through it with the help of people who care about you. You're not abandoned, Kit."

Abandoned.

The word felt like a stamp on her heart, regardless of what Willa said. Unerasable. She simply didn't have it in her anymore to hope.

How could that be his father lying so motionless?

Beckett stood in the doorway of the intensive care unit room. He'd only made it this far last night, when the doctor had first allowed family to visit in pairs. He'd walked with Raegan from the waiting room to here, but he couldn't make himself accompany her the rest of the way in.

Dad hadn't been awake then. He wasn't awake now.

The nurse adjusted one of the tubes protruding from Dad's head bandage. "You can come in, you know."

He made his legs work and entered. The room smelled of clean linens and greenery. So many plants of all shapes and sizes crowded the narrow windowsill, several balloons bobbing above the display. Everyone in Maple Valley must have sent something.

The nurse tucked a pillow under Dad's head, angling him slightly. "I'd ask if you're one of Case's sons, but the resemblance is so obvious, it'd be a silly question."

He couldn't look at Dad's face, not yet. So he looked at the IVs that disappeared into his arms. The pulse oximeter clipped to one finger. The bags hooked to a rolling machine with tubes threading to Dad's bandages.

"This is an EVD," the nurse explained. She fingered one of the tubes. "External ventricular drain. That helps us make sure there's no fluid buildup around the brain. There's an intracranial pressure monitor too. It does exactly what it sounds like—measures the pressure inside your father's head. We'll take that out later today, most likely."

He sank into a chair beside the bed, finally letting himself look at Dad's face. It was pale and slightly swollen. An oxygen mask covered his mouth and nose.

Let him live, God. Just let him live and give me so many more years with him.

The prayer had hovered like a ghost at the back of his mind, flimsy and translucent, since yesterday morning. No, since he'd first learned of the tumor. But now it was a strident pleading, devoid of any kind of elegance.

Please.

"Has he woken up at all?"

"A couple times last night. He was groggy, of course, but he knows where he is and he responded when the doctor asked him to blink, squeeze his hand, that sort of thing. He should be awake quite a bit more today."

Beckett let out a soft breath. "Will he be in any pain?"

The nurse crossed the room, pulled a keyboard from a swiveling stand underneath the computer monitor near the door. "He'll have a bit of a headache, yes."

"Painkillers?"

"We gave him something mild last night. But we need to monitor his pain level, make sure there's no undue swelling. For that reason, we don't want to overdo the meds. Pain is an important symptom. We don't want to risk missing it."

Beckett nodded, now unable to look away from Dad as the nurse typed away behind him. A sudden reversal. "So he's really going to . . . he's going to be . . ."

The nurse's typing stopped. He heard the creak of her stool as she stood. The padding of her footsteps nearing the bedside. Felt her hand on his shoulder. "He's doing wonderfully, Beckett."

He glanced up. "You know my name?"

"Your father gave me the whole rundown on your family in pre-op before the anesthesia kicked. I think it was his way of calming himself. He said you would be the one who looked the most like him."

Tears he'd refused since yesterday morning sprang to his eyes now. The nurse patted his shoulder and then left the room.

Beckett reached for Dad's hand, careful not to move the clip on his finger or nudge the IVs. His father's palm was warmer than he'd expected.

He's going to be okay.

No, they still didn't know whether the tumor was cancerous. They should have some answers on that by Monday. But right here in this hushed moment, he could believe it. *He's going to be okay.*

"I'm sorry it took me so long to get here," he whispered to the empty room, to his sleeping father. "Not just yesterday. I'm sorry I stayed away for so long. I keep wasting time and messing up and then missing out and I'm just so sorry."

There were no wracking sobs today, not like that day at the depot when he'd finally set free so many years of furrowed hurt. Let his dad encircle him with all the strength and comfort he'd pushed away since the day he'd left town. It had been an unshackling. A letting go.

Today was a holding on. To courage in the midst of fear. To faith in the midst of uncertainty.

To a father's love he knew had never once wavered.

"I love you, Dad."

Muscles that had spent tense days coiled inside him loosened now as a lone tear landed on the bedsheet and the hand holding his tightened just the slightest.

18

It was the smell of Grandma's tomato basil sauce that pried Kit from her bedroom. The curiosity about who was making so much noise in the kitchen.

The passing thought that it might be Beckett.

But no, more likely Willa. She'd spent several evening meals at the house in the week since the fire. Whereas Beckett had spent most of those days in Iowa City with his dad.

She missed him. Longed to have a real conversation with him instead of the few brief texts they'd traded. But would it only make things harder? Had the brief foray they'd taken past friendship ruined any chance of going back to where they were before?

The zesty aroma heightened when she stepped into the kitchen. But it wasn't Willa pulling plates from the cupboard. "Luke?"

"Good, you came down. I figured you had to get hungry eventually."

She glanced at the clock above the kitchen window. After seven? That meant she'd been in her room for three hours, sitting cross-legged on her bed, laptop open in front of her.

Screen blank. Seven days and she still hadn't figured

out how to tell Dad about the fire. Unsent drafts congregated in a folder inside her email account. Perhaps it wasn't lack of explanation that held her back, but simple obstinacy. Dad hadn't bothered to show up or to call or to follow-up. Besides, he didn't know about the barn in the first place. What difference was there now?

But it was Friday. Which meant he'd expect a weekly report. And she'd come to a decision: They should accept the offer from Lucas's buyer. Why put it off? They could hobble through the rest of the season or they could be done with it. Dad and Lucas had lost interest long ago. She'd held on for too long.

"You made dinner?" Spice bottles sat in disarray on one counter, and flecks of red sauce stained the stovetop.

"Tried. Can't guarantee it's perfect."

"Did you follow the recipe taped to the inside of the cupboard?"

He nodded as he loaded plates with angel hair pasta and accompanying sauce.

"Then you can't have gone too far wrong."

He handed her a plate and fork. "Let's eat on the porch."

She followed him outside, where he folded onto a porch step, perching his plate on his knees. Chilled, late-October air curled around her as she settled beside him, along with the hazy light of a pastel sunset. The fragrant flowers of the autumn clematis climbing the side of the porch had long since morphed into a silvery mass of fluffy seed heads.

She took a bite, the burst of flavor just right, just like Grandma's. "This is good, Luke."

He circled his own bite of pasta around his fork, the breeze sifting through his thick hair. He'd finally cut it, but only barely, and he'd let a near-full beard cover his cheeks and chin in the past weeks. It gave him a burly look, as if he was ready to hunker down for winter's eventual descent.

But he wouldn't be here for winter. She'd sensed the rise of his restlessness for days. Seen the distance steal into his eyes. But it was better than the haunted shadows of weeks earlier. The fire had somehow pulled him from his former listlessness. He'd spent days hauling debris from the barn, taking over many of Kit's chores. He still woke her with his nightmares every couple nights, but something was shifting—slowly.

They ate in silence while the last sliver of the sun tarried in the west. The gentle colors of dusk reached through nearly bare branches to dapple the lawn, and a scattering of leaves skimmed off the pile Lucas had raked earlier in the day.

"I'm okay with selling."

The scraping of Luke's fork across his plate halted. "What?"

"I said I'm okay with selling. I won't argue anymore. It's probably easiest this way."

"Kit—"

"You need the money to start over. If Dad's willing to give me a cut, too, great. If not, I'll figure something out."

Lucas's pause lingered. "Listen, I'm going to tell you something. And I'm not telling you because I think it'll be all liberating or because Eric told me I need to—"

"You've been talking to Eric—?"

"—or even because I particularly want to or anything. But, well . . ." He pushed his plate out of the way and shifted, angling so that his back leaned against the stairway railing behind him. "Afghanistan."

She stilled.

"My troop was mainly doing humanitarian work, digging wells, clearing roads, that kind of thing. There was this group of kids that would wander out from one of the villages to watch. Saw them all the time, didn't think much of it."

His gaze fastened on the horizon, flecks of light dusting his eyes. Memories trailed over his face until, in an instant, he stiffened.

"It was an IED—improvised explosive device. Obviously meant for us. The kids were coming out to watch again. Stepped in the wrong spot."

"Oh, Luke . . ."

"I saw the whole thing. I was working on a fence. My closest buddy was a mile away. Three of the kids were dead, one was alive. I didn't even think, I just picked him up and started running in the direction of the village."

She closed her eyes, the scene so painful to picture, she couldn't begin to imagine what it must have been like to live it.

"Strangers somehow got me to the right house, but by the time I reached it, he'd died. His mother screamed and wept, and I just stood there."

His shudder was enough to shake the porch step.

"I didn't even realize until hours later my arms were burned. The boy's body had been so hot . . ." Lucas swallowed, his jaw twitching. He pressed his dry eyes closed, tone void of emotion. "His mother took care of my burns. I still can't fathom that. On the night her son dies, she takes care of the man who delivered her dead child to her . . ." He shook his head.

She couldn't help her question. "Lucas, when you got home, when you were on trial, why didn't you stand up for yourself? You'd witnessed something traumatic. Dad got you that lawyer—"

"That's why." His posture turned rigid. "Because he ignored me until *his* reputation with his Army pals was on the line."

Stark understanding settled in. Why had she never considered how Dad's absence had affected Lucas? But while she'd kept trying to find ways to wrench her father into her life, Lucas had done the opposite.

"It was stupid. My thought process was a mess, but I wanted to hurt him." The napkin in his hand was crinkled, sweat-dampened despite the cool of the night.

She inched closer to him on the step. "I was so worried those two years."

He looked at her through eyes clearer than she could ever remember seeing. "I know. And I'm sorry. I'm so sorry, Kit."

She leaned her head on his shoulder, something she hadn't done in years. "Where did you go after that? Why didn't you go back to camp?"

His silence stretched. He wasn't prepared to tell the rest of his story. She wouldn't push. Not anymore.

"Why did you tell me now?"

"When I brought that boy to his mother, she wrapped him in a tablecloth, of all things. When I saw you trying to take on that fire with just a tablecloth . . . I don't know." She felt his intake of breath as he waited a beat, then two, before lifting his arm around her shoulders. "It's not the same thing—a boy's life, the loss of a barn or some land and trees. But hurt is hurt and sadness is sadness. I don't want my little sister hurt. I don't want any more sadness."

With the sun now fully abed, the sky was a quilt of blue, silver stars its twinkling stitches. A mellow wind breathed through swaying branches.

"Sorry I forgot to make dessert."

His comment was so out of the blue, she couldn't help a snort of laughter. "We could steal an apple pie from the orchard store."

In a tentative move, Lucas gripped her shoulder before moving his arm. "My buyer's official offer came in yesterday. But I'm not going to send it on to Dad. Obviously the buyer can just go straight to him if he wants, but I'm taking myself out of the equation."

"But—"

"If you want to tell Dad you're cool with selling, feel free. But only do it if it's the right thing. Not just the easiest thing." He stood, gathered their plates. "Oh, also . . ." He reached down to set something beside her. A recipe card? "This fell off the cupboard door. Something told me to give it to you."

She picked it up, its words coming into focus as the screen door closed behind her brother. Of course.

"Dad, I don't understand why you won't let us make up a bed downstairs." Beckett stood behind his father, facing the stairway that led up to the second floor and trying not to stare at the shaved patch around the bandage on the back of Dad's head.

They'd been home for all of twenty minutes—most of that spent moving like a herd to the front door, carrying in bags and plants and balloons. The entire family had camped out in Iowa City for most of Dad's stay, even Seth and Ava.

"I won't let you make up a bed downstairs because I just spent seven nights in a lumpy hospital bed. Now that I'm finally home, I'd like to sleep in my own bed, thank you very much."

Beckett had to resist the urge not to reach out for Dad's arm as he stepped up. "But the stairs—"

"If I can handle having my skull broken into, I can

handle four or five steps."

"Nine steps."

Dad gripped the railing. "You counted?"

"You know how many times I sat on this stairway in timeout as a kid? Trust me, I know how many stairs there are."

Kate stood at the second-floor landing, hands on her waist. "Would you two stop bickering? You're like an old married couple." She looked past Dad and Beckett to where Colton still stood in the living room. "Promise me we'll never bicker, Colt."

"Promise, Rosie."

Beckett glanced over his shoulder. "You call her Rosie?"

"You've been home almost three months and you just now picked up on that?"

Dad had made it up three steps. "Look, I appreciate the fanfare and all, but I really can make it up the stairs without a crowd of assistants. I love you kids, but give a recovering man a break, will you? Raegan asking me every two seconds if I need a Tylenol, Logan texting and calling so much he might as well have just stayed in Iowa, Beckett driving like a senior citizen."

"Hey—"

"Anybody notice he didn't mention me?" Kate asked smugly.

Colton snorted. "My fiancée, the golden child."

Dad paused halfway up. "Oh, you're the worst of all. Going on and on and on about wedding plans."

"Because you've said eight hundred times you're sick of being treated like an invalid. I was trying to give you a distraction."

"By talking my ear off about how many details there are, complaining about how expensive it all is? Take a cue from your family, daughter. Seth and Ava planned a wedding in two weeks. Your older brother eloped. It doesn't have to be that hard."

Another snort from Colton. "I'd be okay with eloping."

Kate glared over the stairway railing. "Hey, you're the one with the publicist and the famous friends and foundation sponsors who all expect this to be an overblown celebrity event."

"Careful, love, I think this might count as bickering."

Raegan stood in the front door, a bright yellow "Get Well" balloon bouncing against the frame. "Welp, I think it's clear we've all been in the same space a little too long."

Yet Beckett couldn't help the thankful warmth pulsing through him all over again. Same warmth that had taken hold of him on Monday when they'd all gathered with the doctor and heard the best news ever: No cancer.

It'd played over and over and over in his mind since then. *No cancer. No cancer. No cancer.*

Just standing here in Dad's house, the scent of cinnamon that somehow always filled the house, the pile of shoes in the entryway, the playful squabbling of his siblings, all of it together cleared a path toward that hollow space inside him—the one marked *home* that'd echoed with emptiness for so many years. The one Boston, his career, his goals had never been able to fill.

Dad reached the top of the stairs; surprisingly, he allowed Kate to tuck her arm through his. Raegan followed, balloon bobbing against the wall.

"Hey, Beckett?"

He turned to Colton. Had to admit, the guy was going to make an okay addition to the family. He'd barely left Kate's side the entire time they were in Iowa City, only ever leaving long enough to fetch coffee or bring food. Beckett hadn't missed the way he watched out for Raegan, too, as if he already took seriously his upcoming role as an additional big brother. A good thing considering Logan now lived in Chicago and Beckett would eventually . . . what?

He had no clue where he'd be months or even weeks from now. He had no job, had more than likely wrecked his chances with Army. He still had a week until the application deadline, but was there even any point anymore?

"I wanted to say thanks for what you did for Webster. I haven't been around for him as much lately as I'd like to be."

"I don't know if I'd be thanking me, Colt. If I hadn't taken him to that apartment, he wouldn't have spent an evening being questioned by police." At least the investigators had eventually come to believe Webster and Beckett's story. It helped that Amanda had corroborated once she was clear-headed. Last he'd heard from Webster, Amanda had gone back to her relatives in Illinois, and Jake, thankfully, was still in police custody.

"If you hadn't taken him, he would've found some other way there and who knows how much worse it could've been." Colton's phone buzzed and he gave it an exasperated glance. "If someone had told me launching a nonprofit would mean so many schmoozing conversations with potential donors, I'd have shied away from the whole thing."

"Beck, Dad wants you," Raegan called from upstairs.

Colton ignored his phone. "Listen, before you go, things at the foundation are moving faster than I ever thought they would. We're opening another house soon, probably four or five more next year, all in different states. There's always lots of paperwork, zoning issues, contracts—all stuff I hate. You ever want to do some legal advising, just say the word and you've got a job."

"You serious?"

"It's a nonprofit. Couldn't pay you near what I'm sure you were getting at the law firm. Not sure I could even offer full-time, at this point. But if you ever want to talk, offer's on the table."

"I don't know what to say."

"Say you'll think about it, and in return, you can promise me when it comes time for Logan and you to give me the whole, 'We're Kate's brothers and if you hurt her, we'll kill you' speech, that you'll go easy on me. I figure it's coming one of these days."

Beckett grinned and reached out to shake Colton's hand. "Deal."

A job offer. Just like that. One that would likely allow him to live wherever he wanted, might even include some travel.

And yet, would it actually be all that different than his previous job? And say he jumped at it, just hastily signed on some dotted line, another impulsive decision. Wouldn't that prove right everything he'd been trying to prove wrong for so long? That he was rash and impetuous. That he jumped first and thought later.

"I'm not like you, Beckett. You got a phone call from an Army officer in August and within twenty-four hours hopped a plane to Iowa. I spent a month deliberating . . ."

Would he ever be able to get Kit's words out of his head?

Or the needling conviction that he'd hurt her all over again, handled everything wrong. He *knew* Kit. She took decisions slowly. She needed time to mull, always had. How had he expected her to react when he barreled in and took her off guard?

Plus, she was right. He hadn't even known what he was asking her that night in the barn. To date him? To drop everything and follow him to Lord knows where? To *marry* him?

No, because you didn't ask a girl to marry you when your life was a mess.

But you also didn't ask a girl to commit to something when you didn't know what that something was. He'd been swept away in a moment, fraught with desire and desperate to hold on to what they had . . . or *could* have.

But his recklessness had only succeeded in pushing her away. Again.

"Oh good, you're here." Dad. He sat in his bed with his legs bent and his head resting against a mound of pillows. "Kate, Raegan, give us a minute?"

His sisters complied while he crossed the room. "You need something, Dad?"

Dad reached for his water glass. "Yes, I need to confess I lied back there on the steps."

"Say again?"

"It's not Kate who's been the worst lately. Hate to tell you, but it's you, son."

"Huh. Seems like if you hate to tell me, you could just, you know, not."

Dad swished his water around. "You've been hovering for days. You're so tightly wound, it'd be funny if it wasn't also concerning."

"You shouldn't be concerned about me. You're the one who just had brain surgery."

"Yes, and I'm going to be stuck taking things slowly for the next six weeks, at least. I don't think I can handle that with you under the same roof pacing your way through the ceiling."

"You trying to kick me out, Dad?"

Dad took a drink, set his glass on the bedside table. "Listen, Beck. That night in the depot a few weeks ago, when we talked about your mom and both . . ."

"Fell apart?" He felt a twinge of a smile.

"Yes. And when you asked me why I didn't tell you to come home. I've wondered since then if perhaps it wasn't only the night Flora died that you were talking about. These past six years, if I hurt you by not urging you to come home—"

"*Dad.*"

"You have to know, there wasn't a week that passed that I didn't consider hopping on a plane and dragging you back. It's hard to know how to parent adults sometimes, when to give space and when to step in and heaven knows I don't always get it right. I am so sorry if you ever felt forgotten or disregarded. Please know that I'll never stop loving you."

"I know that, Dad. I do. I'm the one who chose to stay away."

"But maybe you needed to hear the words *come home.* I was too worried about getting it wrong, pressuring you. I should've just said what was on my heart. I missed you, son. I'm never happier than when all my offspring are right here. Which is going to make what I'm about to say sound ridiculous, but you asked if I'm trying to kick you out and, well . . . Beckett, you've gone from college to law school to community service to I don't even know what all here recently. You need some time alone. Go fill up your gas tank and get away. Take a trip just for fun."

He plopped onto the end of Dad's bed. "I don't have time for that. So I need to figure out what comes next."

"So go do some thinking somewhere where you're not distracted by a hundred things."

"You really want me to leave. You're serious."

"I'd say 'as a heart attack,' but considering how much time I've just spent in a hospital, I'd rather not jinx myself." Dad shifted on his bed, humor seeping from his expression. It was replaced with a firm-but-gentle prodding. "As for the JAG Corps, Beck, I think sometimes we parents forget the staying power our words have in our kids' brains. Your mother never would've wanted you to feel limited to this one career path. She would've wanted you to listen to your own heart. Even more, to God's voice."

Beckett's gaze drifted from the photo of Mom on Dad's bedside stand to the Bible on its shelf underneath. "I'm not sure I know how to hear God's voice these days."

"Tell me this: When's the last time you thought you might've heard him? The last time you sensed his presence."

He didn't even have to think. "This spring. On the coast. Salt Island." When he'd muttered a halfhearted prayer about his future. It'd been the impetus for his eventual homecoming.

Dad grinned. "On the coast, you say?"

Kit stood outside Beckett's window for ten minutes, trying to decide whether to make the climb. Turned out she didn't have to.

The window slid open, one leg ducked out, then the other. With his arms propped against the frame, Beckett pulled himself the rest of the way onto the porch roof. He caught sight of her the second his head came up.

He grinned.

Moments later, he was on the ground, standing in front of her and clearly just as conflicted as she was about what to do next, hang back or hug or—

He went for the hug. Light and brief. "I was just

going to come over to your place."

She stepped back. "Great minds." She tried to remember why she'd come over here. To see how his dad was settling in. To see how he was settling in. To see . . . him. She just wanted to see him. "Beck, I wanted to say—"

"I'm sorry, Kit."

Their words collided and turned into stilted laughter that turned into taut silence. It lasted so long the motion sensor light over the garage flicked off. Crisp night air nipped at her cheeks and nose.

"I shouldn't have asked you to give up the orchard."

"Beck—"

He lifted his finger to her lips, the movement enough to wash them in light once more. "You found what makes you come alive. As your best friend, I should be one of the people most supporting that, not asking you to leave it behind."

"You have supported it. Like crazy."

Just hours ago, she'd been ready to give up on that dream, though. On the thing, as Beckett said, that made her come alive. Amazing how one heartfelt conversation with her brother and a couple hours of quiet on the porch could make such a difference.

And that Bible verse. The one on the card Lucas had handed her, without having any idea how much it'd stuck in her head ever since finding it that first week home.

The thing was, these past months, every time that verse had rambled through her brain, she'd paid attention only to the first part. But when she'd reread the whole thing tonight, it'd taken on new weight.

"Let us hold unswervingly to the hope we profess, for he who promised is faithful."

She'd been hoping for a dream. Hoping for the orchard's success. Hoping for Dad's return.

Hoping for Beckett.

But real trust, real belief—it wasn't about what she hoped for . . . but *who* she placed her hope in. A faithful God. A God who never promised perfect circumstances, but who did promise his love.

She may doubt from time to time, but that was where Willa's assurance came in: When she felt like letting go, God held on.

"You're drifting, Kit."

Then she remembered—the papers in her jacket pocket, the other reason she'd come to see Beckett, even knowing it might be difficult. She pulled out the stapled pages and handed them to him.

He scanned the top page, forehead wrinkled. "My JAG app? How did you . . . ? What'd you do, break into the house while we were in Iowa City?"

"I know where the house key is hidden. I also know you've been using the same computer password since you got your first laptop. Lucky for me, you left the browser open with the online application."

"But . . . why?"

"Because you're a horrible speller, and even this many years later, I haven't kicked the habit of proofreading all your stuff. I marked all the typos, reworded a few things, too."

He opened his mouth, closed it, looked from her to the papers and then to her once more. "I wasn't even sure I was going to send it in. Kit . . . I . . ."

He must have given up on words, because he pulled her into another hug. But this time, he didn't let go so quickly. She'd molded into him without a second thought, cataloging the feel of his arms and the smell of his skin and the beating of his heart.

"I'm leaving tomorrow," he said into her hair. "Dad

kicked me out."

Somehow she was able to laugh. To tuck away the sadness before he could see it. To release him a minute later.

"Where are you going?"

"West Coast. I'm going to take the trip Mom and I used to talk about. I don't know how long I'll be gone. I don't know what comes next. Even with your proofreading, I don't know about my chances with the Army. I just know I need to go. Maybe it's impulsive, but—"

She interrupted him with a kiss on his cheek. "Just make sure to send me postcards."

"Promise. Come on, I'll walk you home."

"Actually, Beck, I think I'd like to walk alone."

"You sure?"

"I'm sure."

It'd give her a chance to think about how to save the orchard and rebuild the barn and tell her father she wasn't giving up. To pray. To figure out how to hold on to hope while letting go of her best friend.

19

"You need to come see this, Kit. Right now."

Lucas's voice bounded through the first floor of the house, followed by the sound of the back door slapping closed and his steps seeking her out. Not that she was hard to find. The dining room table had transformed into her workspace over the past weeks. Better than the office attached to the orchard store, the one with the perfect view of her scorched barn and stripped trees.

Lucas appeared in the room. "Come on. You need to get over to the orchard with me."

"No, what I've got to do is find an insurance plan that isn't so expensive. And I think I found a new vendor. They don't pay as much per pound, but they'll take more and they don't require as high of quality, so we can unload a lot of what we salvaged after the storm."

"That's great, but take a break. Believe me, you'll want to see this."

Lucas wore a hoodie and jeans, and he'd pulled his shaggy hair into a ponytail. His cheeks were ruddy—most likely from the chilly wind that'd been racing past the windows for the better part of the day.

She'd loved listening to the wind as a kid. Lying in bed at night as it shook the old farmhouse.

It'd turned unfriendly there for a while. Ushered in the hailstorm, aided the fire. She was only just beginning to enjoy it again.

"Not joking. I will throw you over my shoulder if I have to."

An urgency underpinned with enthusiasm laced his tone. It was, perhaps, the most like his old self she'd seen him since he'd returned home. And it was the only reason she forced herself to her feet.

Well, that and the fact that her work wasn't nearly distraction enough. Thoughts of Beckett were never far off. It made no sense—how she could feel such peace at the decision to keep fighting for the orchard, an undeniable belonging, and yet at the same time, experience such an indescribable ache at Beckett's absence.

But surely part of loving Beckett was wanting him to find a sense of his own belonging. Discover *his* purpose, *his* place. Even if it wasn't at her side.

Still, it hurt. Which made distraction a welcome companion. She followed Lucas from the house. "If something else has gone wrong, I'd rather not know. If the second floor of the store caved in or one of the maintenance guys ran a tractor into the shed wall—"

"Shut up and get in the truck."

The wind whipped through her hair as she rounded the vehicle, her steps crunching over fallen leaves and hickory nuts. Seconds later, they were on the span of gravel lane that led to the orchard grounds. The early-evening sky was as golden as a cornfield still waiting for harvest. It would've been the perfect fall night for a bonfire. Or a mug of cider on the porch swing.

The tires bumped over a pothole and Kit grasped the door handle. "I can't believe I haven't heard anything from Dad." She'd emailed him the day after Beckett left town. Told him about the storm and the fire and then, with bated breath, bared her heart:

> *I'm not giving up, Dad. I love it here and I want to stay. I know you only gave me until the end of the season to make a profit. I know the outlook isn't good, and I know you've got a buyout offer. But I'm not giving up. I just thought you should know.*

She'd gone on from there—paragraph after paragraph about what the land meant to her, how she planned to nurture the trees and what little crop remained. She'd told him about the state tourism funds Maple Valley had been awarded, despite the fire, and the role the orchard had played in making that possible. She'd made her case in a written argument that would've made Beckett proud.

She tapped her fingernails on the armrest. "Maybe he's just going to go ahead with a sale and one day someone will show up here and send us packing. Even with all that's gone wrong, I wouldn't blame a buyer for being interested. It's been a tough season, sure, but Grandpa always used to say the good thing about tough seasons is it means better ones are just around the corner. Good from bad. The trees will be stronger next year."

She was babbling, but Lucas didn't interrupt. Didn't respond either. What exactly was going on here?

She didn't have to wait long to find out. Within a minute they were passing under the orchard's welcome sign and the parking lot packed with cars was in plain sight. "What in the world?"

As soon as Lucas shifted into park, she hopped out. Her hair scrambled every direction around her face and the unbuttoned flannel shirt she wore over a tee flapped in the breeze. Her gaze raked over the scene unfolding in front of her. Townspeople wearing grungy clothes and boots moved in a herd toward the barn.

"What's going on?"

Lucas's door clanked shut. "Looks like a good, old-fashioned barn-raising to me."

"B-but . . . I don't understand. Who's in charge? Did you do this?"

He shook his head as he rounded the truck. "Uh, no."

"Then who—?"

"Kit, you finally made it." Eric Hampton broke free of a group of people standing by a long table set up several yards in front of the barn. Was that Megan the barista serving coffee?

"Eric, hey. What's happening?" People were moving all around her, so many people, offering smiles and waves as they went about their work.

"What's it look like? We're putting up your barn." He motioned behind him. "Drew's heading up the actual construction, so no need to worry that you're going to end up with a rattrap. Seth's bringing over a catered meal from The Red Door later. I'd guess we'll have walls up by sunset."

Was that actually *Sam* bent over a blueprint with Drew? Beckett had told her about his daughter. She still could hardly believe it—Sam, a father. He seemed to sense her stare and looked up. His amicable nod said more than she could fathom. "I don't . . . I don't understand. Who's paying for all this, Luke? Who got everyone together? Who—"

"Kit, it was Dad."

She turned to Lucas, slowly, mouth gaping. "I don't believe it."

"Believe it. He called me a little while ago. Apparently your email made an impact on him."

Her argument, that ridiculously long email—it'd

worked? Her heart hammered so loudly she was sure everyone could hear it over the sound of saws and voices and the cold and wonderful Iowa wind. "I think I'm in shock."

Lucas draped his arm around her shoulder. "There's one more thing. He's signing the orchard over to you."

Her focus jerked from the crowd around the barn's foundation to her brother's face. "*What?*"

"He said to tell you to talk to Jenson Barrow. He'll help with the paperwork."

"I don't . . . I can't . . ." She should smile. She should laugh. She should cry. She should . . . something. But all she could do was lean into her brother's hug and let her gaze try to take it all in. The people, the activity, the aroma of Megan's coffee drifting in the air.

And the trees, weathered and strong and watching under a brilliant autumn sun.

"I don't know why he didn't just call you himself. But I'm past trying to understand anything Dad does."

Flynnie pranced to her, mewed, and butted her head into Kit's leg. No way was she letting her pet near the construction site again. "It's a start, though, isn't it?"

Arm still around her shoulders, Lucas shrugged. "You never know."

Maybe things with Dad would change. Maybe they wouldn't. But her hope was grounded like never before. In a God whose love was enduring as this land.

Her land.

For once, aimless felt just right.

The wind raked through Beckett's hair as his classic convertible curved around the Bixby Bridge in California's Monterey County, one of the most picturesque bridges along the Pacific Coast and one of the tallest single-span concrete bridges in the world. To the west, the ocean unfolded into the horizon—foamy white to turquoise to breathtaking blue as far as he could see. Green hills rose and fell in waves to the east.

Mom would have loved this.

This was the trip they'd always talked about taking together.

He tipped his sunglasses over his eyes, his hair brushing against the back of his neck and his shirtsleeves flapping against his upper arms. A low-slung sun bathed the scenic roadway in an orange glow, splashing color against the craggy slope that dipped into the Pacific shore.

As his car neared the north end of the bridge's stretch, he slowed and looked for the scenic pullout indicated on the map he'd picked up at a rest stop outside Carmel. According to a tourist he'd chatted with, it was better to park on the graded gravel road directly across from the pullout. *"You'll get a better picture that way,"* the tourist had assured. *"The whole bridge and the ocean."*

He found the spot the man had mentioned. Pulled over and parked. Grateful for the view, the freedom, the silence.

That tourist he'd run into at the rest stop had talked his ear off for a good ten minutes about this bridge. Told him about the guy who'd built it.

"Name was Charles Henry Bixby, served in the Civil War and then raised cattle, later established a major lumber industry. 'Course then there was no road to get his logs to market and the government wouldn't approve one. So he went and started building his own. And get this, when he was older, long after he'd sold off his land

and moved to Monterey in the early 1900s, when most people would've retired, he went to work for the postal service."

Apparently the man hadn't lived long enough to see the completion of the bridge Beckett stared at now. He'd certainly drifted from dream to dream, though. Had he planned his steps ahead of time or simply stayed flexible, following wherever life led? Had he prayed, hoping to hear God's voice, as Beckett did now?

I'm here, God. I'm listening.

Beckett reached for the brown bag in the passenger seat, the one with the postcards he'd picked up at the rest stop. Needed a pen, though. He opened the glove compartment and fumbled around, its contents spilling to the floor.

And then he saw it. An envelope, crinkled, yellowed. His own name in familiar handwriting.

Mom?

Hands shaking, postcards forgotten, he straightened in his seat.

"I wish I could hear her voice, just once more. . ."

He'd murmured the wish to Dad weeks ago. Was it coming true now? He skimmed his thumb under the seal, pulled out a single page. His focus hooked on the first words.

To my Beckett.

The breeze carried away his gasp. All this time, right in his own car. Years of sitting in his Boston garage. Movements slow, heart thudding, he rose from the car. He rounded to the front, slid onto the hood, its sun-warmed metal sleek and glinting. He laid back, knees bent, eyes squinting.

To my Beckett,

I've prayed for days to find the words to write to

you, my youngest son, my spitfire, my charmer. I'm not sure why, but I feel deep down that you're my child who will need these words most. I've prayed, I've drafted, I've started and stopped and started again . . .

I've cried until my tears splotched and wrinkled the page.

But now I think I finally know what I'm meant to write. And so I start again and pray God gives me the grace and wisdom to say what your heart needs to hear.

Can I tell you a story, Beck? I'll never forget the day in second grade you brought a note home from your teacher. You'd gotten in trouble at recess . . . again. Apparently you were playing sailors and you'd decided the jungle gym was your ship and you climbed to the top and yelled something about mutiny. You had a whole crowd of students swarming around you, cheering. And when a teacher told you to come down, instead of climbing down the jungle gym's side, you jumped and called it "walking the plank."

In her note, the teacher called you reckless and wild.

I remember scanning that note and trying so hard not to laugh as I scolded you for disobeying the teacher. I remember reading it a second time when you'd left the room. I remember smiling.

"That's my Beckett," I thought.

What your teacher called reckless, I called fearless. What your teacher called wild, I called passionate.

You are my passionate son, Beckett. My spirited son.

You are my son who jumps.

I love this about you—oh, I love it. And I am praying right now as I write this that you will realize what a gift it is—what a gift you are. What your teacher might've seen as a weakness, I see as your greatest strength. Don't hide it, Beckett, and don't fear it. Allow God to mold your passion, yes.

But don't deny it.

And when you feel lost, remember God's extraordinary love . . . his reckless love. That's your starting point and your finish line. That's your home. Hold onto it.

I love you, my wild son.
Mom

By the time he reached her signature, tears streaked down his cheeks. Tears of sadness and joy all at once. Who knew why Mom had put the letter in his car instead of just sending it to him whenever she'd written it, probably when he was away at college and she knew her days were coming to a close?

Who knew why he'd never found it until now?

Who knew why she'd even written it in the first place? Had she somehow known she might not have a chance to say goodbye?

Maybe she didn't. But Someone did.

Extraordinary love.

It seemed to envelope him now, like the colors of the sun swallowing the landscape and rippling over the water.

Expansive.

Embracing.

Enduring.

As strong as the steel and concrete of the bridge in the limelight of dusk. Love that spanned myriad mistakes and mishaps, falters and failings. Impulsive decisions, career flounderings, relationships he just couldn't seem to get right.

A love that persisted, held on even when he'd lost his grasp.

And maybe a love that pointed toward the purpose he'd been seeking all this time. Just like Mom said—his starting point and his finish line. Something to receive, but then give . . . no matter where he was, no matter what he was doing. He'd wanted to know what he was made for. Well, this was it.

Extraordinary love.

His purpose wasn't about a career. It wasn't about earning respect or finding his identity in a title and uniform. It was about love. It was about home. It was about a weightless, wonder-filled jump.

Finally, he knew . . .

He held the letter to his chest, closed his eyes, breathed in the ocean air. "Thank you." A whispered prayer. And it was enough.

20

"Beckett Walker, I could kill you."

Kate came storming down Dad's staircase before Beckett barely made it into the living room. A flurry of white and lace and tulle swished around her and she nearly tripped over the recliner.

"Whoa, careful, sis." He reached out with hands still numb from the December chill. He'd driven most of the way home with the convertible top in place. But about ten miles from Maple Valley, impulse had taken over. Despite the cold, despite the flurries floating from the sky, he'd raised the top and driven the rest of the way with red cheeks and winter nipping the air around him.

Kate swatted him away now. "I could kill you."

"Yes, but it's your wedding day and it'd be a shame to stain your pretty dress with my blood."

Buzzing activity filled the house—the sound of laughter drifting from the second floor and a cluster of people gathered around the kitchen island for a brunch that tantalized his senses.

"The wedding's in an hour, Beck. An *hour*."

"Right. And I'm here and look, I'm already dressed." He pulled open his coat. He'd stopped over at Seth's to pick up his waiting tux before coming here. He'd caught a glimpse of Colton trying to pin on his own boutonnière with shaky fingers and Logan stepping in to help.

"Do you know how worried I was you might not make it?"

"It's December, sis. There was a blizzard in Colorado. Wouldn't you rather I have stopped and holed up until it passed than risk my life to get here for the rehearsal dinner?" He'd hated missing it. Would've been fun to give Colt that "Kate's my sister, and if you hurt her, I'll kill you" speech they'd talked about.

For once, though, guilt hadn't eaten away at him as he waited out the storm. He hadn't sat in that Denver hotel room beating himself up for not heading home sooner. Sure, if he'd left earlier in the week, he might've outraced the blizzard.

But he was here now and Kate's glare was more mock scolding than it was truly angry. "You look very pretty."

"Resorting to flattery? You think that's going to earn my forgiveness?" Her eyes narrowed.

"And your hair is really nice all, like, twisted up and stuff."

"Keep going."

"And Colton is probably going to faint at the altar when he sees you."

She gathered the excess of her dress behind her and draped it over one arm. "He better not. I'd prefer he be conscious when I pledge my undying love." With her free hand, she reached forward to straighten his bow tie. "Now, if you'd managed to make it home a couple days ago like planned, we would've had time to catch up and you could've filled me in on all your travels. But since you're *late*, we'll have to wait until the reception. For now, I've got to do the whole 'goin' to the chapel' thing. Or, orchard, as it were."

During her spiel, his gaze had wandered the room. Dad was around here somewhere, right? They'd exchanged phone calls at least once a week—often more—in his five weeks away. Voices, the opening and closing of the fridge and dishwasher ambled in from the kitchen. Pounding footsteps sounded overhead—probably Kate's gaggle of bridesmaids in heels.

"She's not here, little brother."

His focus whipped back to Kate. "Who—"

"She's at the orchard now, probably running around doing last-minute stuff."

"Actually, I was looking for Rae."

"Right." Kate's voice didn't hold an ounce of belief.

Understandable, especially considering just the mention of Kit was enough to set his heart pounding. Truthfully, it'd been sheer willpower that'd kept him from racing out to the orchard first thing upon his arrival in Maple Valley. He'd felt every one of the miles between them these last five weeks, an ache of longing that only grew in strength with each day that passed.

And yet . . .

He wouldn't have traded these soul-cleansing weeks for anything. He'd checked off every one of the sights he and Mom used to talk about. He'd spent nights out under the stars and mornings watching the sunrise.

He'd reveled in the space and the solitude and the sense that he was doing exactly what he was supposed to do. Praying, listening for God's whisper. Simply trusting.

He'd managed to be of use to his family, too. He'd overseen the sale of Logan's LA apartment. He'd met with several of Colton's potential big-name foundation sponsors. Turned out the schmoozing Colt hated, Beckett was more than a little good at.

As for his younger sister . . .

"Yes, I'm dying to see, Kit, but I seriously was looking for Rae."

Kate's grin was full of doubt, but she pointed to the stairs. "Up there." Careful so as not to mess up her dress or veil, she gave him a quick embrace. "I really am glad you made it."

"And I'm ridiculously happy for you, Kate."

Raegan was already coming down the hallway when he made it up the stairs. "You made it. I knew you would." She flung herself at him for a boisterous hug and then stepped backward, slipping off her shoes. "I don't know why I'm wearing these yet. I can barely walk in them as is, and by the end of the day, I'm pretty sure my toes will be a mangled mess."

Her shimmery dress was a deep red that matched her lipstick as well as the streak coloring her blond hair. Classic Raegan.

"A perk of being male. No ridiculous shoes."

"I'd berate you for being late, but I'm going to guess Kate already got that out of the way."

He shrugged. "She threatened my life, so yeah, I guess she's got it covered."

"So what are you doing here? Shouldn't you be over at Seth's with the rest of the guys? Or, better yet, finding Kit? She's been pretending for days she's not anxious about you coming home."

Anxious as in worried? Or . . . excited?

Please let it be excited.

"She's got all your postcards taped to the inside of her kitchen cupboards. And though she's been painfully obvious about not asking when you're coming home, her ears perk every time someone mentions your name."

Why *hadn't* he gone there first? The gnawing desire to see her was about to cut off his air supply right here in the hallway.

Raegan. You're here to talk to Raegan. Hurry up and

give her the ticket and then get to the orchard and . . .

And if he was lucky, find Kit before the ceremony started.

"Listen, I just wanted to give you something real quick." He pulled the envelope from his suit jacket.

"You know I'm not the bride, right? Cards and gifts go to Kate."

"It's not a card, and it's not exactly a present, either." He thrust the envelope toward her. "Just take it."

Raegan accepted the envelope and slid her thumb under its flap. She took out the folded paper, eyes skimming its text. "A flight voucher?" Her forehead wrinkled even as understanding played over her face. "Beck, I can't . . ."

"You can. The dates are flexible. Make an international call and tell Bear you're coming. It's simple as that."

She shook her head. "I haven't heard from him in months, Beck. He left almost six months ago. And we haven't been a . . . a thing in more than a year. Now I'm supposed to just show up in Brazil?"

"Yes."

"And do what? Say what?"

"Figure it out when you get there."

"Easy for you to say."

He placed both hands on her arms. "Rae, you don't have to go if you don't want to. I won't be offended. I just don't want my little sister hurting over a situation that could change—change for the better—if she was only brave enough to do something about it."

"You think I'm a coward?"

"I think you've lived in Maple Valley nearly your entire life and the thought of leaving scares you. But I also think doing the thing that scares you might end up opening the door to a dream come true."

He felt a quiver travel through her as the possibility dawned in her eyes. And then he glimpsed a shaky smile. Raegan rose on her tiptoes to kiss his cheek. "Thanks for this, big brother. I'm not entirely sure what I'm going to do with it, but I love you for it." She stepped back, reached down to pick up her shoes. "Now go find Kit."

"I'm serious, I think if I ever get married, I'll take a cue from Logan Walker and elope. I've already been through all the planning once and it's just way too much work." Kit lifted her hundredth battery-operated candle and flipped the switch under its base. Real candles might've been a tad more romantic, but she couldn't get past the fire hazard of it all. And anyway, Kate Walker couldn't have cared less.

Not so, Megan. The self-appointed wedding planner had declared them tacky and refused to light a single one. Instead, she simply followed Kit around the decorated barn with a clipboard, rattling off the final tasks that needed to happen before the wedding began in a little over half an hour.

Who would've thought the snarky barista would turn out to be a wedding-loving romantic at heart?

They shuffled along the side of the barn, each windowsill crammed with fake candles of all sizes. Kit's midnight blue dress with the ripple of silver running down one side rustled with each step.

"I just can't believe she chose to get married in a barn." Megan sniffed.

Said barn smelled of vanilla and lavender and had been ornamented to elegant perfection. A few guests already dotted the rows of white-slipcovered chairs. The barn was the exact same design as before—same windows and skylights and crisscrossing rafters. Same beautiful wood floors.

It was too bad Lucas had left before seeing the completed project. He didn't seem to have a plan, but at least he'd begun to heal. Slowly but surely. Maybe someday he'd tell her the rest of his story—about his two years hiding away in Afghanistan, about prison and what had happened after.

But for now, she'd had to let him go, trust that God would hold on to Lucas in his wandering the same way he'd held on to her . . . even when she hadn't realized it. And slowly, her hope, her trust, her faith—it was all growing roots.

"A *barn,*" Megan reiterated.

"There's not a scrap of hay nor a four-legged creature in sight."

Megan's jet black hair whipped around her chin. "Not so. I saw that goat prancing around earlier."

"Flynnie is properly penned as of twenty minutes ago, I promise."

Megan only harrumphed and resumed her review of the last event details. "We already did a sound check but I'd like to test the mics once more right before the ceremony. Did you make sure the photographer has ample room for his tripod? I want to speak with the ushers before they start escorting family in."

"Like I said, easy elopement." Kit flicked on the last candle. "Or maybe I just won't get married. I've got my orchard, after all. My trees. They'll never demand endless lists of detail after detail. What do you say to that?"

"That I sincerely hope you're not serious."

Not Megan's voice. Definitely not . . .

Kit thrust the candle toward the windowsill as she spun. The careless movement sent the entire display tottering and spilling, rolling to the floor.

Megan's gasp was no match for her own.

Beckett.

The skylights overhead sent beams of light pouring through the rafters to dance in the agate eyes of her best friend. His tuxedo's bow tie bent askew, as did the little flower pinned to his jacket. He'd shaved, for once, and even had his hair trimmed, though any attempt to smooth it down had been outdone by the wind.

And his smile. His dazzling, familiar, just-for-her smile.

"Hey." Did her voice sound as reedy to him as it did her?

"Hey, yourself."

She barely noticed Megan picking up the candles, muttering about how she had to do everything herself. Kit stepped over a candle to move closer to Beckett. "Another homecoming for another Walker wedding?"

"Another homecoming for another Walker wedding. Only this time, I'm sorta hoping not to get arrested."

"You're consistent, though. Showing up at the last minute again."

His lone dimple appeared. "Why does everyone keep saying that? The ceremony hasn't started. The bride isn't even here yet."

"The bride isn't here?" Megan budged to Kit's side, her voice shrill.

But Kit couldn't take her eyes off Beckett. She'd known she'd see him today. But the knowing had done nothing to prepare her for the thrill swirling through her now, nervous delight so intoxicating it rendered her wordless and useless and . . .

She couldn't help it. She threw herself into arms that opened just in time. "Oh my goodness, I missed you. I mean, I thought I'd missed you years ago when I was in

London, but that was nothing compared to this." His vest and shirt muffled her voice, but she didn't care. "There's so much to tell you. Dad deeded the orchard over to me, can you believe it? I wanted to call you, but I knew you were trying to think and—"

Beckett silenced her with his hands on her cheeks. He leaned back as he cupped her face, smiling into her eyes. "When did you become the talker of the two of us?"

And then he kissed her, gently at first and then with a stored-up hunger that mirrored her own. Her arms rounded his neck as his circled her waist, his hands warm through the light fabric of her dress.

"Not getting married, my eye."

Kit giggled against Beckett's lips at Megan's sarcastic words and then pulled back, but only far enough to take in Beckett's smile closer up than before. There was something new in his gaze. Not just the daze of having kissed her breathless. Something tranquil and settled.

Megan's heel tapped in time with the music playing over the speakers. "I suppose this means I'll have to finish this list on my own."

Beckett glanced around Kit's shoulder. "I'm afraid that's exactly what it means. I've got some business to discuss with Miss Danby."

"Business. Right."

Beckett reached for one of Kit's hands, still locked behind his neck, and brought it down. "Come on."

He tugged her toward the back of the barn and then outside the sliding doors. She gasped at the sight of glistening snow tumbling against a crystalline landscape, a blanket of white already covering the ground. "I've been in the barn for the past hour and a half. I had no idea it was going to start snowing this quickly. I mean, I knew it'd snow eventually. I could feel it in the air this morning—the cold front and the low pressure—but I thought it'd hold off until later and—" She broke off as Beckett stopped around the side of the barn, out of sight of the parking lot now bustling with cars. "What?"

"I just really like it when you talk weather."

Goosebumps trailed up her arms, and before she had a chance to rub her palms over them, Beckett shrugged out of his jacket and draped it over her shoulders.

"So this business you need to discuss . . ."

"Right. Okay." He reached into the pocket of the blazer around her, pulled out a piece of paper, and handed it to her.

"What is it?"

"See for yourself."

She unfolded it, trying to ignore the wind ruining her hair and her heart trying to pound its way out of her chest. "A résumé?" She looked up at him. "Handwritten?"

"Yeah, but you have to admit it's a step up from last time I asked you for a job. I'd kind of like to be paid this time, by the way, but there are things I'm willing to accept as compensation other than money."

"Beck!" The cold couldn't stop her flush.

"Also, I should mention I'm really only available part-time. I'm going to do some legal advising for Colton's foundation."

"Slow down for a sec. I don't understand. The Army, your application—"

"I never sent it in, Kit. It just didn't feel right."

"But all that preparation . . . it checked off all the boxes. You said you wanted something with travel. Something with variety. Something exciting and meaningful."

"I can get everything I need right here. As for travel, we'll take vacations. Besides, there's a checkbox I was forgetting all this time." He stood close enough that she could feel his warmth embracing her. His voice was soft. "Something I'm crazy about. Something I'm absolutely, wildly passionate about. Something I love."

She blinked rapidly—tears or maybe snowflakes wetting her eyelashes—and the wind, the cold, the crowd of people humming in the distance, it all simply dissolved from her awareness—like water molecules exposed to heat and evaporating into clouds. "Isn't that three more boxes?"

"Are you going to give me a job or what?"

"You're wildly passionate about the orchard?"

"Try the orchard owner."

Her heart sung. "But your dream . . ."

He closed the last sliver of space between them, slipping his arms under the tuxedo jacket that hung past her waist. He kissed her forehead and then each cheek. "You've been my dream since I was eleven years old."

There was nothing left to do except let herself burst into tears and bury her face in his neck while her heart lifted a thousand whispered prayers. *Thank you. Thank you. Thank you.*

He pressed his face against her hair. "I probably should've waited to even talk to you until after the wedding. 'Cause any minute one of my sisters is going to come around the corner and lecture me for making you cry and ruining your makeup and—"

"Found him, guys."

Her crying turned to laughter as Raegan's voice broke into their moment. More footsteps trampled in the snow behind her. She didn't have to turn to know it was probably Logan and Seth and their wives and maybe even Case and Kate if Megan hadn't found them yet and . . .

"Someone might as well go tell Megan it's going to be a few minutes." Logan's voice. "Blame Beckett."

Kit tipped her head to meet Beckett's gaze. Beckett Walker—who was *staying*. "Burn your ships, right?"

His smile could melt every last sparkling snowflake. "Burn your ships."

She smoothed his wayward hair from his forehead, whispering his name with enough wonder and joy to warm her forever . . . and kissed her best friend.

THE END

Acknowledgments

This is my third full-length Walker Family book. Throw in my prequel novella and, wow, I have spent a lot of time with this made-up family. They feel real. And in a weird but oh-so-cool way, they have changed me.

The fact that you, wonderful reader, have taken the time to get to know them, spent a few hours here and there in their world . . . it means more to me than I could possibly say. From the bottom of my heart, *thank you.*

An extra special shout-out and a bazillion virtual hugs to early readers, reviewers, and influencers. You rock, that's all there is to it!

I'm also incredibly grateful to:

Mom and Dad—You always top my list of acknowledgments! For as long as I can remember, you have supported and encouraged my story-love. For that, and for all the practical ways you support my writing journey, I will never stop being grateful.

My siblings—You get a shout-out in every Walker book because you have influenced these characters in both big and little ways. My life is richer because of you.

Grandma and Grandpa + many other extended family

members—A lot of readers tell me they love how close-knit the Walker family is. I'm always happy to say they take after my own.

Charlene Patterson—I am so, so thankful for your editing expertise. This story is much stronger and more polished because of you.

Bev Baedke at the Community Orchard in Fort Dodge, Iowa—Thanks so much for answering all my apple orchard questions. I can't wait to visit the orchard this fall!

Laura Musyoka—Thank you for being my medical expert and coming up with a good health crisis for Case. Who would've thought back when we were painting our faces with watercolor and playing "save the princess" in the hay mow, one day you'd be an ER doctor saving real lives while helping me complicate fictional ones? :)

Susan May Warren and Alena Tauriainen—That weekend at Susie's last November was just everything I needed . . . right when I needed it. Thanks for the brainstorming help, but even more, for your friendship and support.

Katie Ganshert, Courtney Walsh, Cara Putman, Hillary Manton Lodge—All four of you weighed in at different times with ideas and thoughts for this story. Through Facebook and Voxer and email and in person and, wow, you were just so crazy helpful. Thank you.

Lindsay Harrel—Thank you so much for reading a draft of this and for all your helpful feedback, as well as all the encouragement along the way. I'm immensely grateful for your friendship.

Terri Simmons—Thanks for being an awesome proofreader! I appreciate your help SO much. See you at the office!

My coworkers, aka friends, at Hope Ministries—You. Are. Awesome. (All together now: “Yes, we are!”) Rachel Hauck and Beth Vogt—thank you for uplifting and inspiring me so often. The Grove Girls—oh, how I <3 each one of you. Gabrielle Meyer—thanks for being such an encouraging friend and for hosting the best retreats. Raela Schoenherr and Amanda Luedeke—your continued cheerleading is just the greatest. Jenny Zemadek with Seedlings Design Studio—this cover is one of my very favorites ever. Thank you!

And to the One who is still teaching me how to hold on . . . thank you, forever and always.

About the Author

MELISSA TAGG is a former reporter, current nonprofit grant writer and total Iowa girl. She's the author of the Walker Family series, the Where Love Begins series, and the Enchanted Christmas novella collection. Publishers Weekly named her book, *Like Never Before,* to its Spring 2016 "Religion and Spirituality" Top 10 list. When she's not writing, she can be found hanging out with the coolest family ever, watching old movies, and daydreaming about her next book. She's passionate about humor, grace, and happy endings. Melissa loves connecting with readers at www.melissatagg.com.

You Might Also Enjoy

WALKER FAMILY SERIES

FREE prequel e-novella
Three Little Words

A charming story of romance between polar opposites in this exciting introduction to Melissa Tagg's series about the charismatic Walker family and the endearing town of Maple Valley!

Walker Family Book One
From the Start

Kate Walker writes romance movie scripts for a living, but she stopped believing in "true love" long ago. Could a new friendship with former NFL player Colton Greene restore her faith?

Walker Family Book Two
Like Never Before

Widowed speechwriter and single dad Logan Walker never expected to inherit his hometown newspaper. But the change of pace, a town mystery, and working alongside scrappy reporter Amelia Bentley, might be exactly what he needs.

Other books by Melissa Tagg

Made To Last
Here to Stay
One Enchanted Christmas

CPSIA information can be obtained at www.ICGtesting.com
Printed in the USA
LVOW07s0408191016

509279LV00001BA/197/P